LIME SQUEEZE

MARIUS ENESCU

ISBN 978-1-966012-35-1 (paperback)
ISBN 978-1-966012-36-8 (hardcover)
ISBN 978-1-966012-37-5 (digital)

Printed in the United States of America

CONTENTS

CHAPTER I

STORMY NIGHT

Commander Igor Andreevich Polivanov was enjoying the chilly breeze on the starboard wing of the bridge. He slowly produced his Capstan square metal tobacco box, grabbed a cluster of wet noodles between his fingers and pressed it gently into his shortly curved Briar pipe, not before sniffing it with obvious satisfaction.

Both pipe and tobacco had been coming as a gift from a friend he deeply respected and feared in the same time, if only for uncommon wealth and influence, spelled power in his notebook.

Maybe the word friend was not entirely appropriate, yet he unwillingly had been choosing this definition as coming closer to his own expectations.

He put out his thumb and gently pressed the tobacco inside the pipe, like his ancestors did with the popular "mahorgka" in Siberia, lit it with a match, puffing vigorously, then threw the burned stick into the smooth, dark sea, splashing some 40 feet beneath.

Polivanov was in his fifties - a true Russian at heart, even if his Gruzyn mother's heritage was obviously betrayed by his medium height, dark-grey appearance and thick moustache, all rendering a stunning resemblance to Stalin himself. Well, maybe Stalin in his earlier days!

He had quickly buried his communist youth and all Cold War slogans under his permanent preoccupation for his job and a satisfying income.

His Russian Navy education made him a worthy sea wolf and his later experience in the Middle East and South-East Asia, an equally valuable and cunning merchant. Countless voyages aboard suspect smuggler tankers or multipurpose cargo ships under various flags, brought to him unprecedented expertise during the Serbian war blockade and in the Oriental seas around Iraq, Iran, Egypt, Bahrain, Somalia, Mozambique or India and China. He and his 9 mm Beretta had made it through a lot of.. delicate – so to speak – situations.

On the other hand, he had always been clever enough to never deny contact with his former comrades in the GRU*. Hardly a choice to consider, however! The only known way out of the organization were feet first or in the form of thick smoke passing through the chimney of some abandoned factory! They did not bother him a lot with information harvesting anyway. By the time he passed on the requested data, it was most likely already on their map and he was convinced they frequently used him just for back up checking. If it meant double checking on other guys, it was all the same to him, but he did have sometimes the creepy sensation they were checking on him, too. With these people, you could only mistake once and never lived long enough to regret it! Obviously, orders were not to be discussed, but obeyed immediately. Yet he was surely in no danger, as he still accounted for one of the best operatives in his area and maybe the only one doing the kind of dirty job he was enabled and supposed to.

Right now, on the other hand, he enjoyed the distinctive sensation of combining orders with his own interest in the most effective and - proudly admitting it - pleasant way.

Sharing sometimes the company of the richest and most devious, yet publicly unknown weapons or oil smugglers – the hated DAESH or ISIL entity leaders included – he did manage to keep secrecy over his business and making a lot of money in the process.

---

* *GRU – Glavnoie Rasvadivatelnoie Upravlenie – equals to Army Secret Service. This organization, more discrete and less well known than the infamous KGB, has actually been the main training and operational structure of Soviet Russian espionage. Apparently, the collapse of the Soviet empire brought only minor change to its structure and objectives (see Ukraine war and the Russian potential to interfere in democratic proceedings in other countries).*

He already owned a 4 star hotel in Arenal, the joyful resort of western Mallorca, and an exquisite restaurant in Greece, in Porto Carras, Khalkidhiki, not to mention his big fat Panama offshore transactions and Cayman bank accounts. To his few friends, he used to say his fortune was already "big enough to buy a small African country, elephants and pigmies included".

Both tourist locations he invested in have lately been jammed and swarming with Russian tourists in spite of the blockade against Russia, and especially after the Turkish tourism was impaired by internal political turmoil. He felt very comfortable with this, while having either fun or work. Work was most of the time at sea. Fun meant a jar of smooth quality Russian vodka and three Moldavian or Lithuanian blonde club dancers, able to massage all the parts of his body for hours on end. His dream was to retire after few years and spend all his time and money within the two locations, taking care of his commerce.

Looking around in the dark night, Polivanov sighed and noticed his pipe had burned out. He filled it only half this time – too much smoking could be bad for health, he thought – and lit it again.

In such rare moments of introspection, Polivanov used to think about his life. For instance, he remembered again to have been married once to a girl in Odessa, when he was young and sailed for the Russian Black Sea Navy fleet. He also recalled she was seven months pregnant when he left, never to come back. "High" GRU orders were for him to "defect' in the port of Marseille and "build" a new life; he was supposed to never contact his family again and he did obey orders without any second thoughts.

She never really knew what became of him and she was better off like this. Probably hating him? Most likely! - He thought. With a touch of softness in his rough character, he had been thinking sometimes whether the child was a boy or a girl, and often imagined himself playing in the yard of a cozy little house with some 5- year -old kid. He had even promised himself to have a discrete inquiry sometime in the future in order to identify his child – now aged about 28 or 29, according to his calculations - and help him or her to a better life, with himself as the unknown benefactor in the shadow, like some sort of Count of Monte Cristo.

Polivanov smiled and waved away the thought together with the smoke around his head, with the pipe.

Too little, and too late for a lost life, a life he was not prepared for, and would have never been, as it were not part of his training!

Maybe too complicated even! Probably too dangerous for his blood; enemies in his line of work often take trail of family and use your beloved ones to destroy you. He could not afford to become soft – not then, and certainly not here and not now! "I'm getting older anyway!" he thought and a surprisingly gentle smile spread on his rough and dark face, making his thick moustache spread towards the grayish half-shaved cheeks.

His thoughts went back again. Eventually, after officially "defecting" to the capitalist world, he was hired in Marseille aboard the "Le Dauphin", a small tug boat belonging to a certain Jacques Didal.

Didal taught him everything he needed to know about running boats and fishy business in a great harbor and by the time he left France, he was better than his master. Apparently, Didal never guessed his true commitment. Polivanov was never sure about that, as Didal was both clever and discrete and he certainly was not the kind of guy to complicate his life asking around.

Polivanov's trained discretion and the philosophy of staying out of unnecessary trouble helped a lot on the way and made him earn this last big contract, for example. With the blessing of the GRU, of course! He was satisfied, as there has been no problem within the past 5 years and he saw no problem for the next 3 years to come, even if he didn't really know – or even care – who actually hired him.

Officially, it was a shipping company from the Philippines, the "Nymrod", with a Russian manager – Nemirov – if that was his real name, but God only knew whose money was in it, as well as in the weaponry of all insurgent Arabic militias.

He puffed a couple of times from his pipe, surrounding his head with a thin cloud of spicy smoke. Yes! Business was going very good! His deceptive strategy was paying off every dime. There was little chance his ship would be tracked. The "Luki" – a light 5 800 DWT cargo boat - was officially registered in Panama as a geared multipurpose cargo ship doing service in the East African area, carrying merchandise from as far as Libya in the North to Mozambique, Durban and Madagascar in the South. In dire straits, the "Luki" could change her name and – to some extent – even her appearance, within the hour. Rapid name change on the bow and aft, some fresh paint with different color on the funnel and rust in visible places and the two powerful cranes to move around cargo and other deck structures would do the trick, and it worked out fine twice so far, when the "Luki" was conveniently mistaken for other ships.

It was a cool evening in the Gulf of Aden, one with less mist than usual and full of charm, with the moon shinning into the horizon and creating a silver path to nowhere, stretching out for miles to the South - Eastern horizon.

Polivanov thought of how calm things looked here, compared to the hell that the speed boats he'd launched three hours before were probably encountering. The nightmare of the Eastern African piracy was not going to end soon; not as long as he and his "Luki" were around looking for business.

In fact, there were also other parties sharing this game – some small boats manned by a bunch of Somali hotshots from Puntlands – the poor Somali county situated in the very Horn of Africa, poorly provided and armed, maybe linked to the "Al Shabbaab" and two other bigger teams – one possibly sponsored from India's scrap yards and the other probably from Iran or even the ISIL, the Syrian "Caliphate" (or both) - and killing anyone in the name of money.

The initiators of this piracy business, the skinny nomads from Puntlands and their canoes, didn't really matter anymore these days, as any ship would splash them away with a couple of hoses. But he and his "Luki" were by far the most complex and modern team around.

So far nobody noticed that the "Luki" had been operating in those seas for over 5 years without reporting any dangerous event. He was seriously contemplating the option of reporting a faked & failed attack, just for the sake of credibility.

The "Luki" was a geared cargo ship and so far, only its owner, crew and mercenaries below knew that under the lumber piles or pipe line segments or other cargo stashed as artifacts upon its deck, there was a huge secret storage bunker, holding four 25 feet long stealthy speed boats powered by turbocharged Volvo Penta engines, capable of 100 knots on still sea, and four Yamaha powered zodiacs, riding the waves with speeds in excess of 50 knots. The attack rubber boats were also provided with powerful electric out-boards for stealth approach.

All transformations of the ship had been done with uncommon discretion in the obscure Indian shipping yard called Panjim, south of Mumbai, and everything was paid cash only. No papers or blueprints were issued at the time; it was all arranged as if the ship had never been there. The existing official papers told a very different and dull story, about doing some hull and paint repairs in an obscure Mumbai facility.

Launching any three of the four speed boats took exactly 7 minutes and 30 seconds, according to the latest performance. Polivanov had witnessed the scramble exercise hundreds of times and could execute the launching proceeding even while sailing his ship at 12 knots, so the American Radar units in Djibouti at Camp Lemonier would not get curious about a ship stopping too often in the middle of the Gulf of Aden.

Piracy in Eastern Africa was becoming a fruitful job and he was not going to ask where the rest of the money goes, as long as a consistent part ended up in his pockets, allowing him to pay his crew substantially and to keep his ship running. His conscience was quite clear as there have been only two white civilian victims within the last 5 years and those were two stupid morons who thought they were bullet-proof. Well, of course there were also lost a few foreign mercenaries or black sailors – Gospodin (God) rest their soul – but they didn't really matter as they knew what the risk was and most likely, no one would miss them. Besides that, he seldom agreed to take ransom hostages aboard his ship, as he wanted to keep top secrecy about his operations. The "Captain Philips" story came in handy to blame exclusively the Somalis. He even made a point in keeping clear his relationship with Al Qaida, Al Shabbaab or any other known terrorist entity as a beneficiary; prisoners would be passed on to them on hard cash without delay, preferably without being transferred to his ship. He didn't care if they were killed after; sometimes he even wished that would happen, as secrets remain secret only if there is no witness left. To the prisoners, he would be just an accomplice using his ship for a dirty trade.

His higher rank crew was mainly hard ex-Soviet military, but many sailors were European or Somalis, all hired with official papers according to regulations.

Apart from this legal crew, there were on board another 50 well trained mercenaries who officially did not exist. Sharing wide international origin, the armed men came from very different countries like Germany, England, France, Russia, Serbia, Ukraine or South East Asia. A considerable number had come from Somalia and especially its Northern separatist region of Puntlands. All these were the actual "pirates" that operated the "stealth" boats. The boat captains were ex-Soviet and former Spetsnaz from Afghanistan, war veterans. Some Europeans also shared the same level of confidence, but he always took care to double them with safe Russian comrades.

Many had joined his project to avoid prison, others had just gotten out of it; all carried fake IDs, for being able to leave the ship on very serious reasons during port stays. They lived in special, well ventilated quarters, built within phony walls that separated the holds and their presence on board was as secret as that of the speed boats.

Pirates were supposed to take turns in coming up on the deck, preferably at night time. Even so, Polivanov would not allow any of them out, until a full radar check proved no ship, aircraft or surveillance drone was around. Special corridors bellow the main deck would prevent them from being seen or accounted for by satellite infrared sensors. Those tunnels were also used by the pirates in order to take action stations, as the crew was inside each of the boats and ready to sail by the time they were hitting water, engines roaring.

The "Luki" was supposed to look harmless and ordinary and the dull black paint with a little bit of rust here and there was meant to sustain this general idea. The ship looked like a smaller rusty old

Arab or Turkish cargo ship and any features distorting this image have been carefully hidden. No one would have ever believed that even the smallest electric bulb was functional, that the kitchen chimney would in fact be the exhaust pipe for the spare generators and the funny looking white box-shaped contraption on top of the bridge was in fact a complex collection of satellite recognition and communication systems.

Apart from the ordinary pirates, he "enjoyed" these days the presence of a special passenger, introduced as a representative of the employer, obviously sent to keep an eye on things on this voyage. Polivanov scarcely met the Asian looking guy (he couldn't say if Chinese, Vietnamese or Korean) at any time and started being more relaxed when he saw that Mr. Lu – by his name – was not really talkative and even seemed to be pleased when left alone.

A young sailor opened the bridge door, creating a yellow light square on the bridge floor, and addressed to him:

– Gospodin Komandir! We are approaching the second launch coordinates!

Polivanov looked at his watch and turned towards the bridge:

– Viktor! Prepare them to go in 5 minutes!

Viktor Ignatievici Zarufin, the second-in-command on "Luki", turned his round red face and blonde beard towards Polivanov and nodded. He took a receiver from above his front panel and spoke briefly to it.

A horn-like fire-alarm blew twice and sudden movement started on the main deck, in front of the bridge, as the cover of the middle hold was silently sliding folding open to one side.

The nearest of the powerful derricks on main deck turned lights on and sunk its hook inside the hold, Within seconds, a 12- feet-long Zodiac came out the hatch and was passed over-board close to the hull. Six men, all colored, rushed to embark, four of them wearing hooded dark uniforms and light suppressed machine guns, the other two being dressed in dirty looking civilian clothes. Each of the two civilians was carrying one square tin container, about half meter wide, with some complicated devices attached to it. Once inside the Zodiac, they waved to the crane operator who lowered the boat into the sea, engine running. Upon touching the water, one of them unhooked the boat and waved again to the guys above, as the rubber boat throttled away.

The crane retrieved cable and put out the light. The whole operation had lasted 2 minutes and 20 seconds, while the ship followed at cruise speed its alleged course towards the Red Sea.

– Harasho Viktor! Maladietz! Good job Serioja! Polivanov looked at Serioja, actually Serghei Didenko, the ship's chief engineer, a tall, dark Moldavian from Trans-Nistria and an excellent technician. He had come up to the bridge as soon as the operation was completed and was busy extracting a short plain Camel cigarette from a twisted and torn package, hidden deep in his grease stained blue overall outfit.

Back in the Panjim shipyard, Sergei had managed to mount and install two additional generators in places no ship register controller would get curious about, all in order to have spare energy for the secret crew and hardware. The twin overpowered 7 000 horse power Burgmeister & Wein main engines of the "Luki" had no secrets to Sergei and in case of emergency, were able to render the ship a speed twice the average of any commercial liner and similar to a top speed of a WWII cruiser, plus twin-screw warship maneuverability. The operating speed was, however, much lower in order to avoid curious radar surveillance. The power "reserve" was meant to ensure quick run at 25 knots, on otherwise not wanted special occasions.

Polivanov smiled to his men and turned away, facing again the dream-like moon rise and concentrating upon lighting a freshly filled pipe. He was to reduce speed to 8 knots for two hours, until the armed 4 members of the Zodiac crew would come back.

The large speed boats were supposed to make a deceptive move on a great Dutch tanker, harassing the big ship and making "waves", only to suddenly quit chasing it after the desired interval and the fulfillment of their mission. He was to recuperate them in the middle of nowhere, in a point carefully fed to his GPS computer.

Launching the Zodiac was in fact the main task and the two "civilian" characters were supposed to safely and secretly land on the North shores of Somaliland, somewhere between Berbera and Karin, in Saxaan County of Somaliland, about 15 miles East of Berbera port.

Meanwhile, the speed boats he had launched were enduring hell. Everything went right while they have been visibly chasing the "Batavia" for about two hours – the great Dutch oil tanker registered to Liberia - until suddenly everything took a nasty course.

An American corvette based in Djibouti happened to be patrolling the area at low speed and was mistakenly taken by Polivanov's men and their short range radars for another, yet smaller, merchant ship. The corvette U.S.S. "Astrid" – patrolling some 15 miles away, frantically radioed questions towards the speed boats, now visible to her, and soon launched on a full speed interception course, firing lighting shells in the night above with both bow guns. The speed boats found themselves deprived of the surprise factor advantage and tried to hide, putting the oil tanker between them and the "Astrid". After all, they were not supposed to attack the tanker, but simply make themselves noticed and hang around for some time, long enough to give the Djibouti task force a spooky evening, while covering for the other operation. They had almost gotten away with it and were throttling full speed north when the corvette launched its newly assigned Navy customized Venom chopper hosted on its aft hangar.

Anatoly Kraiciuk, a formerly wanted mercenary from Ukraine, declared dead in his home village, kept steering the leading pirate speed boat onto the right coordinates. His reddish long hair was wet with sweat and the water splashing over the bow and the long tortuous scar on his left cheek seemed purple in the dark, bluish, dim light, coming from the control gauges in front of him. The rumble of the chopper could be distinguished now over the roar of the Volvo engines. Blinded by the salty water, Kraiciuk was often looking over his shoulder to check on the chopper's position and when spot lights were turned on from above, he yelled to the man behind him:

- Ahmed! Call Kurt, Yassef and Michael and tell them to spread! We meet at point Octopus. Message to open fire if this buzzard comes close to them!
- Ok! Try to keep the bird away, Anatoly! Ahmed turned to the radio station and shouted two quick sentences in Somali. Using Somali in unprotected radio messages was no great mistake; it would at least delay the reaction of an enemy who had little, if any knowledge of this language.

Like horses touched by a magic whip, the other two boats swung to a divergent course. For a brief moment, they managed to get out of the spotlight in the air. Then chopper found them again, that is with the exception of Michael and Rahman, who were in the middle boat and managed to clear off, pushing their engine screaming in overload, while the other two boats were closely traced again from the air.

A rough, metallic voice came from above:

- Stop your boat immediately! Drop your weapons! Come up on deck with your hands up! I repeat! Stop your boat or we will shoot!

The message was repeated a few times, as the helicopter started descending towards the targeted speeding boats: a fast pray, but not fast enough for the Venom.

The answer came in the form of a bullet spree that ricocheted from the chopper hull like the noise of hail falling on a tin roof, but the light weapons of Kraiciuk's crew were no match for the partly armored Venom's hull. The chopper instantly cleared away at safe distance from the boats and increased altitude, while locking in on its two targets.

- Ciort! Kraiciuk cursed, steered on a diverging path and looked back to his men: Ahmed! Get the RPG! This bastard has armor! Get him down! Quick!

Ahmed went below and 2 seconds later came up with the RPG on his right shoulder. As he was leaning to one side, to protect the others from the backfiring jet of the weapon, the chopper pilot saw him and two of the clustered side tubes of the chopper's starboard ignited. With a furious swish, the two miniature Hellfire like rockets made their way towards the boat. Kraiciuk saw them first:

- Ciort! - He cursed again! He turned head and yelled to the others, while trying to steer sideways:
- Incoming! Everybody down!

But the warning came too late. As the men turned to him to see what was going on, the two rockets struck home. One of them hit the main open cabin and shredded Kraiciuk to unrecognizable pieces. Ahmed was still carrying the RPG on his shoulder while being blasted away in the darkness like a torn up puppet. The dismembered hand of Ahmed, still squeezing trigger of his RPG, ultimately released the grenade, his body still up in the blast at the peak of its trajectory. The fired round fell helplessly into the sea one hundred yards away, dislocating tons of salty water into a miniature geyser.

The other rocket fired by the helicopter hit – split of a second later – the aft of Kraiciuk's speed boat and turned the engine compartment into a fire spilling volcano. The blast mowed away the other three pirates and they were dead before they even hit the water some twenty yards away from the stalled, disintegrating craft.

The twin boat made almost another mile before sharing the same fate. Kurt and Yassef, along with the other three, were blasted out of the water by other two rockets hitting aft beneath the water line. None of them survived and the red lights of their life waists signaled the place where their mutilated bodies were floating amidst the torn pieces of their shattered boat. The vigilant chopper hovered over the scene for about two minutes before it hailed the corvette to request return and landing permission. The third escaped boat was considered too far to matter anymore. The powerful radar on "Astrid" would sooner or later depict it, preferably at a closer range. Twenty miles away and cleared from the battle zone, the "Batavia" radioed thanks before continuing its voyage, slowly increasing speed.

The corvette maneuvered to come closer to the scene in order to look for survivors and start investigation proceeding.

Two Zodiacs with 3 men each plunged into the dark water and turned on search lights upon the scene. Clusters of choking smoke and still floating debris made it difficult to recuperate the remains of the 9 bodies, dressed in rubber swimsuits and wearing modern light and radio-signaled life waists. No part of the scattered body of Kraiciuk was ever found to be buried.

After all, his official burial had already taken place 10 years before, on a dull rainy day in November, in the small cemetery of a village called Vladimirovka. A deceased drunker from a nearby village was still enjoying the comfort of the cold, thin and cheap plywood casket, 6 feet under the cross bearing his name.

CHAPTER II

DAWN OF DARKNESS

Almost one hundred miles south-west of the scene, Polivanov's last launched Zodiac was sailing at full speed towards the coast, east of Maidth. Closing up on the last thousand feet to the shore, gas engine was cut and the silent electric outboard was turned on.

The water splashing against the boat was the only sound accompanying them, as the men kept themselves low beneath the boat's board, weapons ready in hand. The coast was poorly guarded in the area and it was highly unlikely for them to run into somebody, but early fishermen or wandering inhabitants from the coast were sometimes both armed and curious.

The two civilians dressed as locals laid in the middle, holding carefully the big tin cubes and protecting them from any possible damage. None of the uniformed warriors spoke, as they knew very well what they were supposed to do. The two men with the cans were hired local curriers and were eager to accomplish their task, one for which they were handsomely paid - 500 dollars in advance and another 500 as soon as there was proof the boxes have been delivered, or better said deployed. Orders were for them to place them in an exact spot, using GPS guidance, and leave immediately.

One thousand bucks was a year's pay in Somaliland so they were eager to get the job done and collect. Sadhanny, the man who hired them in Burao, made it clear that if they "forget" everything they saw and did in the last 24 hours, they may get another similar job, sometime in the future.

- Maxamed !– whispered one of the civilians, as they silently approached the beach. I wonder what's in these boxes if they pay us so good! Maybe it is something expensive. If we could just take a look! Can we?

The one called Maxamed whispered in turn, without looking at his companion:

- No way! Don't you see they are sealed, you moron? Besides, these two little tubes on the side look nasty to me; maybe the thing is booby-trapped or something and will go off if we try to mingle with it. What if this is a bomb or something? And you know what, Youssef? I think it is better if we know less about this. If we keep our mouth shut, we may get another job in the future! So keep your ideas to yourself! I swear that if you even try to open the box, I'll kill you myself!
- Hey, you two crows! – one of the armed guys, a brutal voice spoke to them. Keep your bill shut both of you or you feed the fish and we get others to do the job! Understood?
- Sure Boss! Ok, Boss! Yes Sir! Youssef turned to his part of the boat, his black eyes fixing the masked white mercenary with the cold expression of a beaten dog, waiting for the right moment to take an avenging bite.

Finally, the boat touched sand and the soldier who manned it retrieved the electric outboard to prevent it from damage. Maxamed and Youssef carefully took their boxes and connected carrying belts to them. They helped each other to mount them up like back-packs, stepped down in the shallow water and instantly vanished into the mist of the dark shore. Three seconds later, the boat was turned seawards and the four mercenaries set sail. Three minutes later, the electric outboard was detached and the powerful Yamaha engine started driving the boat on an interception course with the "Luki".

Meanwhile, Maxamed and Youssef have been traveling together inland for about one hour, then shook hands and took separate ways, Maxamed turning East and Youssef West of the small creek bordering the city and the moors behind it. Mountains were shadowing the South horizon.

After walking about one mile inside the moors, Maxamed took out a GPS hand device and turned it on. Compass in hand, he made a slight correction to his direction and kept on walking until meeting a bunch of small trees. He then stopped and circled around with the GPS in hand until he apparently found an exact spot. He saw a knocked down tree trunk and placed the metal box leaning against it, top up as he was instructed. He looked behind the box, found the red button and pressed it. A small radio transmitter started beeping signals that ignited the signal spot in the "Luki" radio-room monitor within 0,3 seconds. Confirmation of deployment was there. Dawn was shedding first light, coloring horizon in a spectacular pink-bluish display and things started having a shadow.

On the other side of the moors, Youssef had been doing the same and soon, both signals were visible on screen in Polivanov's bridge monitor. It was the first time that the captain saw Mr. Lu very nervous while the operation was running and very happy after it was completed. In fact, he thought that it was the first time he saw Mr. Lu ever smiling, while watching the two spots on the scanner. Smiling would be an appropriate word to characterize the mimic of Mr. Lu, as his mouth turned from the reversed "W" of a sea bed fish into a thin horizontal line, displaying no lips and just two yellowish twisted front teeth. His eyes accompanied the grimace with a shark glittering glance, sweeping around. After this brief moment of joy, Mr. Lu cleared the bridge and went back to his quarters without saying one word. He was supposed to disembark in Port Sudan and no one was eager to see him on deck again before that.

Polivanov had no idea what the containers were or what was inside. Actually, he didn't even care. All he knew was that they were extremely important and secret and he was supposed to organize a whole circus elsewhere in order to make this operation as stealth as possible.

More than that, in the unlikely situation of failure, he was supposed to dump the tanks into the water, but only after setting on the self-destruction mechanism. Mr. Lu had been very specific about this part of the job, as well as the obligation to keep the boxes clear from damage and crew curiosity. He had also mentioned that any intruder who would open or damage boxes would be shot on sight, so the metal cans stirred no imagination.

After recuperating the rubber boat, the "Luki", still sailing constantly, was heading towards point "Octopus" supposedly to meet the speed boats. Polivanov had been already radioed on special frequency by Michael and Rahman, who gave him the bad news: "The Sardine and the Tuna are lost! I repeat, the Sardine and the Tuna are lost. Shark proceeding to Octopus as planned". While reading the freshly decoded message, Polivanov's face got even darker. Kraiciuk and Kurt had been some of his best men and the rest were well trained soldiers. They will be hard to replace, not to mention his need to justify the loss of the two boats – some 300 K worth each – during an otherwise common cover up operation. Mr. Lu said nothing of this, as if the sacrifice had been accounted for or he didn't care anyway. But Polivanov did not like a stranger thinking his men were expendable. Still, there was nothing he could comment; the whole thing was no regular business, it came as an order from the GRU superiors and had top priority.

He sighed and filled up his pipe again; he soon decided he was not in any trouble after all. After debriefing Michael, he would find the right way to present things. It was the first event of this kind in 5 years of successful activity and he knew he was too valuable to his contractors to get any reproach.

The two pirate boats being destroyed, there was only one likely to be traced to base, but studying the event sequence, Polivanov realized the "Shark" got away without being followed, as the corvette was too curious to inspect the other two shattered boats.

Actually, he thought he had been clever enough to discretely flee the hot area, while busted power boats would be taken for an independent longer- range pirate group. He even hoped to get a bonus to cover for the expenses and buy two new boats in a very discrete manner.

But Polivanov was still upset for losing his good men. He was not being sentimental, but he knew he was going to need at least one year to find matching replacements. That was bad for business, not to mention the other problems, for instance, the risk of positive identification of some of the possibly recuperated dead men. None of the crews carried ID on a mission, even if fake, yet some might have been under international search for more or less important felonies, being hand printed and all. Kraiciuk, for instance, had been declared dead one decade before. He could only imagine the surprise of the investigators while and if identifying his body. One could only hope that most of them sunk with the boats. However, any speculation prior to Michael's debriefing would simply be pure and unnecessary theory.

Polivanov raised his head and looked around. Kolia, his steward, stood in the door frame with his haystack of yellow hair, sleepy eyes and sneezing every 2 minutes, as he usually did.

–   Skaji (say), Kolea! Igor Polivanov turned to the suddenly awakened sailor, who was nervously blinking and squeezing the white towel in his hands. Do you know what the Russian peasant asked the golden fish to get him as his first, second and third wish?

Kolea opened wide his blue eyes and raised eyebrows in disbelief, with the understanding expression of a boiled fish head staring at you from the inside of a soup bowl.

Captain Viktor Zarufin witnessed the scene with bored eyes. He moved his head sideways and rubbed his backbone with a tired face, then spoke with calm and harsh voice:

–   Kolea, go to the galley, you moron! Get a glass of good stuff for the Skipper! Bistro! Bistro! (Quickly! Quickly!)

Kolea vanished like smoke from the door frame. Polivanov smiled; Viktor Zarufin was a man to his heart. Not the kind that stabs you in the back! Viktor needed the job to keep a hungry family in Russia, a family he visited only once in 5 years, as they officially knew he worked on a sea oil rig platform, far away.

Polivanov, officially a tug owner at the time, and unofficially – a GRU agent spying the Italian Navy units in the port of La Spezzia, one day wondered the streets around the harbor. While doing so, he encountered a stiff – drunk and desperate Zarufin.

Viktor was jobless and miserable at the time, but Igor immediately hired him and made him 1ˢᵗ mate on his tug. He trusted the 6 feet 3" tall and powerful Russian and what he got back was not only blind obedience, but an attitude full of respect, deference and some sort of delicacy in every approach. Zarufin had been an excellent student for the Navy Academy, but some family misfortune placed him under a great deal of debt. He borrowed money from black-market loaners and mafia, until he was unable to pay back and had to flea for his life, relocating his family deep in the countryside.

He then took the large world to his feet. When Polivanov met him, Viktor was broke and prepared to put an end to his misery under the cold waters of the Spezzia Gulf, but the skipper gave him money and hope, and now the commander was second to God for him.

Kolea came back with a tray filled with small glasses and a bottle of ice cold Stolichnaya. Zarufin took it and waved Kolea away.

He then turned to Polivanov and put out four small glasses on the front panel board next to him. He filled them all with slow, respectful moves, watching how the glasses walls nearly freeze while receiving the colorless fluid.

- Gospodin Komandir! Na zdarova! We drink for our lost comrades so their soul can rest in peace!
- Zdarova Viktor! Polivanov hesitated while accepting the glass, took a long glance to it like being diverted by inner thoughts, then suddenly looked around like being surprised. The vodka went down the hatch with an elegant wrist move.

The other two glasses shared the same path. After a sigh of relief, Zarufin filled the glasses in silence with a new and generous portion of ice-cold oily vodka.

– You know what the American say, Komandir! You cannot make omelet without breaking eggs! Kurt was a fearless man, and he defied death! I also knew Kraiciuk and he was a fierce man, too. I confess I did not like him at all but I'm sure he would always have preferred to go in such a way, while being strong and fighting, rather than suffering from rheumatism in a hospital bed!

Zarufin saw no reason in mentioning that he was not the only one who disliked the presence of Kraiciuk and sometimes feared his moods, the only fragile comfort for the others being that they all shared the same side. For the time being! Kraiciuk had been some sort of loose cannon; there would hardly be any mission without him scoring some kill. Most of them had been covered by the events, but sooner or later the monster in him would have taken over and at such moment there would be just one single choice for Polivanov – terminate Kraiciuk while giving a message to the others, before the mad dog could endanger any other operation.

Polivanov smiled, took another large sip and put his hand in the right pocket in search of his pipe.

– Davai Viktor! Pour me another! He lit his pipe and puffed a few times. Yes, they were good men, he continued. And yes, the Americans are right about the omelet. But when the eggs are rotten, smell can go far and spread fast! Let us hope no one sniffs our omelet!

CHAPTER III

THE GIFT

Close to the Northern Somaliland moors east of Berbera, Abdel-Moussa, a skinny little goat shepherd, barely ten years old, was so amazed that he almost forgot about his animals. They grazed the stinging short and dry yellowish grass or the even less nutritious leaves of the dwarf bushes scattered around, while trying to lure their master towards the tastier grass around the moor, but the moor was evil and Abdel-Moussa kept clear from it and its cursed waters.

Only now he had suddenly discovered something far more interesting than his goats. He put his hand above the eyes to shadow the blinding light of the rising sun, already strong in the clear early morning. As this was not enough, he took off his yellow cap – the one he was so proud to wear since he's gotten it from an oil exploitation team – and held it above to get a better look. There, somewhere at the margin of the moors, something was glittering in the sun and he was wondering what that could be. It was shinning like polished silver or a mirror in the distance. It could be something dropped by someone – he thought – but who would venture so far from any road in the wilderness to dump something so visible and maybe precious? He then thought it might have fallen from an airplane, like the ones he saw on TV, at the village shop, but there were no regular flights in that area and their poor country had no planes, as much as he heard. Regardless the source, he decided it was something intriguing and it was worth investigating. One thing he knew for sure: he would not go home until he found out what that was! He whistled twice to his goats and waved the stick in his hand to direct them closer to the moors. The goats did not wait twice and gladly took the new direction, spreading towards the more colored grass bushes.

Abdel-Moussa knew from his parents it was not safe to go to the moors. Manny people had died there by quicksand and even if one survived that, you could get sick by breathing the evil fumes and still die because of fever and shivers. Venomous snakes and insects were waiting there to bite the person who would be so reckless as to get deeper in swamp territory. He promised himself to be quick; he would not stay long – just a few seconds – but long enough to see what that thing was.

He slowly approached the object, looking around to see if there was any human presence and his eyes grew bigger as he saw the silvery metal box. In an instant, his childish mind started building up a wonderful dream, in which Abdel–Moussa, the lucky little shepherd, finds a treasure and he saves his parents and other six brothers and sisters from hunger and disease. He realized his hands were sweating and wiped them on his already dirty T-shirt. The uncertain yellowish color could not hide a formerly red commercial saying something about Coca-Cola. Reaching near the object, he completely forgot about the goats, which scattered around randomly, some of them dangerously close to muddy area.

He found a bigger rock to sit on, five or six feet away, and started looking at the tin box with his large black eyes, where amazement was now overpowered by childish greed. Yet the box looked like nothing of this world and he realized that even if he touched it, it would be impossible for him to decide what it was. The shape and the things attached to it were so unlike everything he had been seeing so far!

As he sat staring at the box, now deprived of any shadow from around, the sun started warming it up directly. Suddenly, without any warning, a click on the top of the box made him attentive. A little rod moved around and switched the cap of one of the two little tanks attached to the box. A small cloud of bad smelling yellowish vapor came out of the box and was taken away by the gentle morning breeze. Soon, Abdel – Moussa heard another click and the little rod moved again, this time the other way around, switching on a lever of the second tank. The hissing sound that started went on for about one minute, but no vapor came out, like it was going inside.

The young boy was starting to wonder if his coming there had been a good idea after all, when he thought he heard something like an increasing humming sound from inside the box. As the sound grew, two or three more unexpected clicks moved other little rods on the side of the box and two lateral windows came open, still protected by a thick metal net. The humming suddenly grew and it was at this time that Abdel-Moussa got scared, fearing that the whole contraption will blast.

That box must have been the doing of Shaytan (Satan) and he was not going to wait and see it blow up or casting some spell on him.

He ran away from the box, desperately trying to get together his goats, but one of them had gotten stuck in the mud. The boy came near and started pulling it by the horns, but his maneuver scared the poor goat even more than the sticky mud. As a result of the boy's effort, the goat started kicking randomly while going lower and lower in the grey mud. Abdel feared that if he stays more he would share the goat's fate. Desperate to save the others, the boy abandoned the goat and ignoring its scared and desperate cries, managed to get his feet out of the mud. He started driving the herd as fast as he could farther away from the moors towards the small, unnamed village where he had been born and lived ever-since. The village was only 1 mile south of the moors and had exactly four clay half-buried houses and a dozen tents, hosting some 100 extremely poor and hungry people. The central stone building – having one room and one storage barn outside, was the shop, the only facility having electricity from a tiny gas generator, a refrigerator and a TV set, their main connection to the world

Meanwhile, the humming in the box reached to a peak. Soon, another click and the third rod moved about five millimeters upwards. Inside the box, the rod's end pushed a little crank that twisted around and unlocked a safety pin. The safety pin was retracted and freed a knob that let a little window open wide in the sunny side of the box.

For several seconds, nothing happened, but soon, a pair of hairy antennas and the head of an inch long insect came out to the light. The creature looked like a mosquito – a very large one – and had golden rings around the belly. After checking around with the little antennas, the insect came forward and took- off, circling the little opening in the box like a bee from a hive would do, before taking the direction of the moor. Soon, more and more insects came out, until the little hole was jammed by them. As soon as they were getting out, they swarmed around for one minute, heading on to the moor for water or in search for fresh food.

The humming grew and clusters of insects got loose from the box, swarming like a dark cloud in the thin morning air. Two millions of them had been jammed in the anesthetic filled atmosphere inside the specially built recipient, patiently waiting for a chance and now they were free, at last. The cluster dispersed as some of the insects headed for the water and many others spread out to find any warm blooded, carbon dioxide- exhaling creature within reach.

But the giant mosquitoes were not alone. Some early birds rose from the bushes and came to feast, gorging themselves with the still dizzy insects. Even so, most of the mosquitoes dispersed before the bird attack could get significant. One of them was speeding in the thin morning air on a fresh scent trail, left by a running and sweating creature, exhaling carbon dioxide. The mosquito instinctively climbed to some ten feet to look around and it saw a group of creatures running away and leaving a tasty fresh scent that made hunt even more imperative. One naked creature with apparently softer skin, partly covered in a light color cloth, became particularly interesting for the insect and the mosquito dived in for the attack.

As Abdel – Moussa entered the gates of his village, he felt a small sting on the back of his neck. He quickly responded with the palm of his left hand. He looked to his palm and saw an insect looking like a mosquito, only much larger and oddly colored. He noticed the critter had already bitten him and threw it away with disgust as he kept on walking, trying to find a credible story for the loss of one goat. What little Abdel-Moussa didn't know was that from that moment on, he was going to live only four more days and helplessly die by undeserved suffering.

About half an hour had passed since the release of the giant mosquitoes and at this moment, if anyone would have been near the deserted box, he would have seen the third rod moving again and releasing another safety pin, placed on the opposite side. The safety pin that was pulled released the red button that initiated the whole thing, only this time, instead of going in, it went out for about two centimeters. A click followed and thick acid fumes enveloped the box, which then suddenly went off with a small but vigorous explosion that tore it off to dozens of pieces and scattered them hundred feet around. The second box went off within two minutes, as well. Aboard the "Luki", Mr. Lu smiled again while seeing the two beeping spots disappear from his scanner. His neon tube shape smile meant the mission was complete and all he had to do was to report and wait for the results. Mr. Lu was very satisfied. Without saluting the persons on deck he went back to his cabin, and even if he were not Vietnamese, opened a bottle of "Ryon-De" – one of his preferred Vietnam strong rice-brandies. He hated Russian vodka which – in his intimate opinion - was tasteless. He took a satellite communication device from his closet and placed it in front of him, connecting it to the small tin dish mounted on top of his cabin. He turned it on and hailed his HQ with the known code. A man with a harsh, but somewhat young sounding like voice asked in Korean:

- Bogoseo? (Report?)
- Everything went perfect. We are in good time.
- When is it time to harvest?
- First crops in one, maximum two weeks. We already installed feed-back communication.
- Very well. Proceed as planned.
- Sir, Yes Sir! Over and out!

Mr. Lu turned to his bottle and poured a generous portion in his glass. Yes, everything was going on as planned.

Mahamed and Youssef rejoined on the dusty road to Burao. They were both natives and dressed like any Somalilander in the area.

Youssef was even more representative, as he revealed all the local biological characteristics: his skin was brown black, not pitch black like the Ethiopians; he was tall and slim, with fragile looking articulations, his face displayed a thin nose and lips, unlike colored locals from the western coast of Africa. His larger clothes were waving in the late morning breeze like hanging on a tall fence.

As they went on the dirty road, an old truck – probably the Grandpa' of Mercedes trucks – came thundering from behind and raising clouds of dust. They hitched the ride to Burao and soon arrived to the central market. A mix-up of colored clothing hanging on boards, old shoes, metal scrap or shinny odds and bits, half covered cloth tents and animal smell from the chicken and goats wandering around, came together in a overwhelming supra-realistic picture. The wondered a bit around until they found the right tent. The man named Sadhanny, their contractor, was waiting for them. Sadhanny, a typical Ethiopian, with black skin, large head and one foot smaller than Youssef, was a ka'at vendor. Although proven to western world as being a drug, the ka'at was brought from Ethiopia in ever increasing quantities and the green leafs would be present on the table of every Somalilander, sometimes instead of lunch or dinner. Chewing the stuff made you feel stronger and more confident, pretty much like the amphetamines, but the individual consuming it would also become noisy, overconfident, reckless and liable to risky or unsocial acts. Not to mention brain deterioration within a number of years. Hospitals were already jammed with people with permanent brain damage, unable to quit the drug or get back to reason. But nobody would be able to stop this commerce soon, as it brought half a million dollar income to the small country's budget every day.

Once identified, Sadhanny smiled with all his resting teeth (far from a complete set) and greeted them.

–   We did the job – Insha'Allah! – said Youssef, cutting off any polite conversation. We came to take our money and we'll be on the way. It's already afternoon and we have to get to Hargeisa. Maybe we find a car or a truck to get us there.

- Ok, ok! You did good job, my friends! Sadhanny smiled again. But the money is not with me. I do not work alone, you know! We are a serious institution that provides good jobs for capable guys like you. Here! Have a seat and drink some tea! I'll call the man you need to meet. He will give you the rest of your money and then you can go.

He took two extremely dirty metal cups and placed them in front of Mahamed and Youssef. He went then to the back of the tent. There, on a small improvised charcoal stove, there was a former green paint can that served as a pot. It was full of boiling goat milk. He poured one spoonful of black China tea inside and waited till the content turned brownish. He took a fistful of sugar cubes and threw it inside. The hot Somali tea was then served. He took another larger cup and scooped gently from the pot, ignoring his dirty right sleeve that dipped into the drink. He used the cup to fill the smaller ones in front of his guests, then smiled to them again and excused for going out to make some calls. After Sadhanny silently vanished outside the tent, Mahamed and Youssef sniffed a little the cups and – pleased with the preliminary inspection – started noisily sipping the tea, satisfied and relaxed, thinking only about their triumphant home return while disregarding the complicated financial arrangements of Sadhanny.

But Sadhanny was quick; he was back in less than 10 minutes. He let them finish their tea with a greasy smile on his face and then showed them out of his tent:

- Look – he said. You must follow the main road South. Once you pass by the hospital, turn right on the road to Hargeisa. As you leave the city limits, there will be a big red house on the right and lots of scrap iron in the yard. The man's name is Tahoot and he is waiting for you with the rest of the money. Maybe he can also put you on a car to Hargeisa.

Mahamed and Youssef thanked for the tea and hurried along. The prospect of getting home was so energizing they got to the scrap yard in less than 20 minutes. One large and old red Toyota pick-up truck was parked in front of the house. The vehicle looked like it had seen better days, but then thousands of similar trucks roamed the dusty roads of Somaliland. Old and dusty the house looked too, but at least it looked like stone built and some of the walls were even painted.

The two men slowly entered the yard, looking around for someone in the dimming sunset light. A huge and powerful man, head all shaved, about forty, came out shortly from a tin shed next to the house. His dark skin and strong body line betrayed long hours of bending iron or some long forgotten military career, possibly under the command of General Aidid. He looked at them with a cold, less well-coming face. His massive forehead shadowed a pair of inexpressive black eyes, now aiming back at the two travelers. He took a short glance to the deserted street.

Everything seemed still at sunset; even the regular and noisy kids were absent, called in for the evening prayer and the eternal goat milk. Tahoot, for the dark man was Saddanny's friend, waved to them to get closer and invited or rather directed them inside the shed with a decided thumb, without blinking or saying anything. In spite of the rapidly dimming sunlight and the growing darkness of the night, there was no light turned on inside Tahoot's workshop and the dirty small windows allowed in just a couple of weak beams of light, glittering with slow moving dust.

Mahamed and Youssef were both too tired and too cheerful about their recent success; eager to take their money and leave, they were speaking about their trip back, failing to notice that Tahoot gently locked the metal door of the garage once all three of them were inside. They tried to see something in the dim light, maybe a place to sit and talk. They turned towards their host to ask something, but froze instantly when seeing Tahoot two steps behind them and carrying one nasty looking huge machete in his right hand. Youssef happened to be closer to him and tried to back up, unwillingly pushing trembling Mahamed to a darker corner of the shed, eyes fixed on the sharp edge of the weapon.

Before any of the scared couriers could say or do anything, two vigorous swish sounds were heard and the machete opened wide Youssef's neck, blood flowing furiously from the split arteries, while fallen body was shaking off its last spasms. Mahamed, speechless and with a terrified look in his eyes, took some more steps back until he felt the warm tin wall of the shed behind him and realized there was no place to go. He instinctively made a desperate leap forward trying to grab Tahoot's hand, the one holding the machete. The furious swish of the massive knife was heard again, the terrified Mahamed watching in disbelief as his right forearm and hand were dropping on the sand covered floor, fingers moving. He tried to scream but the steel fingers of Tahoot clinged to his throat. Mahamed found himself on the floor chocking, crawling in the sand that was mixed with Youssef's blood as he bitterly understood his fate was doomed too. He tried to look up and the last thing he heard was the swish sound, followed by darkness.

Within few minutes, the sand and dust on the shed floor had already been sucking dry most of the blood from the two beheaded bodies. Without a word or a blink, Tahoot cleaned his machete with a wet cloth. He then undressed the victims, taking care to put aside the five hundred dollars each of them carried. He took the two men's coats and trousers and all other garments and threw them along with the bloody cloth in a rusty barrel outside. He poured gasoline inside and lit it. A thick cloud of smoke rose over the yard, but neighbors were used to his habit of burning all sorts of garbage.

Tahoot took some large plastic bags and put the bodies inside, wrapping them tightly to avoid blood leak. He then backed up the pick-up to the shed entrance, loaded the two bags in the back of the truck without visible effort, and covered them with a blue rubber canvas. The whole lot looked like a small pile of junk that nobody would take a look at.

He went inside the house, cleaned himself up and went to the car. While turning on ignition, he called Sadhanny by his Telesom mobile. After a brief wait, Sadhanny answered.

- Sidee tahay (how are you), partner! The job you asked for - It's been taken care of! I'll be at your place in one hour! Taxadaar! Ha ciyaaro kulan ila! (Be careful! Don't play games with me!) He hung up before Saddany could answer anything.

He drove carefully out of the yard and took to the fields, driving for about ten minutes on a country road that was leading south, towards a bunch of small hills with dry and nasty looking bushes scattered around. The landscape was dull and deserted and looked gloomy in the sunset light, especially the savage looking valley lying like a deep bowl with steep sides, right between the hills.

When looked from the cliff, the valley seemed bottomless and always dark, even in daytime, due to the thick dry overgrowing bushes. There was no road sign and most people there knew that the dusty trail passing by would lead somewhere far south – east, towards the border with Mogadishu Somalia, and only the military or the smugglers would use it once in a while. Beyond that, the valley was the ideal environment for a large hyena family and Tahoot knew they actually roamed that area and knew where to seek for them. He parked on the cliff, above the small valley between the hills, killed the lights and unloaded the two bodies. He smiled while removing the plastic bag wrapping. He didn't want to give the hyenas any indigestion! He liked the hyenas a lot, especially the brown - grey spotted female that led the pack, which he had nicknamed Shakka. Shakka was a bit larger than the rest and with a lighter brown shade. He would come now and then to the hills; sometimes to feed the hyenas with the dead bodies of the people he'd killed and sometimes just to sit and watch them eat or play. He would always try to look for Shakka; he observed the animal looking at him in the distance, showing no fear or emotion, until evening made its eyes red in the dark. Shakka was an animal to his liking and sometimes he felt the urge to go out and talk to the female and scratch her on the head; he would expect some tolerance since he often fed them, but he knew better that going alone inside the den territory of a hyena pack would be suicidal, even if you carry a weapon. He wasted no more time, he dragged the naked and beheaded bodies to the edge and then pushed them rolling down the steep slope. He even took the effort of throwing the heads farther away in the mingled bushes, laughing like a kid when he saw them rolling and bumping down to the bottom.

After a few moments of silence, a chorus of ever increasing growls and short barking sounds came from across the valley and Tahoot thought he could see some pairs of red eyes glittering in the darkness of the bottom. He decided it was too dark to stay and watch the show; darkness and the presence of fresh meat would lead the hyenas into a feeding frenzy mode, and when that happens, the difference between friend and foe becomes irrelevant to them.

Tahoot got back to his car and drove silently away. Back in the city, he followed the main street downtown, towards the marketplace. He went straight to Sadhanny's ka-at shop. Making a silent entry into the tent, he sat down and grabbed the nearest tin cup around; he dipped it into the Somali "tea-pot', then took a few noisy sips emptying the cup. Satisfied with the taste, he picked from the plastic bucket on the ground a branch of cha'at full of green juicy leaves. Five or six of them ended up in his large mouth, strong white teeth chewing them, then produced 1000 U.S. dollars from his pocket and handed it out to Saddany.

The Ethiopian took bills one by one, looking carefully at them into the light of the only lit bulb, with a discrete smile on his face. He finished his inspection and count and handed over the bills back to Tahoot.

– Lacag fiican! (good money)!

Tahoot grinned, grabbed Sadhanny's shirt by the collar with his heavy hand, pulled him 3 inches close and said:

– You do not know them, I do not know them. If someone asks, two men came asking for a ride to Hargeisa; since I had no transportation, they walked on. I advised them to stay overnight in a hotel or something but they refused and went on. Souhar, my nephew, who is my mechanic, was witness to that. I'm afraid something bad could have happened to them in the fields, but we'll never know, sax ah? (right?). Oh, and, by the way, I stopped by to see my favorite hyenas in the hills. Shakka seemed happy to see me and I brought presents to her! Ha ha ha! A sudden burst of laughter meant that Tahoot found his joke very funny. He then released Sadhanny's shirt and arranged it around his neck:

- I'll take you to see them once, sax ah (right?)?

Sadhanny grinned while feeling chills down his spine. It was hard to know what Tahoot had in mind the next minute. He rose from his plastic chair and said in a more common voice:

- Ka dib! (later!). It was good doing business with you, saaxiib (friend)! I'll call you when I have another job for you and he handed him the rest of the money Youssef and Maxamed were supposed to receive. Tahoot took the other thousand dollars and vanished in the night.

Four days later, a bored local policeman, was doing field inquiry in Burao. Two Hargeisa men had gone missing for one week and a truck driver remembered he drove two resembling guys from around Maidth to Burao a few days before. He also said that both men were in a hurry to get to Hargeisa and may have possibly taken the road at night somehow. Along with others, Sadhanny from the market place and Tahoot from the car repair shop, said they do not know the two Hargeisa men who possibly disappeared in the area.

After one week of questioning the neighborhood in the merciless sun heat, the old policeman decided Thursday afternoon he'd put too much sweat into this investigation and signed final paper. Case closed!

CHAPTER IV

BLUE MOOD

Stephen Hicks was a meticulous man with a meticulous mind. A prominent microbiology scientist can afford to have his customary gestures and idiosyncrasies, like anybody else or even more, perhaps. After all, he had been working with GERMINA Inc. for 30 years or so, ever since he was a student and the company became a power of the North-Eastern biochemical industry. Now he was a key factor in its Milwaukee located industrial laboratory.

Officially, GERMINA Inc. was a company dealing with the production of agricultural biological ingredients, veterinary drugs and bacterial suspensions for ecological sewage or soil treatment for accidental oil spilling, but few people knew well about its intense activity on a much more sensitive type of products, ranging from powerful toxins with restricted pharmacological use to biological warfare – another 19 persons, to be exact. And he was the one responsible for all this activity which, despite the rather poor official recognition - which he sometimes yearned for - did pay very well! Well enough for him to quickly become the happy owner of a nice mansion house in Springdale Estates, just North of Waukesha, and lots of luxury cars, like lately a powerful X5 BMW that would carry him downtown Milwaukee by Highway 94 in less than 1 hour and to his job in less than half that time. He had even considered during time buying a boat on the Michigan Lake, but he realized he loved so much his comfortable – read lazy! – style of life, that he might never set sail. Besides, he was not very fond of water – even if that meant drinking water – except for the one he sometimes used in his large Jacuzzi bathtub.

Practically – Germina was him and he was Germina – no matter who stood up-front – and he enjoyed a lot playing indispensable.

The company's industrial facilities – otherwise totally ecological – were situated on route 16, between Bristlecone Pines and Hartland, on the northern part of the road, and didn't even look much of a factory. There was a group of office buildings with a wide parking and three large, narrow, windowless, bunker-like cubic-shaped constructions, with no visible chimneys or other exhaust systems. No one would have ever suspected the three level underground facilities lying beneath the parking lot and the beautiful garden surrounding the buildings.

His house was also minutes away from the local Capitol Airport and the Waukesha County Airport and this was giving him a pleasant sense of mobility and independence.

His only problem was boredom, sometimes. He was a single man and convinced he couldn't stand marriage. The kind of slavery marriage meant to him would ruin his cozy, yet quite irregular program, as sometimes he would work nights in a row or choose to rest for a couple of days in the middle of the week, enjoying sleep, personal massage or long drinks in his Jacuzzi, accompanied by some carefully selected local hooker. How would this look compared to "Yes, honey!", "Right away honey", "Yes, Dear! I love your cooking!", "No dear! I can skip the football game, if you want me to!" or sleeping forever on the same side of the bed! And next to the same person, as well, until that person would end up growing leg hairs as long as his own, snore like a pig, exhale a carnivorous dinosaur breath and fart like an old horse after eating wet corn! Or use his razor and after shave for the legs first and later for an equally strong beard. No sir! Besides, no regular wife – much less an aging one – would enjoy his sometimes peculiar habits like picking his nose while watching his favorite game or wondering around the house in his shorts – occasionally the same he'd been wearing the whole last week. Or was it the one before? There was also another issue Hicks would strongly disagree with, and that was sharing money with somebody else, regardless whom. He was getting the shivers thinking of how a "mistress" would have chopped his bank account daily, all for very serious reasons, of course. In his opinion, married sex was definitely the most expensive one!

Otherwise a very suspicious guy – he never opened door without looking through the sight first - he had a list of preference from a friendly escort company and took pride never choosing twice the same girl – or at least – never twice during the same month. Part of his foreplay was enjoying fidelity discount, as he was a lousy tipper, girls would say.

Quite careless about his looks, his long grey hippie – like hair was spreading a little amount of dandruff on his rather narrow shoulders and his thick lenses & black rim glasses apparently increased the size of his blue, boiled fish – like, expressionless eyes. His vulture – like thin nose was no help in improving the image and only the large mouth with solid white teeth and a sincere looking smile made some correction. Far from being an athlete, Hicks was over 6 feet tall and dressed clean when getting out, but always in obscure brown or grey clothing. His slim appearance always made his clothes look like having been borrowed or inherited years before.

Stephen Hicks didn't need to be happy, as he was a deeply satisfied man. He had been involved in many ways and in various actions with his company. He was confident the Board trusted him, being above any suspicion or doubt. He never asked about the company's clients or why sometimes bizarre chemical or biological products were leaving the facility safely canned in fertilizer brand crates towards some even more obscure destinations. He had his own suspicions and sometimes he collected copies of interesting papers and kept them safe in his home, but he never talked about them and that kept him clear so far. The fact that certain military divisions of the US Army were interested in their products and were discrete clients from time to time or even sponsored part of company's research for their exclusive benefit, was so much more reassuring to him and proved helpful during unwanted events. Yeah, unwanted events, unfortunate accidents, side-effects, collateral damage, he had it all in his vocabulary and he was convinced that you need to break the eggs in order to make an omelet. Or just for practice purposes, sometimes! There is no success without experiment, right?

Like in many other evenings, he stretched his back in his armchair, yawned and picked up the evening favorite pastrami & pickles sandwich. While chewing on a huge bite, he tapped the pause bar of his sleeping computer and selected mail. The evening local news was pouring endlessly on the mute TV screen on his side. A small half emptied Budweiser can was located down on the floor, next to his armchair and a large, half emptied bourbon bottle stood proof to the evening's ritual sacrifice.

Bruce, his huge black Tomcat, yawned as well and slowly walked to its feeding dish where a huge pile of greasy cat food was supposed to satisfy sixteen pounds of appetite. After smelling the food, Bruce started eating with a disgusted attitude, tail up and taking obvious care to avoid dipping whiskers.

Funny how these mail computer programs run these days. They can bring to you a lot of crap as important messages but throw away potentially essential info or from important persons. Curious to see if he was right about it this time, he switched to junk mail and picked on a message from his professional forum. There was a text about a medical organization taking care of water disseminated infections in Haiti, bla, bla – just another pile of crap! Nervously, he deleted the message and jumped to the next one.

This one was more "exciting" – a much more documented allegation on the HIV immune persons in Swaziland along with a clinical trial..– God, what a mess! These morons think they could take some miraculous serum from the naturally immune and pump it into the exposed ones like in the movies, so they could fuck each other's asses happily ever after, without any fear. So much for the rubber industry! Jesus!

Next junk mail didn't look very exciting either, but he suddenly grew attentive.

It was an obscure allegation of a physician from Romania (Hmm, Dracula's layer – he smiled). The guy had a private hyperbaric oxygen therapy facility and was reporting treatment success in the case of a 15 year old girl diagnosed with a version of Lyme disease. Lyme disease was again closer to his preoccupation and to that of some military officials, at least ever since the Iraq post-war disorders of

American troops were proven to be connected to some of these nano-bacterial infections and the percentage of autism affected kids sky – rocketed in their families. Nothing new though, at least for him! He already knew this, and even more, but was not supposed to brag about it, as officials thought it might trigger mass hysteria and the media would turn to "feeding frenzy" mode.

- How boring - he said loudly and yawned again. He turned to his coffee cup – more like coffee syrup, as he preferred it light and with lots of sugar. This would save a lot of coffee as well. He took a long sip and looked at the message again and suddenly found the coffee sour and difficult to swallow. With frozen face and moving like a robot he enlarged the message font and looked again in disbelief.

"…According to the special tests performed by the National Infectious Disease Center in Bucharest - Romania and confirmed by the similar facility in Vienna, Austria, the girl suffered from a neurological infectious disorder caused by Borellia afzelii …."

He looked down rubbing his chin. How the hell did that get so far? The germ had been indeed "engineered" by a much younger Hicks and his lab in the early 80's and this put them ahead of the Massachusetts competition. However, there was an "unfortunate event" that caused the death of 2 lab technicians and it was some time until they figured it out and decided to put an end to the "experiment". It was supposed to be covered and buried by now and yet, some 20 years later, it emerges as a random case in Eastern Europe? He had a feeling that something was not right about this and he needed some answers before he went to sleep. After hesitating for a moment, he picked up the cordless phone next to him and furiously dialed a long number:

- Hello! Yeah, it's me! Listen, I have to talk to you. Something strange happened. It seems that the bugs we were working on in 85- 90 …. Remember the story? Yeah, I know you were young and came later to us….Well, somehow they broke free in Eastern Europe, Romania to be more precise. What do you make of that?

A longer silence exposed the slight electrical hush of the telephone. Then a rough, metallic voice answered:

- I don't know; like you said I came to the office years after. As far as I know we were careful about the known consequences and nothing else happened. Do you think the information is reliable?
- …Err…I don't know… It's something from a forum…., but the physician guy who wrote this seems competent! And they have back-up tests in Austria, some hospital in Vienna! Do you realize what this could mean to us as a corporation, if they start tracking the disease back?
- Stephen, listen to me, don't get excited!… the voice pleaded equally…
- No, no, no, no – you listen to me! Hicks was literally spitting words out, walking to and fro like a caged tiger, telephone in hand! This is serious for me – I was the project manager at the time and when the whole shit- bag bursts out I'll be held responsible and they'll put me on the never-come-back-and-keep-your-freakin'-mouth-shut-up disposable list! I'll rot in jail to the end of my days! Do you understand what I'm saying? Hicks was already shouting and trembling with fury while bringing the telephone in front of him and looking at it like facing an enemy.
- Stephen – get a grip on yourself! Who would know anything about this project after so much time? Listen to me! Your behavior will start looking suspicious only if and when you overreact!

The voice on the phone turned firm and harsh; no shade of patience in it this time!

- So far it is nothing official. Let's see what they've got there? Some peasant in "Moronia" decides he found a special case. So what? Can't you see he tries to connect his crappy career to the Austrians so that his sorry ass can get more clients? Come on Hicks, what the fuck? Are you depressed or something? Why don't you call one of your girlfriends and take a long refreshing bath…I'd say that would cheer you up! Tell you what! Give me a call tomorrow morning and we'll talk about this over lunch? Come on! What do you say, huh?

-   I don't know…err.. Guess it's all right! – The answer came with rather unconvinced tone and interrupted by hesitations. I'll… huh!… I'll call you tomorrow - but we'll have to make a decision about this! I'm not scared, but preoccupied by this shit a lot more than you can imagine!

Hicks was visibly escalating his mood while talking and the voice seemed to realize it.

-   Go to sleep Stephen; get fuckin' laid or drink yourself to reason! You sound like an old parrot and apparently think like one or even less at this moment!

The metal voice was followed by the unmistakable click.

Hicks interrupted his nervous walk and stood next to his armchair starring foolishly at the receiver. He finally put it down so gently as if it were ready to explode. He realized he was sweating a lot more than usual. With slow motion gestures, he took of his blouse and unbuttoned his shirt. His narrow chest displayed a disgraceful solitary bush of whitish long hairs, now moving up and down underneath his larynx with every hectic breath.

How was he supposed to make them understand that this could be a disaster to him? He remembered the whole story as if it were yesterday. At the request of some highly ranked officials in the Army, they were supposed to do some study on various types of Lyme disease and their complications, prevention, risks, blah-blah! And yes - including inflicting scenarios! Lyme disease is a traditionally scary illness for the Americans, but the truth as he knew it now was even freakier. The common disease is generated by the well known Lyme bug - Borellia burgdorferi. Living as a parasite inside ticks, it reaches by stinging in a human being or other mammal, where it settles sometimes for good. The infection develops as local inflammation around the tick bite, which eventually goes away within weeks, but that doesn't mean it is over. Later on – and this could mean years – new manifestations of the infection could be revealed and they can occur in almost each and every system of your body, sometimes discovered as already inflicted late complications. You face disorders that mimic paralysis or madness, muscular or joint inflammation. It also affects your hearing, eye sight or skin as well. Hicks knew that fierce immune reaction lacked on account of small genetic print of the bugs and that such feature increased tolerance. The bad part is that it takes a lot of specialized tests to reveal such infection – that is if the physician happens to think of it! The good part is that ticks are practically the only natural carriers and it is only under some climate and vegetation circumstances that you get exposed to ticks. Or at least it was so until he, the respected Professor Hicks, worked on some strains of Borellia bugs (the afzelii rare type) in order to make them portable by mosquitoes as well. And Hicks did even more by genetically enhancing their aggressiveness and penetration power, thus turning them into acute and fatal disease developers, able to kill human in only a few days.

Some of these bugs must have been taken to Europe or gotten out by chance and took years to cross the ocean; eventually they did it somehow.

He smiled at the resonance of the words – Hicks rimed with ticks! The general idea was that mosquitoes live practically EVERYWHERE and if infested with unexpected germs like, say, Borellia, they can poison in turn a whole nation in a couple of years – a nation that would be diseased and dying within the next few years, being preoccupied by its health problems and lacking the determination and the finance to face war preparation and arm race - hence the interest of the Army's Strategic officials. Needless to mention the powerful pharmaceutical companies that became interested in the aftermath scenery, when selling their cure to the "poor affected nations!" would grunt them billions. Billions out of which they agreed to share some with his lab in advance, so to speak, in the name of ever encouraging prevention for public health.

Third World War may have ended without firing a round towards the Russians, but if such ideas come to life, the Fourth might take place in hospitals rather than trenches.

Fact was that during the experiments, his engineered mosquitoes proved reliable hosts for the engineered germs that survived in active mode, inside insects, for at least 7 days, sometimes more than 2 weeks. This was anyway long enough to transform one container with two million hungry insects each, into a deadly time – bomb. One could think what can happen when several such containers are strategically deployed inside a city holding 2 million inhabitants.

More interesting even, spores of bacteria would survive inside each insect to its death and beyond. Each hungry mosquito female would sting humans several times even within the first 24 hours, not to mention the capacity of inflicting disease to other warm blood hosts that would become additional long term sources.

To conclude this, according to his calculations, some 10% of the population would suffer from at least one sting within the first week and out of them about one third would get infected. Some 100 000 people in a city of 2 million will live in hell within the next few weeks, only to end up crippled or dead, after consuming all financial resources of both their families and community. Secondary transmission of the disease will get other 50 000 within 6 months, enough to create havoc in the whole region.

This would become a national health problem to deal with and paralyze a great percentage of a country's budget. There will be less money and interest for weapons and army training and the genius part of it is that nobody will be blamable, as it could always be taken for a natural insect spread-out followed by epidemics, as it happens so often. Once they find out about the germ, they will concentrate on ticks and only years after they may realize it was something else, still not knowing where it came from and being unable to collect evidence for an intended biological attack.

Nothing like the West Nile virus though, which may kill faster, but it is much more difficult to deploy. Certainly, West Nile was not a very subtle testing solution when more or less accidentally deployed in countries like France, Spain or the former Eastern Block, being much too far from the virus endemic regions, but the idea of the mosquito vector proved right and saved the day in their effort for finding the new and ultimate carrier.

Yeah, the idea was pretty sneaky and Hicks was the perfect victim of anti-Russian propaganda at the time. As a student in biology and later, young specialist, he had always thought that Russian cities, many of which placed near rivers or lakes, would surely become legitimate targets for biological weapons with insect deployment. As Soviet President Brezhnev was about to die, rumors had it that his tough communist branch of the Party was determined to pursue the hard external policy line, in conjunction with the tough North – Korean regime of Kim-Il-Sung. Yap! Those were good times and young biologist Hicks was doing interesting research work, for even more interesting pay after graduation and signing in with Germina.

The mosquito – Borellia carrier project was still going on in the late 80's and early 90's. But things went terribly wrong when two of his employees – capable technicians unfortunately – got accidentally exposed to highly infested mosquitoes, while manipulating insect containers inside a safe bunker. One container cracked open after falling to the ground and hundreds of thousands of infected mosquitoes broke free. As soon as danger was detected, armored gates closed in less than 5 seconds and waves of strong poisoning gas were blown inside to instantly kill released insects. The two men were trapped helplessly inside without wearing gas masks and fell down coughing their lungs out. The ventilation and door opening proceedings took long minutes with all the checking and double checking. The men were carried out later, both terribly stung and almost poisoned to death. They were extricated alive but in unstable condition. Even so, they were not rushed to a public hospital but to a "friendly" military medical facility.

Hicks knew that the ultimate cure against gas intoxication and massive bacterial infection would be the hyperbaric oxygen therapy, but for this American standards imposed official proceedings and maybe unwanted publicity on the case.

He was still assessing the effort of saving his valuable men against the inevitable rumors and questions raised about the project

– especially if the technicians survived and talked - when they conveniently succumbed days later to Herxheimer reactions and irreplaceable damage to their brain, inflicted by the poisoning gas.

Stephen suddenly remembered he had been fasting and staying awake for the whole week and only after the families received a generous financial compensation and they managed to keep outsiders, including the press, out of this business, was he able to eat and sleep.

He was devastated at the time by the idea that such accidents could terminate his career and above all - his present job, but in the end nobody blamed him for what seemed to have been a common negligence of the technicians who ignored their obligation to wear gas masks, gloves and full protective gowns while inside deposit.

Fortunately, nobody mentioned or even observed the out-of-scale high level of bacterial infection acquired within just a few hours. He had been able to relax later, spending some very refreshing days and nights taking long baths with Lila, one of his already favorite girl companions at the time.

It was one of his first projects – he smiled thinking about the young Hicks – and yet it was the only one he had to cancel in '88!

Sebastian Reading, the manager at that time, called him and told him that the corporation cannot afford to be exposed in such way so he should better slow down engines or refresh his research program, otherwise severe cuts will follow. But Hicks knew that Reading was no master in his sector, as his true boss was the "Special Programs Executive" Stan Gorman. Stan Gorman was already thinking about retirement. He had little – if any – interest in whatever Hicks was doing there and would take his word for grunted at any time, "in the name of superior interests". Such argument would make his enemies drop any challenge. Years after the accident, Gorman suddenly decided to retire and he was to be followed by Archie Donovan, a very young and talented nobody at the time, but with surprising credentials. When Hicks was already working for Germina Inc. as a fresh and talented Assistant Professor in his forties, Archie Donovan was hired as simple trainee in the Supervising & Security Division, lead by a modest professional called Nathan Holmes. Some 15 years younger than Hicks, Archie was the kind of ordinary fellow that had something nice to say to everybody. A well proportioned athlete, always in excellent physical condition and a bit dandy looking, he was brilliantly intelligent, reckless and full of nerve. Rumor had it that he scored on all eligible female colleagues in the company before Hicks could even learn their names. That could have been one reason for the jealous Hicks to quit seeking a female partner in their little community and choose the more comfortable solution offered by the escort companies, to which he became addicted ever since. Archie was a person of strong personality and very soon – rather abruptly, Hicks remembered – grabbed hold of a good position in Special Programs. He later gave apparently little notice to what Reading said or ordered and Hicks noticed that sometimes Reading would step back on his decisions when Archie Donovan disagreed, as he did with Gorman. He would always back up Archie in front of Reading. Archie would never confront Reading during meetings, but it was interesting how a couple of phone calls could turn everything upside down. Hicks realized soon who held the real power and the fact that his fresh boss Archie placed him as project manager for very sensitive research cases gave him the possibility to readily choose the winning side. His relationship with Archie grew to apparent friendship and a very comfortable one, in deed, especially after Archie became big boss on Special Programs by replacing Holmes. Archie gave him complex and sometimes secret projects to deal with and Hicks knew that he would never be asked to hurry or to do this or that. He was completely free and Archie apparently tolerated his crazy program and his weaknesses on the condition of ultimately getting the job done before deadline and according to contracts.

Archie would give him information on a need to know basis and he was not supposed to ask questions, nor was he inclined to. He was perfectly satisfied with his income and his way of life.

Sometimes Archie would give him huge bonuses and they would celebrate together in crazy parties that degenerated in little orgies. He ended up wasted and sleeping naked in someone else's bed and in somebody else's house, but now that he thought of this, he realized that – in fact – he never saw Archie drunk! Archie was either tougher than he thought or he was cheating on shots.

Hicks smiled thinking of the good years. Young Archie's first serious assignment was to take care of the accident aftermath, solving problems in a very discreet and professional way. Sure, they had to dump the project anyway. Soviet President Brezhnev had passed away, quickly followed by Andropov and Chernenko, all put to rest one by one under the walls of the Kremlin. The bullying attitude of the Russians was starting to fade away and their project failed while finally Gorbachev had taken over in Russia and was applying his glasnost policy of the 90's. Much of the same trend was kept by Eltzin and his follower. It was hard to define the present line, but there was no essential come back for the iron curtain policy, at least until the recent blow over Ukraine. The Cold War was then over and money consuming projects – especially ones with complications and problems like this one – were no longer regarded as being appropriate.

Nevertheless, his own friendship with Archie grew in the late nineties – even if it wasn't a time -consuming relationship. He could not understand how Archie made him feel so comfortable. Of course, there were times of doubt, too. He was deeply impressed once about Archie's behavior when two niggers tried to mug them. Oops, he giggled – he had thought of the bad word! So, two African American (still black!) persons attacked them. Archie had a gun, but didn't use it. He beat the crap out of them instead; one of them finally ran away but the other couldn't, and Archie continued to hit him even after he was out. He didn't stop until the man was a mass of comatose flesh, face turned into a giant hematoma that his own mother would have failed to recognize. And he wouldn't have stopped if it wasn't for the police patrol car that came rushing in. They decided it was better to split, trying to avoid publicity.

The second time he worried a little was when he heard about the accidental death of one of his technicians' brother, who sued the company in spite of all previously decided arrangements and had been very annoying for about ten years after. Archie was very furious because the man refused to give up the complaint like the dead man's wife did in the past. The trial went to a stall after the guy made a trip to Europe to visit some relatives and died in a terrible car crash on a highway somewhere in Holland, between Amsterdam and Utrecht.

His car burned up entirely before he could be extricated from the wreckage and the carbonized body could be identified only by dental records. The car said to be responsible for that traffic incident disappeared, driver never to be found.

Hicks thought then he had a too vivid imagination to see any involvement of Archie in this, but some inner feeling kept giving him the creeps when thinking that Archie could have had another face – one he would never like to see.

Yeah, that was an able man and so far, his friend. Archie Donovan, the man with a pleasant metallic voice.

Waiving away his thoughts, Hicks turned to Bruce, the cat and saw the dish turned over and a pile of cat food spilled on the carpet.

– You are no cat! – he yelled at Bruce who was licking his right paw in the open window with the mysterious tranquility that only cats can display on a Sunday afternoon. You suffered a pig genetic mutation and you behave like a pig, trust me! – he kept on shouting to Bruce, cleaning the floor with a piece of cloth. I don't know why I keep you – he mumbled going back to the armchair.

It had been a lousy evening so far and Hicks feared it would carry on the same way. He needed to relax. He thought for a moment at the net information that caused this turmoil, staring at the cloth in his hand. Maybe he became paranoid about all this and the fact that he saw and heard many things did not help, given the suspicious nature of his character. After all, it could be just another coincidence; maybe that girl travelled in endemic areas or maybe it was a mistaken diagnosis. Possibly – thinking about the obsolete technology of the Romanian lab – hardly, if considering the Austrian back-up. But one single case doesn't mean anything and Archie had to be right.

He must have been very tense to react that way, like a school boy before the exam or a first timer teenager before getting laid. He knew who could boost up his moral – somebody like … Lila. Skin to skin therapy like he did with a nice blonde called Lulu almost 30 years before, when he was a lot younger. Yes, he will call to see if Lila is available. He went to the phone, dialed a number and waited:

- Hi, it's me! Can you put me through to Lila, please? 'Yeah, I'll wait …While waiting he poured a generous amount of bourbon from the bottle on the table into a crystal glass, his hand a little shaky.
- Yeah,… Lila? Hi, it's me, Stephen! Can I invite you to a private party tonight? You can? Okay. My place then, 9.30! Bye sugar!

Satisfied that he found Lila free, Hicks turned to his computer and silently dialed Google.

He had been browsing for some time, taking large sips from the bourbon on the desk when the door bell rang twice. That must be Lila – he thought and rushed to the door. No matter how impatient, he would not take chances, so that he first slid open the cap of the sight in the door and then got closer to take a look. Yeah, it was Lila all right and giggled as he opened and smiled at her:

- I thought you'd never come! What took you so long? Here, let me take your coat. Come in and make yourself comfortable! If you want to …freshen up you know where the bathroom is!
- Thanks Stephen! Lila made an imperial entrance with her long fur coat negligently thrown on her right shoulder and waiving her hips the way she knew would steam up his glasses.

He slammed the door shut and unconsciously rubbing his bony hands, he went to the bar and picked up a bottle of champagne from the little fridge beneath.

- Surprise – surprise! He yelled to Lila in a harsh and unconvincing voice, as she took her time to undress and slip into something more comfortable.

The old goat didn't waste any time – she thought as she heard him pop up the champagne. She packed her gear carefully, so she would not take too much time leaving. Of all the clients she knew, it had to be him! This is because Stacey didn't ask her first, so she could have said she's busy! Stacey was the Madame's niece and had a deep respect for old customers. So deep that she volunteered in times of shortage – thought Lila with a grim on her face! Of course her own name wasn't Lila, but Mary-Ann and she was in fact dark-haired even if she appeared as a sumptuous blonde. She would carefully hide any trace of that by removing hairs from her arm-pits and legs and shaved her loins twice a week.

She refreshed her lipstick and slid into a heavily perfumed black and vaporous negligee, even if she knew that she would wear it only for a couple of minutes. The old parrot knew nothing about foreplay and she wondered if this is not actually a blessing. But his known passion for Jacuzzi and underwater mating would keep girls wet until pickled and she hated to stay wet.

- I'm coming – she cried, feeling sorry for her elaborate coiffure that will soon look like a wet cloth. The younger girls mocked her on Hicks' preference for her. "Does he need to "dive – dive – dive", so you can order – "periscope up" - Lila?" or "Lila, you should do your manicure more often; you already have grown skin between your toes like ducks!" And now - "Another "Bay Watch" episode, Lila?" – asked Jenna, smiling viciously when she got out of the massage parlor.

Screw the old goat and his ideas! After all, that's exactly what she was supposed to do – screw him! But as she was passed 30, she found out that she had to be more often rendered available for older guys. At least she would spend more time socializing and less playing the sex machine for weirdoes. Hicks made no difference, but she could not afford to refuse a client like him. Dianne – her daughter - was only 12 and she knew that without the money she put aside it would be very difficult to raise her.

His sexual practice was infantile and he would rarely demand oral or anal intercourse, fortunately, for this made him cum too soon! As if it made any difference! He would invite her to a drink and then plunge into the bath where he probably enjoyed a booster effect from the bubbles, while having the usual speech about how good he is and how fortunate she should feel to get screwed by a personality like him. Then he will briefly penetrate her for two minutes or so (sometimes much less), undecidedly aroused, on the bathtub bench, in 3 inches deep water, only to take her place for the usual body massage. The massage part was relaxing, but only for him, as she hated touching his wet long grey hair and the bone-bag appearance of his body.

Another quick and even less enthusiastic intercourse two hours later will conclude the ceremony and she would be free to go home.

- Are you ready yet, my dear? - asked him with an unctuous voice.
- Coming! She said and made a glamorous appearance out of the steamy bathroom. She was indeed well made and she knew it and exposed her Greek statue like forms in a way he could not resist. His face turned pale but spotted with red on the cheeks and on his slim, vulture neck. Sweat drops sliding on his back-bone, he smiled and showed her the sparkling wine in a tall glass.
- What should we toast for? – she asked, smiling and apparently ignoring the fact that her negligee slid outwards exposing her flat belly and the tiny black bikini hardly covering anything.
- We'll toast for …err.. luck, this time! Yeah, this is a toast for being lucky! He took a great sip and swallowed it with a gulp, followed by a sigh of relief. She took a glance towards the half-emptied bourbon bottle and the large glass next to it. "It's gonna' be a synch tonight if he insists drinking the whole bottle" she thought to herself. Bourbon and champagne made a dynamite combination, but she didn't really know how resourceful Hicks were on drinking.
- Let's go to the glass house… You know I'd like us to relax in the Jacuzzi tub, right? Please don't say no! His ridiculously childish tone made her sick.
- Yeah, sure – she said smiling and pretending she was sharing his preference.

They entered the glass house through a transparent double door from the ground floor lounge and got next to the Jacuzzi tub that was softly "boiling" with foam. Hicks turned to her and grabbing her arms, made her face him. With slightly trembling hands he took off her negligee and let it drop on the floor. He then put out his hand to feel her cheek gently but as he reached towards the chin, he suddenly and violently stuck his pointing finger deep into her mouth.

- Tonight, we're gonna' get crazy baby! He whispered in a harsh voice, sweat pouring from his forehead! We're going to do it all! You're my doll, baby and I'll make love to you all over….. With robotic movements he tore away her bikini and threw it over the exotic plants surrounding the scene.
- What took you so long, cow boy… she whispered, desperately trying to get his dirty finger out of her mouth while still smiling. She stepped into the warm water and leaned open arms against the marble margin, displaying the best of her generous breast floating in mid-water. Looking upwards to him she spread her legs into an obscene posture that granted full view to her shaved, pink loins. She shook her pelvis a few times like in a mating movement, displaying amazing perineum details that made him blink and whispered:
- Come and get it!

CHAPTER V

GETTING SERIOUS

- I'm not supposed to eat all this shit!

Archie Donovan, the man with metallic voice, said this loudly, raising discrete attention from the other tables in the restaurant. Some of the eyes were turned towards his plate, hoping to observe the dish they should avoid next time, but the plate in front of the angry character was actually empty. After some time a woman answered:

- What did you say, honey? The pretty looking brunette, apparently in her 20's, yet much older in reality and staying next to him at a remote table in the Lake Park Bistro on Newberry Blvd., Milwaukee, seemed to be at least 2 inches taller than him when standing, but now she was leaning against the cozy armchair in a lazy and a bit cheeky attitude.
- Nothing dear! I had an unpleasant discussion with a moron! Archie smiled charmingly, lowering his voice to a decent whisper.
- Seems the moron was a friend of yours, I guess! – she giggled – 'cause you talked to him for a long while… Honey…! You have a lot of moron friends lately, dear! She slowly turned to her glass of cheap Chardonnay and took a miniature sip, licking her lips with the tip of her pink tongue.

She is getting wise, Archie thought, while keeping his adorable smile on. I should end up this charade – he decided. After all, the girl made no mistake in imagining that a handsome and rich guy – almost twice her age – picked her up simply for her unique metaphysical analysis capacity, overlooking the amazing talents emerging from in-between her thighs.

- No, I have in fact very few friends, if any… - and he was not lying at all. He suddenly made a decision:
- Hey Adam! He turned to a man passing through the lounge. Is Zack on duty today?

Adam Stiegel was the main "chef" of the joint and smiled back to Archie:

- Sure is, Mr. Donovan. Would you like something special?
- No, Adam. But everybody knows that Zack Binder is the best cook on the Eastern coast when it comes to foie gras de canard and anything about duck anyway. I'll have one of these and also the spiciest duck he can produce, with some veggies, but no broccoli. I hate broccoli!
- Would you like to have another wine to go with that Sir? Adam said, taking a disgusted glance towards the Chardonnay cup. He knew that Archie's taste in wines was a mess, but he pretended to appreciate his connoisseur appearance, as Archie qualified as a stable customer.
- I wouldn't know Adam. Maybe you suggest something fit?
- But of course, Sir! I would suggest Châteauneuf-du-Pape rosé. It is a Grenache vintage and it proved an ever increasing interest in the United States lately. I have a five- year- old bottle for you. Bien chambreé…and goes perfectly with roast duck!
- Spare me the details Adam! I trust your taste. Is it okay, sugar? He turned to the young lady, preoccupied at the moment to light a slim cigarette!
- Hm, hm! Adam pretended to cough while looking expressively at the cigarette.
- Oh sugar,… we can't smoke here.. so sorry! We'll go outside later, right?

Absently, she extinguished the cigarette in the plate in front of her and put it away. Adam removed it with deference.

– We'll try this wine of yours, Adam! Archie said enthusiastically. He hoped to drink her away from her intuitional questions. It was true to him that women had the curious talent of guessing by sheer intuition deeply buried secrets, and revealing them publicly at the worst possible moments.
– I'll go out for a cigarette – the girl said.
– Okay Elizabeth, I'll prepare the wine for you! Archie answered smiling cheerfully. Maybe next time he should try a blonde… something more refined – he thought.

Elizabeth! Bullshit! She was known in the clubs as Betty-the-Sword-Eater, but because she came from a rather honorable family, he agreed to show her some respect. Not that she deserved it when she was drunk and acted like a crossroad hooker! But she was such a good fuck that he simply couldn't resist and had been tolerating her moods for … yeah, one year now. He had other "resources" of course, but when it came to feeling really good, Betty was the queen… Boy, did she know it all! He looked at her fine curved lipstick-painted lips as she was making her way out on the wide balcony and pictured in his mind her deep-throat technique, instantly having a transient lumbar shiver.

His forehead darkened as he remembered about Hicks. This spoiled his evening. This moron was an extraordinary biologist, but a pain in the ass sometimes. He was easy to conduct – he would do anything for money and a hooker from time to time. But he had a big mouth and after all those years he proved to be less and less reliable when it came to doing things discretely. He had a list with all his preferred whores and their reports and took care to have them scared enough or paid enough to forget what they heard from Hicks during the voluptuous liquid frenzies they shared with the old crook. But this last call gave him poisoned food for thinking. Hicks didn't seem drunk when he called – he may have gotten wasted later. He remembered that Hicks was very scared years after the Borellia project went wrong. But no matter how young Archie Donovan was at that time, he proved efficiency and discretion beyond any expectations, if we disregard the "accidental" death of that technician's brother in Holland, which was followed by a routine police inquiry. That was how he got the leading job from Alistair Thorndike – the Big Boss. Sebastian Reading came in a couple of months later and found it difficult to swallow the kind of trust that Thorndike showed to Archie. And Archie Donovan earned it entirely, as nobody ever suspected Germina Inc. or somebody inside the company, when a private jet of some hard-to-deal-with filthy rich client blew up above the Atlantic or when the exquisite yacht of a Russian general sunk unexpectedly with everyone on board in the middle of the Aegean Sea. There were many other unfortunate accidents on the list but only Archie knew them all.

It was quite difficult until Reading learned to stay in his box. He was supposed to be the able manager of the visible part of Germina Inc., the one that publicly developed ecological solutions for agricultural needs. But the other side was the "Mr. Hyde" of the company and there was where he came in. The special products were engineered by Hicks (who officially dealt with common biological research) and his small team in a secret lab underneath the north side of the parking lot. The area was restricted to other employees and the blueprint of the factory displayed just an uninteresting compartmented warehouse in that area.

What Reading didn't know was the fact that Archie had been "planted" there by a secret hand (Reading ended up by suspecting CIA) and that he continued to work for both Thorndike and his former organization, whichever that one may be. Apparently Thorndike not only knew about this, but made Archie's work easier by rendering him powers that sometimes defied Reading's, all in the name of superior interests, which for him meant more money and thriving Republican policy.

This is how Archie ended up making major decisions and in spite of his care to avoid confrontations with Reading, he couldn't help feeling like the real Boss – and that was sometimes visible and irritating. He attended extraordinary meetings with American

Generals, Senators and State Secretaries, European politicians amongst which more recently the British prime Minister Brown, Indian Maharajahs, Pakistani officials, Israeli IDF responsible officials, Russian generals, African leaders and Arab Sheiks, all in the name of good will, friendly help and money making. And the money kept pouring! But the more it came, the more he needed. He was a man of Epicurean convictions and his main care was to be fit for any adventure. He enjoyed his life and his life was full of unpredictable events as he liked to let a certain amount of unpredictability to invade his privacy, that is not more than he was able to handle.

Archie was friend to everyone but nobody's friend in particular and his own concern was his person. Above all, son of an obscure postman in New York City, he was yearning for the noblesse touch and the glamour of the high life he never experienced as a kid and he was convinced that only more money can bring it. Obviously, in spite of his native intelligence and his service credentials, his doubtful taste in various domains was visible from time to time and Betty made a good example. He turned his eyes towards her while taking a sip from the recommended wine – too dry for his taste – and he thought again about his business evolution. He was good and the best part was about to come, but only if he managed to complete his work and this meant that those who stood against this goal will have to be eliminated. Soon, the Germina Inc. and his duties will be forgotten and he will enjoy spending a fortune for the rest of his life in Bali. With the comfortable thought that such development is his second nature, he relaxed and concentrated on the steaming roast duck in front of him, smiling.

– Honey! He cried waiving to Becky – food's here!

She joined him wearing the face of an Egyptian Sphinx, but he totally ignored her while eating the duck using his bare hands. She would have to comply with her formal duties and the main one after such dinner was to fuck him dead.

Popular ice cream and water melon plus some stinking French cheese followed the silent ordeal of the duck.

– Are you going to work tomorrow? – She asked looking doubtfully at her ice cream cup and delaying the moment when she was supposed to taste it.

– Sure thing! He answered absently. Why do you ask?

– I'd like to go to the gym and then I'll do some shopping! I'd buy something fancy to eat for lunch… Maybe I can lure you home… she turned towards him displaying a pretty smile, one that couldn't be guessed given her previous mood. She was starring at his slightly grayish hair and his black eyebrows, wondering about the heritage of his dark blue eyes that were restlessly moving around while halting upon her from time to time.

– I'm sure you wood, but I'll be busy. He recalled some of the days when, after having lunch, they would vote for a quickie and it all ended out into a sexual frenzy during which they devastated each other the whole afternoon. Yeah, she was good, but she talked too much and now she had started thinking, too. He will have to revise this and maybe find another option, but for now she was no danger. Besides, she wouldn't know about his business meetings – the official ones and those he kept in the deepest secret.

– Tell you what – he continued – we'll go someplace else tomorrow. Your choice. We'll have to celebrate, remember?

– Celebrate what?

– We can celebrate 446 days since we met; isn't it lovely? He gave her the most contagious smile he could and she responded readily with hers. You know how many days passed without making love?

– You fuck! I thought you were serious…Okay, do it your way. But don't say I didn't try!

– You're my kind' a gal! He felt so emotional that he kissed her hand, something to melt away her rigid mood. Will you excuse me for a moment? I'll have to make a private call! Hey! Garçon! Bring me another bottle like this one! He yelled while crossing the room towards the balcony.

Once outside, he produced his smart-phone and dialed a number that was not in the agenda.

- Hi, it's me. Listen, I have a problem that needs some clarification. When can I see you?

The other voice mumbled something.

- No, I can't tell you now. I have to talk to you face to face! Can I see you tomorrow at 2.30? No, I can't make it earlier!....Ok? Meet me at the Harbor House beer pub, downtown.

He switched off and stood undecidedly for a few moments, then dialed again.

- Hi Lenny! It's me, Archie Donovan! Yeah, long time no see.. Listen Lenny, I'll come to have lunch at your place tomorrow 12.30. A friend will join me and we have to talk business – undisturbed! Would you fix me a small table for two in a discrete corner by the window? I adore the channel view!

The voice at the other end confirmed as Archie smiled and thanked, putting his phone back into his pocket.

As he slowly went to the balcony's green area to sit down for a while, he tried to imagine Lenny's face. Channel view! Yeah, that was one of his best places for a comfortable chat with friends, but mostly with sensitive persons. The place was a rather isolated block on the Eastern side of the channel, near Pabst Theater. When seated facing the channel, someone with keen eyes could literally see everyone around, so there was little chance to be followed by anyone or to have anyone with listening gadgets parked around. While relaxing in a white and comfortable plastic armchair, Archie took out his phone again and – taking advantage of the freshly lit evening lamps – he sent a brief message to Hicks, giving him the place and the time. He needed to speak to the old wizard and figure out what was his problem before attending the second meeting. He thought it would have been very embarrassing to forward a false alarm to his friend, not to mention that it could even turn dangerous. They would think he's out of hand and lost control inside Germina and he could not afford or permit that to happen. His goal was not only to make a lot of money, but to have enough in order to become a meaning person – somebody people should ask about before confronting. And of course – he smiled to himself, all by trying to stay alive in the process.

Even if already handsomely paid by the agency, he put up a hard salary negotiation with Germina Inc., especially after Sebastian Reading had been replaced a couple of years before by Oliver Schuster.

Schuster was a younger engineering specialist, recruited by Thorndike because of his credentials and mostly because he was painfully earning his buck as a second hand local crop dusting agent. He was a third generation German Jewish on American ground and except for his fair complexion and his rigid attitude he was rather easy to deal with. He proved to be a man of principles, understanding that Archie enjoyed total freedom with his departments on solid grounds and was smart enough to never make a move on that. He was supposed to do what Reading did before, but there was a personal touch in that because Thorndike made him somebody and he felt extremely indebted for that. Things were cool with Schuster and he didn't want to disturb them. But Schuster and Thorndike were not supposed to know all of his doings. He smiled and thought that if they were to know it all and speak about it, they would end up in solitary confinement or reclusion in an anonymous psychiatric facility that nobody heard of and nobody cared to visit. That is if they would still be alive! Nope, the distinguished Mr. Thorndike and the obedient Mr. Schuster will never know what's on his mind and when they'll find out, it will be too late and probably irrelevant.

He suddenly remembered about Betty and their meal and rushed back to the table.

– Sorry honey, just some annoying call from the office! I get so busy these days! Sometimes I fear I'll never get enough of you! – he smiled charmingly, watching the rather acrid look on her face while still chewing mechanically on a piece of pie. But the wine had already done its thing! There was only half of the second bottle left and first half finally started smiling at him.

–   I thought you left! She said licking gracefully her fingers. She took a generous sip from her glass and returned to him with an understanding smile: We'll never get along like this! I'm greedy – I want you for myself full time! She pushed away the plate with half eaten parts and smiled: Some more desert, maybe? We'll have to go! This wine turned me on.

Archie smiled back and waved the garcon:

–   Desert menu again, please!
–   Yes Sir! The boy vanished and returned like two seconds later with the menu booklet. Archie pushed it towards Becky, who grabbed it with less than sure hand.
–   I think I'll have …ice-cream! Yeah, vanilla ice-cream with strawberries!

The waiter dimmed his smile when hearing the ordinary choice – again!; after all, the chocolate mousse with Chinese caramelized fruit and fresh lemon cream was one of the most regular deserts and came practically at the same price. He swallowed his comments and answered with a professional smile:

–   Right away Madam! Anything for you Sir?
–   No thanks! …..And send me the check, please!
–   Certainly Sir! Would you be paying cash or card, Sir?
–   Cash! Thank, you!

Archie was very careful about using his card. Maybe this wasn't a very strategic meeting, but he knew the amount of information you can get tracing people's cards and he didn't want to become subject to that. Besides, it was impossible for his passion for Betty to go unnoticed indefinitely and his subconscious triggered an alarm signal concerning her becoming one of his weak spots – maybe the only one! He was definitely going to do something about it! Yeah – a major change! Starting with the color of the hair or something! But not tonight! No, tonight he was in for it. He felt an arousing sensation while she smiled at him licking on her strawberry ice-cream. There were parts of her very difficult to replace and right now he needed all of them.

He turned to the waiter and gave him the money, with the usual "keep the change!" stereotype and the convenience smiles.

She finally finished her desert, rose up and stretched a little, pushing her breast almost out of the cleavage and spread imperceptibly her extra-long impeccable legs, to the satisfaction of the still smiling waiter. She then pulled on her soft, short haired fur coat that resembled no well known animal and stepped towards the exit with exhausted gait. She grabbed Archie's arm and hung to it, pushing herself into his body until she made him feel her animal warmth. The couple walked away towards the silver Mercedes Coupé that was being parked at the entrance and the woman got in by pulling up her skirt until her long and slim legs uncovered the black lace garters.

"I'd take a ride on that beast!" – thought Nick, the waiter, still smiling about this double meaning. He than turned back to the table to clean the mess they left behind. Thinking about Maria, his Latino wife who was easier to jump than circle around after giving birth to three kids, he scratched his forehead and grinned. "I guess some things are only for some people" he sighed – "and I'm definitely not one of them". John smiled again at the thought – impeccable philosophy!

Archie drove elegantly towards their downtown suite, apparently ignoring the 400 horse power gently humming under the hood of his muscle car. There was no rush; he had been drinking, they were in a quite crowded area and there was no need to impress Elizabeth, who seemed already impressed by the Châteauneuf she placed on top of the Chardonnay.

–   So you'll be busy all day long, right? She was making a slight, but visible effort to articulate words correctly.
–   Yeah, I guess so! He answered his mind miles away.
–   Then it's time to start saying good bye for tomorrow morning, baby! She smiled and extended her hand pass the gear lever towards his pants. Still thinking to himself, Archie didn't seem

to realize what she was up to. She searched a little until she found the zipper and forced it down. With impressive dexterity and a rather cold hand she extracted the object of her interest and leaned down until her head was between Archie and the wheel. One short kiss and some tongue play and then she aspired the whole of it, keeping it tight until she felt it growing. This move made Archie smile and look down to her, as he was driving on their front alley towards the garage.

–   Now you have my undivided attention, he said to her, petting her head and gently forcing it towards him.

He made a final turn and parked on the left side of his big hangar for a garage, next to a black Porsche. The always red Ferrari wasn't missing and the shadowed part of the hangar displayed a special edition Range Rover Vogue, with shiny accessories and a large yellow Harley with fine leather harness.

He thought it was just in time, as her effort had started influencing his ability to drive. He unbuckled his belt and pushed the seat backwards to make more room. His right hand tore at her underclothes and reached a place as warm and humid as her mouth, still having the odd sensation of acting like a kid at a drive in. He leaned backwards in his chair trying to enjoy the sensation she gave with her tongue play and aspiration movements, enhanced by expert hand play. His fingers kept penetrating her as he enjoyed letting her lick them from time to time. After a short time of mutual effort, bright colors sparkled in his eyes as his seed came through. Betty felt him loose and accelerated her moves. Once cleared, she rose and visibly swallowed the whole load, smiling while performing some convenient after play hand tricks.

He took a deep breath, raised her head and smiled at her face, all messed up with lipstick:

–   Come on honey! Let's go inside. It's getting cold here and I need to drink a hot coffee. Already sobered up, Archie's mind was cooking things that a sumptuously drunk and willing Becky could not flush away with her well trained abilities.

CHAPTER VI

One month before

A WIDE WORLD

It was a regular early autumn day for London; mist and fog almost all morning, a bit of rain in the afternoon and a feeble, golden sun, which shined good-bye as early as 3 p.m., followed by grayish, but less arrogant clouds.

Marble Arch area was as crowded as ever, most of the people diverting towards Oxford Street, pouring up and down the "tube" entrance, near the "Prêt-a-manger" shop facing the Hyde Park entrance. The Cumberland was almost in the corner, with its classic and massive appearance, but with its futuristic hallway lights, changing colors every 3 hours or so. The downstairs bar was as crowded as ever, filled with the people courageous enough to step down the transparent glass stairs. It is a good place for a meeting – enough people to feel the public spirit, but not so many as to bother you. The light is always a little dimmer, so you don't have to worry about a loose tie or a too colored sports jacket. It is also a good place to have a drink, if you overlook the fact that beer was commonly as expensive as scotch; an elegant precaution against ordinary booze addicts.

A remote table in the corner hosted two characters. One of them, a bald tall man in his late sixties, with some resting shortly trimmed blond hair around his ears and a rich moustache, the size of a sparrow, across his reddish face, was dressed in a dark ultramarine coat and white shirt, on top of cream white trousers. He was also wearing a pair of oversized dark brown shoes that – judging by the frequently changed position of his feet – were difficult to accommodate in the limited space under the table. He was holding a giant beer mug in his right hand and was directing his speech with the left one.

The other, seemingly in his early thirties, medium dark complexion with some isolated grey hairs bordering his temples, looked more elegant in his appearance. He was wearing mustard - brown coat and black shirt, wisely fitted with the black trousers and shoes. A quite tall person – as one could judge from his seated position – but remarkably well proportioned and inspiring a sense of inner strength that had nothing to do with bulky muscle, his appearance was rather antagonist to the man sharing his table. He was absently starring towards the half -consumed coffee in front of him. His green intelligent eyes looked somewhat sad, but glowed in the obscurity of the bar as he turned to speak to his companion:

- So that's what you say, Henry - that I should take the job? What if I fail! So many before me fucked up and had to leave!

Henry Sutton took a deep breath - followed by a gulp from the mug - licked his lips and said:

- Yes, Pete! You should definitely take the bloody job! If a dozen scoundrels fail and have to go, why should that bother you? You are much better than they'll ever be. Besides – he took another sip from the recipient in front of him – if I come to think of it, I don't remember having anyone better than you, ever since we've been cooperating with the Office. For God's sake Peter, what do you want them to do – beg you?

Peter Bud was still looking beyond his coffee cup, slowly spinning it in fractioned 90° turns with his fingers, as if it were a "chanoyu" *

---

* Chanoyu (chadou) represents the "tea ceremony" for the Japanese. Honored guests may be invited to a ceremony which is much more than simple tea drinking; it becomes a ritual of exquisite complexity that includes tea

cup. His thoughtful look matched his softer voice, at least when compared to his companion's.

– I don't know Henry! If I do my job right and with honesty, I might upset somebody and I'll get into some kind of trouble. Come on, old man! We're not kids anymore! You know we talk about money, a lot of money – and when money is at stake, pressure is due to come; it's either the easy way or the hard way, until you finally do what they say! It's not the job, it's not the country, and it's not the first time, after all! For Heaven's sake man, this is a WHO job, not a countryside paramedic practice! Peter seemed to steam up his mood.

The older man named Sutton looked at him and smiled like a grandpa':

– You've always been the responsible type of man, haven't you? He shook Pete's shoulder with sympathy and continued: Well I've got good news for you; your breed is highly appreciated by anyone, even if they do not say… or do not pay! The bad news is that your kind is very rare, so rare they would put you stuffed in a bloody museum and have a good laugh at you every Sunday on open door Scouts festivities!

Peter Bud, the younger man, smiled and shook his head in disbelief.

– You're wrong, Henry! There are many decent people around us. They see what happens and understand the dirty "subtleties" of politics. They do not react simply because they are fed up with this misery and therefore refuse to be part of it or so they think. Look! In my country, people are so upset about politics right now

---

preparation, special and rigorous cup manipulation, spiritual conversation and careful courtesy. Generally, guests are required to officially express their appreciation for the invitation by a next day telegram or post-card.

that a candidate can get elected on a presence of 30% only – or even less! Tell me Henry – is this democracy? A guy that puts together 50% of the 30% coming to the poll gets to be elected mayor of a large city! In fact, he is voted by 15% of all the electors, and those 15% will decide the fate of the city and of the other 85% - who chose to stay home! - for the next 4 years. All the 85% say afterwards has no meaning, because the whole crap pile is legal!

Henry Sutton smiled again and gently tapped his lips and his huge moustache with a paper napkin.

– Tell you what, Buddy boy! He knew that calling Peter like this was rather irritating and wouldn't have gone unnoticed if it came from somebody else. Peter was Romanian by father origin and his family name – Bud – came from somewhere in Transylvania – Dracula's land! But now he wanted him stirred up and Henry was a specialist when it came to psychologically drive someone to do something. Of course, Peter would not protest about Henry's calling him Buddy, especially when that meant Henry was about to deliver to him an important message - and he was willing to accept it under these terms.

– You know that the WHO is a bloody complex institution! Right now, it is managed as one of the most apprehending international companies on the face of the Earth and the amount of money that goes into it is beyond your wildest imagination. Think only about the chronic diseases programs that most countries have and that's worth tens – maybe hundreds of billions for each state. Think about malaria drugs, AIDS or yellow fever vaccination – how much do you think that costs? We're talking here about 70% of the world's population depending on those, and the companies producing them can change governments in their countries – or others, for a fact – if they wish to! This is why inserting more decent people - like you – inside, can help us save some of that money, otherwise ending up in private and very selfish pockets. Do you think that Dr. Chang, the appointed Director General knows all about it, while sitting in her chair in Geneva? Well I'll tell you what! – Henry's face turned reddish! She knows nothing – I mean practically nothing – about the real dimension of the disaster – and this is because it happens that some relevant things are missing from her official incoming reports!

Henry stopped for taking a large sip from his beer. Peter was still looking at him attentively.

– Do you think Akamoa – the deputy, or the assistants like Aysward, Chestnovinski, Jamal, Nakatumo or Fujimori know exactly what is behind this? They are essentially good people, my friend, but like all other good people, they have the bad habit of trusting other people below them and sometimes this is not a good thing to do, because other people do not share at all the same kindness. Take for instance the swine flue! All affected countries went hysterical about this, but things calmed down only after the large serum producing companies started selling the "adequate" vaccine and the world felt safe once again! Even if they know something's fishy, they have to put the money in for adequate measures. Or they become vegetarian!

Henry looked down to his almost finished beer and said in a softer voice:

– But now, I'm sure that my information is reliable and something even uglier is cooking. By Jove, Peter, do you think the Russian president suddenly considers his country a community of independent states? Do you think the Al Qaida have weekly gatherings just to eat spicy "Camel aux champignons", drink tea and watch belly-dance? How do you think the whole ISIS dirty business started in the first place? Didn't you hear that Iran had no rain in the last fall because the European countries stopped the clouds from passing over their country? Think they're happy? The Chinese army has so little room in their garrisons they have to take turns when sleeping and eating, but I'm not afraid of them; what I'm afraid of is the many thousands I can't see dwelling in unknown labs experimenting something secret and nasty… Henry stopped to renew his air reserve and took a large gulp.

Peter knew that Henry was not bluffing. Henry may have been his friend, but he also happened to be one of the most influential inspectors of the Yard, when it came to "external" affairs cooked by MI 6. He had earned the specific type of independence allowing him to "poke" his nose into various domains of activity, some of which could hardly be guessed – from aero-spatial to cosmetics, from food – poisoning to art smuggling, from mining industry to health-care, you name it – you have it. Peter was frequently surprised about the amount of details – some of which very specific and deeply technical – that Henry Sutton operated with, regardless the subject or the moment. This thing inspired Peter's highest respect, along with that of many others, among which the MI6 officials who discretely, but constantly cooperated with Henry. Pete even wondered if that was not his real affiliation, after all. Apart from that, Henry was a straight speaking man, with a reputation of good balance between honesty and temper and a large dose of dry English humor; his popular style attracted friends and deceived foes, to the benefit of his office and his country.

- I'm supposed to work for the "Health security and environment" department – broke in Pete. The manager is a Japanese guy – Director Fujimori or something. Of course, I know about things that happen, Henry, but my concern is that they will expect of me to act "kindly" as you say, like stay in my little corner like the nice competent public clerk I am and let the authorities bother with the ugly things whenever they want, they can or happen to care about, which means I'll be out of action, most of the time. Nothing good will happen, either way. I'll get bored.
- Wrong again, my friend! You will see things, know people, experience problems and try to find solutions and then finally, you will know exactly what to do and when to do it! It is very

important not to rush! Act according to the law, cover your actions lawfully even when you cheat or lie – I'm sure you will do it only for a good cause. If you try to hit an enemy – do it only when your file on the subject is unbreakable and "shoot to kill". Remember – this is like open war – no side is taking prisoners. And, of course, I'll always be there to help if needed! You see, the term "security" is magic to me and I'm interested in everything connecting to it, especially after the bloody bus - bombing here, in my city! So, if you ever come across something peculiar or smell something fishy, don't forget to let me know – I won't barge into your business, but I could be very resourceful with information and adequate help! Speaking about this, here's a card with another telephone number you can use to contact me – a special one. You can use it for sending messages, too. I must warn you that any call or message from you may enable me to track you within a lot less than 30 seconds. Better keep it in your mind and destroy the card. You also have here a delegation very different from the ones your office will give you; it enables you to enter any restricted area in all national institutions from airports to museums, not to mention hospitals and laboratories. However, it will not be valid for private facilities, but I'm sure you'll manage somehow. Look Peter, I used to know your Grandpa for more than 15 years and became his friend when he came to England more than 30 years ago, hoping for a better and safer life. I still have deep regrets about his death, as he was a good friend, man of his word and taught me lots of things. Despite your father moving to US and his early passing while fighting for the US army against terrorism, you chose to follow his character footsteps. That comforts me for losing him as a friend, but also makes me feel responsible for you like you were my nephew. I know this is the kind of job you like to do, but this time you will have a lot more to deal with than common health security programs and computer statistics, that is if you chose to get involved. You're in for a great job; secrets will be revealed to you and sometimes you might be in danger. Nobody will touch an Assistant Director with spot-lights on him, but the rest of the team could become targets.

– Henry, stop this melodrama or you'll make me cry! Peter smiled. I know you were a good friend to Grandpa, but my life is not your responsibility; just need some sound advice sometimes. I guess it's nothing wrong if I'm fulfilling my career and I also use it to find out what's happening back home or at least in my area! I want you to understand me correctly – I do not regret my coming here! But I can't afford to remain totally disconnected to the land where my ancestors were born. Something fishy is going on up there and I intend to find out all about it! Don't worry Henry; I'll try to keep myself out of harm's way! Peter took another glance to the card in his hand and returned it to Henry:

– Here! You can have it back! I'll call you!

Henry Sutton sighed and stood up, waiving to the waiter, who presently showed the check. Peter interfered:

– My turn, Henry, remember? Peter smiled and left a ten- pound banknote on the table.
– All right then! I'll see you next week, Pete! Tell me how you're doing!
– Sure thing Henry! Have a nice evening!

They shook hands and departed the Cumberland in rather opposite directions – Henry chose Oxford Street and the crowd that helped him cheer-up and think better, whereas Peter entered Hyde Park and took an alley that led towards the Serpentine lake. He was carrying his trench coat loose on his arm; the passed rain did manage to warm up the atmosphere. He was in no hurry, or at least he made it look so, as he was trying to buy some time for thinking. It was not the first time he had to make a difficult decision; one of the most important was giving up on returning to his father's country - Romania. He was interested about the Communist past of the country and understanding it was not easy task. All the sordid secrets of the communist regime were being revealed one by one, using powerful media channels. What puzzled him more was that it didn't happen naturally, due to a legitimate aspiration of people to find out who tortured them or why, and to see the responsible ones punished or at least banned from political life. No, the weird thing was that dark secrets about someone seemed to "accidentally" make it to the press whenever that person was running for elections or was nominated for an important job! It all looked like a carefully directed hybrid war scenario and it sure looked like the Russian influence still lingered on. His Grandpa found a police activity councilor job in UK during the regime of the communist dictator and this seemed to be the best choice for all of them. His father chose to leave for US and married there his mother – an elegant, beautiful and educated young lady he met in DC. His father had a military career in US as a technician for mechanized infantry radio warfare and had left this world prematurely during the first Gulf war, leaving Peter a disoriented young man and a wife that was sick with breast cancer and died soon after.

Peter had been an excellent student and his outstanding results happened to be highly appreciated in the US, UK and in other few countries where he applied. He had graduated "George Washington University of Medicine in DC, along with some others, but only outstanding ones like him received scholarship. He went through a very serious testing in order to start his specialty studies in public health at this Medical School. His father was no longer near him and he wanted to honor his memory and please his terminally ill mother with such achievement. Meanwhile, he kept in touch with Henry Sutton, the friend and colleague to his late Grandpa, a man of extraordinary respect for principles and friendship.

After the Revolution in 1989, Romania represented – at least for a number of years – a heaven for fire-arms dealers, terrorists, Italian mafia leaders, international crooks and human traffic.

Remembering all these made Pete smile; he has always been so proud of his Grandpa and father. Walking along the alley, Pete heard the noise of loud voices and saw two workers in protection overall suits, engaged in a vivid dialogue over some bushes and little trees at some distance.

They had tools and an electric car nearby, but argued fiercely about the exact place of the implantation of some young trees.

– Nice evening – he said to them, hoping things were not already out of control. Do you need help or something?

The two workers turned to him quite irritated about his interruption, but soon one of them exposed something like a smile:

– *Dobry wieczór! Mi nie rozumiemy! My jesteśmy Polscy*!* Good bye!
– Oh, sorry! …. It's all right! Pete said – waving to them. So, I'm definitely not the only one – he thought smiling. So much for the Polish plumber! Looking at the massive trees in the distance shedding yellowish leaves in the evening twilight; he wondered why East-European's conversations always ended up looking like fights.

The large alley took a gentle right turn while directing towards the bridge across the Serpentine; the restaurant nearby the small boat and hydro-cycle pier was quite animated, but there was no boat on the lake at this time. A colder evening breeze was chasing away passers-by, as well as the low clouds on the evening sky.

Peter kept on slowly walking towards the middle road bordering Kensington Gardens. His shortly cut dark hair showed better the grayish shade. His slightly curved eyebrows were frowning. He could have been taken for a clerk or a police official with his reading glasses hanging loose on his chest, but few people would have guessed his advanced skills in martial arts. Peter was not married and his vivid activity was some excuse for it. Besides, he considered himself still too young and emotionally unstable for such commitment. He would generously step into a relationship with attractive and interesting women, but ended up alone as his professional activity and his habits made him more like a lone wolf than a socializing good catch. Many of the charming young ladies he met and even lived with, would eventually urge him to take a decision, but he wasn't ready for it yet and he didn't believe it mattered so much if bonds are stable enough

---

* Good evening! We don't understand! We are Polish! (Free translation from Polish language))

or safe-guarded by a simple ring. They were not strong enough; they left even if passionately regretting him. Besides, after the death of his father, his mother was entirely depending on him. She was always so kind and thoughtful, carefully leveling the inherent asperities developed between him and his severe father at a certain age, that he enjoyed showing her his undivided attention until her timely passing at a time when people enjoy a stable life surrounded by grandchildren, relatives and friends. People in the US had precious family values, but didn't share the same enthusiastic gathering - around that governed traditional Mediterranean or Balkanic habits. His mind flashed back again.

Peter was too upset to enjoy the fact that his grandpa had been inspired leaving in due time and avoiding to see all this aimless post-revolutionary drifting of his origin country; his father had seen it as a child all before time and warned him so often! He frowned while walking outside the park area towards the nearby museums. The Natural Science Museum and the Technical Museum were his favorite in the area. Even if carefully assessing painting – and sometimes experimenting it – Peter was no scholar and placed classics in a more boring drawer, in spite of their being located inside the Royal Galleries. He stepped mechanically down the street, noticing the fallen leaves attached to the side-walk by the evening moisture and returned to his former thoughts.

Fact was he had to make a great decision now, and this decision – despite the obvious complications and involvement – still represented a coronation of his efforts. He was a highly praised graduate in public health and he had crowned all this with his doctoral degree. Once refreshing his CV with the PhD degree and being a US citizen welcome in UK, new horizons opened for Pete and soon he was being selected as faculty for the institution he graduated. Few months later he was given the chance to complete his job capacities by acting as counselor for public health issues for DC metropolitan area. Some interesting and irritating issues for the authorities were solved with the help of a young and competent advisor of the municipality, who also managed to save significant public funds while doing so, hence Peter's opportunity to get in touch with the Health and Human

Services and expose some of his ideas. A more mature Peter Bud received the challenging job of deputy Director in the regional Public Health Institute and was in close touch with the WHO within the last couple of years. And now this – his being proposed as counselor for Dr. Fujimori -Director - at the "Health Security and Environment" Department of WHO! Not a bad way to build up a sound career – Peter smiled. He had reasonable suspicion that back in Romania, such development would have been impossible if he weren't somebody's son or nephew or even so.

But there was more to it than his will and merit; Peter had inherited from his father the urge to be the best and completed it with his determination to be worth something, to do something remarkable and to leave behind something remarkable. He was not a career chaser; his good results came in naturally and success did not alter his personality. Like all intelligent people, he grew up even more modest, never embarrassed by self-criticism and perspicaciously employing quality humor. He was perfectly aware of his capacity and the amplitude of his capabilities, yet shared the reasonable doubt that comes with common sense in decent people.

His father had been an intelligent man and a patriot. He had been graduating psychology and was familiar to English, Russian and French language. A distinctive intellectual and specialist in military information area and a tenacious tracker, he desperately fought to keep his family away from communism and terrorism.

His intelligence work in the US Army and preparation of the Gulf war often brought him close to Henry Sutton and many a fruitful cooperation led them to a stable and respectful friendship. In fact, it was Sutton that inspired Peter to proceed with full study advance in the US, easier to sustain as his parents were there with him.

He suddenly realized he was already reaching the crossing of the Exhibition Road with Cromwell Road and he resumed his forward direction towards Old Brompton Road. He had managed to rent a small apartment nearby, within the Sussex Mansions.

While walking and enjoying the fresh evening air, Peter realized he was hungry and it was time to eat. While going towards the middle block of the complex where his apartment was located,

Peter wondered where to stop and grab something to eat: at the "La Bouchee" or the "Rocca di Papa". He ultimately chose Italian and Luigi – the supervisor at the Rocca di Papa - greeted him and welcomed him, as Peter was a frequent customer. Peter suspected Luigi to be anything else but Italian, by the lousy "Bon giorno, Signora! Bona sera, Signore!" he managed to produce from time to time. There was an easiness of a Latin person to observe accent fault in Latin language use, in persons not sharing the same origin.

But Luigi was there to stay and he did a good job and for all it's worth, he could have been Vietnamese at that time; that wouldn't have had the chance to spoil Peter's appetite for "Pasta con le Sarde" and Chianti. Peter grabbed the bag and went to his block entrance.

He felt tired and acted accordingly. He opened the door, lit everything in his small suite and dumped the bag on the kitchen table. He took off his coat and refreshed before getting seated. He turned on the TV and switched to SKY news, which seemed too crowded with complicated politics – and he realized it didn't go with his appetite. He took the remote and browsed a little until he found a fresh episode of "Mrs. Robinson's sons". But his mind kept refreshing Sutton's words – "I'll be there when you need me!". What could be so important as to capture Sutton's undivided attention? He knew Henry to be one of the rare persons able to create a rock-solid case simply by putting bits and ends together, only now it seemed more than small potatoes.

He waited with his fork lifted in the air, as trying to pick a correct answer to his question, but then concentrated on his plate again; tomorrow will be another day and the first thing he'll have to make will be a clear decision. He felt a great deal of his pressure lifted from his shoulders as he lived with the impression that the decision had already been made.

CHAPTER VII

In the same time

SOMEWHERE IN AFRICA

Surya Abdilgani was looking into her microscope and gently moved the slide laterally to catch some details of the exposed insect. It was a mosquito, a female with rather peculiar characters.

She raised and wiped her forehead with a towel. It was warm weather even in autumn and the coming rainy season was not supposed to help; not in Somaliland. The Community Hospital in Hargeisa – the capital city of the independent province – had lived better days. She thought of her responsibilities as a General Manager and the lack of drugs and materials that threatened to close the gates every single day. She imagined how far from her friends' imagination her life was here in Somaliland, but it was her native land and she shared the call that many other fellow citizens from UK, other European or foreign countries obeyed.

Surya was an MD, PhD in infectious diseases and a Canadian citizen. She had left Somaliland 30 years before when she was young and scared and became a successful physician in Canada. She was married to a fellow countryman – successful engineer himself – and had a very good life so far. They had two kids, now both in college and wondering what is ma' doing back there. She smiled – Ma' was doing fine on an $ 300 monthly payment and she was doing fine because she was again close to her people and could finally help them directly, as she swore to herself she would do when she made her escape from poverty and social misery.

She had been born in a Somaliland freshly freed from its status of British protectorate in the 60's, but the hopes and ideals built by the citizens were soon dismantled by the power greedy communist regime of Siad Bare. Her parents did not wait for the known finale of the socialist soap opera and fled to Djibouti, then Egypt and later to Canada via France. How the unification attempt of Siad Bare failed they learned from TV, as well as about the desperate move of the Somaliland people to take again their destiny into their hands. Suffering bloody retaliation and devastation from their Mogadishu cousins, who stormed the country and made a shameful retreat stealing even the tin covering the houses, the citizens of Somaliland found themselves again poor in a rich country, but free from the ongoing abuses of General Aidid. The American involvement in Mogadishu proved to be a failure in the end and the power of the UNO forces was still limited and unable to control economical disaster and extremist behavior that led to the formation and development of Al Qaida branches like Al Shabbaab. Back South and in the Horn (Puntlands), trigger happy desperados have formed combat units that went to sea and experienced piracy, roaming the Eastern coast and getting enough prey as to feel encouraged to continue. The American military outpost in Djibouti was reassuring enough, at least for the shore of Somaliland at the Aden Gulf, including the port of Berbera, as the rest of the Eastern Coast belonged to the already mentioned independent province – Puntlands.

Surya thought of her local problems again and sighed. The Emergency Unit was still a mess; there were not enough stretchers and patients were placed on the floor at times. The X-ray unit was away from the ER and first aid was sometimes delayed and inconsistent. But basic drugs were available at least for emergency cases. It was difficult to understand and even more difficult to accept in the name of a poor society, at least after her Canadian experience, the lack of a sound health insurance system in Somaliland. It was true that their religion would not accept such system as well as interest banking, for a fact, but some state coverage for the emergency cases was necessary, far more than the actual contribution.

There was a knock on the door – few people would disturb her after ten o'clock at night.

- Come in! She said.
- Salaam! It was Faisal, the resident on duty.
- *Ska warran, Faisal*? (How are you Faisal?). She smiled. Faisal was a "fresh" comer in the unit. He was of the last year's graduates of the Prague Medical University and he was very eager to perform. His father was a bank owner in Hargeisa, but the son was not in for an easy life. He was industrious, well prepared and he had signed up for a future specialization in cardiology. Faisal smiled standing in front of her:
- Fine Madam! I was wondering, since you are here, could you come to the internal disease department to see Mr. Ahmed. He is not feeling well; he is a little feverish, sweating all over and grew shivers. But there are some neurological symptoms I'm worried about. He is originally a Maydh citizen, coming by transfer from Burao – I wonder if he is not one of those cases…

Dr. Surya Abdilgani sighed and rose, grabbing her stethoscope. It couldn't be another; not another in the same day!

- Very well Faisal! I sure hope you are wrong this time, but I fear that you are too good to get fooled by the symptoms.

They both walked uphill towards the internal diseases pavilion and entered the large patient's room. All patients were asleep at the time, with the mosquito protective canopies on top of them.

The cruel neon light made some of them blink and turn on the other side; some sighs made their way to their ears. They approached Ahmed's bed. Ahmed was a slim man in his forties, all soaked in his thin cotton blouse. His face was like carved in wet stone and his eyes glittered over the bedside. At times, short shivers and unwanted movements shook both his hands, yet the right one clinging tightly to the canopy. She also noticed that his right eyelid was slightly lowered as compared to the opposite one and his mouth was slightly drooling.

Dr. Abdilgani touched his forehead, then listened to his pounding heart and asked him:

- Ahmed, can you hear me? He nodded slightly. Please take my hand! She extended her right hand to grab his. Apparently, Ahmed was unable to open his fist and shake hand with her. He was trying to move his feet, but obvious movement was present only on the left one. She smiled to him.
- You're going to be well Ahmed! She said. I'm going to transfer you to another room, that's all! She made a discrete sign to Faisal and then talked to the nurse:
- He will be transferred to Pavilion C, along with the others. Same treatment! Please take blood and urine samples and do test it for malaria plasmodium, but also for bacteria like the ones I told you about. I want him seen by the neurologist right away – and yes, you will call him up and have him come here from home because I said so! Faisal – she turned towards her trainee – you've done a good job! She smiled – Keep an eye on them; we might find other cases. Remember all of you – keep clear and respect aseptic measures until we know what we are dealing with!

She went out of the suddenly airless room to a fresher air outside; this was something she had never seen

It was the ninth case this week. She was used to having 15-20 cases of malaria every year, sometimes even more, but this time all came from the same area and in a short time. The moors near Maydh were endemic area for malaria all right, but this was something else. Probably malaria, ok, but something extra as well. The question was which one came first. Her medical common sense told her that another disease started first and the crisis was triggered by malaria on top of it. She might have been less interested about this if it weren't for that mosquito's structure she recently discovered. She was familiar with all the local species and knew them for years. And now, a new one acting within the same area just like that, coming out of the blue. The insects she suspected were much larger than common mosquitoes, bearing some Amazon like features and the content of their digestive tube was full of bacteria of different shapes, many of which she could not identify. To her it looked like the Psoraphora Cilliata – a Caribbean species – but it seemed impossible to encounter it here. The laboratory she had was limited in action and it was not provided for extensive research. If her suspicions were right, she would have to report this to the Ministry of Health and perhaps suggest solutions. But treating something you don't know anything about would be impossible, so that Dr. Abdilgani thought about her chances. The local hospital lacked both money and time in order to improve its lab performance. They could ask for help from abroad. It could come cheaper from Djibouti or Addis Ababa, but it could be more sophisticated and pertinent when coming from the Emirates. This would mean Government involvement and budget clearance for something that others might say it's only her imagination building up a case on top of regular malaria outbreak.

But she knew her haunch was right; all the targeted cases had been seeking medical care during the months prior to this crisis, but now they came with various complaints that showed no common pattern. She registered random arthritis, eyesight troubles, kidney problems, tegument eruptions and a whole list of neurological disorders. The only thing that connected the patients – otherwise randomly distributed according to gender and age – was the place where they lived – the neighborhood of Maydh and later on, in the outskirts of Burao.

Once she has a case on this, she would of course have to discuss the matter with the authorities.

She stepped back towards her office, only to be approached by a young nurse coming her way:

– Madam, please! She raised her white long coat and her long dress in order to climb the stairs quicker. She sighed to catch her breath and wiped her wet forehead with the back of her hand, careful not to disturb her black and red head cover. She looked weak and thin, but her black eyes had an intense look that could not be shadowed by her ebony face or her beautiful reddish lips bordering pearl white teeth as she smiled.

- Please Madam! Could you come to see Suad, you know, the pregnant woman who was in labor yesterday. The child was born all right, but she is still bleeding a little and she has pain. I'm afraid to let her like this until tomorrow morning...

Dr. Abdilgani smiled and gently grabbed her shoulder:

- It is all right Nagwa! Let us go to the obstetrical department! What did the specialist say when he left?
- Dr. Ali Mohamed said we should carry on with the antibiotics and beware of hemorrhage and since you were here, I thought I'd call you first!
- Aha! Very good Nagwa! I'll check on her but do me a favor. Please call Dr. Ali and tell him I want him here by 11 p.m. to check on this patient. His decision comes first and we can't take any risks.
- All right madam! Thank you Madam! Nagwa already turned away to leave down the stairs, when suddenly she came back and looking at Dr. Abdilgani she said: I'm very happy we have you here Madam! Without you we'd all be dead by now!
- I'm happy to be here with you too, Nagwa! This is why I came back, after all, and I am here to stay!

Sweet child – she thought! Nagwa was 18 and an orphan practically grew up in the hospital. Her parents died before Dr. Abdilgani came as manager. Nagwa felt deeply indebted for the protection and the education Dr. Surya Abdilgani provided, and studied to become a nurse and always be around her benefactor. Nagwa already earned her own salary of about 60 dollars / month. She smiled; life will be harsh on Nagwa. Soon she will have to marry a hard working but probably less educated youngster, as she had no parents to provide a dowry. As any man sharing Muslim religion, he would become reluctant to her attending day and night nurse job in the hospital and she might be forced to stay home and raise children. Dr. Surya sighed

– these were some things still difficult to comprehend and even more difficult to solve. Not now! Not there! Not by her, she was afraid!

Nagwa left with her soul filled with love for dr. Surya. She was so generous with her and everybody else, for a fact– the Canadian woman was practically her mother. She found it difficult to express her love and admiration but this was a moment when she had the courage to do it and that made her feel happy. Her only hope was that Dr. Surya would never go away; she knew that was impossible, as the doctor's family demanded her presence a few months every year and for all she knew, the madam could simply go on a trip back home never to return. But she hoped that maybe Dr. Surya would decide to move back to Somaliland for good. Nagwa smiled – How naïve she could get! Who would leave from a developed country where one can enjoy a good life, only to experience the poverty in Somaliland, where even drinking water is scarce?

She would be satisfied is Dr. Surya would stay for a few years more. If it weren't for all those people bothering her! She remembered as Dr. Surya was very upset some days before when some unpleasant people with journalist credentials came by the hospital and started asking about patient statistics. They were particularly interested by malaria, but also other diseases she hadn't yet heard about, too. Dr. Surya had to cut short the talk sowing a visible discomfort. Some of them seemed to be Americans, but the next day some Russians came asking the same questions. Nagwa recalled that with one exception - the guy who spoke – all the rest seemed more like military than journalists. And with the second team it was the same problem. One better dressed and polite man, but the rest had brute faces. She was pleased when they left and prayed to never see them again.

Going up to the mother & child pavilion, Nagwa called the infirmary maid:

- Yasmine! Yasmine! Dr. Surya is coming to see Suad and her baby! See that she has everything she needs! I'll be in the other room to call up Dr. Ali! This won't make him very happy - she thought dialing the number.

After checking on Suad, Dr. Abdilgani went back to her office and her thoughts. The new events were rather puzzling. She thought she knew almost everything about the diseases of the place, at least after so many years and yet she was contemplating now something different. It didn't fit in the picture; she couldn't tell why, but something was out of place.

She turned on her microscope and started looking again at the female mosquito under the slide.

- Where are you from, girl? She mumbled! I think you would have an interesting story to tell if you could speak, but now I have to figure it all myself. She looked at the whitish color of the legs and antennas and the light brownish color of the body. Quite typical for light deprived organisms! What could keep such insect away from light? Even if crepuscular in feeding habits, mosquitoes spent a lot of time in daylight and other local species were proof as they had a much darker shade of brown, especially the anopheles. She smiled when the idea came to her and set back on her office chair, gently rubbing her chin:
- Who kept you in the dark, girl? The ones who fed you and taught you how to sting? She rose from the chair and started walking wall to wall – it made her think better. The hypothesis she contemplated was so crazy that she was afraid to go on within the same logic. If that was proven true, the consequences would be disastrous. But who would do it and why? Suddenly, it became clear for her why she found no plasmodium trace inside that mosquito. It was no anopheles, but then it was also not from Africa. What were the bugs inside – the ones the insect was supposed to spread – she would have to guess from the list of diseases linked to mosquitoes.

Dr. Abdilgani smiled again and she decided to make a medical report for the next morning; she felt she would be guilty if she didn't react. If she would prove to be wrong – so be it! She could take this kind of failure, but not the one presumed by inaction. She grabbed the phone and dialed a number; the phone rang repeatedly until a sleepy woman voice answered:

- Yes! Who is it?
- Dr. Abdilgani speaking! Rooda, my friend, *Ska warran*? (How are you?). Rooda was the senior pharmacist of the hospital; a nice person and a dear friend to Dr. Surya, always ready to help and full of ingenious ideas when it came to provide the "shop".
- I called to ask you something. Tomorrow morning when you get to the pharmacy please process the orders I am going to leave on your desk. I'm going to need a lot of antibiotics: Amoxicillin, Rocephyne, third generation cephalosporin, quinolones, doxacycline, and others I'll mention on the list. And when I say a lot, that means tons! Don't worry about the money; I'm going tomorrow to the Ministry of Health and I'm going to get it even if it's last thing I do! Why? Rooda my friend, because we're going to need them and fast! My only worry is that we could react too slow! Maybe it is already too late! Ok! Now go to sleep! We'll have a lot to do tomorrow!

Dr. Abdilgani hung up as she held her forehead with the other hand. How was she going to explain this? A haunch? Little if any medical proof! Just her medical expertise and her Canadian education that broadened her views! Knowing about what happens in the wide world keeps you informed…. and prepared. She decided to build up a legal back-up and set down in front of her computer, starting to write her report. As if remembering something, she got up again and went to the phone, dialing furiously a number she found in the book next to it:

- Hallo! Salaam, Dr. Ahmedin! Sorry to disturb you so late! Dr. Surya Abdilgani from Hargeisa state hospital calling!
  There was a man's voice speaking.
- Yes! Of course I wouldn't call you without having a serious reason. We have a confirmation of aggravated form of malaria of a ninth case from your region! All cases come from the Bahramat

neighborhood of Maydh and three more from the outskirts of Burao. According to my testing, there is something more or else than malaria about it and I have reasons to believe that you are bound to see more of this. We are going to give strong antibiotics along with malaria drugs and no, we did not identify the germ or germs yet. All I can tell you is that an alien species of mosquito could be responsible for this new complication or outbreak, so adequate measures should be taken immediately, until we figure out what we are dealing with.

Dr. Surya listened for a while and then she replied:

- Dr. Ahmedin, I do not have solid proof at this time, but I'm willing to risk my career on this. Yes, I'm dead serious, so serious that tomorrow I'll pay a visit to the Ministry. Hope she will listen to me and believe me! And Jamal, buy all the mosquito spray you can find tomorrow! We may need an entire shipload soon! …..The interlocutor said something more and Dr. Surya replied: Ok! Maybe it's better so; we could go together! I'll be around when you come!

Dr. Abdilgani went straight to her computer and continued writing with firm hands. She had reached the point beyond doubts; while explaining things to Dr. Jamal Ahmedin, she clarified some of the aspects in her mind. The few important questions resting in her thoughts were: Why? Who? And how?

Her only hope was that the Ministry of Health, Mrs. Fadumo Saaleh, would trust her reasoning and her expertise as she always did. Dr. Saaleh would be suspicious in the beginning, but Surya's Canadian credentials and her patriotic commitment would make her position hard to deny.

She soon finished her report and then she activated the printer in order to get two samples. She knew about the power of a piece of paper and she intended to keep track of each file she had to make.

By now, it was too late to go home. She picked the phone and dialed the ward room:

– Hallo! Samsam? Good evening my child; sorry to disturb you but I'll stay here for the night. Please bring me some biscuits and a jasmine tea for the night, will you?

Nobody knew how Samsam got in this unit and now nobody really cared about this. She was – according to needs – cleaning maid, infirmary maid or cook helper – she had knowledge of all practical things and she was worth her rather excessive weight in gold for this hospital. No one could imagine how things could have gone without Dr. Abdilgani, but they were pretty sure it would have been hell without Samsam! No more than five minutes later Samsam came to the office door and knocked gently:

– Hello! Madam, how are you? I brought you some chestnut honey to go with this tea. You will see how refreshing it will be. You will sleep like a baby and….
– Samsam, thank you but spare me the lecture. I'm tired my dear! Dr. Surya gently took her by the hand and pet her cheek. Grayish short hair could be guessed beneath her head covering scarf. I love you my dear… she continued.

Samsam took her hand, kissed it and put it on her forehead:

– Madam, I know you are upset. We all see it. Bad people came to you and I know we have problems. For us it is important that you are here to try to save us, Insha'Allah! Maybe some people will die, but then they always do! We're used to it. Allah will protect us! And we are close to you, so sleep tight and be fresh tomorrow!

Dr. Surya smiled to her and slowly embraced he for a decent hug. Samsam was no public speaker but she had her way with words and she always made herself understood.

- I'll be all right Samsam! Just remember to wake me up at 5 for the Morning Prayer. And Samsam! She paused: If anything goes wrong with the patients in Pavilion 6 let me know immediately!
- So be it Madam! Samsam made her exist in silence and Surya remained with her twisted thoughts. How long has this been happening? Who did it and how? Her mind was still busy with such thoughts when she fell asleep. It was late in the night when a gentle knock in the door made her get up.
- Yes! Who is it?
- It's me Madam! Samsam came with a sad smile on her face. I just wanted to tell you that Mohammed Ali Aksalla – you know – the one who came first from Maugh, died one hour ago. There was nothing to be done! Dr. Faisal was very upset; he tried to revive him for 30 minutes or so, but it was no hope. We can only pray to Allah for it to stop!
- It is all right Samsam! I was quite expecting it to happen! We're going to get to the bottom of this somehow, I promise! I'm sorry for him, but I sure hope to be able to save the others. Now, Samsam, go back to your quarters and make sure you bring me my morning tea at five, okay? And have Nagwa call the debriefing tomorrow at 8.30 sharp.
- Yes, Madam! Samsam departed the quarters. I sure hope you are right! Life gets so complicated sometimes for us, normal people! – She mumbled as she walked away.

Dr. Abdilgani smiled – the rest of us are the abnormal people, the ones bringing havoc in other people's lives! But this time it was going to be different! She will try and she will succeed!

Leaning above her computer screen she made her conclusion in the material for the Ministry of Health:

"In support of my theory, honorable Minister, I take the liberty of pointing out the main arguments:

    a) malaria outbreaks are not uncommon in the Maydh area, but this one is special because of its possible yet unlikely association with another infectious disease; We have registered an ever increasing death toll and now it rose to 1 patient per day; the total number is 37 at this time;

b) as the clinical aspect is similar, the crisis board implemented in Hargeisa concluded that all dead patients suffered from the same disease, probably spread by the same type of insect that disseminates malaria (mosquito); we also have indications and suspicions about the possibility of person – to – person contamination or perhaps stung by same contaminated insect;

c) a strange and practically out of place mosquito was accidentally caught and registered in the Maydh area; the mosquito resembles the species called Psoraphora Cilliata, normally located in the Caribbean and it is believed that it might be related to the disease outbreak;

d) with respect to the national security of Somaliland, we strongly believe and advise that natural migration does not explain the presence of this mosquito species and it is very likely that the insect was brought here accidentally, even if we have poor air travel connection ; however, the number of such insects suggests a possible alien deployment, which makes this a problem of national security;

e) in view of the above mentioned, we request your help in conducting a nation-wide investigation in the following 2-3 days over this peculiar incident; if the results sustain our point of view, we strongly advise requesting immediate investigation and help from the WHO. I take the liberty of emphasizing the importance of quick decisions and action upon a matter which can turn into a national health disaster.

While waiting for your immediate response, please receive my deepest respect and appreciation for the work you are doing.

Dr. Surya Abdilgani; MD; PhD;
Consultant - Infectious diseases"

"She must trust me on this – she sure will. It is too scary to be overlooked anyway!" Surya thought and sighed.

With a last thought on her determination to do the right thing, she fell asleep for another 45 minutes.

CHAPTER VIII

At the same time

SOMEWHERE IN EUROPE

It has been a long day and a long night. Dr. Georg Cristian, also German citizen, enjoyed his first morning coffee in his office, at the Hyperbaric Medicine Facility in Constanta, the greatest Romanian port city at the Black Sea. Life was different ever since the economic crisis began.

He had been a close to genius student in high school and a very successful medical school graduate in post-revolutionary Romania, but chose to launch his career elsewhere. He had set his mind on Germany. He made it big time there, working his way up to the position of Chief of the Hyperbaric Medical Facilities of Bielefeld, covering for the whole Northern region of Germany.

A man of wide medical proficiency, he was able to describe clinical assessment, physio-pathological theoretical subtleties and a significant number of treatment proceedings in various diseases, regardless the item. He was also a man of quick thinking – well, sometimes too quick, one would say - but he proved right almost every time and – again to some people's discomfort - he had a pleasure in showing it publicly and defiantly, which made him less efficient in making friends.

Dr. Christian took another sip from his fresh Latte Macchiato and looked around. This was all his doing! The house, the lab, the hyperbaric chamber that was worth $ 1,5 million; they were all his and they signified a fresh start.

As soon as the European crisis restricted health funding – that was under the keen eye and ordering of Germany's "Iron" woman Chancellor – originating in East (Communist) Germany– his hyperbaric center went to a stall and everything turned to pieces. He had to give up some of the chambers and took one of his own back to Romania. It had been very difficult to complete all paperwork, especially because he soon got officially recognized as the one and only specialist in this medical branch in Romania, yet still being a German citizen. But now he was working as a private entrepreneur on his facility; more and more patients came to seek advice or treatment and the chamber was full 365 days / year, most of the time by two proceedings per day. He already had good cooperation with trauma & orthopedic surgery specialists, surgeons, neurologists, one talented PhD in transmissible diseases and had contact with the laboratories of the local Medical University. He was also fighting a savage war against the ignorance or jealousy of many colleagues and the suspicion of numerous patients. Yet some of the projects he started with his close friends already paid off. Research and medical reports were on the way concerning the positive association between the mycoplasma infection and certain less well- known diseases like lupus, avascular necrosis in bones (and especially that of the femoral head), spondylitis, random arthritis syndrome, lateral sclerosis, some neurological disorders and even autism.

Dr. Cristian was thrilled about gathering so much data; it would have been very difficult to do it in Germany. However, he owed his skills and his expertise to the German proceedings regarding Nano-bacterial infections, especially Lyme disease, which was a real problem in Northern lands. Apart from borrelia, dr. Cristian had already identified a number of other similar rare bacterial agents possibly involved in the diseases he was treating by his hyperbaric chamber: Mycoplasma, Babesia, Ehrlichia and even well- known parasites like Toxoplasma.

The principle involved in hyperbaric oxygen therapy treatment was the capacity of oxygen with increased partial pressure to boost its diffusion inside the organism ten times compared to normal.

But Dr. Christian was also concerned about other facts. Ischemia was a good and spectacular indication. And profitable, for a fact! With infections, things were rather different. He had been part of the German offensive against Lyme disease and of the Federal Government plan to control the disease. Now that the danger was no longer so great, authorities started losing interest in this type of treatment, especially under the indications of the Saxon Chancellor that ruled not only Germany, but the whole Europe during this strange crisis. Yet by his coming back to Romania fully equipped and prepared to do business, it didn't go bad. He smiled: not bad at all! Anyway, the new borrelia strain he depicted in one patient puzzled him; very different from the Burgdorpheri, which was the traditional culprit in the area, this afzeli type created havoc. He found again the same strain in a 5 year old child that developed a tremendously rapid neurological involution. The poor girl was practically comatose within 10 days and sent home from the highest clinic in Bucharest to die in peace, and only the desperation of her mother brought her to his facility. His experience and eroded feelings didn't help when he saw the little girl walking again next to her mother only 7 proceedings and a week later: they all had tears in their eyes! A skilled practician and a cunning scientist, he did not believe in coincidence. The third case with similar symptoms was the daughter of a known cardiologist in Bucharest and blood tests ran in Austria disclosed the truth: it was the same germ – a certain Borrelia afzeli, otherwise not very different from the rest, but this strain seemed strangely aggressive. There was something wrong with this germ; he had a bad feeling about it, but as it always happened, it was his haunch against the good old books! The question that kept his mind busy was only natural: How can a quite well- known germ – even if rarely encountered as infectious agent – suddenly grow more aggressive and invasive than it ever was during the previous 200 million years? While everybody was concerned and occupied with Borrelia Burgdorpheri, this minor cousin suddenly decides to become more powerful and a potential killer! The logical answer was crystal clear in his mind; somebody mingled with it and made it more powerful and more resistant, but who and why? Why did it start striking now? Why did it strike in communities not related to ticks or the appropriate geographical environment? He had heard about some US labs dealing with Lyme disease research; his suspicious nature made him think it was not impossible to consider this research more than treatment related and bearing active trends. One American scientist – a Facebook friend called Hans Stebinger – from Massachusetts, even admitted having had some related research in the 80s, but he said their contract went to a stall as financing was switched off. He assumed there was no more interest in the subject or maybe somebody came up with better results. Either way, he was surprised to find out about the early and distant spreading of such strain.

Maybe Stebinger was right. The lack of interest is not a likely option for this century, Cristian thought. He smiled: scientists always being tributary to sometimes childish jealousy! Obviously, some other lab came up with more fruitful research, but even this was not something of ravishing importance. The problem was how the germ got inside those patients. Even if not totally reliable, patients declared no tick sting within the previous 5 years or as far as they could remember! Again, logic must take over and come up with an answer. If there were no ticks, some other being – most likely an insect – played intermediary. The only common insect to blame within the area is mosquito. It was known that West Nile virus had outbursts every 2-3 years or so, but they were somehow predictable. But if contaminated mosquitoes did this, his first thought was he could get more patients, yet suddenly realizing that such development could trigger mass disease, far beyond his logistical capacity. Maybe far beyond anybody's logistical capacity! "I must be raving mad" he thought to himself and smiled. Mosquitoes did not carry borrelia! Everybody knew that! Maybe this was the reason for which some people did not take him seriously; maybe he had this inclination towards exaggerating or daydreaming as he saw things beyond normal comprehension. Well, it was all right! He couldn't change now and he wouldn't do it even if they urged him to! He had lost much but gained more by being himself. He took his notebook and marked some observations he intended to comment with his friends first. If there was one harsh lesson he learned on his way back to

Romania, it was the one that you shouldn't brag about something unless you are positive about it and it is better to disclose facts first and then, when everybody is desperate about answers, come in with reasonable explanation. Preferably without criticizing anyone! The last part was the one he could not master properly, as his irony flooded conversation every time he would catch someone off guard and out of the subject.

The facility was slowly getting to motion. Yvonne, the know-it-all secretary, a sweet brunette with interminable legs, came in waiving hand:

- Good morning doctor! She stumped her feet on the entrance door carpet and tic-ticked her high hill shoes towards the large console with 2 computers, faxes, scanners and printers all around.

Cristian recalled his first meeting Yvonne under circumstances his wife Sylvia would find very annoying and then thought about her efficient job at the facility. She was there practically 16 hours a day, even if she was paid a handsome salary for 8 plus bonus for weekends. Work at the hyperbaric facility was 7/7, 365/year; there was no Christmas or Easter break; there was no stopping of the proceedings on which the patients depended. It was hard to do, but not impossible, it seems. He looked again at her impeccable legs dressed in black stockings and sighed; sweet memories do not stand the trial of time. He smiled and answered:

- Hi Yvonne! You're beautiful today and you look very energetic!
- Ta, ta, ta! Doctor Cristian, careful with compliments! Mrs. Sylvia could come anytime now and you'll get only a sandwich for lunch, if you carry on like this. Here, I'll fix both of you a new coffee.
- It's okay Yvonne! I don't know what I could do without you! Please fix the files for today when you finish having your coffee. And check the mail; I'm waiting for an interesting message from the States! Well – that is if they decide to answer!
- All righty! Just wait a little until I get my clothes off! Not all of them dr. Cristian, do not worry! What is on your mind?

– I don't know! I keep thinking about these new cases. It's odd to find this strain of bacteria now and here. It seems out of place! Pretty severe complications, too! Here, Yvonne! Please give me another cup of coffee! Black, this time!

He extended his hand to the pocket where he held his cigarettes – "chopped straw" – he called them, much to his wife's dissatisfaction.

– Come on girls – this is nothing compared to the plain Camels I used to smoke! He extended the slim lady cut cigarette that he burned by 1/3 in one single sip. This is junk; I'm smoking more paper than tobacco! – He complained. It's no big deal; I'm just doing 4-5 a day! Hope the paper's not recycled!

Dr. Cristian was already caught in a fierce conversation with a fellow colleague from Germany, as he requested some new information on the etiology of Lyme disease- like syndromes in the past five years. Not that he expected any surprise, but he wanted to be convinced that the presence of the new strain was quite isolated and consequently carried a different meaning.

– Yes Yvonne! He mumbled and mechanically crashed the remains of his cigarette in an ashtray nearby, eyes on the monitor. A new idea was coming to him; he was going to call his former post-university PhD education colleague Peter Bud, freshly hired by the WHO according to the latest Facebook posting. "Yes, Yvonne, why don't I call Peter?" he mumbled again.
– Never mind! She said and closed the door gently behind her. After all, first patient group was due to come within half hour and everything was to get started. She produced a small phone from her pocket and dialed a registered number:

Yvonne felt that something was rather unusual about Cristian; he was very tense and preoccupied about something, possibly related to the new cases he had to treat. She was very fond of him as a dear friend and boss; never tried to control him. Maybe he was no Prince Charming, but he was a tall handsome guy, short hair, "barba –de-quarto-giorni" – a four day beard, and with slim, elegant appearance; a little unpredictable – she thought, but that was something meant to make life so less boring. She would have acted differently with him, that was for sure, but that was a distant thought, as his wife did not waste any opportunity to show her that they belong to different classes.

Dr. Cristian was talking over the phone to someone in the States.

- Thank you Professor Schuster! Thank you for the e-mail address! I will write about my points of interest! Once again, I am indebted to you, Sir!

He hung up and smiled:

- Well, it all starts making sense, after all!

CHAPTER IX

One month before

WHO'S AFRAID OF THE BIG BAD WOLF

One month later, Stephen Hicks was still under the impression of the animated lunch dialogue he had with Archie Donovan. It was the first time in many years he felt rather unsecure.

Again, it was the first time he perceived Archie as a different, terribly strange and menacing entity, so distant and cold and even aggressive to him, in a way he would never have believed it before.

Archie was not rude to him; on the contrary – he was smiling and friendly as always, but despite the encouraging words, his eyes told a different story. The suspicious nature of Hicks took over and after so many days was still ruling his conduct. The alarm bell in his head has started buzzing and the fearful Hicks kept on hearing it day and night. Especially during nights! And more frequent relaxing Jacuzzi experiences did not help; he was even more tired than before!

Archie had tried again to minimize things by playing the reassuring act, but it was something so professional in his way of doing it and such obvious lack of personal involvement, that Hicks was caught by surprise. Donovan was also very evasive about solutions. Maybe he had been day-dreaming about his relationship with Archie; maybe he had just seen the good and happy parts and was deliberately blind to the real facts he should have never ignored.

He had been so naïve to think they liked him; maybe they just needed him meanwhile and Archie was cold enough to socialize with him as long as he was useful to the organization.

It was all turning into a nightmare. Few days after his talk with Archie, his frantic round the clock search on the Internet paid off: new interesting interventions on the forum displayed the particular interest of the Romanian doctor – in fact a German citizen called xy – concerning his patients with infections inflicted by peculiar Borellia strain. And even worse than that, his most powerful competitor and personal enemy, Hans Stebinger, from the "United Chemicals" in Massachusetts, had entered the dialogue. He even disclosed the interest and the activity of his lab around Lyme disease and the involved germs, until they lost contracts for this job.

Stebinger also admitted cooperation with army officials during experiments.

Another very alarming fact was that officials in Eastern Africa had recently described a suspicious outbreak of malaria, complicated with what was believed to be a strange and acute development of an infectious disease, which already had killed more than 30 people. Local investigators blamed alien insect species for the outbreak and had been making steps in demanding a WHO investigation.

The obvious lack of funds – common reason for poor nations to reach for the WHO – would not deter Hick's mind from two significant details adding poison to his tormented mind: the emphasis on "alien' insects being blamed for the outbreak and the severity of the disease. Malaria was carried by mosquitoes and the other disease came – most likely, in his opinion – the same way.

"Oh, yes!" he thought – that is the missing link! The malaria bug and the Borellia carried by "Hicks" mosquitoes! The Pandora box had been opened – Hicks thought. He had been unable to sleep that night and spent the day after pinned in his armchair, heavily drinking whatever came to his hand, as long as it had alcohol in it.

Two days later he had to replace his liquor reserve and went out. A suddenly older Hicks wondered the streets, his pale smile towards the shop attendant making him look freshly unburied. Hicks was a very afraid man; he had been striving to establish a personal universe where he enjoyed total satisfaction and now, he was scared stiff that everything will be shattered to pieces by this old history.

The worst thing he was afraid of, was being ignorant to facts and letting things happen their own way.

Even if the bug had gotten out somehow – or maybe was taken out, who knows? – he could not understand the severity of the disease and the quick occurrence of consequences. As far as he knew, the Borellia he had engineered had the capacity of being parasite to mosquitoes, and spread much easier, but otherwise it was not more dangerous than other similar strains, once you managed to identify the strain. Or was it? He never had time to verify before if the financing of the project was indeed cut.

What had happened along the way? Slight mutations are likely to occur in no less than 20 or 30 years, but the question was if radical ones like those inducing such aggressiveness were natural or came with that modification he was responsible for?

The conviction that he couldn't have been responsible for such development had been rather comforting and helped him pull together. He started working again at the lab and beside his increased nervousness, his sometimes- unpredictable actions and occasionally controversial decisions, he seemed again the old Hicks, only weaker – if that was possible – and uglier – which was even less convenient for him..

His mind was made; he was going to see what happened after the Borellia accident and try to figure out whether this could be dangerous to him in any way. He had his info sources; he wasn't regularly using them, thus trying to avoid suspicion, but sometimes, as the cautious person he was, he needed some answers able to protect him. Each of some three notary legalized letters he wrote was safely closed in one prominent Milwaukee bank (Tri City, Pyramax and Bank of America) and its content was to be referred to the police as well as the local and national press, should something nasty happen to him.

His allegations were solidly backed up by crucial document copies in each of the three letters that were supposed to be opened and remitted to destination in the highly unlikely – he hoped – event of his untimely violent death.

That was not supposed to be a defense mechanism, as he told no one about the letters, but a deadly late revenge to those that supposedly killed him. He may have been naïve, but not so much as to imagine that the products he made were sold only for crop dusting.

He needed some security, yet being unable to speculate on it. He did feel tempted once or twice to tell Archie about the letters, but failed to do so, realizing he didn't know Archie that well – at least, not well enough to trust him on this. Now he was pleased he had told no one about the letters – especially to Archie, whom he was currently growing afraid of. It looked like a cunning revenge, yet Stephen was not seriously contemplating this M.I.A. scenario. He always wondered if he could somehow savor the outcome after or the whole thing was just supposed to help him pass away in a more dignified manner.

He felt pretty sure that such danger could only come from his company's discrete security system, but only if he did severe mistakes! News on the net suggested he somehow did it, but he was still the only one to know it. Crap! Apart from Archie, of course! He and his big mouth! No one was reacting yet and this made him happy, as it seemed much less important than he thought before!

But now he felt somehow that Archie was no longer the good story telling friend he knew and would not hesitate to harm him if necessary! So much for a long friendship! They have shared bar shots, joints and cigarettes and later on cigars, pussies even, yet now he felt better when thinking about the letters.

Maybe he should tell Archie about them and see how he reacts. Or maybe not! What if Archie would overreact? He had seen him before mutilating people when blinded by fury! No! No! No! It was much better to keep this secret to himself!

He needed to keep a clear mind and avoid panic! He would have plenty of time to bring up this subject if forced by unwanted opportunities and he hoped none of those would occur.

But Hicks was no longer in control of his life and he knew it. The temptation to flee and leave it all behind was massive, yet reason instructed him that drawing too much attention on his person right now would be equally inappropriate and dangerous.

He was sure he had lost Archie's confidence – not really knowing when – and he sensed that the next logical step would be to cover his ass. He was sorry he now he overreacted during his talk with Archie. There were embarrassing scenes at the restaurant when they met and the result had been far from satisfactory. It was true that Archie had no possibility to calm him down as long as he was terrified by his own demons, but then it didn't mean that he will also forget this terrible encounter. They were alone in the restaurant, so that nobody had seen the unleashed and hysterical Hicks, but the cold look in Archie's eyes was one that later gave him chills up and down his spine.

– Hey! Be careful with that! Stephen hicks yelled to one of the workers inside the depot who was trying to stack some crates with a small Caterpillar fork-lift. The man acknowledged and lowered his speed, setting the crates on top of a huge pile of similar ones.

All labels were blue and had a Germina Inc. mark with a "Fertilizer' under-word. Regular stuff – Hicks thought, but with foul smell and able to stain everything around till doom's day!

He continued his walk towards his laboratory and stopped in front of a coffee machine to take a sweet filter. He grabbed the hot cup holding it with a fresh paper towel and took a sip burning his tongue. As he went towards his office he stepped inside his secretary's room. The young man behind the counter smiled to him:

– Anything wrong Sir?
– Nope! Just wanted to tell you to prepare some older files for me; I want to see the older studies and experiments we had on Lyme disease. I'm interested in biological assessment concerning germ multiplication rate and toxic enzymes. Search in library shelf no. 4, CD recordings from 1985-1990! And David, I need the genuine info, not the ones released for officials and media!

- Very well Sir! Just give me half an hour and I'll make a file on those!
- Very well David! Take your time! And make sure you find a list with all interested contractors and dealers we sold any stuff to. I just want to study them this afternoon; I may start a new research on that in winter! Just one more thing: don't register this request! It's just for refreshing my memory! I get so confused with all this stuff around!
- Right Sir! David, an ex hopeless chemistry teacher in his thirties, short hair -cut, ear ring and fancy clothes, smiled to him. By the way Sir! Mr. Donovan said you should call him when you get to the office!

Hicks wiped out the smile from his face. He turned back to David and, recomposing his voice, he answered:

- Oh, yeah? Ok. I'll call him! Just get on with that file, please!
- Sure thing! I'll live it on your desk if you're not there!

Hicks waved to him and went to his office, some thirty feet across the hallway. He entered the large office with mahogany covered walls, went straight to the refrigerator and took out a large straight bourbon bottle. He poured a generous amount in a glass and took a long sip before crashing in his armchair. He extended a trembling hand to the phone and dialed Archie's number.

- Hi, Archie! Fake optimism wrapped his voice while speaking. How are you? Just went to grab a coffee!
- Listen Stephen! Could you come to my office…say…in about ten minutes? I've got something to talk to you about.
- Sure Archie! Sure thing….I'll be there in ten…Bye! A more trembling voice ended the conversation.

Hicks extended his chair and lay back, holding his glass of bourbon with both hands. How official Archie sounded today! Old fears and newer shivers reached to Stephen's spine, as he gulped the rest of the liquor like water. He poured another one, thinking that he had another seven minutes to pull himself together. The worst possible thing was to let Archie see how afraid he is! After all, he was Professor Hicks, a man with strong reputation and a real wizard in microbiology and no one would dare touch him. All he did was by direct orders (which he accidentally managed to record and register) and if Archie had a problem with that, he should find another scapegoat. After all, he simply blew the whistle on a subject much too sensitive for the company to be blamed by anyone. Yeah, no one could have the nerve to confront him and he was still too valuable for the company to become disposable. Adequate action was needed to wrap up this thing properly so that nothing would happen to the company's name (or to him, for a fact).

As he stepped out the office towards Archie's, he thought that this job was, in fact, perfectly fit for the Security Exec., in other words, the ball was in Archie's court and now he was called to be informed about the next move. After all, Archie had been officially informed about the infectious events in Romania and Africa, so that neglecting such information was out of the question.

In a twisted way, Hicks was confident that he had managed to manipulate Archie on this one; the man was to solve a mandatory security problem for the company and Hicks would largely benefit from the results. "Yeah, pal! This time I hired you to do something for me", he thought, entering Archie's office with a large smile on.

– Hi Archie!
– Hi yourself, Stephen! Have a seat! Archie pointed out to a smaller chair in front of him. Putting invited people in the position to look upwards to him was one of Archie's old but efficient techniques of intimidation.

Hicks collapsed into the narrow armchair, combing his long grayish hair with the right hand and lifting his white lab gown. A comfortable coat color, for dandruff pouring from his scalp would not be visible anymore. Meanwhile, Archie was pretending – or maybe not – to read from some files in front of him. Hicks froze when he saw the mark on the file covers: they were the very same he had been asking David to prepare for him minutes before!

- Surprised, Stephen? I had a feeling you'd ask for these, right? Archie raised his head with a broad and satisfied smile on his gentleman's face, but his eyes kept a sad, expressionless appearance. You'll tell David to get it from me, but only when I'm done with them. Understood?
- Su…sure Archie!
- Oh! One more thing – from now on you have restricted access to older contracts on this matter! Security decision; I expect no comments on that!

The trembling voice of the mouse inside Hicks was making its way to his lips again. He coughed twice conveniently, and then continued on a more masculine and reassuring tone:

- What's the big deal anyway? The documents are done by my office and signed by me, so there shouldn't be any problem! After all, I'm the one who got interested in this issue and I'm the one who signaled this potential problem for the company! Stephen was raising the voice as he felt he was right and brought argument in the dialogue.
- Shut the fuck up, you moron! Archie rose from his chair, eyes glittering and his fist turned white while hitting the table. The problem is you – only you – because you've got a big mouth, a brain the size of your bugs and got way too much interested in this issue!

Hicks became even smaller in his chair and bowed the head like a cornered dog towards the stronger enemy. He didn't have the power to look into Archie's eyes at the moment, so he simply sat there twisting his wrist watch metal brace like counting coins.

As if regretting his previous explosion, Archie turned to a cupboard behind him and took 2 glasses and a bottle of single barrel Jack. He poured a few drops in his glass and filled half of Stephen's.

- Hicks! I know you've worked on the item long ago. Remember this: it was LONG ….AGO! It has nothing to do with the things you uncovered recently. What you found out has nothing to do with the company, so stop bullshitting me and pretending you are a man of sacrifice! I know only too well you're preoccupied by your own ass and nothing else, so spare me the lecture on this!

Again in control, Archie smiled once more, but his evil eyes did not follow the rest of the face.

- Here's to you Stephen! Cause you are a VALUABLE ASSET of this company! He touched Stephen's glass with a slight crystalline kliinnngggg- noise and took a sip.

Hicks took the glass, apparently disregarding the proportion of liquor compared to the other one and took a longer sip, almost cleaning dry the glass. All this time he was unable to take eyes from Donovan, who seemed to hypnotically attract his attention.

- But Stephen, if you stick your nose one more time into this matter again, I promise you to become a DISPOSABLE asset of the company! Have I been clear enough, Hicks?

Stephen took some time to receive and process the hit. He suddenly looked at his empty glass and rose slowly, like a rheumatic old man. He went to the bar and poured another whiskey, took a gulp and turned towards Archie trying to put up a smile.

- Don't worry Archie! I may be a pain in the ass sometimes but I'm not crazy. I'll leave it up to you! You were right about me! I'm growing old and selfish… Stephen made a pause……and afraid! But any stupid allegation can turn the focus on our company and such scandal means termination, for me surely, but also for you. I may die sooner than you will, Archie, but I do not want to die poor, that's all!

Stephen took the glass and finished his second drink.

- Thanks for the drink! I needed it!

He then turned his back on Archie and went out the door in silence.

The two men parted, taking very different thoughts with them.
As Hicks left the office, Archie stood behind the desk for some time and then went to the bar and poured himself a more significant drink than the first one. He was hoping he succeeded in scaring Stephen enough in order to calm him down and bring him back to his regular activities. The old goat did not want to die poor!!!, like he would vote for that himself! What Hicks didn't know was that Germina Inc. may have been the only money source just for him, but no longer for Archie! In fact, at this time Donovan couldn't care less about the future of the company! For what he knew, it could close the next day after he completed his business. He would be far away by then, spending a lot of money under a new name and enjoying a fresh and more relaxing career. The important thing was to finish collecting the information he needed and send it to the right place in due time, which meant within three weeks.

Maybe Hicks would be getting suspicious about being banned from access to some files, but he should be too scared by now to try to even think about this, and by the time he would be reacting somehow, it will be too late. The fact that Archie knew everything from his office was no big surprise to anyone; what they didn't know was that Archie could also see and hear them in the rest-rooms and – valid for a great number, including Hicks –even at home. Like this he would know everything about their profile, from diet to sexual fantasies and all this information served for just one purpose – his personal interest and ability to manipulate and use them.

On the other hand, Stephen's interest in the contracts puzzled him and proved to be the only somehow worrying aspect: Hicks smelled something and his nose were trained to sniff money. Under a calmer perspective, Archie had to admit that banning Hicks all access to contracts had been a momentary and maybe rushed decision! Yeah! Maybe this would paradoxically make Stephen's interest grow even bigger! He had to get softer on that somehow. He would pretend forgetting about it in a couple of days and maybe even meet Hicks in a restaurant; chat again like the "nothing- happened-between-us" type of meeting! That would be a good idea, but Hicks should learn very carefully not to poke his vulture-like nose into his business or else…risks to be eliminated from the equation.

Stronger men had been trying to defeat Donovan or catch him guard-down; they were all memories now and none lived to tell the tale! He'd been having the idea for some time, ever since Hicks started this hysteria over the Lyme disease contracts, but the professor was still valuable in his research, provided he worked like he used to. Yet Archie had also sensed that Hicks was no longer in his normal mood – he seemed scared, elusive and paranoid. This was a poisonous combination for Archie's interests and for the company's welfare, yet Hicks still was a hard to crack nut, not so easy to replace. More like the rabid coyote trying to bite you even after you put it down!

Some of the already commenced research could have been finished by his colleagues, and especially by John Plunket, a PhD degree in microbiology, who promised to become a new Hicks, even with less peculiar behavior. That would give them one year – he thought at the time – to rebuild the team. But now it was a different story. Hicks was suspecting something, and was not going to give up that easily; he must have cooked some B or C plan for his future meanwhile! Yeah! The sneaky old fox was better off close to him than knitting something fishy out of his view!

Big boss Schuster must also have smelled something, but conveniently kept his nose out of Archie's business as usual; he would interfere only on very obvious things!

Even his "friends" from the Agency had started asking some irritating questions concerning a number of contracts and some unexpected meetings he failed to report about.

He was keeping it all under control, or so he thought. After all the time and the risk, three more lousy weeks there and he would be free to quit and leave, never to return! Obviously, no one knew – or was supposed to know - about his planning to quit on a very short notice! As for Elizabeth, she didn't matter anyway, as she was either gone shopping or drunk most of the time! She was not part of his plans for the future, anyway!

He finished his drink, then took out his prepay mobile and dialed a number:

– Hi, it's me. I have prepared the material you needed. Deal and delivery as usual!

His words were extremely significant, as deal meant another half million American dollars and "delivery as usual" meant the parking lot of the Harbor Beer House, at exactly 7 p.m., in the first and the third Friday of the month, which happened to be the next day.

Sometimes, it was just about receiving orders, but most of the time he would deliver papers or evidence of accomplished missions. And of course, receive cash pay. Always small bills, different bag every time! He never met his contractors twice in the same place. He commonly connected the parking meetings to his stopping for dinner, so he would have a perfect alibi in front of his "colleagues" from the Agency, whom he shared with other meeting places. Daylight would be avoided as the eye in the sky could see anything these days and at least three hundred feet free space around.

– I see! He continued. Most likely we will conclude our contract next time, so make the necessary preparations. We can settle details when we meet. Have a good day!

For Archie, the "details" meant the rest of 50% or another 10 million bucks, due to be received on completion of his mission.

Archie was confident that the whole sum would be more than satisfactory for him to open a hotel and a casino in Brazil and happily live ever after. He adored samba girls and had always fantasized about having sex with one while she is dancing!

Smiling at this thought, Archie closed the cell phone and called another number from his office phone:

– Hey Lenny! How are you, pal? The voice said something back. Listen, Lenny! I want a table for three, next week, on Wednesday, okay? Make it in my favorite corner! Yeah! And put away a bottle of good champagne, ok?...What? ...I don't know, something French, anyway!.. Right! See you Lenny! And Lenny...First I'll have dinner tomorrow! Alone! Just a steak and black beer!

Archie smiled again and went to the back wall of his office, where he held a rather cheap copy of a sea painting of Eivazovsky, the best marine landscape Russian painter. Beautiful, even if peculiar for taste, it had been hanging there for about three years now. As expected, the painting was the cover for a quite well hidden safe. He slid the painting to the side, then dialed a long series of numbers and opened the thick door.

He practically did not need to take anything away from the safe, but enjoyed to look at the small shinny special canisters of about one liter each, with their little security green led safely blinking on one end. Two things – weight under 2 pounds – still worth 2,5 million bucks each. All in a long number and carefully packed in a regular silver suitcase. But the stuff inside could enable a bio-lab to produce poisonous germs capable of killing entire cities. Plus instructions for use!

Satisfied with the view of his next day's delivery, he closed the door of the safe and scrambled back the electronic lock. He went to the door, picking his jacket along the way and turned the lights off, gently closing the door.

The image of Archie getting out of his office, taken from a skillfully deployed detection proof digital camera, inside the eye of an African statue placed in front of his office, was replaced – split of a second later – by darkness, on a monitor situated in a small room full of computers. The dark guy in front of it puffed out a cloud of smoke, crushed his cigarette in a large bronze ash-tray, made out from the bottom side of a navy gun shell, then relaxed in his chair and picked up the ringing phone:

–   Yeah, it's me! I saw where he keeps it! I think it's gonna'be soon, maybe even tomorrow! Keep an eye on him day and night; we need to know the place!

He hung up and went out of the office, lighting up another cigarette.

While getting out of Archie's office, Hicks felt a little bit better. He lived with the impression that he somehow scored on Archie; pushing on this older-guy perspective was a reasonable and expectable approach, only he felt deeply entitled to it.

He stopped to call David on the cell phone and told him he would need the papers later, maybe even the next week.

In spite of Archie's attitude, Hicks felt some type of uncertainty in the thin air inside the office. Archie wanted desperately to scare him off something – so there must have been something wrong with the Lyme disease research contracts. Donovan was afraid of what he might find out, that's why he insisted on banning him from access to them. Hicks smiled and went out towards the parking lot above. Yeah! Maybe Archie will try to soften things within the following days. And if he did, Hicks would be sure Donovan is trying to cover for something fishy – something maybe outside the company's interest; perhaps something personal?

Hicks went to his car and took his place; while buckling up, he thought of another serious aspect: if Archie tries to cover something and he finds out about it, he will be in danger! Any sign of interest or inquiry on the subject could mean his own elimination – and Hicks knew now that for Archie, that meant physical! Suddenly his mouth turned sour and his throat dry. Now he finally understood that his allegedly strong position was in fact feeble and on a delicate balance, ready to be sacrificed by Archie, for his personal interest and at any moment, if needed. He turned on his engine and started taxiing towards the gate. "Yeah!" He thought "I may be in danger, but Archie is also vulnerable, because he is afraid of what I know!". The future was going to be complicated. He had to gamble on this and the odds were not very favoring. If Archie was indeed afraid of his knowledge about the facts, then the more he knew, the greater would be the fear! Hicks felt he had to do something about this and the best he could do was finding out even more.

Next Wednesday evening, the Harbor Beer House seemed cheerful enough for the three persons seated at a table overlooking the river.

Archie Donovan was playing host and his loud enough laughter was penetrating the separating curtains from time to time.

Elizabeth was seated next to him on a cozy armchair, shifting her superb legs in black silk stockings from one side to another, in front of a desperate Stephen Hicks, who could barely take his eyes off her knees. It is not that he wanted to stare like that, but somehow he felt attracted to the view beyond his control and he was even more disturbed and irritated by this.

Still under the impression of his last discussion with Archie, Hicks had promised himself to be extra careful about this relationship. He accepted the invitation after Archie had softened a bit over his last decisions, only to see what would be Donovan's next move.

The suddenly polite and detached Hicks was determined to follow his last decision, pleased with the fact that he correctly anticipated Archie's play. His intuition was telling him that Elizabeth was merely a decoy and a disturbing factor, to prevent him from focusing over the facts, but he had to admit that she was really good at it, and everything she did turned him on in a way he could not explain.

Archie had been ordering sea food – langoustines de San Lucar de Barameda – pâté de "foaie gras", grilled salmon with baby carrots and "coquelette au vin", all to go together with several bottles of "Brut d'Akermann", as cold as an iceberg and dry as the sand in Sahara. Archie seemed to be in a good mood, like the old times. He had been saying jokes, laughed a lot and made frequent insinuations about their working together and getting rich.

When the first two bottles finished, Hicks started to wonder if he had been thinking right or maybe he felt inclined to become a little bit paranoid. After all, with the fresh information and all, nobody had been reacting so far and everything seemed like it used to be. The bell in his head was still ringing, but it was becoming just an annoying sound – something like a buzzing fly hovering above your meal – definitely preventing him from enjoying the view that Elizabeth chose to share with them. Hicks even requested permission to take off his coat, after she accidentally spread her legs a few times while laughing, long enough for him to notice the dark color of her bikini and make him sweat consistently.

Archie did not react or maybe he pretended not to be aware of that; anyway, he was behaving like he didn't care. He was leaving the table from time to time to order something or make telephone calls, and this gave Hicks the opportunity to chat with Elizabeth.

- So you are a journalism graduate? Why didn't you carry on this line of work? Hicks smiled taking a sip of his wine.
- Oh, yeah! Let me think! I've got a bit smarter after I became the well-known local Miss Milwaukee! I learned how to fuck important persons and get something out of it! As a journalist, I would have had to repeatedly fuck my old, bald and sweaty office manager to allow me to publish a small fashion article. Satisfied?

She leaned backwards and pulled her skirt so high, that her thighs were uncovered up to her silk underwear.

She took her glass and then slowly crossed her legs in front of Hicks, making sure he is closely watching the scene. Hicks was turning red in his cheeks and his heavy glasses started sliding down the slope of his sweaty long nose.

- Of course you're not satisfied – she smiled picking up a long bread stick. She dipped it in the sauce in front of her and then licked and sucked on it languorously in front of the hypnotized Hicks. He blinked and seemed to sober up the moment Elizabeth bit the stick with a cracking noise and started chewing on it. She leaned forward towards him, spreading her legs and watched with satisfaction as his eyes lowered to the view she offered. While holding the wine glass in one hand, she extended the other one and grabbed Stephen's chin in it. Her hand was cold and somehow refreshing, Hicks thought!

- I know what you want right now! She showed down to her departed knees. You'd like to know how it is to be right here, between them, right, comrade?...... Don't you find me attractive? ...Huh?

Hicks realized she was leading him to a trap and shook vehemently:

- No, no, no! ...I mean, yes! Sure I find you attractive, but you are with Archie and Archie is my friend; I could never.... Excuse me for staring like this.... He made a move to get up; I guess I'd better go!
- Tat! Tat! Tat! You bad old fashioned boy! ...She filtered her look towards him through heavy eyelids and pointed her right index to him, while getting another thirsty gulp from her glass. Archie would fuck your girlfriend while she's holding your hand saying I love you! – believe me! Don't tell me about Archie! She added, waving her finger in denial.

She filled again her glass almost finishing the fourth bottle and took a long gulp. Her wet look and uncensored gestures signified that she didn't care anymore what she was drinking, as long as it kept coming.

- Hey, waiter! She cried loud – come over here! Get me another one and make it fast! I'm thirsty!
- Yes Madam! Right away, Madam! The young waiter did not seem to notice her acrid tone or her glued tongue. He disappeared after the curtains and ten seconds later he came with the fresh bottle and a towel. He let the cork burst to one side and filled a fresh glass for Elizabeth.
- Anything else, Madam? – he said, with a professional smile on his face.
- No thanks! You may go! She waived him away.

Hicks found the brake welcome for his need to recover as he was chewing on their interrupted conversation. Something had been scratching his ears and he wanted to make sure his haunch was right before Archie came back. Elizabeth was becoming conveniently drunk to help him. He leaned forward, avoiding looking beneath her skirt, now almost up to hip level, and poured another wine in her rapidly emptied glass:

– Miss Elizabeth, when we talked before, why did you call me comrade? Hicks tried to put on his friendliest smile ever and pored himself a new wine, to accompany her. Just curious! He added.

– Lover boy gets curious, hmm? Well I'll tell you why, lover boy! She took a sip and stared towards the dark window. Archie has a lot of moron friends, some of which I fuck from time to time, like the Russian mother fucker who bit my tits once! Your grey hair reminds me of him, comrade; His moustache was very ticklish and my pussy waters when tickled. Hey, maybe I'll fuck you too, sometime! She smiled, giving him a friendly wink with her left eye, while the right one was staring at him without a blink, like the glass eye of a broken rubber doll.

She leaned back giggling and shifted her legs to a more comfortable position, one that required no effort for observing the quality of her underwear and its vicinities, at the exact moment when Archie came back. He instantly registered the scene and noticed that Elizabeth was wasted, but managed to smile and rub his hands:

– Okay! I can see you got along fine without me! Anyone for desert?
– No thanks, Archie! Hicks raised and took his coat! I think I'd better go! It has been a lovely evening. Thanks for the meal! He turned to Elizabeth before Archie could say anything:
– Miss Elizabeth, I wish you a pleasant evening!

She waived him away, preoccupied to finish her glass and looked aside before he walked out.

- I'll see you out! Archie took him by the shoulder. Sorry about Elisabeth! It happens to her when she has a good time, but we're between friends, isn't it, Stephen? Thanks for coming! It's been like old times for me! We'll talk things over a cup of coffee tomorrow morning, say ten thirty? I need to speak to you about a project.
- Yeah, sure Archie! Ten thirty! I'll be in your office. Good night!

Hicks stepped out steamed up by a different energy than the fine wine induced. He was almost sober when he got out in the cold and went to the parking lot. He got in his car, buckled up and relaxed while cleaning the lenses of his glasses:

- Yes, Comrade! It will be like old times again -He said loudly and gently drove out of the parking lot. He was sure now his suspicion was right. Now it was time for him to play ball!

Fighting demons

In a cozy conference room of Ambasador Hotel close to Hargeisa Airport, it was cool because of small windows and the AC. The oval table in the middle was surrounded by 5 persons, all invited by the Ministry of Public Health himself.

One of them was Dr. Abdilgani, the manager of the Hargeisa Hospital, the other was dr. Sani from the Burao Hospital, and the other three were guests. There was an epidemiologist responsible with transmitted diseases, a representative of Ministry of Housing and Internal Affairs and the President of the Senators in Parliament, his Excellency Mr. Ali Maxamed Xoosh, the formal leader of the Jacub tribe community nicknamed Waran Madow (Black Spear) after one ancestor that successfully confronted a lion in the desert alone armed with only a spear. The tribe leader was in his sixties, with grey hair and beard stained with henna, according to tradition. He had a hat and a stick, paying tribute to the old elegance requirements and enjoying deep respect from all those at the table.

– The conclusion of my report is that we are confronted with a new disease that has an unexpected carrier – a species of mosquito which is not indigenous. We have 54 mortality so far and have been unable to save any patient. By the time we realize the correct diagnosis it is already too late, as they develop multisystem failure. We sent samples to specific labs in Abu Dhabi, Djibouti and Addis Ababa. Preliminary results indicate a borrelia strain, but I never saw one so aggressive and destructive. We are currently reconsidering our therapy protocol by introducing Rocephyne as primary choice antibiotic, but protection against insects is of great importance. We rely upon our cooperation with public health authorities for area disinfection and need help in prevention for population.

– I understand ! The health Minister was presiding the gathering. He took one sip from the Somali tea in front of him and continued:

– Any clue regarding the origin? I understand Lyme disease is not endemic here, like malaria.

– Indeed, Sir! We barely have a few cases, as Lyme disease is transmitted by ticks. By the way, the alien mosquito we captured in the infested areas seems to originate in Caribbean area and we have no explanation for its natural migration in our area. The only possibility that does not defy logic is that the insect was brought here somehow.

– If I may interfere – rose the epidemiologist. We have gathered samples from Maydh, and Burao infested areas. We collected a few dozens of such mosquitos. They are indeed alien and we found this species as being usual in Caribbean islands. Dr Abdilgani is right, we find it hard to explain its presence here. It is not about a few insects carried with the plane. Besides, for the time being the only functional airport in Somaliland is Berbera, and we had no case there, Inshallah! However, if we already caught dozens of insects, we have to consider the entry of a much larger number and their invasive potential in populated areas, especially those with precarious hygiene.

The Health minister took a deep breath and sighed; it was going to be a large team work to solve this problem.

- I am going to contact the Ministry of Economy. We are going to need extra funding for this matter. For now, we must make sure we have enough mosquito nets on the market to advise population to use them for the next 90 days, and we will arrange Government subsidies so they come in cheap like 1-2 dollar / piece. We will augment funding for necessary medication for the hospitals but I strongly advise to maintain for this job only the two larger facilities in Hargeisa and Burao. These two hospitals will arrange a special isolation pavilion for these cases – as we do not know yet the inter-personal contamination rate – and I will have every morning after the morning prayer a report from each. I also want a report on the bug when identification is completed and any details that might help me take the right decision. Please inform all personnel in the hospital to wear masks at all time. The patients with such disease will receive no family visit and – turning to the epidemiologist – your people will go in the field to make epidemiological inquiries starting with the families of the diseased ones. Maybe if we identify contaminated patients earlier, we can give them a chance.

All those at the table were silent; some took notes.

The Ministry of Internal Affairs – his excellency Bashir Cawaale – spoke:

- I leave to the specialists the delicate burden of identifying and dealing with this germ. For us it is very intriguing the fact that we deal with an unknown and new to us disease, allegedly inflicted by uncommon insect which does not belong here. The possibility that such contaminated insect reached our territory by chance is close to zero- I would say - so we will try to find out who brought it. We have reports of two groups of medical specialist who visited the two hospitals and were interested in malaria like diseases. The reports are not clear yet; they came by Daloo Airlines in

Berbera and they spoke English, although our people heard them talking Russian between them. They took evasive information concerning some of the first patients, who already died. But we still do not know if they are related somehow to the event. It could be a coincidence.

– That would be a very strange coincidence- Dr. Abdilgani smiled.
– Anyway, I also ordered extensive search and contact with medical entities that can help, together with our colleague – the Minister of Health. I took the liberty of asking for help from our friends in UK, as usual. They did not forget Somaliland was once British protectorate.

Everybody looked at Ali Maxamed Xoosh who was gently combing with left hand his short henna stained gray beard. Eventually he rose his eyes and looked at everybody in the room, before speaking with a soft, but cutting voice:

– If the things we discussed here are proven to be true, as I think they are, we must face a very severe danger: someone is using our fellow countrymen as Guinea-pigs. They probably are testing new cures for diseases, but they inflict disease first. May I remind you the words of the Prophet: "There is no disease on the face of the Earth that Allah dis not leave a cure for". This was not the doing of God, this is a calamity inflicted by men. I have decided to alert my colleagues and we will pass within 2 days a Superior Chamber motion enabling our Secret Service to activate our agents abroad and cooperate with foreign intelligence agencies to get to the bottom of this. First we will ask for help from UK, but we will also inform our cooperators in US, France, Italy, Djibouti, Emirates and China.
– So that everybody knows what to do in the next 2-3 days. We thank you all for your help and will certainly keep you informed. My ministry formed a crisis cell and HQ will be my office. My mobile will be active day and night for any communication – the Health Ministry rose from his chair as a sign the meeting has ended.

The people around the table rose and went out, shocked by the powerful heat of the afternoon.

They got to their cars and one by one left taking the main street and then the dusty roads of the city – a 2 million inhabitants city having no current water, sewage or electricity, but a lot of projects and no funding for them.

Ali Maxamed Xoosh went to the dusty grey Toyota Landcruiser that brought him. His driver was seated comfortably and was taking a nap, when abruptly woken up by the Superior Chamber President:

- Hadi, wake up. Let us go across the Creek, pass by the Mansoor Hotel and drive me to the military barracks in the outskirts. I need to meet someone there.
- Haa Mudane! (Yes Sir!) and the young driver set the car in motion, integrating in the crazy traffic that rose dust to 50 feet above, covering houses and cars like ashes from a distant volcano.

It took half an hour for the car to reach the opposite side of the town. The car was admitted at the entrance barrier and the sentinel there performed an approximate salute for the VIP.

The car was parked in front of a more modern concrete building, the HQ of a large military compound. President Waran Madow was wearing his long khameez and macawiis, with a wide leather belt, his felt hat and cane. He was welcomed by a soldier who presently guided him inside. He went straight to the commander in chief of the military facility.

- Your Excellency, how kind of you to do me the honor! General Ilmi Abdile smiled. The general was a tall slender person with a short haircut and a little grey goatee beard. Hs black eyes were as severe as his voice and the smile he put on did not succeed in warming up his presence.
- Salaam alekoum! My dear general, how is your life here?
- Alekoum salaam, your excellency ! We are ready to do our duty, but I take this opportunity to remind you the things we miss: spares for engines (half of our vehicles, including tanks are old

and we have no parts for repair, no hydraulic fluid for the recoil guns, little ammo and obsolete guns and we lack technology to repair them.

- That I know my dear general! Trust me when I say we are doing our best to convince the minister of finance to direct more funds to the army, in general. We have a plan to buy 3 helicopters soon, for police use, but we are looking for platforms that can mount some weapons on. And soldiers?

- Otherwise men have upgraded moral, especially after they received the new camouflage uniforms. We have one company ready for deployment at all times because of the Al Shabab roaming into the South and West, but then we had no serious trouble yet. They somehow get new weapons ahead of us, because we are blocked by Somalia Mogadishu embargo all the same.

- That is a problem that is entirely on the hand of politicians. You know that our demands depend on our recognition as independent state from Somalia. So far, we are recognized by Djibouti and South Sudan (which is fighting for recognition itself) but the African Union did not respond to our call yet. I am afraid this will take a longer time and we have to prove our stability and commitment against terrorism to become trustworthy.

- We will try to do our best! What can I do for you Mr. President?

- General, I would like to speak with Major Maxamuud Bashir, the one in charge with special operations.

- I will call him immediately! He is in the building. Meanwhile let me offer you some tea! The general turned to the soldier near the door and shouted a quick order. The young soldier disappeared and came back after 4 minutes with a fresh trey holding three cups of Somali tea.

After another five minutes, a tall slender character in a camouflage uniform knocked at the door.

- Come in Major! At ease! Have a seat ! Mr President Waran Madow does us the honor of a visit.

- Salam alekoum ! Glad to see you again Sir!

The major was a man with a slicing look in his black eyes. He had his head completely shaved but carried a thin moustache which gave him an even more severe appearance. He extended a hand with long and thin fingers. He looked made out of steel chords and muscle but his self sufficient presence showed wit and action readiness.

- Alekoum salaam. Major! Likewise! Sorry I usually come to you only in times of need. We need to talk!

Then he turned to the General and with a kind voice said:

- General, do you have a room where I can talk privately to the major? It is a matter of particular interest for state security which does not involve the army, if you do not mind!
- Not at all Mr. President! Responded the General with a somewhat acrid voice. Please follow me!

He guided the two men to another locked room on the same hallway. Inside the room walls were fitted with copper nets to obtain Faraday cage effect and silenced with soft materials.

- This is the strategy planning room! Nobody can hear what you talk here!
- Thank you my dear general! We will take only a few minutes!
- As long as you wish, Mr. President! I will be in my office !

Waran Madow took the larger armchair and sat down, sipping with visible satisfaction from his steaming tea.

- Major Bashir, we will have to solve a delicate problem. Here are the facts. It seems that an unknown entity has brought on our territory insect vectors that carry an unknown yet disease which already killed almost 50 people in Maydh and secondary Burao area. Strangers came to collect information on the impact of the disease and we cannot exclude Americans – the mosquitos involved are from the American continent – but also Russians, as some of them were speaking the language. I do not think this was done by American or Russian states, but I believe it to be a demo for bio-warfare commerce, involving some private interest. We are currently searching to find the origin of the disease and its germs and your mission will be to identify and eliminate this source.

- But this means acting outside our country! The Major observed.
- Yes! This is why we need skillful men like you! You will take only 2-3 good men with you and go anywhere it is needed as tourists visiting your relatives from abroad. We have Somalilanders in the US, UK, Canada, Scandinavian countries, Denmark, France, Spain, practically anywhere, so that will be no problem. If needed you will receive weapons from our people there, but I would like you to be creative and make things look like accidents or well-deserved lessons for those using our citizens as Guinea pigs.
- Mr. President, I will be up to the requirements to serve our country. I will choose two skillful men and will be ready whenever you decide.
- Thank you, my dear boy! Needless to say, this conversation did not take place! I will send you all relevant information at your home by currier. Hadi, my driver will pas by and leave you data on usb.
- Agreed Mr. President. It has been an honor to have tea with you.

The two men returned to the general's office. The general was busy studying some papers and politely rose from his armchair:

- Mr. President, I have ordered a quick lunch if you will do us the honor to join us…
- Sorry to disappoint you dear general, but I am in a hurry to discuss some papers we have to vote in the Chamber tomorrow. Perhaps some other time, maybe! Have a nice day and God help you for all thing you have to do! Inshallah!
- Ilaahay ha nagu anfaco! (God help us!) Please visit us again!
- Do not worry! We will have the opportunity to discuss army needs in the new Parliament session next month.

They shook hands and Waran Madow went to his car, ordering Hadi to return to Ambasador hotel, for a political lunch with two councelors of the President of the Republic.

Meanwhile the General recomposed his serious posture and spoke to Major Bashir:

- So Major, what was this all about? Can I help you with something?

Major Bashir smiled gently and answered instantly, as any hesitation would mean concealing something to the eyes of the mighty general:

- Nothing out of the ordinary! Some politicians are suspected of cooperation with Al Shabab. We need to know if it is willingly done or it is blackmail. And by the way Sir, I may need some vacation days shortly. I was planning to visit my daughter. She is a student in UK preparing to become a specialist in international commerce.
- Hmm! This Al Shabab is consuming all our time, resources and energy! Sure you can go! Just let me know when you plan to leave so we can appoint someone to replace you! Thank you! Dismissed!
- Haa, innu noolaado! (Yes Sir!); Waan fahamay! (Understood!) and he stepped out.

The afternoon sun was blinding. On the dirty road outside the barracks, a herd of goats was slowly eating its way in the sidewalks invaded by dry grass and discarded pet recipients.

The buzzing of a district electric diesel -generator could be heard in the vicinity. It was a cozy afternoon, most people preferring the shadow of their little clay houses as the whole neighborhood seemed deserted.

Decision time

A week later, the Health Security and Environment offices of the WHO were unexpectedly free that afternoon. Few people passed from time to time, paper files at hand, from on office to another or stopping at the office station to use the copier machine. The last door on the hallway was the office of Dr. Fujimori and he was deeply concentrated in reading some documents in front of him. As a personal favor, he organized his office in this smaller room, with forced ventilation and the fire detector was off because he was still addicted to smoking. More than that, he somehow procured plain French "Gitanes" cigarettes which were his passion when confronted with office problems. His colleagues and co-workers advised him to quit, but he resisted in saying it was his only vice and tried to avoid lighting cigarettes when having company.

Today he was having guests: Peter Bud, his new counseling secretary and Henry Sutton, who was glad that after the long airplane trip to Geneva, he was welcome with a cup of coffee and could openly enjoy his regular cigar. The dry smoke of Gitanes was mixed with the sweeter and thicker aroma of Sutton's cigar, creating a smoke curtain slowly dissipated by the exhaust fan. Problems were as mingled as the smoke from the two men.

After the usual compliments, Fujimori opened dialogue:

- I have already had a preliminary discussion with the Director of the WHO-Africa office. Things appear to be serious – we actually have two main problems to solve: one I identifying a germ in a strange outbreak and its best cure and secondly – where it comes from and how did it happen. I confess I have other concerns on my table right now – for instance a serious SARS type outbreak in Wuhan region of China. They isolated a new strain of coronavirus – possibly zoonosis. I sent Ben Johnson with a team to verify on that one and I want Peter Bud to go to Africa – in Somaliland to be more precise or wherever it is needed to get to the bottom of this. The Director of WHO Africa will assign a small team of 3 epidemiologists to accompany you. You have to verify also some cases of Marburg fever in Kenya and some incidents with water disseminated entero-colitis in Ethiopia. You will return from Addis Ababa within 10 days, but your first stop will be in Hargeisa – Somaliland. I think you will have to transfer in Dubai airport.

- I heard about the outbreak in Somaliland- Peter said. I have a friend in the Emirates – their lab work detected some strain of borrelia afzeli, but with unprecedented features. It carries more toxins and enzymes than the usual species, and multiplying faster and more aggressively. They found only a third generation cephalosporine to be effective and that if you have an early onset of treatment with increasing dosage to avoid Herxheimer syndrome. Isn't it Henry?

- The British Agency for Tropical Diseases has indeed confirmed this finding by processing the samples sent from Somaliland. The features of this strain of Borrelia are different enough from the common type to trigger the suspicion of bio-weapon testing, hence the MI 6 involvement and my presence here, which is to remain as discrete as possible. Not to mention our concern on the incident of the coronavirus zoonosis in Wuhan, China, where we suspect the involvement of a local lab, allegedly trying to develop a vaccine against coronavirus. Probably a mistake or a mishandling of the virus, I can't imagine the Chinese infecting their own people, but I wouldn't trust their reports. Thy will try to push garbage under the rug, as usual.

- We believe that, too! - answered Fujimori. We must be very cautious, because the Chinese are very sensitive. I sent Ben because of his expertise in sensitive cases and his skill in socializing with difficult partners. We hope to obtain some samples of proteins to develop our own science on it, possibly find a vaccine until we have a new pandemic on our head.

He sighed, he lit a new plain cigarette, puffed twice with visible satisfaction and continued:

- Do not worry Mr. Sutton, our cooperation will remain discrete. In here, everybody knows you are Peter's uncle- and he smiled. So, we will wash this laundry inside family.
- If I may interfere Sir, -Henry Sutton spoke. According to our information a similar, but common strain was reported in the US – Milwaukee to be more exact, also Illinois, Indiana and Michigan. We are currently trying to contact specialists in UK, France, Hungary, Austria and Romania, who signaled the presence of this strain. We strongly believe the strain was engineered somehow, but the puzzling thing is common disease is transmitted by ticks. In Somaliland ticks are not present, and they blame a rare species of mosquito, not indigenous. Actually, the alleged species lives in Central America and besides being interested how in the world the bloody germ was carried by a mosquito (normally not possible), we would like to know who brought it there. We have our own list of suspicions and we believe we must start by identifying the source. But Peter here – my nephew, that is – he said smiling – is going first to find out relevant details from the very exact place. We are also eager to investigate and we are cooperating in this with the American NSA and maybe the CIA. They will provide assistance inside the States, as we think if we want to find the source, we have to concentrate on the states with maximal incidence there – Wisconsin, Illinois, Indiana and Michigan. We will also have a specialist as a member of your team, presenting as an epidemiologist from UK.
- We agree on that, answered Fujimori! We need all the help we can get to prevent this thing! If what you imply with bio-warfare turns out to be true, only God knows where this can strike. Mosquitoes are everywhere and if this gets epidemic, it will be twenty-five times deadlier than the most severe malaria. So far, we have reported 80 cases and 60 are already dead. Maybe we will come up with better recommendations and medical help and diminish the impact, but we fear that even with most adequate treatment the survival rate will be 50%.
- When do you want us to leave Sir? - asked Peter.

- Yesterday! Answered Fujimori smiling like the Cheshire cat! I have instructed my people to prepare airplane tickets and visas for the team. They will do the same for your envoy, Mr. Sutton!
- Henry, for friends! - said he with a smile.
- Glad to meet you again Henry! You can call me Arinobu!
- Ok then, I will prepare to leave as soon as I get back to London. Henry, we will discuss some tactical details on the way.
- Sure thing Buddy Boy! - smiled Henry. Let me finish this blessed cup of coffee and my cigar with Arinobu here, if he doesn't mind.

Peter went out and closed the door behind him.

- Not at all Henry! Besides I wanted to talk to you about the thing in China. I sense danger there, as we receive confusing reports from there. One family physician posted on his Facebook account some worrying details, but it was quickly retracted, which makes it even more intriguing. He was talking about already dozens of cases and unprecedented contamination rate with 10% mortality. The whistle blower conveniently died from the disease days after. The disease is similar to the SARS outbreak in Hong-Kong and more recently, the even more deadly MERS outbreak from camel – born virus in the Middle East. This coronavirus seems to be able to trigger more than diarrhea, I guess. I need protein antigen to prepare a vaccine, but we will see how quickly we can obtain that.
- I know it is hard for you. We did not have a serious epidemic, much less a pandemic ever since WWI. We have a concern too. You realize that air travel can spread it across continents within hours.
- It is air travel we fear most. It will prove very efficient for spreading a disease. However, the bad part is we can do no prevention on this, as you have to have a good reason and physical proof before banning air travel on any direction.
- And by the time you have proof, it is already too late to prevent contamination, I understand. Well, we'll do our best to get to the bottom of this, Sir. It has been a pleasure meeting you – said

Henry, gently pressing his cigar stump into a metal ash-tray. I have your telephone number and e-mail address – you have mine. My dear Arinobu, you can call me anytime you need, day or night!

– Likewise, Henry! Let's get them! Fujimori smiled, wiping his glasses and seeing his guest to the door.

He returned to his desk, picked the yellow phone in front of him and dialed an interior number:

– Hello! Fujimori here! Did you solve travel documents for dr. Peter Bud and the other two? Ahah! Working on it…. Please, add one person to the delegation, an American epidemiologist. Marguerite, my secretary, will call you to provide details. Same plane, same itinerary, same hotel, etc. Understood? Very good! Arigato!(Thank you!). And see that they can leave within 3 days or as soon as dr. Peter comes from London.

One last cigarette was lit and Fujimori leaned back in his chair, his hands raised and palms crossed behind backbone. He was more confident now – good men worked with him. He was sensitive to Henry's advisory activity, although they knew each other only by telephone until now and Peter was a good asset for the organization. He was an intrepid young man, well educated, with extensive theoretical knowledge and a distinctive ability for thinking "outside the box". He was very satisfied with such secretary. Ben was good too, smart, agreeable, excellent in theory but more prone to base his actions on protocols and recommendations and less interested in personal initiative. Equally useful anyway. Efficiency would come if he knew how and where to use each of them. He had other helpers, too, and for example the Korean Huan Seoung was a good catch, too.

Fujimori cleaned his ash-tray, opened window to enable fresh air replace the smog inside the office. When room was cleared, he closed the window and went to the hanger in the corner to get his coat. Another day's work was done.

Unrest

Stephen Hicks was home in a lazy Friday afternoon; he was yawning while staring at his half full "Jack" glass, thinking how he could manage things to his favor.

For a brief moment, he felt tempted to call for an escort, but he knew he had missed the weekend programing and he will end up with some fat and ugly cowgirl, unable to smile even when penetrated, so he dropped the idea.

It was important for him to know what Archie Donovan was cooking behind him, and most of all, if this secret doing of Archie had the potential to affect him. He wanted to build some protection for this, as he knew that Archie had no comrades when it came to getting something he badly wanted, and that would end up by pacing Hicks on the disposable list.

Now that Archie has blocked his access to the contracts. there were few ways to check on what was happening in GERMINA Inc. But he was a resourceful man, and he would come up with some idea. Besides that, he was nursing the crazy thought he would be able to make Elizabeth talk and maybe find out some interesting details from her. He would also understand if the colder approach Archie displayed was caused by her. That meant he would have to contact and meet her, without Archie knowing about it. He was not very hopeful about this maneuver, but he promised himself to try if and when the time was right.

– Hey Bruce, go eat your food! …. You, filthy animal – he shouted to the cat that stood motionless on a chair.

As Bruce did not even blink, he took of one of his sleepers and threw it to the cat, which watched with bored eyes the shoe fly-by.

I'd better think about my problems and live the cat alone. He waved disgustedly towards Bruce (no reaction from the cat yet) and turned on the Jack glass, taking a serious gulp from it.

Meanwhile, he did not find any worrying internet activity regarding the borrelia strain causing turmoil and he was happy about it – like the saying "no news is good news". Maybe everything is going to be forgotten and buried within other events, like the new respiratory coronavirus they unleashed in China. He knew very well the behavior of coronavirus, mostly inflicting digestive infection and was aware of the "significant" outbreaks of SARS in Hong Kong and MERS in the Middle East. Zoonosis – my foot! He thought- let the people of the Wuhan lab speak – for sure whistle blowers would disappear, like it happened here, right, and his friend Archie was no stranger to the fact.

He was still staring at his window, which displayed a large vision of his less tidy garden. Rose bushes wildly grew here and there and the grass was high, not mowed for months during the past summer and trees were all rusty in color and their empty branches gave the place a gloomy appearance. Stephen's mood was equally blue and he decided he will spend time alone intoxicating himself with the rest half bottle of Jack and think his next actions over the weekend.

He did finish the bottle and fell asleep in his armchair, TV set on, in front of him, and the laptop on the small table next to the armchair.

He suddenly woke up three hours later, switched off everything, and went towards his bedroom and bathroom, almost stumbling over Bruce, the Tom cat who was slumbering in the doorstep and was in no mood for bothering to move aside.

Saturday noon was a sunny, yet chilly day and Stephen realized it was late when Bruce came to his door and was restless because of hunger.

–   Ok,ok – I am coming, you, filthy animal! He yawned and found his mouth gluey and dry!

He scratched with one hand the long grey hairs on his chest and went to the bathroom to take a shower – a concession to the fact that it was weekend. Blinded by the hot water inside, he searched with a trembling hand for his glasses on the shelf in front of the steamy mirror. He put them on and was displeased to see that his wet head displayed two large green eye balls – possibly enhanced by the thick lenses – giving him he appearance of a giant hairy frog.

He dried his hair and went out to the kitchen, presently followed by a desperately hungry Bruce, and opened a can of cat greasy cat — food which he poured in the cat's plate on the floor:

- Here you are, filthy punk! Stuff yourself!

He washed hands and took two eggs, cheese and ham from the fridge and started cooking a typical English breakfast. He felt hungry and especially thirsty after the booze consumed last night. He took a small canteen with orange juice and took a few gulps directly, without using a glass.

Art this moment his mobile rang. He extended a trembling hand and answered absently, without checking first who called. The next moment he was instantly sober, as he heard Archie on the phone:

- Hi Stephen, hope I did not disturb your beauty sleep! His metallic voice emitted a short laughter, like he could see Stephen barely awake. Can you talk?
- Sure! Sure I can Archie!...I... did not expect you to call today, being weekend and all.... - he managed to mumble.
- Ok, now that you are functional, listen to what I say! I am leaving today to New York to meet some potential clients.
- Oh, yeah!... Ok! Do you need me to do something?
- Oh, no big deal! Check on the production status of those "fertilizers" we are to export to Belarus and Pakistan. I live with the impression our guys are behind schedule. Sorry to ruin your Saturday. And Stephen, something personal... I booked tickets for a movie on Sunday and made reservation for 2 for dinner at the Opus of Belfry House. As I have to go, I am afraid Elizabeth will not be able to go alone, so I ask you to accompany her!
- Opus at Belfry House! But that is a very expensive place...
- Don't worry, Stephen, I am buying. I left Beth a shopping card she can use to pay for everything. Please do not let me down, I do not want to spoil her expected leisure time or I'll be busted — you know how women are! And you know how unpredictable she is — I wouldn't trust anyone else for the job, bro!

Suddenly awakened by the opportunity of meeting Elisabeth alone, Hicks regained his normal voice and energy and answered:

- Oh, it's ok Archie! My time is available for this, I don't have anything better to do anyway. I'll text a message on the "fertilizer" production rates tonight.
- Ok. I talked to Elizabeth and you can call her around 1 pm tomorrow to set up a meeting. Movie is at 3 pm and restaurant table reservation at 7 pm. Thanks a lot!

Archie hung up before Stephen could say anything else. Stephen had a large smile on his face – his wish of seeing Elizabeth alone was accomplished. Of course, he would be very polite and respectful but also very curious about some things. For a brief moment, he felt a cramp in his lower abdomen when he thought he could lure her into a sexual intercourse, but then shivered and shook his head in disbelief. Not for me, not the time, not the right person. For a moment, he realized this thought turned him on and he took the phone and called Dave.

- Hi Dave, sorry to disturb you on weekend!.... What? You are working? Are you at the office? …. Ok. Listen, I will come in half an hour or so, too. Until I come, please prepare for me the production file for the last 2 years and the shipment report for the products in class S for "Sensitive". I know that I no longer have access to the contracts, but I am not interested in those. I want to make sure we safely meet the deadline with our production. Ok? Thanks a lot Dave, see you! And wait for me with a large coffee – black and sweet! Bye!

He took a large breath and pored himself a large glass of orange juice - to go at noon with a slice of cold pizza he found in the fridge.

He dressed up casually and he chose a dark brown coat over his black shirt, sort of matching well the light blue jeans and the brown shoes he wore. Before going out he dialed a known number and spoke:

–   Hi! Stephen here! Tell me please, is Lila free tonight? Yeah, I'll
    wait!.... Aha! Tell her I am expecting her around 7 pm! Yeah,
    thanks a lot! Bye!

Satisfied with the program he designed, Stephen thought he
should shave for the date in the afternoon, but he was too hurried
now to go to his office. He went in front of his house, where his
BMW stood waiting and got up into the car thinking what type of
conversation he should have with Elizabeth. He drove carefully to his
office and parked close to the main entrance of GERMINA.

He went downstairs in the restricted area and used his fingerprint
and eye retinal reader device to go inside, where the second office on
the left was bathed in warm led light. Dave was there and he was
working something on his laptop. He rose his eyes, nodded to Hicks
and extended a huge jar with mild black and sweet coffee.

–   You have the files on your desk ! said David, concentrating on
    his work. I have to catch up with some personnel files, seems the
    IRS is not satisfied with the taxes paid by some of our employees.
–   Aha! Said Hicks, rather absent, while taking over the files. You
    know what, Dave? I will also need the report of last week's stock
    for the products in the warehouse – I mean what we have in the
    warehouse now. I want to have a feed- back on our productivity
    and storage capacity.

Dave gave him a long look as it was a rather odd request
from Hicks - commonly busy with production itself and less with
administration – but he answered promptly:

–   Sure thing, Professor! But in order to see them you have to sign
    the Q-23 form according to regulations. I am supposed to report
    access to these files.
–   Yeah, whatever, just let me know where do I have to sign!
–   Dave extended a piece of paper which Hicks presently filled in
    and signed.
–   All right now?

- Yeas, of course! … And here you are – this is the file of warehouse stock.

Hicks took the heavy folder and the other files under his arm, while keeping coffee at hand.

- I'll be in my office, Dave! Call me if you need me! In one hour, we'll go check on the production labs.
- Ok Sir! And Dave, displaying his usual Sphynx smile, went on writing.

Hicks entered his office and literally crashed into his armchair – first he would take time to enjoy his coffee looking on the files, then he would go to check on the lab production. The productive lab in the restricted underground area worked 24/7 as that was a strategic branch of GERMINA's activity.

First, he started looking in the production figures. He was interested in very sensitive products (odd fertilizers, bacterial mud for sewage control, other bacterial products (some of which labeled as bio-enhancers, bio-nutrients or bio-corrective flora) and he noted down some figures. He took then the expedition reports and also noted down the corresponding figures. Following this approach, he started calculating the remaining stocks. Meanwhile, Dave passed by his office and politely knocked his way in. As he stood in the doorstep, he put on his wax statue smile:

- You were saying we go to check on the lab in one hour. I am ready to accompany you Sir.
- ….One hour already? Hicks acted like being surprised. Ok, here I come. He put on a white lab gown and a pair of hospital-like polyethylene slippers.

The two men marched on a long corridor and had to use ID and fingerprint to pass to the lab, which was concealed as a water reservoir with no apparent entrance. However, some part of the concrete wall slid to one side as Dave pressed a hidden button. The view was that of a vast hall, with countless partitions on the margins. Some were air-tight enclosures with separate ventilation systems and they all had yellow beacons for emergency status and could automatically close if anything contaminating happened.

Hick went to the nearest booth where a tall and handsome African American all dressed in protection suit studied something on the microscope.

- Hi Nelson! How are things going?
- Fine Sir! The colonies meet the dimensional standards of the contract. The bugs are strong! And he smiled, displaying a perfect line of front teeth.
- Ok, keep up the good work! Who is doing enzymes testing?
- I think that would be Paul Trang, booth no 14, Sir!

Hicks waved a bye sign and crossed the large hall towards the indicated booth. A slender man dressed in overall protection suit and with an Asian appearance – actually second generation of Vietnamese American – greeted Hicks.

- Hi Paul! Any problem?
- Well, this strain looks good, but we have to grow another 10-15 generations after we alter a little the lithic enzyme. It is still too weak for a good tissue penetration.
- 10-15 generations? What is the multiplying rate on this strain?
- About every 19 hours, Sir. We need 3-4 days to get the good result. I think we will be on schedule with the first batch around the 15th of this month.
- Aha! Be sure to remove the preceding gene before you place the altered one. If there are two, the efficiency of the germ will be compromised, as the micro-organism will try to produce both types of enzymes and none will be perfect for the requirements.
- Yes Sir, I know that Sir. Besides, that would also imply the likelihood of random mutations beyond our control and expectations.
- How about antibiotic sensitivity? Have you tested it?

–   We do it on each strain and each bacterial generation. It only responds to rare and very expensive medication like Tienam. It works for Legionella* as well as for modified Yersinia**.
–   Good! Try first the common antibiotics and make sure they do not respond to those. Especially third generation cephalosporines like Ceftriaxone.
–   Okay Sir! I'll talk to Robin from the genetic lab. We will enhance the antibiotic defending enzymes, but we must leave room for an antidote like Tienam. You can check the situation of the guys working on the vaccines. We may have some good results in some strains. Of course, we will not report anything and leave that to you and Mr. Donovan.

Hicks nodded and was quite satisfied with the result; he would report to Donovan things were going well, and within a few days they will have the ordered product and will need one additional week for adequate packing and shipment.

He returned in his underground office and resumed his calculus. When he finished, he opened the registered storage files and started to compare figures. He went to the present day and soon discovered some problems. For instance, 3 kg of packed microbial cultures of the sensitive type missed, even if they should have been in the deposit. This means they were shipped somehow without being recorded in the shipment register. He traced back when this difference occurred. What he found was deeply disturbing. The last extraction of this material must have occurred days before – 1 kg to be more precise – two thermally protected cans of about 1 pound each. Before that, another two were gone missing two weeks before and the same 14 days before that. So that meant someone extracted 2 cans every 2 weeks lately. He was afraid to even think who must have been, but he knew that apart from him, there were few persons with access to that storage room, among them the department supervisor – Greg Lowry and Archie Donovan, actually only them. Workers would come to

---

*   Legionella – the germ inflicting "Legionaire's disease"
** Yersinia – the germ causing plague

manipulate boxes and crates only when door was opened by one of the three persons.

Question was: should he ask Greg about this ? Maybe Greg was involved himself and it was out of the question to ask Donovan. He was confident he already pushed too much on the guy's nerves and didn't want Archie to react violently.

He decided it was not something he should tell Greg; this might turn him into a passive whistle blower and expose the guy to God knows what, not to mention his personal involvement in the mess. No, that was a thing he must dig out himself. Dave would be useless to inquiry as he probably doesn't know anything and the next second, he would tell Archie.

Stephen felt uncomfortable at the thought he had to sign the form for having access to the files, after he was already banned from some of the archives, but hoped Archie will not get that curious.

So far, he had to admit the most likely suspect for taking the cans was Archie himself, but how, when and for what purpose, Hicks was unable to say. He had to find out more, maybe talking to Elizabeth he would see puzzle bits falling into place.

Why would anyone need to take modified bacteria – liable for biological weapon use – and do it so discretely so that his own company does not find out, at least for some time?

That person can sell stuff on the black market and the subtle coverage of the operation suggested the money from this deal was not going in the company's cash box, but in the pockets of the thief.

Stephen was struck by the logic of the situation.

Oh, dear God! Archie was selling modified stuff to unknown beneficiaries and cashed the money for himself. Judging by the market level, such stuff was worth millions and he was sure that if Archie did it, he must have gathered a few million, not to mention the contaminated insects bonus. According to the papers, the altered mosquitoes carried the bacteria of his nightmares, the heavily modified borrelia afzeli, turned into an infectious monster able to kill 70% of the patients. He knew only too well how that works.

That was it. It was nothing he could find out more from here. He returned the files to Dave who was still very concentrated on whatever he was doing on the computer, waved "good-bye" and went to his car in the parking lot. He drove carefully towards home and stopped at Hank' diner to grab something to go for his late lunch. He was in no mood for cooking at home so he took the package with a hot hamburger and fries, food dispersing an appetizing smell in the whole car. He reached his home in another 15 minutes and went straight to the living room, dumped the package on the table and removed his clothes, putting on a Heffner type of home gown and sleepers. He then went straight to the bar and took a new bottle of Jack Daniels ready to open it, when he suddenly stopped.

No, it was not going to be so. Today he had found out important things and he felt he was powerful in front of Donovan for the first time in many years. This called for a celebration – he placed back the Jack and extracted a bottle of Scotch – a purple case of 12 years old Aberlour. He had been receiving it on his last birthday from a visiting epidemiologist from UK.

He opened the case, took the bottle, opened it after some hesitation and poured a giant portion in a water glass. No ice to ruin flavor – word went and he tasted it by a huge gulp. He made a face in the beginning – it didn't have the sweet aroma of Jack, but the after taste was exquisite and pleasant. A sensation of pleasant warmth dropped to his lower limbs. He took another sip and turned his attention to the hamburger, while opening his laptop in search of news.

He was still scrolling the MSN news when he finished his food, when he saw something almost paralyzing: a short article stated in few lines that WHO is concerned about a recent outbreak of infectious disease in Northern Somalia – province of Somaliland. The new disease was likely transmitted by insect sting and was a deadly mixture of symptoms between Lime disease and malaria, which was not possible because one is given by bacteria and the other by a parasite. It was still unclear if the disease was transmissible from person to person, and the WHO was determined to investigate the case.

So much for celebration; he took a gulp of whiskey and it seemed sour. He must calm down and think how to react with Donovan.

He decided to think about this until he fell asleep in his armchair. The door bell ringing woke him up. He went towards the door, followed by a curious Bruce cat. On his way he grabbed a jar with water and drank a few gulps like a thirsty horse. He approached the door with caution and looked on the door sight lens. His fear diminished, and he opened the door wide with a large smile on his face:

- Lila, welcome! I thought you were not coming anymore! Here, let me take your coat! Come in and we will start by offering you a sip of quality Scotch! I'll use Jack – I feel more comfortable with it, he continued, pouring the drink in her glass.
- Ok Stephen, do you have some ice? I like it on the rocks – Lila said.
- Sure thing, dear! I do not have cooked food but I have a can of Foie Gras somewhere and I prepared a bottle of Champagne for later.
- Easy on the booze, cowboy! I'll have to drive back home later.
- Or you can stay for the night – rushed Stephen warmed by whiskey and her presence.

She smiled and asked:

- Are you ready to pay for program extension, Stephen? And she hoped he will realize that meant paying more than 700 dollars. Stephen heard the question, took some time to assimilate it and after a small shiver smiled saying:
- You were always a well balanced person – I said we will taste some Champagne, not get wasted!

Lila sighed in relief and took her bag towards the bathroom:

- Okay, Stephen, I go change into something more comfortable. Can you turn on the bubble bath – I like them tickling me all over! She smiled and showed him the tip of her tongue.

– Anything you wish my dear! Stephen took another gulp of Jack and that made him feel in control of things.

Bruce – the cat - yawned and slowly went towards his pillow; it was going to be boring for him.

The next day Stephen woke up with a sentiment of unease; he was so happy to spend the evening with Lila, who was skillful enough to make him cum twice. Nobody else could turn him on the way she did and her final squirt drove him crazy. Of course, he would have to change water in his jacuzzi mini-pool but that can be done easily and was worth the effort. And the money. He had a short shiver thinking he would have to pay her only to sleep there with his hard - worked money. No! Fun is separate from rest, and shouldn't be mixed together.

He went to the bathroom and started to shave, using a shaving brush and foam, followed by a careful maneuvering of a classic razor like 50 years before. The razor was inherited from his Grandpa and was a piece of an interesting collection of old coins and medals – some of which from WWI he kept in a locked drawer. Those artifacts were more precious to him than jewelry and nobody knew about his hidden treasure.

He finished shaving and cleaned the foam resting on his face in some places with a fresh towel. He took a glance at the clock and observed he slept late again. He went to the kitchen, filled Bruce's bowl with some cat food and started the coffee machine.

He took a large cup, threw three cubes of brown sugar in it and poured generously from the coffee jar. Then took the cup with him and went to his armchair to think better, not before grabbing two cinnamon powdered donuts from the cupboard. Light breakfast he thought he would eat better for lunch on Archie's money.

He finished the coffee rehearsing the questions and answers he would deliver during his meeting with Elizabeth and deep down he felt an intriguing mixture of feeling: she was very uncomfortable now and then and an unpredictable bitch sometimes, hence his nervousness and secondly, he was thrilled to be next to such beautiful and sexy woman, able to turn heads on any street while walking. What could happen beyond that is a matter of imagination and the only way he could approach such vision was in his dreams.

Finally, he decided there was no point in being late. He took a marine- like dark blue coat with metal buttons over cream trousers and white shirt, even used his exotic Arab scent after shave and carefully drove his car towards Milwaukee. While in the outskirts of the city he dialed Elizabeth's number.

- Hi, Elizabeth! I came to the City to accompany you as previously discussed with Archie. I am almost downtown, and I can pass by your place to take you.
- Oh, Hi Stephen! What time is it? Oh, must be 1 o'clock if you call me. Here's what: give me half an hour to get ready. You can come to 1300 N Prospect Avenue. It is in Upper East Side close to Lake Park.
- Ok. I'll be there in half an hour. Bye for now.

Stephen made a rough estimation; as it was Saturday, he would have no problem to reach Upper East Side in half an hour from the place he stopped. He dialed the address in his GPS and drove away.

The city was quiet this time of day and weekend kept people inside, a chilly covered atmosphere on top of it all, leaving no option for those who were voting for a stroll. He finally drove on an alley in front a huge block full of luxury apartments and parked on a free space in front of the entrance. He took his mobile and sent a short text to Elizabeth – "I am here".

He was looking at the small park in front, observing the signs of fall – trees in yellow green shades and a rusty carpet of leaves on the narrow grass spread around them.

She came with a fresh appearance, dressed in a trench coat, over an exquisite grey deux - pieces and long black stockings with oddly colored high heels shoes by Christian Louboutin. She gave him a smile of recognition and stepped to the car. She went straight to the right front door, opened it and climbed in, raising elegantly her short skirt until Stephen could see the black garters of her stockings.

A cloud of exquisite perfume – maybe something Arabic Stephen thought.

She set herself comfortable in the seat and buckled up, while Stephen unexpectedly sneezed and looked at her with tearful eyes.

- What's the matter with you? This perfume is Baccarat Rouge 540 by Francis Kurkdjian ; cost me 700 bucks for a vial. What do you want me to wear? Chanel number 5?
- No, no, excuse me! It is not the perfume – it is exquisite and fits you, but I have problems with my old sinusitis. And Stephen put out his most friendly smile. Where do we go ?
- It the same place where we went the last time, Lake Park Bistro on Newberry Blvd. Not very far from here, and the cinema hall is within walking distance from there. Come on, I am already hungry.
- Ok – said Stephen as he set the address on his GPS. Hang on!

The drive was short, about 15 minutes, traffic lights and all, and soon they were seated at a table in separate booth with some view to the dance floor.

- What do you want to eat? She asked, grabbing the menu. Hey, waiter, she raised the hand and gave a short but penetrating whistle. The gesture was observed by the waiter and few other clients who were curious about the whistle but would have never imagined a fine woman like Elizabeth would be capable of such thing. The ugly looking character next to her must have been the culprit and Stephen received some sour glances, while Elizabeth looked very amused by the scene.

The waiter arrived in time to save the moment:

- Welcome Miss Elizabeth! What would you like to have today?
- I think I need a small espresso first to wake up completely and a large G&T, but make it 50/50! I will order food after!

- Understood Miss! Half gin and half tonic! On the rocks! Any preference on the gin
- Tanqueray! If you have it!
- Certainly Miss! And for the gentleman?

Stephen looked in the menu and decided to accompany her:

- I'll have a Scotch, large, no ice! This LAGAVULIN 16 years old should do! And some tonic water and one cappuccino for me!

Elizabeth smiled viciously:

- Nothing without the morning milk! Mama's boy eats and drinks only healthy stuff!

Stephen was ready to respond then he realized it would be worthless and smiled as if enjoying the joke.

- So, what have you done lately?
- Nothing much! I go out shopping, hit the gym, see a movie from time to time and fuck whenever I can. Mostly Archie, when he is around. And you? I heard you are active and willing to revive some of your older projects. How is your love life, Stephen? Still using taxi-girls? .....You know it's not too late to find a Mrs. Hicks!

Stephen almost choked and answered presently:

- Oh no. no! I am too old for that! I have given up family life prospects and sacrificed all this for my career. But who told you I want to revive my older projects? Was it Archie?
- Who else? He seemed very worried every time you speak on the phone with him.
- Well, that would be unusual ! I mean, we've known each other since Archie came to the company as a young apprentice and we got along fine ever since. But that was long before he met you!

– was Stephen turn to score on Elizabeth. On the other hand, I wanted to talk to you, anyway.

At this moment, the waiter came with the ordered drinks and carefully placed them on the table in front of them:

- Can I get food order now, Miss? It will give enough time for the Chef to prepare it.
- Yes! I want to have this – and she pointed to a dish on the menu, avoiding to read it in Italian.
- Oh yes – Lobster capellini with leek-Tarragon cream sauce – very good choice Miss! And for the gentleman? - he turned to Stephen.
- I'll have a beef steak – medium rare – with chips and tomato salad. Get me some hot barbeque sauce, too!
- Certainly! And the wine to go with them?
- We leave that to your appreciation, Mathew! Said Elizabeth, after looking on the waiter's badge.
- Okay! I recommend a more consistent, not too dry, white wine for the pasta – say a Louis Latour – Montrachet Grand Cru Blanc. And a Bordeaux for the stake – I have a Chateau Margaux from 2012 which is outstanding.
- Ok Mathew, thanks! Elizabeth smiled and waved him away with a bored gesture. So, you were saying – she turned to Stephen who was busy sipping on his coffee.

Stephen almost choked with the coffee after this brutal interpellation; he smiled again and took out his glasses to wipe them and buy some time for thinking:

- What was I saying … Oh, yes, I wanted to tell you that I've known Archie for a very long time and I know him quite well. We may have had a disagreement or two now and then, but then we have a long history of friendship and trust behind us. I lived with the impression you are not pleased with our relationship… and Stephen smiled again, taking a huge gulp from his Scotch.

The velvet taste of the reddish whiskey gave him more courage and was clearing the fog in his head.

Elizabeth was busy sipping on her gin and raised an eyebrow while Stephen talked, then smiled and said, looking at him straight to his eyes:

- Stevie boy, I am an independent woman. I like the good life Archie provides me with it and he is able to satisfy me in almost all aspects. We are not planning to get married, as both of us enjoy independence. I owe him my financial status, that is true, but I don't give a rat's ass on whatever he is doing with his friends. Come, let us go outside on the terrace! I need to smoke and I am not drunk enough to do it inside.

They grabbed the glasses and went to a small table for two on the terrace. It was a bit cold and windy, but the booze was warming the atmosphere enough.

- So, Steve darling, and she extended her fine hand with perfect manicure and gently caressed his right cheek, grabbing his chin and forcing him to look her in the eyes. For all I care, you could fuck with Archie in the ass or do whatever you boys are doing.
- Oh no – Stephen was trying to back up – it is noting like that, but I have seen he was kind of upset lately and he seemed to be picking on me….and I thought maybe I take too much from his time with you.
- Nonsense, Steve! I know you are straight – girls from "Mount Venus" parlor speak a lot and you can find out a lot of funny stories about people. Their Madame is my friend – she concluded, finishing her drink and crushing the cigarette but into the ashtray. Let's go inside ;I think they brought food.

They went inside and the dialogue was sacrificed to eating; Elizabeth pouring glass after glass of wine after every morsel and being visibly affected before she even emptied the plate. Stephen was more methodic in his approach to the steak and consumed half of the red wine even before feeling its taste, which in his opinion was too sour and left his mouth dry.

- You know what, pal? Most of Archie's friends are morons, especially those he deals contracts with! But you are nice, Steve, and you are not dangerous, that's why Archie left you as my nanny! He knows you are too old and ugly to stir me up and besides, you would meet him again next week.
- I assure you I have no intention of this kind, I only promised to accompany you as a friend, hoping you will get to also see a friend in me…
- Ta, ta, ta… Elizabeth silenced him, but turned towards the passing waiter and yelled at him: Hey Mathew, bring me another wine like this and vanilla pistachio ice-cream, baby!

Mathew stopped abruptly, memorized the order and nodded shortly, then rushed to bring the goodies.

- Why is it so, Stevie boy? Don't you find me attractive enough for you? Hmm?

Stephen thought the situation becomes uncomfortable for him and she was bringing him to a corner where he was helpless. It was clear now that Archie's attitude had nothing to do with her, most likely it was triggered by his particular interest in company production archives.

- Not at all! I mean it is not that, I think you look awesome, hot even, but it is not my privilege to approach this issue.- Stephen tried to face the assault. We should conclude lunch here, there is half an hour till the movie starts.
- I know when it is time to go and I won't go without another coffee… Elizabeth was looking around to see the waiter, who understood and proceeded to the order.

- You said some time ago that Archie presented you to some of his friends…
- Oh yes, darling. He needed to have female company. That did not prevent him from advising me to be nice to some of them. This is how I got to fuck some hotshots from God knows what country or organization. Naturally. Archie couldn't mind because he was the interested part, and I helped him for fun and because those goons paid extremely well.

She took a sip from her second coffee and smiled:

- It was bad with the Russians – they have little care for the right procedure and even minimal hygiene. And lousy tippers too.

She waved off some bad memories and took a sip from the fresh coffee in front of her.

- Like I do not want someone to stick his finger into my mouth and bite my tits. I do not exactly enjoy anal, although I noticed it stirs men up. And I don't squirt!

Then she turned to Stephen, who was listening like mesmerized her confession, thinking hard about the last time he saw any contract with Russians, but he didn't recall any. Maybe that was one of the anonymous deals responsible for the missing stuff from the depo.

Without realizing how close to a plausible explanation he was, Stephen put on his best smile again and replied:

- Why, I really think these details are rather personal but tell me, how come Archie agreed for your escapade with those people? Having a woman as beautiful as you are would have made me extremely jealous…
- Nonsense, Stevie boy! Elizabeth was determined to finish the second bottle of wine as well as the coffee. Archie and I are independent people and we do services for each other. He said please and I could not refuse him! Looks like some kind of

contract depended on how much that guy was impressed by me! And he was, baby, he was! I gave him a lesson he will dream about for years! She giggled stupidly, like all drunk people do sometimes! But tell me, Stevie boy, why was Archie pissed at you last time we met?

Stephen heard an alarm bell ringing in his ears. He smiled again and answered with an equal voice:

- How the fuck should I know? Thought it was because of you but now I see you cannot be blamed. Maybe it's that old story with some stuff we produced many years back and things went wrong.

Elizabeth seemed to focus her attention on his words. "Me and my big mouth" thought Stephen and he rapidly added:

- But thing turned fine, we were able to fix all problems, especially thanks to Archie's efforts.
- Glad to hear that, but I believe he was not upset on memories only…
- Oh no, I was clumsy enough to bring up a related topic, that's all ! "Old big mouth moron" Stephen thought about himself, while carefully trying to shift her interest from the item.
- Look, we got only 20 minutes to get to the movie! Shall we?
- Okay Mister! But I'll go when I'm good and ready! Hey Mathew, take this card for the pay while I get dressed.

She made her way gracefully to the wardrobe, in spite of being almost drunk and took her coat on her shoulder.

- Come along Stevie boy, I'll show you the way!

It was short walk around the block to the quite, small, but elegant cinema hall. Elizabeth showed the booked tickets and went straight to the bar to order sodas and popcorn. Happy, with a whole bucket in hands, she accompanied Stephen inside the already dark hall. The film was already beginning when they finally found their seats somewhere in a rear isolated booth, but with perfect visibility and audition.

She made herself comfortable raising her skirt to the hips, crossed her long legs and removed the jacket, remaining dressed in a thin shirt which was barely trying to hide her black bra, which was just the right size for her rich breast, without exceeding a plausible oversizing. Stephen was mesmerized by the view, having trouble to choose between the silver screen and the marvelous view next to him.

The movie was some thriller, but loaded with a lot of sensual activity or plain sex scenes. Elizabeth seemed to enjoy, crossing her legs on the right or on the left every 5 minutes or so. A violent scene on the screen made her shiver and she grabbed Stephen's hand, squeezing it tight until the suspense finished. Stephen thought she would release his hand, but instead, she pulled him closer to her. She grabbed his hand and lowered it until she placed it on the front side of her panties and along her things, above the garter level. She caressed the area with his hand, then suddenly, she took his hand and placed it inside her panties, until he distinctively felt the silky touch of her shortly cut pubic hairs. She extended her other hand, unzipped his trousers and grabbed his organ with a mild and soft touch. Stephen was conveniently aroused, so she started a mechanical pumping movement, in a rhythm which she knew would trigger a quick and satisfying result.

Stephen was no longer able to understand what he saw on the screen, and was sweating abundantly. The lenses of his glasses looked steamy, but he was concentration only on his tactile sense now.

Elizabeth felt his nervousness and she decided to tease him a little; she caressed her loins using his hand along the middle cleavage, but she would stop his hand short of reaching the entrance to her vagina. She must have moved his hand a dozen times to and fro before allowing and directing him to palpate the wet area and insert the tip of his middle finger inside her vagina. While doing so, she had a small shiver and sighed, then continued to use his finger like a dildo, getting more and more passionate in the process. Stephen had already cum and was regretting his hasty reflex. At times, she moaned quite loud and some heads turned in their direction.

Finally, she was a little sweaty when she had a shiver, exhaled relaxed and smiled to Stephen:

- You have a handkerchief, Stevie boy? I have a whole load of your grandchildren in my hand.
- Sorry, but it was impossible to resist! Here you are, and he gave her the handkerchief from his pocket.

The film finished and lights were on, forcing them to get their clothing tidy and recompose a decent attitude.

- Steve, get me home darling!
- Certainly! We have to walk to the car, though!

While parking in front of Elizabeth's apartment, she grabbed his hand and caressed her loins again:

- You are cute like a Teddy bear! Why don't you come up with me to have a coffee. I'll have one! Got to sober up before I speak to my mother tonight. She always calls me around eight.
- But I,....
- Never mind, told you I am independent and besides, we know each other better now, don't we?
- Yeah, sure! He gave up and closed his car, accompanying her on the hallway to the elevator.
- You know, Archie never came to my place, if I come to think of it! Here, take a seat! She invited him in a large living, while crossing towards the open space kitchen and turning on the coffee machine.
- Nice place you got here!
- You bet! One bedroom, but it is expensive – I think around 5000 per month. I wouldn't know, Archie takes care of it.

Stephen smiled. He was happy because he had a conformation for some of his suppositions and having a sensual experience with a woman like Elizabeth was a great achievement by itself, even if technically, it was not sexual intercourse. From this point of view, he felt drained and powerless, unable to get another boner soon, but then the conversation could prove useful enough.

At this moment, his mobile rang:

- Yes Archie, Hi! Like I said in the afternoon, everything is ok and they will meet the deadline, I am sure. .....Sure, we'll talk when you come back. Miss Elizabeth? She I fine, we went to the restaurant and saw a boring – for me – movie, and now I am seeing her home. I want to be home by 10 pm cause tomorrow I have a lot of things to do. Aham! Okay, Archie!.. You too!

Elizabeth was smiling while sipping on her coffee:

- What do you know! Maybe Prince Charming turns jealous after all! Maybe he fell in love with me!
- That wouldn't be so hard to achieve, if you ask me! Tried Stephen to joke about it.
- Relax Stevie boy! Archie fell in love with himself long ago and there's one thing he could possible love more – and that is money. I do not blame him - she softened the critic – I'm a material girl myself!

Stephen was holding coffee cup with both hands, seated on a cozy armchair, with a little sturdy wooden coffee table in front of him.

Now it was Elizabeth who had to answer the mobile:

- This must be my mother!

She stepped towards the shelf grabbed the mobile and answered speaking very quickly:

– Hi Mom! Listen I wanted to tell you about this awesome costume I saw the other day at Serena's shop. Yeah, it is red, deux pieces, and you can use black lingerie. Tell you what, I call you back in one hour, I have some stuff to do. Bye!

Stephen was miles away with his thoughts, still smiling and turning the coffee cup in his hands, nursing the satisfaction he might actually guess the secret partners of Archie and guess what? They were Russian and only God knew who else was mixed in this shit – he thought.

Elizabeth seemed to enjoy the moment and she poured a Gargantuan quantity of Martell Cognac in her coffee, tasted it and forced Stephen to taste it:

– This is Yumee! She said – I like coffee like this – it turns you on, isn't it, Stevie boy?

Without any further word, she stood in front of him and slowly, very slowly let her panties drop down. Freed from them, she stepped to the music corner and put on some whiskey blues vintage pieces.

Her lower body was perfect and her hips were shaped like Greek amphoras, flat belly and when he removed her bra, her breast sort of broke free in a cheeky upwards pointing attitude. The sight could make a eunuch faint, and it was devastating for Stephen, whose red spots on the face and neck took a purple nuance. He was still seated in the armchair when she got seated on the coffee table in front of him, spread her legs so he could see her pubic region close to his face. The pubic hair was trimmed in a small and reasonable triangle on her Mons Venus and her split pink was wet and inviting.

Stephen was paralyzed at the thought he wouldn't gather strength for a new boner, but she saved him by saying:

– Okay, Stevie boy, I noticed you did not order any desert at the restaurant so I can offer you this. Remember, I like it when you take time, and do not bite, please!

Like remotely controlled, Stephen got down his steamy glasses, bent over her and kissed her pink. She tasted sweet and a little bit sour and the perfume was driving him mad, so that he started a frenetic tongue dance inside her pink, licking it upwards to her clit and going in as much as he could. She sighed in the beginning, and after she started moaning louder and louder, the deeper he went with his mouth-work.

- Hey Stevie boy, you are a young talent and I can teach you more! But you haven't told me the real reason Archie was pissed….Oh yes, there …. Sure, right there… oh it's so good!

Stephen was so busy he could hardly speak, but he answered anyway:

- Beats me, maybe the missing stuff from the depot, I mean we always have poor account of all and things move everyday…he mumbled, but his regrets for saying this faded at the thought that his treatment would divert her attention from such boring details. He started chewing and licking even more vigorously, obtaining a chorus of moans from Elizabeth.

In the end she started sweating and pressing his head between her legs furiously. When almost ready to reach climax, her telephone rang, and she interrupted the push to pick up the phone, while Stephen continued his tongue exploration:

- Yes, Hallo again mother!

She suddenly rose to her feet, leaving Stephen who was searching with blurred vision some napkin or tissue to wipe his mouth, blood pounding in his skull.

- Yes darling, I have a lot to talk to you about! I've been out today! Hold it for a couple of minutes ! I call you back!

She turned to Stephen, who meanwhile had managed to put on his glasses and was moving like a discarded Muppet.

- Steve boy! Thanks for the "massage"! Maybe we meet again some time! Off you go! I got things to do! Thanks for the day Steve – and she came next to him and gave him a kiss on the cheek!
- Okay… Sure, bye Elizabeth….He took his coat and went to the elevator, with the distinct impression that something was wrong.

He walked few steps to his car and got in, trying to relax a little after the bumpy ride with Elizabeth – one crazy bitch – he thought.

Suddenly he realized what triggered the alarm bell in his head. When her mobile rang and she answered - he could swear he heard a man's voice, even if she spoke to "mother". So that a man was "mother' and she was going to call him again to talk to him. Not Archie, he could recognize his voice on the phone any time of day and night, no, no, it was somebody else and she sent him away to avoid any interference or curiosity from him. So that Elizabeth has secrets, too, right? He realized he fell into this like a fish in a bowl of soup and it would take time to understand and put things together.

Business as usual

The Luki was sailing Eastwards close to the tip of the African Horn. Commander Polivanov was "patrolling" those waters in search of pray and he had sent two of his speedboats to check on a radar target sailing in the opposite direction ready to enter the Gulf of Aden.

Odds were in his favor. The boats reported a 25 000 DWT bulk carrier registered in Malta, but belonging to an iron Indian company.

Indian business people were keen on saving taxes and fees, Polivanov thought, and probably were buying their fuel from the black market in Saudi ports, so he gave them green light.

The two boats approached the ship, the Indian crew opposing little resistance with some water hoses. The whole attack lasted 10 minutes and it was very rewarding m as they found in the captain's safe box 220 000 USD. His hunch about the business of this ship was right – they were buying fuel from black market with cash. Unfortunately, the captain of the ship had the bad idea of defending himself with a gun and his boys had to shoot him, but this was the only casualty.

When they left, the second in command took over and the ship continued course, probably reporting the incident in the nearest port.

By the time this happened, the speed boats were far away on an interception course with Luki. The big ship did not even stop, but kept cruising at 8 knots to avoid any suspicion of the military radar operators. In the darkness of the night and after checking the presence of foreign surveillance (like night vision drones), the mobile crane of Luki extended overboard and raised one by one the two speedboats, placing them deep inside the middle hold. A metal cover rolled in and covered the hangar, and some pipes and cargo crates had been conveniently scattered on it as if it were the bottom of the hold.

A pleased Polivanov sent the sentry soldier to fetch the vodka reserve and he called Zarufin to celebrate success.

Viktor Zarufin came shortly and was happy about recovering the two speed boats while on course to Durdura, around the Horn of Africa.

Viktor was les cheerful and by the second glass of vodka, he told Commander Polivanov he was afraid they will be exposed. Polivanov explained he was sure about surveillance and used ship's own drones in order to secure action. Viktor observed that, even at night, they were still exposed to satellites. Polivanov waived this off:

– We are not that lucky! You become interesting only if you stop!
– Whatever you say Commander! I am afraid of modern technology!
  – smiled Viktor, accepting the third ice cold vodka. Then he apologized and left the bridge.

Seated on his chair next to the radar screen and the helm and staring outside in the darkness, adjusting his clothing appearance with rather trembling hands, he thought that apparently, things were going all-right and his superiors were satisfied with the results, yet something didn't go right as planned and he couldn't tell what. Maybe this was something physiological, he thought, trying to remember what he ate and did before, trying to find a reason for his bad mood.

What Polivanov did not know was that a tiny surveillance satellite was targeting the Gulf of Aden that evening, registering images of anything moving at sea and on the Northern shores of Puntlands and Somaliland. The course of Luki, the phantom ship, as well as other around 20 ships, including the attacked Maltese flagged bulk carrier, had been registered in the device memory and were to be disclosed on demand.

Polivanov felt confident because of his intel services – he had been organizing a vast and efficient system of information regarding the ship traffic in the Red Sea, Aden Gulf and western Indian Ocean, a huge sea surface which had become his hunting ground. The Indian ship flagged in Malta was a tip he received from a friend in Mumbai. He will give him something when they meet face to face. But he remembered of the dozens of fishermen who were his informers. He had informers in the Red Sea in Port Sudan, in Jeddah – Saudi Arabia, in Al Mukalla, Aden and Al Hadaydah from Yemen. In the Gulf of Aden, he had some informers in Djibouti, Berbera (Somaliland), Tooxin and Bosaso (Puntlands). Further on, he was in contact with informers in Kihshia in Kilmia Island, Gishub and Steroh in Socotra Island, and going South he had a powerful network in Dar es Salaam (Tanzania), Zanzibar, Merca and Mogadishu in Somalia, Nacala and Pemba in Mozambique and he had a friendly resident in South Africa as well.

Like this, Polivanov had time to get info on target, rather than blindly attack anything or targets proving too big to "chew". He had been informed about traps – ships that came full of armed soldiers or accompanied by war vessels sailing so close to generate a single spot on the radar. His communication system was GMDSS, state of the art performance, he could call or receive calls via satellite anywhere in the world and he strongly believed he had thought of everything. His five years uninterrupted activity were proof to it, and he was satisfied with the way he was moving. He did not like the casualties

– the death of that ship's captain was unnecessary and bad for their business, but he hoped it will go without any important reaction. He needed to take a break in order to purchase two more speed boats to replace the destroyed ones and to recruit some people. He thought he would find some good mercenaries in Dar es Salaam, Nacala or in Yemen – where it was swarming with Houthy rebels. He was reluctant in taking Iranian soldiers – they were not very well trained and they were religiously brain-washed and would have started skirmish with the two Jews he already had on his team.

He also had a promise to choose from the crew of a Russian large ship that was coming in the area within two weeks. He had 4-5 recommendations from his comrades in GRU and he was eager to welcome the designed personnel – those were verified and he could trust them.

If it weren't for these shortcomings – boats and men to replace – he almost had forgotten about the incident on the Northern coast of Somaliland. He remembered he was happy to get rid of Mr. Lu at Jeddah and he celebrated this with Viktor by sacrificing a whole bottle of vodka.

He would give men a break when they reach Egypt; keep the ship there for some "repairs" in a small yard, while waiting for the speed boats delivery. He planned to take a plane ride to Thessaloniki and then get to Porto Carras to enjoy staying at his hotel and restaurant for a week or so. After this, he will be back to business, with fresh boats and personnel.

He lit his pipe again and after puffing a few times, went in the command room and said to the young officer there:

-   Ship is yours! If you need anything call Viktor! I am going below! Keep same course! We should be entering the Red Sea by tomorrow evening.
-   Tak yesti! Comandir! (Understood Commander) the young officer answered, concentrating on the radar screen, while the helmsman did not make any move, looking outside and to the compass in front of him. The helm was a small and delicate half steering wheel, something similar to that of the old airplanes, and

the throttling handles of both engines, also resembling airplane ones, were fixed at ¾.

The Luki was cruising at more than 16 knots, but they did not want to drag attention with their speed, preferring to use it only in complicated situations.

Uneventful days have passed, with the usual meeting of his close officers for the customary evening vodka and discussions about the repairs and necessary supplies.

They finally docked at Ain El Sokhna port, close enough to SIDC Industrial Park and even Cairo, where they could order spares and have access to an airport. The mercenaries, almost all with fake passports and sailor cards, took two weeks off and they were glad of escaping their hot "prison" – the hidden quarters below deck.

Polivanov himself talked to them when they left the pier:

–   Listen to me men! We will be ready to sail in 14 days so I expect you to be on the ship by then. We wait for no one! Be careful where you go and what you do! I strongly advise you to avoid regular international flights – they are very careful with ID's. If anybody gets in trouble, he is on his own and we will not interfere – it is our policy to keep away from publicity. Now line up and go to Viktor's office to receive your monthly cash pay. Who wants to send money somewhere – use MoneyGram, and avoid the banks. Better send smaller sum several times, instead of a single larger deposit. Never send more than 10 000 in one transaction.

He was watching as his mercenaries were turning to go to Zarufin's office:

–   And do not forget one thing: you are in a Muslim country and you must avoid public alcohol drinking; do it alone in the hotel or bar, or wait until you come back aboard the ship. Should anyone ask you anything – you're unemployed sailors looking for a job! Vai paniemayete? (Do you understand?) Good luck!

The ceremony went similarly with a part of the crew of Luki, those fortunate enough to enjoy a brief 7 days -vacation. They would come back within 7 days and replace those who remained aboard for repairs and organizing supplies.

Didenko, the talented Chief Engineer, was standing in the main deck door, with his always lit plain Camel stuck to the corner of his mouth. He was not smiling, his thoughts were very practical – he was planning to do decarboxylation of main diesel generators and if possible, he would do some maintenance work on auxiliary, secret ones. He also had to check on a main separator and a water pump for the cooling system of starboard main engine. The hold electric covers had to be cleaned and lubricated for swift functionality when extracting and reloading the speed boats. Finally, he was supposed to contact friends and organize full fuel bunker. There was time to do stuff, but no vacation for him. He would go out occasionally to send some money home. And yes, he was preoccupied by the unrest between Russia and Ukraine and figured out Trans-Nistria would become a legitimate target if and when war broke. He would have to try and relocate his family asap and he promised to do so on his first leave. He would take them to Moldavia first, and maybe try to get a Romanian passport and move on to Europe someplace. He had enough money to relocate and he did not need to cover his identity, as he kept away of any compromising operation. He was an engineer and his job were on this ship. He was not interested about the activity of the ship – even if he understood too well its criminal nature – but he kept away from anything else than mechanics. He was doing a good job and was one of Polivanov favorite employees, perhaps also because he was keeping silence and never asked questions.

A very confident Polivanov, carrying little luggage, stepped inside the Thessaloniki airport and quickly went to the exit door, passing through the "nothing to declare" gateway.

He was careful not to carry his gun when travelling – besides, he had a concealed one in every of his hideout locations. Sometimes, and in some unstable places, much more than a Beretta – we talk here assault rifles like AR 15 and hand grenades, explosives, detonators and even modern crossbows with little poisoned arrows or spring blade throwing knives. That was "Home, sweet home" gear.

Polivanov stepped out of the car in front of the hotel he owned – the "Meridian" and left a currier boy to park it and bring his bags.

PortoCarras was warm enough and dry. Plenty of people were taking a walk in the surroundings and in the distance, he could see the deserted beach and the port full of private boats, all looking shiny and luxurious.

The automatic door opened in front of him and he entered the pleasant reception hall, swarming with people, full of exquisite clothing and fancy perfumes. A few distinguished gentlemen were seated in the smoking booths with huge cigars in their hands, patiently waiting for their families to reunite. He noticed that many of the guests spoke Russian, which was good. Besides, he would have the opportunity to make new friends, imagine new deals and possibly find out some interesting facts for his comrades in the GRU. Frequent reports keep you interesting and alive – he used to think.

He made his way towards the bar, where a tall handsome blonde woman, wearing a silk blouse that was unable to properly cover her huge breast and a pair of metal blue trousers, bent over the bar table, was filling some glasses with a transparent liquid – looking like vodka.

- Olga Kuznetsova – dorogoy moy (my dear)! Chto ty delaiesh devushka? (how are you, girl?)
- Igor Andreevitch – Dobro pozhalovat! (Welcome!)

Olga Kuznetsova was the hotel manager appointed by Polivanov, to take care of the place while he was missing. She was apparently doing a great job.

- No pozhaluysta! (Please come !)

Olga showed the way to her office, without forgetting the small tray with ice cold vodka shots.

– Udachi I budem zdorovi! (Good luck and good health to us!) she
took the first glass and kicked the one in Polivanov's hand.

He smiled and approached her with a vigorous arm then kissed
her on her mouth and then noisily on both cheeks. Olga Kuznetsova
was not in her prime, but she was a ripe and had the experience of
the woman who knows what the wants from life. Their relationship
started with a genuine love story some more than two decades back in
the slums of Marseille, but the nature of Polivanov's erratic activities
did not enable them to comfortably consume their love then. Soon,
Olga discovered her appetite for money and they had the revelation
of a very successful business relationship. Of course, this relationship
was spiced with some leisure activities and occasional friendly sex,
but they had no time for serious commitments or jealousy. Olga was
faithful and vengeful, and had the reputation of savagely defending
Polivanov against all enemies.

– Na zdorova! (Cheers) Replied Polivanov, drinking the second
shot and taking seat in an armchair. I think I will go and have
a shower, maybe take a nap. I am tired! Tonight we eat together,
you tell me about things and we party! He smiled at the prospect
of this program and Olga smiled back.
– I missed you! I was afraid for you! And she combed his rough
gray hair with her fingers. Then she kissed him affectionately on
the lips and said:
– Come, I'll help you take a bath and give you a bit of massage! You
seem tense! But first, let us finish our drink!

He gave a good example pouring the remainder of the Stolichnaia
vodka in the glasses and drinking one of them in a single gulp. Then
she extended her hand to a bag on the table and extracted a cigar
(black but not so large) and lit it, puffing vigorously until she created
a blueish cloud around her.

They finished the drink and moved on to Polivanov's quarters.

There Olga turned on the shower and came back to undress
him. Polivanov stayed on the bed staring at the wall in front of him

and finally seemed to observed her after she finished to undress him and she stripped her own clothing. He suddenly observed how her generous -read huge – breast hanged in front of her chest and lust sparkled in his eyes. They went to the shower, where Olga started covering him with soap with her strong but gentle hands, occasionally rubbing her Rubensian body against his until she went to his lower parts. She bent over and started a skillful hand job and after he was aroused, she went on using her mouth. When she felt he was ready, she firmly pushed him against the wall, then came over with one leg around him and impaled herself on his member, moaning with satisfaction. She kept on steadily moving up and down for a number of minutes and feeling him ready to go she got free and kept on working on her knees until she received the full charge of cum on her face and in her mouth. Then she smiled and rose to her feet, starting to rinse the remaining soap from their bodies.

Polivanov smiled and buried his face between her huge tits; after a moment he looked up and smiled:

- Olga, I'm getting old! This should have taken one hour!
- Nonsense, Igor Andreevitch! You are tired, but it was all right anyway! I will call you when I need more! Until then, I have prepared a surprise for you after dinner!
- Surprise? What kind of surprise?
- You will see ! Until then, rest! Here you have fresh underwear and some clothes. Why don't you take a nap and I'll pick you up for dinner.

He approved and dragged her by the hand. When she was in reach, he buried again his face in her generous breast and gently bit her by her left tit. Olga jumped back and pushed him away, laughing:

- Nu pagady idiomy!(You wait and see, you peasant!)

She kissed him like sucking life out of him and covered him with a blanket, then stormed out of the door, shouting something to the room-service maids.

It was dark outside when Polivanov woke up and he felt himself rested and without any stress. He went to the bathroom to refresh himself and found with satisfaction his toilet kit. He trimmed his moustache and shaved, brushed his teeth – stained in front because of his habit of keeping there his pipe – and splashed himself with an expensive and exotic smelling men perfume.

He found a clean white shirt, cream light trousers and a dark marine- blue coat, with metal buttons. He looked like an elegant middle aged business man and there was no trace of his buccaneer personality. Sharp dressed while still being comfortable – that was the way he liked it. Hi thoughts were interrupted by a knock on the door:

- Commander Polivanov Sir!
- -Yes – he opened the door and saw a young apprentice dressed like a waiter.
- Madam Olga sent me to tell you she is waiting for you downsairs at the casino bar! He saluted and ran away, without waiting for any reply.

Polivanov looked around the room, grabbed his tobacco box, his pipe and matches and went on the hallway, letting the room door close automatically with a loud click.

Olga was waiting at the bar with fresh frozen shots on a small tray in front of her. She smiled, this time refreshed and dressed in a long dark sari-like gown, allowing a provocative view over her body. The side cleavage showed a firm and still young thigh and it was like a political speech – long enough to cover the most important facts and short enough to stir imagination. She also had fresh ear rings and lipstick, looking ten years younger than the forty she had in her ID card.

She smiled and showed him a chair next to her.

- How was your rest? Are you Ok?
- Okay! He smiled. What shall we drink for?
- First, we shall drink to us and our friendship – may it last forever!

– Zdorova! He acknowledged and they threw first shot over.
– To our friends and families! – she continued.

Another shot followed the same ritual.

– Hey Olga, this vodka made me hungry! Let us go eat something!
– Ok, Igor Andreevich! Follow me! She led the way into a more discrete hallway and the smell of food betrayed they were heading towards the restaurant, which proved to be large enough, cozy and airy. The smell betrayed quality cuisine.
– Let us sit here, Olga suggested, showing a small table for two. Then she waived a sign to one of the waiters who came presently.
– Listen Evghenii, we want to eat something good. Bring us a bowl of borsch first and then a steak with sweet potatoes and pickles,

Evghenii – the young waiter – nodded and left like a ghost. In a split second, another young man came with a small tray with frozen little glasses and a bottle of Belluga luxury vodka, which he poured generously.

It was a matter of minutes before another waiter came with a couple of steaming bowls and placed them in front of the guests, together with toast and spices. Polivanov attacked the specific acrid soup with visible satisfaction, noisily sipping the soup according to Russian tradition, while looking around in the restaurant for fresh faces. From time to time he would stop to smile to Olga, who seemed very happy to please him. He was her hero and we might say – a very generous one. In a manner of speaking, her life depended on him like the one of Zarufin and like him, she would never dream to betray Polivanov.

Steak came together with a bottle of Champagne.

They ate and drank until full, then asked for some Rusian tea for desert, together with a Hennessy for digestion.

At this moment Olga invited him to go to the casino for a spin. He accepted and they went to the roulette table, where Polivanov made a bet on 17 red and placed 1000 USD. He lost that and another two hands, but he won the forth one when he bet on 7 red. With a bagful of chips which he handed to Olga, he left for the restrooms.

Upon coming back to the bar, a sharp dressed man in his early forties, wearing a red tie, got in his way and asked him in Russian:

- Gospodin (Mr.) Polivanov?
- Da! Ya Polivsnov!(I am Polivanov)
- Proshu proshcheniya! U menya yest' soobshcheniye ot druga! (Excuse me! I have a message from a friend!) and he raised his hat and went towards the back door, leaving a small white envelope in Polivanov' hand.

Polivanov was very curious about the letter and in his mind was already guessing who the "friend" would be, but this was important and nobody had to know about it, not even Olga. He went back to the bar and finished the drinks with Olga.

- Listen Olga, I am still tired from travelling, I think I'd better hit the sack. We'll call it a day! Thank you for this wonderful welcoming party! You are my best friend and the best woman I can wish for!

Olga was blushing a little, but it was hard to say if it were from the emotion or the booze. However, she decided to rectify her emotional appearance by lighting a new cigar, from which she launched a cloud of blueish smoke towards Polivanov and smiled to him:

- You are my Prince Charming and my master! Working for you and loving you was my hiring job, but now it's my reason to be. Have a good night!

Polivanov smiled and made his way to the elevator. He was indeed physically tired, but satisfied, He was curious about the letter but he wanted to read it in his room, to have time to think about it.

He opened his door, threw the coat on the bed and removed his shirt to get some fresh air. He sat on the arm chair in front of the little office table and the TV set and opened the envelope. The address of the sender placed on top of the page caught his eye:

"29155/ 76 Khoroshyovskoe shosse, Khodinka, Moscow"

Yap! He thought. Unit 29155. That was it. The most discrete and subversive unit of the GRU. The cream of the cream of the Army spies – his comrades.

The address was the HQ of the GRU (Spetsnaz) – and that made it clear what the orders were and the text was a typed message, not very long – and Polivanov observed that securitizing protocols were respected. Message personally handed to him, meant top priority. The note had been typed on a typewriter not a computer, thus any internet breach would have been prevented. This document was unique and that meant he had to obey orders and destroy it after reading it.

Inside the document he read:

"Commander,

You are to sail with your ship to Jeddah and be there on the 19th of the month; see that your repairs are ready by then. You will take a group of 5 persons led by a man called Yuri Semionovich Sokolov. The identity of the other members of the group is not of your concern. Upon positive identification of Yuri Semionovich at the Golden Camel Café in Jeddah port, you will embark the whole group and launch them in the 5th night (24 to 25th of the month) on to the northern coast of Somaliland, at the same location like last time, at coordinates 10.97/ 47.02, between Xiis and Maidh. You will report launch and come to the same location after three weeks to pick them up. You will be contacted by radio-telephone for extraction, 3 days in advance, by code: "500 ton charter party offer Aden Gulf area; stand by for details". Stealth and discretion are mandatory. Avoid any suspicious behavior and armed engagement at sea. Any objective reasons to interfere with this plan will be reported to our office in Bandar Abbas in Iran, in due time to order corrective measures. When recuperation of team is accomplished, you will file a complete report of the operation. The recuperated team will be transported to Bandar Abbas and team disembark will be reported. Unless further notice, this is a priority mission! Read and destroy message!"

Polivanov sighed and rose to his feet, paper in hand. So, his next moves were already decided. At least he was given time to finish repairs and rest his men. He decided to communicate to their charter party broker to search for credible contracts in Nakala of Mozabique and Bandar Abbas of Iran, to justify his presence in those waters. They would be on a tight schedule. Maybe find some pray on the way there. Beyond mandatory orders, business is business. He decided to call Viktor in the morning to take adequate measures to make the ship ready to sail on the 15th so they would reach Jeddah without problems on the 19th.

He took both envelope and paper and placed them both in the ashtray on the balcony table. He lit papers with a match and witnessed them burn to ashes, then returned to the room, as somebody was knocking at his door. In his hotel, he felt secure like if it were his home and Olga's bodyguards were more than able to face any intruder before reaching his apartment. But who knows, and Polivanov had the healthy habit of trusting no one. He got his gun from a drawer next to his bed and stepped in the safe angle behind the door, then asked"

- Who is there?
- Room service – he heard a woman's voice and though he heard her laughing.

He opened the door and he saw two young ladies, very beautiful and dressed in sexy outfits, one blonde and one brunette:

– Hi! They said – we are Georgia and Julia ! We are your surprise from Madame Olga! She instructed us to put you to bed and make sure you get a good night's sleep! Can we come in?

Reasonable proof

Director Fujimori was assembling the delegation for investigating the Somaliland epidemiologic incident. Delegation was to be led by Dr. Peter Bud, and had four other members, now present in the room.

A younger character, with a stack of mingled blonde hair – Jason Barr – was a lab specialist and a computer wizard. In his late twenties or very early thirties, he was loosely dressed in large colored clothing, sort of "flower-power" style. Although he may have seemed superficial at the first glance, the vivid intelligent look in his eyes told a very different story.

The second person was a tall and slim African American – Joseph (Joe) Cooper. He was a PhD in epidemiology and with a passion for exotic diseases and African life. Joe Cooper was also a well- documented literature amateur and he had published some poetry himself lately.

The third member of the delegation was a French parasitologist, who was a member in the WHO parasitology board. Jean- Yves Durand was a sharp dressed elegant man in his early forties, with a pleasant smile, but less sustained by his eyes, which preserved a distant look on other things and persons.

Finally, there was Liam Johnson, a tall and silent true Texan, specialized in molecular biology and bacterial metabolism. He was in his early forties and induced a calm and steady, stable sensation to the people around him. He was a genuine Texas citizen with Lone Star State convictions, hat and boots included and a wide belt that could easily harbor a holster with a gun in it, if you had that kind of imagination.

All of them stood in front of Fujimori and listened to his words:

- You will be and work at all times as a team; wherever you go, you go together, even if you need to cover more objectives. Dr. Bud, I rely upon your wise correlation of the actions of this team. I will be waiting for a daily report each evening after 8 p.m. Geneva time. Any questions?
- Sir! Liam Johnson – the silent member of the group suddenly spoke, with little respect to protocol – what if we stumble upon some big problems and we catch the bad guys red handed?
- You will take information only – as significant and detailed as possible. Then you will report and law enforcement will react promptly. Your further task will be to imagine ways to solve the health problems, only – at least on the short term. We will provide advice and help on a wider scale after. It will be our task to seek and implement lawful actions. Do you have other questions?
- No Sir! Peter answered after checking an eye to eye acknowledgement from the others. We will go to prepare for departure.

As they were going out, he spoke to the others:

- I accepted this assignment for its responsibility; for the rest, we are equal partners and we will decide together what is best to do. I wanted to have this cleared before we go. I'll meet you at the airport tomorrow at 1 p.m. We got two hours to clear check-in and we travel with hand luggage only. See you, guys!
- Bye for now, tubib*! Yves Durant smiled generously! We talk over coffee at the airport.

The night was not very cold, but Peter has been unable to sleep properly. He was not worried about the travel; he was contemplating his role in the team and he wished there were more time to consolidate relationship in it, for now just a gathering of outstanding specialists in various sciences related to healthcare, but meeting and supposed to work together for the first time in their life. Mixed thoughts and

---

* Tubib* – doctor, in Arab; currently used in Maghreb ex-French colonies

uncertainties kept him awake until 4 am and after that, he managed to take 2 hours of restless sleep.

He got his luggage and took a cab to the airport.

The first he saw was Liam Johnson, seated on a bench, feet hanging over his backpack and hat covering his face, in a slumber attitude.

He simply moved his hat to one side and said:

– Oh, Good morning! You made it ! Have a seat!

And he put his hat back on the face, like avoiding the contact with external environment. Peter sat down next to him, eagerly searching the landscape for a known face. Finally, he noticed Jason Barr, the IT specialist who saw them and came along and later on, they were joined by Joe Cooper and Yves Durand.

– I take the window seat! – said Liam, from under his hat.
– I take the aisle seat – said Jason Barr, smiling like a spoiled kid. I have to go to the bathroom often, I have a restless bladder! – he added.
– Middle seat suits me – Joe Cooper said – I don't mind where I seat, provided I get where I have to go.
– I am glad we have an agreement – smiled Peter with an acrid face. Now you grown- ups take your gear and move to the control booth.

Speaking loudly and lamenting about the early hour – although it was almost eleven am – they lined up for the check. Everybody removed metal gear, belts, glasses, watches, everything that may have triggered alarm.

On their way out, the border control agent stopped Liam and said:

– Is this your bag Sir?
– Yes, it is!
– Kindly remove your knife from your beauty-bag Sir!

- Knife? Christ, what kind of knife? I have no knife – said Liam extracting the beauty bag from his backpack.
- Sorry Sir, please remove the knife as instructed, or we will retain the whole bag.
- Ok, ok, let me look what kind of freakin' knife you saw!
- Here it is Sir – the custom agent picked with wo fingers a small Swiss penknife and showed it to Liam.
- Oh, come on! That is a little toy my mother gave me on my last birthday. It barely has a two -inch blade!
- .Rule is less than one -and- a- half inch Sir – either give it up or bag stays!
- All right, all right! Forgive me mother! Liam said, as he took the small penknife and threw it on a pile behind the counter, where dozens of similar objects were gathered in a large crate.
- Here, satisfied now? He posed in a menacing attitude towards the border agent, one head shorter than him. The clerk did not even blink as he continued:
- No Sir! Please follow me! He led Liam to one side, and he dressed one rubber glove to his right hand. Everybody was stun, as they all were thinking: Is he going to do that kind of checking here, now, with all the people around?

But the border clerk took a cotton pad of some kind from a tin box and started touching with it Liam's body, arm pits, belly, hands and then placed the pad in some kind of electronic detector meant to trace forbidden substances (especially explosives).

Joe Cooper smiled like a Cheshire cat and approached:

- Like carrying a knife was not enough! Now you are a suspect for explosives! How long do you plan to embarrass us, Liam Johnson?

But Liam was in no mood for jokes:

- Oh, shut up, Joe. Your Massa must very proud of you since they hired you at the WHO; be happy they let you speak! Now give me a break, will you?

Joe smiled mechanically, but the joke seemed too gross for his sensitivity. He turned his back on Liam and pretended he had some texting to do on the phone.

Peter noticed the incident and he promised himself he would keep an eye on this. For now, it only seemed a friendly skirmish, but it was important to prevent it from degenerating, as Liam came from a Southern traditional environment.

Flight to Dubai was rather boring; six and a half hours of uneventful airplane routine, with Jason Barr stuck to his laptop, Joe Cooper mostly sleeping or pretending to do so, Yves Durand enjoying endless conversation with neighboring passengers and Liam Johnson isolated with his whiskey flask next to him and reading from a NRA magazine. Inspiring pictures of various types of guns and ammo, apparently required his undivided attention. Peter took some rest, ate a sandwich and then ran through his notes again and again. A number of questions were becoming clearer by the hour in his head and answering them was nothing short of accomplishing his objectives. Some of them particularly bothered him, and he wrote them in his notebook:

- Was there any connection between the strange infections registered in Somaliland and the odd mosquito species depicted there?
- Was there any biological assessment to identify the incriminated germ inside the insects, in order to prove their role as vectors?
- If so, how did the insects get infected and where did they come from, given the fact that their natural habitat was 10 thousand miles away and across the Atlantic Ocean?
- What were the odd characteristics of the incriminated germ, otherwise liable to inflict milder and chronic disease, not toxic and acute with life- threatening severity within days? Besides, almost half of the diseased patients died and a 50% toll is a disaster in any infectious outburst, not to mention an epidemic development.
- Is it possible that the germ has been "engineered"? And if so, by whom? Did it accidentally infect the insects or it was loaded

within those mosquitoes on purpose, turning them in powerful and virtually impossible -to - stop biological vectors?
-   Finally, why did this development take place in Somaliland and not elsewhere?

Peter felt that answering these questions would mean the decisive step forward in depicting the mystery and connected to it, finding a way to solve the problem.

After a few long hours of waiting in the crowded Terminal No. 3 of Dubai airport, with the team resting on a bench surrounded by Pakistani nationals, slumbering next to their refrigerator sized luggage, the old Air Gorilla Boeing 737 took them over the sea. There was one mandatory stop in Djibouti, then an unannounced short stop in Berbera airport, where they were supposed to disembark. Upon embarking through the front door, Peter looked inside the old, but sturdy airplane and realized that, with the exception of Joe Cooper, they were the only white passengers on board and they already enjoyed curious looks from the others. To his restlessness, he observed the poor lighting inside the cockpit, with a lot of detached wires in the dashboard and a couple of Russian speaking blonde pilots, one of them visibly drunk. He preferred not to mention it to the colleagues and after a nightmare session of having everybody seated in the right place, they had a delayed take off, remarkably smooth otherwise. Smooth and a bit boring was the whole three-hour journey to Djibouti. A few people got down and there was a rather disturbing incident. Peter noticed the airplane was awaited by an ambulance and a police car. The first to disembark was an old man who occupied one of the front seats, who was declared dead on arrival. Very likely a cardiac arrest, he heard passengers say. He was taken away and some other four-five people got down, being replaced by others.

Upon taxing towards take off position, Peter observed the dozens of airplanes and helicopters of the AFRICOM American air- force parked along the strip. That was a force to reckon with, he thought.

Finally, after half an hour, they descended to the isolated airstrip of Berbera airport. Quite rough, made out of concrete tiles, surrounded by sand and no tower in view.

A red pick-up that had seen better days followed the airplane: there were some extinguishers in it, a few sand bags and two shovels in the back and Peter realized that was the fire-department vehicle in case of emergency.

Civilian cars and a small ugly bus, waiting for travelers, were parked next to the strip. They went, as previously instructed, towards a grey Isuzu with police beacon on the roof top.

A slender character in military uniform got down to greet them:

- Dr. Peter Bud? He extended his right hand, with thin and nervous fingers. I am major Bashir and I welcome you to Somaliland. Please follow me to the car.

Peter introduced him to all the members of his team, and then they drove outside the airport facility.

- I know you must be very tired, but I think we should take advantage of our being here. We are going to pay a short visit to the Berbera hospital first, if you do not mind. You will find out some first -hand details about our problem and after that, we can go to Hargeisa, our capital city, where you will have an important meeting.
- Ok major! Lead the way! Peter smiled. The others were silent, partially because they were indeed very tired. Besides that, the heat of the Berbera sunshine was close to unbearable, especially because of the high level of humidity, which made the environment a breathable "warm soup". Sweating desperately, they sighed with relief when Major Bashir turned on the AC.

The dusty road led them towards the city, with small houses on the sides, flocks of goats here and there, sometimes obstructing traffic. Finally, they got to a more crowded area, with a large market place, where vendor tables full of colored stuff were mixed with animals for sale and people swarming by. After extensive use of the horn to clear his path, Major Bashir took a larger street towards a less crowded neighborhood. A two - level building, all painted white and surrounded by smaller pavilions, welcomed them – the Berbera Hospital.

The car was allowed promptly inside the parking area and everybody stepped down from the car.

– You can leave your luggage in the car! It is ok – major Bashir smiled, and continued. Please follow me!

They were invited inside the building, which displayed open space hallways and went to an office at the top floor. Inside, a tall and handsome character in his forties invited them in:

– Glad to receive you! Dr. Musa at your service!
– Good day Dr Musa! I am Peter Bud and these are my colleagues: Dr. Joe Cooper, Dr. Yves Durand, Dr. Liam Johnson and IT specialist Jason Barr. We are assigned by WHO to have an inquiry over the epidemiological events within the last couple of months in this area.!
– I take it you have been introduced – Major Bashir came from the outside hall and brought with him a nurse holding a tray with Somali tea for everyone. Somali tea is a variant of African tea. Actually, it consists of goat milk mixed with black tea, sweetened with honey. Practical advice says you have to boil the goat milk and simply add a few bags of black tea inside. That's all! The taste is awesome and it doesn't finish as fast as a small cup of coffee. Now that everybody was comfortably seated in an armchair, talks were initiated.
– Dr. Musa, we came here as a result of the invitation expressed by the Ministry of health of Somaliland. The matter is politically sensitive as you probably know, given the fact that Somaliland province enjoys poor international recognition, yet. You can imagine we had to additionally demand official access from

Somali- Mogadishu authorities, but thanks God, there was no problem with that, given our domain of activity.

- I understand all this and you can go into deeper detail with our Ministry of health in tomorrow's meeting. Right now, I would like to show you something and for this I invite you to accompany me in a short visit of our hospital, as soon as you finish your tea, that is! And Dr. Mus extended a friendly smile.

- Ok. We are ready for it! They did finish their tea in 10 minutes and they were off visiting the pavilions.

- - I want to get you to the isolation pavilion, where we have separated those carrying the disease. According to our observations – not backed up by vigorous science, though – it is not transmitted from human to human, but we suspect insect vector could do it. In other words, until proven otherwise, we suspect that even local mosquito species can unwillingly carry the bug, not only the alien one.

He walked forward towards a narrow pavilion with dim lights inside.

There were almost 30 beds inside, each one having an individual net cover, and patients were lying on their beds, apparently paying no attention to what was going on around them. In their emptied eyes, with fixed look, and the sweaty foreheads, Peter could read fever and dehydration, accompanied with despair. One bed was covered with a white sheet and dr. Musa nodded – another helpless victim succumbed to the unknown disease.

- Technically, we have isolated some strain of Borrelia, but we lack the proper lab facilities to differentiate it. However, it seems much different from the one described in all books. The invasiveness and toxicity reach staggering levels when compared to the standard strain. We wonder what could trigger such mutation and the only available answer for now is it might have been modified while infecting the mosquito vector, but we do not have sustainable proof.

All members of Peter's team were impressed by the visit.

- The infection rate is still impressive, even if not as large as it were in the beginning. It is decreased somehow and reached to a new, but stable level. We get 20-25 new patients every week. It is unlikely that local mosquitoes took over the "task" of spreading the bug, but that is my personal feeling, and I have no scientific arguments to back up this idea, except for my hunch.
- I see, but never the less it is interesting and it should be researched! - said Peter. We have no clue at this moment about the origin of this disease and that bothers us – and the WHO for a fact – a lot.
- There is something you will be informed about. Some time after the outbreak – maybe 2 weeks later or so – a team of biologists and doctors came to visit us and asked about it. The interesting thing is that happened, according to my knowledge, before we even made all this public, so there is little chance, if any, for hem to have been informed about the outbreak from here. It is as if they have known about it all along. They spoke English with us, but some of them spoke between themselves in Russian and had military aspect – you know, like short haircut, silent, coordinated and very disciplined. I could not talk to any of this group except for their speaker, who was very detailed in explaining us his mission to gather info about new infectious diseases for an NGO, allegedly situated in Malaysia. They left no cards, but they were interested about the ill people and the number of deaths. I forgot the name of the NGO, something about promoting health and disease prevention anyway.

Peter and his colleagues were silent, listening to him and looked with compassion towards the patients who were staring at them from their beds.

- What treatment are you using now, asked Peter, looking with interest in a patient's file. To his desperation, everything was written in Somali, so the only thing available to guess was the fever curve and the blood pressure chart, both seemingly affected by the disease.

- We are using a protocol with Rocephin and an Aminoglycoside, later – if we see some recovery – we may continue for some weeks with Minocycline. But we do not seem to make a great difference. The survivors have severe complications like pulmonary emphysema, pericarditis or rhythm alterations, allergies, kidney failure. Anyway, they are not getting fully healthy and remain crippled. There hasn't been any case of *"restitutio ad integrum"**, as the book says.
- Are these people from Berbera, doctor? Joe Cooper asked, while looking at a shelf with dozens of vials placed in boxes with patient name on them.
- Not really, most of them are from the eastern region, close to Maydh. This hospital was the closest available for them. But the number of patients in Berbera is slowly growing, so we asked the health authority to cooperate with environment agency and the local administration to work for pest and insect control within the Berbera area. We hope to minimize the number of potential vectors, especially mosquitoes. We are finally not afraid of malaria, but this thing proves to be much worse.
- Doctor Musa, I believe we've seen enough. I think it is time for us to continue our trip to Hargeisa now. Thank you for the visit and the excellent tea! Pater smiled as he shook dr. Musa's hand and greeted the staff around them.

On their way to the car, Yves had comments:

- Mon Dieu, those people do not stand a chance! What can the doctor do? They do not even have a detailed diagnosis on the germ!
- Yap! Pretty messy stuff! Liam Johnson agreed.

---

* *"Restitutio ad integrum"* = healing 100%, as it was before;

Major Bashir took his automatic sub-machine gun next to his driver seat, and he gesture did not go unnoticed by the others, who chose not to make any comment.

They left on the dusty road, a quite narrow asphalt path, whose poor quality was frequently interrupted by holes and gaps demanding special driving skills to avoid.

They expected to need almost 3 hours for the 160 Km trip, but before the 10 km milestone a barrier was closed in front of them and they stopped for the checkpoint. Major Bashir showed his papers (the uniform did not seem to impress the sentry) and they were free to proceed, only to observe such check-points every 15 kilometers or so.

Major Bashir explained that such measure was considered necessary and effective to control weapon smuggling and deployment of Al Shabab terrorists, considered the greatest danger to Somaliland.

- Thanks to our prevention, we did not have any terrorist attack in the past 14 years when the last suicide bomber threw himself up in front of the presidential palace.
- How about smugglers?
- Hm! We are quite careful with those. See that truck loaded to the brim in front of us? It is loaded with ka 'at. This contains a powerful substance similar to amphetamine. It is very customary to chew its leaves especially after a meal. People find it stimulating, but it is a drug nevertheless, and I understand in Europe and western countries it is prohibited. There are hundreds of people who lose their mind after years of consuming this weed brought from Ethiopia. Commerce with it is so powerful, these trucks are protected and excepted from even obeying traffic rules. Everybody uses ka 'at, even the Government clerks, and we have a problem with this. The drug is cheap, 2-3 dollars a bunch of leaves, and there will be a revolution if we forbid it's use abruptly.
- I take it you don't use the stuff, asked Jason with a smile on his face.
- No Sir, I do not! Major Bashir looked at him for a second. I was informed about the harm it can do and I try to stay free from it. Also advised my family to keep away from it. I also think it is

bad for the economy. After the noon prier and lunch, most people chew ka 'at and their capacity to work is greatly diminished in the afternoon, if any of it resting at all.

Everybody was silent for some time. They passed through tiny villages and Peter's colleagues were horrified to discover two dead hyenas in the middle of the road, most likely hit by speeding cars.

The sun was setting when they entered the mountain area and the increasing number of lights showed them Hargeisa city was close. They finally reached on a large boulevard with no sidewalks, then crossed a bridge over a dried channel and stirred to higher ground, towards the Hargeisa airport - which was not opened yet. Next to it there was Continental Hotel, the safest place in the country, with a group of permanent UN personnel hosted there.

The car was directed through a maze of concrete obstacles, and finally was checked beneath with a lamp and a mirror by a sentry. They got in and passed a rigorous metal detector control, after which they took their luggage and were permitted to enter the reception.

- These guys do not joke about security! Observed Liam Johnson, trying to locate his room.
- That makes me feel safer – said Jason Barr, smiling. I sure hope there are no mosquitoes. I took the malaria prevention pills they gave us, but the other disease looks pretty scary to me.
- All right gentlemen! Peter accompanied them to their rooms. You got 30 minutes to have a shower and unpack. I'll meet you in the lobby. I hear they have a swell restaurant outside in the park. We'll dine there and discuss our program for tomorrow.

The next morning Peter welcomed them at the breakfast table:

- Good morning sleeping beauties, how was your night?

Everybody smiled, but there was no immediate response.

- Camel steak was good! Said Liam Johnson – but not as good as a Texas steak! He smiled with an understanding smile.
- It was fine- also stated Jason – but with no good salad and poor desert!
- These guys plant mostly sorghum – so it is understandable they have little available green leaf – Peter said. Stick to the Somali tea and the scrambled eggs. No cheese, in the regular sense of the meaning.

They took some time to enjoy breakfast and coffee, and then Major Bashir approached the group and said :

- Good morning everybody. I am supposed to invite you to the meeting taking place at 10 am at the Ministry of Health. Important people will be there – the head of Somaliland Senate in Parliament, Ministry of Health, of course, Ministry of internal affairs and I will represent the National Security Agency. I will be waiting for you in half an hour in the lobby.
- Very well Major! We'll be there! Peter answered.

In half hour everybody was embarking the large Isuzu SUV and heading towards the Health Ministry.

The building was not impressive, however it had three floors (two above the ground floor) and had open space lobby areas upstairs.

They were led upstairs to the first floor, to a wider lobby area with armchairs, some sort of a waiting room.

Shortly, Major Bashir came back and invited them in a room where several people were already seated. He made sure everybody had a chair and presented the to the already existing guests, then presented the guests:

- Please allow me to introduce to you his excellency Prime Minister of Somaliland, Mr. Dahir, and the Minister of Health, dr. Fadumo Salleh. Accompanying them, there is His Excellency Sir Waran Madow, head of local tribes and President of the Senate of Somaliland Parliament. To my right there is Professor Sharif

– Executive Director of the Environment Agency, Dr. Abdilgani – General Manager of Hargeisa Hospital and General Diriye – Minister of Housing and Internal Affairs. As mediator, I would ask everybody to have a seat. Tea is on the way! -Major Bashir smiled gently, but preserved his serious look.

After the tea was served and conversation lingered over weather and food and oil prices, Major Bashir took over and gathered attention:

- I hereby have the privilege of informing you that the Government of Somaliland, with Parliament acknowledgement, has declared a state of medical emergency due to the disease outbreak in the North, and delegated us to create a work committee on this issue. We are gathered here in what would be the first meeting of this committee and I am glad representatives of the WHO are here with us on this occasion.

Everybody watched him as he stood up and went to a screen. He made a sign and curtains covered the windows and a projector was turned on, showing a deserted landscape near the sea. Major Bashir spoke:

- As Information Division Chief, O take the liberty of hosting this meeting. To begin with, I would like to greet the presence of our Prime Minister, Mr. Dahir, and I ask him to tell us his point of view!
- Salaam alekoum everybody! Please allow me to inform you first about the fact that his excellency, our President of the Republic of Somaliland, is deeply concerned about this epidemic event and its possible implications outside the public health issue development. I am myself deeply concerned about the information I already have in this topic and I confess I can hardly wait to know more and find a way to fight it. The mortality of this disease is frightening and the prospect of fighting it barehanded is equally scary. Having here our guests from the WHO, I feel reassured that

we will get qualified help as soon as possible. On my behalf and that of the government – and you have here the representative of Health Administration and Environment Agency – I can surely say that we will do any effort and approve any decent measure helping us to put an end to this nightmare, Inshallah!

All the Somaliland participants nodded in acceptance and turned with interest towards Major Bashir, who spoke again:

- Thank you, Prime Minister, we will need all the help we can get! Next, I will do an introduction to the topic, as information gathering is in my domain of activity.

Turning towards the screen and the image posted on it, he continued:

- This is a deserted place near the small port of Maydh. Somewhere, between the port of Maydh and Xiis, there is a small river which feeds a moor surface of a few acres, the bushy area you see in the distance. According to our information, most of the cases of this peculiar infectious disease originate in the villages around these moors, like the moor turn to be the center of a circle of deployment of the cases.
- Can there be a connection between the moors and the type of alien insect – in this case a mosquito – that you found in the area? – asked Yves Durand. I am asking because I am a specialist in parasites and insect vectors and I would like to study the insect you have found and the place it came from.
- But of course! You are welcome! – answered Major Bashir. I think dr, Abdilgani, the manager of our Hargeisa Hospital has gone to the deepest available level with the research in this case and she will share the information with you, but for now, I would like her to tell us about the evolution of the disease. The Hargeisa hospital was the point where all severe and very severe cases converged. Dr. Abdilgani, please!

- Salaam alekoum to all! First cases occurred two months ago. The first case, a young shepherd from the area – a child eleven years old, to be more precise – was admitted to the Burao hospital after 2 days of ever -growing fever and decreasing general condition. When he got to the Hargeisa hospital, he was almost in a coma and died the next day, due to multiple organ failure. A brutal infestation with malaria was suspected in the beginning, but tests showed he was not infested with malaria plasmodium. You have his image on the next slide – and indeed everyone could see the tormented face of Abdel Moussa, the little shepherd in his dying hour. Same situation was observed with all referred patients, none of them testing positive for recent malaria – and dr. Abdilgani scrolled through a dozen pictures of patients with the same disease, all apparently suffering from fever, dehydration and toxic state.
- However, some patients managed to make the connection between their disease and the previous sting from a large mosquito, and even captured some. We had the opportunity to get a number of dead specimens in the beginning, some of which not so badly crushed so we could study them a little. Later on, with the help of the Environment Agency and Professor's Sharif, personally, we were able to catch a few live individuals, actually females and we managed to demonstrate that all of them carried the same germ we found in our patients, starting with the dead ones. You can observe the insect in this slide.

There was a close- up image of a huge mosquito – maybe the large image made it scary – but the aspect was frightening. The golden belly with black rings was very peculiar and made, beyond larger size – another differential aspect of the incriminated insect.

- Mon Dieu! But tell me Madam! Did you manage to identify the species? – asked Yves Durand.
- I think I did. In my opinion it is Psorophora Ciliata – a species of mosquito which lives thousands of miles away, over the Atlantic Ocean, in the eastern part of the American Continent.

- It sure looks like that! Yves Durand exclaimed! But how did it get here? No insect like mosquito can possibly fly across the ocean. It must have gotten here somehow else.

- That is exactly what we think! But we have two more questions to ask. When it comes to a disease carrier status, commonly not all the insects are carriers, but some and this rarely means up to 20%. We know that mosquito females are the only ones that sting – because they feed on blood of mammals mostly - and can thus transmit disease, either malaria, yellow fever or other. But we can never find more than one in three-four infected insects. In this case, absolutely all the insects we found were infected, which is odd and we wonder why and how this 100% selection was made?

- Indeed, there should normally be mostly germ free individuals – added Peter. What was the second question you mentioned about?

- Well, the other question has two components: how did the insect come here and why – of all places in Africa - it came here.

- Do you think there were many such insects? Asked Liam Johnson.

- By the number and distribution of patients and the efficiency of insects – all of them being infectious and active vectors – we estimate there have been tens of thousands or even millions. The moors close to Maydh seem to be a convenient environment and I would be curious if there was any interbreeding with local species males. If so, only Allah knows how we can get rid of them. There will need to pass many mosquito generations until the bacterial charge transmitted among them will be discharged. Imagine how many victims we will have by then. If the alien mosquito species will not multiply, it is likely that their presence will fade away in a few weeks, maybe three months, we think. We just hope that this disease cannot be transmitted directly person to person, but we think such prospect is highly unlikely, because it would need contact with patient fluids, especially blood, like in AIDS for instance.

Dr. Abdilgani took a break to take a sip from her tea, and continued:

- I am talking about a Borrelia strain, a very unusual one. I am familiar with Lyme disease in Canada, that is why I consider this a particular strain. These bugs are far more aggressive, invasive, toxigenic and resistant than common Borrelia. Something is wrong about this germ, like it has superpowers. You can see on the slide a photograph of droplet visualization by Tyndall type microscope. The density of spirochetes is outstanding when compared to common strains. The germs are rapidly multiplying and are very aggressive. Our findings were confirmed and further detailed by a lab in the Emirates, upon our request and I hear that has been the case also in Europe.

- That is something I can confirm, Madam -Peter spoke. We also believe that the germ was genetically modified somewhere, perhaps in the US, according to some information, but we are not sure about the connection with Somaliland and the Russian speaking delegation you told us about.

- Looks like we've got now more questions than answers, Liam Johnson said with a bitter smile.

- If I may interfere – General Diriye, Minister of Internal Affairs rose from his chair. We have carefully assessed all information and we tried to connect this outbreak to some events, many of which may have no apparent relevance, but maybe some could enable our understanding of the facts and drive us to the correct answer, to some of the questions you mentioned. For instance, we have made up lists of all border entries and departures in the month preceding the first case. So far, we did not notice anything relevant, but we keep on checking everybody, name by name. Somaliland has many of its citizens living abroad (UK, Northern countries, even US) and they frequently come to visit. We are currently studying the lists with infectious diseases of all patients from our hospitals in the same period of time. We have also made lists with accidents, suspicious deaths and disappeared citizens in this interval. As soon as we centralize data and find even the slightest relevance, we commonly inform the Government, Parliament and WHO about our findings. We have also taken information regarding the group of "doctors", who arrived approximately in the debut days of the outbreak. Of course, Major Bashir, our Chief of Intelligence can tell you more about this.

Major Bashir rose from his chair, made a sign to a clerk to open window blinds and addressed everybody from the table he stood nearby.

– It is true we were very much interested about this guest group. We have run the list with names and credentials, and they checked all right, but this did not impress me much, as -if someone wants a perfect cover – he will go to extensive details to build it. It was all very simple and precise, almost too good to be true. The only thing I could not understand was the fact that people bearing English, French or Italian names – and I underline their perfect passports and background info – used Russian to talk between themselves. This detail was confirmed by several witnesses, amongst whom I can quote here dr. Abdilgani, the manager of our Hargeisa Hospital.
– So, the whole thing could be set up by Russia? – Jason Barr asked impatiently.
– Too early to say and we do not have facts to back up such possibility. But it is nevertheless a possibility of involvement of some kind!
– Did you check all airplanes, or cargo transport from sea? Peter asked.

General Diriye stood up next to Major Bashir and spoke:

– Of course, we did! We have a list of all cargo entering the country and a detailed material about all the ships which visited the port of Berbera and their cargo that month. We have included fishing boats, as well. So far, nothing interesting.

Major Bashir took over:

- We were interested in designing a pattern of the population travel in and out of the ground zero area. So far, the only significant thing I found about was that two men from a village near Burao were seen days before the first case was registered walking from the seaside towards Burao. A truck driver picked them up on a road connecting Xiis to Maydh and brought them to the outskirts of Burao. Nobody met them or seen them after this and I am afraid it is a dead end. Families tell an interesting story, about them being hired to work on a ship two months before and they were waiting for them because they called and said they returned to the country. They were expected to get home the day they disappeared. I checked the names, but they do not fit in the crew list of any ship that visited us during that time.
- We can assume there is a possibility they entered the country illegally – Liam Johnson said.
- Very correct – and this is what we suspect. But our border, including the shore line, is so vast, and most of our guards are located South, on our border with Somalia Mogadishu, keeping an eye on Al Shabab terrorist. If they cam by sea, we must investigate the ship that carried them here, and for this we decided to ask help from the American base in Djibouti. Most likely, they have real time access to satellite investigation and a diagram of the ships passing by our shores during that time could prove very useful.
- However, Major, Peter observed, investigating the disappearance of the two individuals could prove challenging, but is it related to the disease outbreak and if so, I wonder how.
- Allow me to interfere – Professor Sharif spoke, taking time to take a gulp from the hot Somali tea in front of him. We have visited the area to do some observation from the environmental point of view. I have here some photos – and he displayed them on the table in front of them – showing two areas next to the moors. In these two areas, we found metallic debris scattered around on dozens of square meters. Most of them are small, millimeter to

one- centimeter size, but we found some pipe like fragments and everything looks like stainless steel. In a manner of speaking, it looks like an airplane crash site, only smaller. We thought that maybe we are faced with the site of some drone crash, an UAV being much smaller than an airplane. I strongly suggest we go visit the sites as I believe there is more there than meets the eye.

- Agreed Professor. We will gladly accompany you tomorrow, if Major Bashir will be so kind to accept.

- I am at your service, Dr. Bud. I will make the necessary arrangements for tomorrow. I think his excellency, Sir Waran Madow is willing to tell us his opinion.

The old man rose to his feet, wearing with elegance his traditional Somali clothing – his macawis (some sort of men's skirt) was mostly brown. On top of it, he wore an immaculate white shirt and a kuphyad (embroider hat) on his head. The grey hair on his head and his beard were heavily stained with henna, and he also elegantly carried a stick, although he did not seem to need using it for support. Everybody was silent, as the old man spoke softly in Somali and Major Bashir was translating for the guests.

- Salam alekoum! I hereby welcome our guests and the honorable committee here gathered. I want to underline that the evolution of this disease outbreak is far more important than previously believed, as the phenomenon exceeds the medical territory and seems to have economic and political implications triggering surprising consequences.

The old man removed his glasses and mechanically wiped them with a clean handkerchief. Remarkably coherent, Peter thought and saw that all his colleagues were impressed by the speech. They did not expect an old and traditionally looking man to express himself with such clarity and relevance.

- I strongly believe that the disease did not occur naturally; the characteristics of the involved germ, the way it was transmitted, the presence of an alien species of insect to carry it, every thing points to a biological experiment and maybe the visitor group that came then was there to assess results. What I want of you all is to find out who designed this experiment and who did this to our citizens. We may be poor and uneducated, but I will not allow anybody to use our fellow countrymen as Guinea Pigs. I wish you good luck with your research and may you find good answers to all questions, more urgently now about how to treat the disease! Inshallah!

-   I take it this will conclude our meeting – Major Bashir rose to his feet. Your excellency Mr President of the Senate, Prime Minister, ladies and gentlemen! Allow me to see you out and invite you to have lunch together at Continental restaurant.

They moved together towards the cars and once arrived on the large Continental domain, they went to a closed pavilion, where a low table was set and every body could comfortably sit on a pillow. Peter tried to comply, ignoring the desperate looks of Jason and Liam, who were seemingly unable to find a proper lotus position and ended up by leaning to one side like ancient Romans, to the amusement of the other guests, who were more than acquainted with traditional serving.

The sacrifice was not in vain, thought Peter and he could see everybody appreciated the meals. A huge bowl with steamed rice was set in the middle, and two sheep, cooked in one piece in the oven, represented a wonderful display on large silver trays. Salads, fruits, sorghum cakes and buckets of Somali tea and bottles of ice -cold water, were all within reach, together with lime-water to refresh hands.

In the beginning Peter was afraid the sheep would be a heavy meal, but Somali sheep were small, like 25 Kg at maturity, and tasted surprisingly good, better said extraordinary.

-   Do you like the meat? Major Bashir asked, smiling for the first time that day.

- It is awesome – tastes like game! Jason answered. You cannot guess it is sheep.
- After all, we have some experience with that! Major Bashir said. You know, Somaliland has always been a free province and was never a colony. It has been registered as British Protectorate and they used to call it "The butcher shop of the Empire" because or main activity is animal farming – especially sheep and goat. Somali sheep are smaller, with black feet and they are very resilient with thirst and hunger. Besides, we broke free when greater Somalia tried to introduce soviet-type socialism on our province. The civil war lasted for a few years and the problem is not entirely solved. Officially, many countries fail to recognize us as a separate entity and we are sharing the embargo on weapons with Somalia. Part of our same ancestor heritage is Ogadenia, South from Somaliland, at the present day attached to Ethiopia, but also claimed by greater Somalia. I have relatives there.
- I see! Peter answered, while chewing on his steak. But tell me, I want to ask you something else. Hargeisa city does not have electricity grid, sewage system or fresh water distribution grid. How do you manage to keep food and hygiene, in general?
- Your question withholds the answer. Every morning, animals are being sacrificed at the market place and meat is sold out, mostly being cooked and consumed the same day. So we only eat fresh and there is no danger. Major Bashir smiled.
- The electricity we use comes from a several diesel generators, each of them providing for a few blocks. The majority of the inhabitants only use a few bulbs, maybe a TV set. The more favored economically may have a refrigerator, but commonly bare necessities are covered and people go to bed early. Electricity is quite expensive here, about 1 USD per Kilowatt. As for the water, maybe you saw that all houses have a water tank and manufacturing those tanks became some sort of local industry. Having 150-200 liters of water is a necessity. There is a huge business with water tank trucks which bring water from a source 20 kilometers away. According to our info, water is sold for 8-10 USD per barrel, but costs peanuts at the source. The water business reaches a level of

about 200 000 USD per day for Hargeisa only. But the sewage problem is very acute. Many buildings have dug- in septic tanks but they come to overload and sometimes infiltrate basements.

- That is something hard to solve; Liam interfered, while trying to graciously get rid of the naked bones in his plate. You will need to dig the streets for sewage channels and other ditches for water piping. You need a master plan and it will be messy if you do not take it block by block and street by street.
- I totally agree – said Major Bashir. All this is accounted for, but we are confronted with the more decisive problem of financing such project. We are not going to have the necessary amount of funding anytime soon.

He stopped to take a few gulps from his Somali tea and continued.

- Now you understand that such poor infrastructure and healthcare is likely to enhance the severity of a disease outbreak, especially if inflicted on purpose. One thing I do not understand – of all neighboring poor African nations, why choosing us?

Peter took a few sips from his own tea, and while looking in the eyes of those in front of him, said:

- The reason must exceed the infrastructural shortcomings, perhaps being more related to your geographic position. You have a shoreline to one of the most crowded sea, with shipping routes used by dozens of ships every day. I think maybe this is a direction we should be looking at.
- You are probably right and I will go deeper studying this topic – Major Bashir said. After such meal, please do not feel offended if many of our guests will be serving ka 'at for "desert". He smiled and went to see his excellency Waran Madow to his car, where the slumbering driver got back to life and opened the door to help the President of the Senate. They shook hands, then the car left and Major Bashir returned to the table where the dialogue had

started being more vivid thanks to the bundles of ka 'at spread on the low table.

- If you think you need some time for yourselves, I think you can leave. We will be staying for final, more personal talk. I thank you for the participation at our meeting and lunch. Major Bashir smiled for the second time that day and extended right hand to everybody.

- The stuff does not seem too dangerous, said Jason chewing a few leaves of Ka 'at.

- That's swell! Joe Cooper answered. It is good they have no weed here. I guess you used to smoke it as a college boy!

- You bet! Smiled Jason. Hey, it happened only at parties! But then we had times when we were partying almost every day! This stuff is not bad either!

Everybody laughed.

Liam Johnson and Jason Barr were especially happy about abandoning the uncomfortable position at the table and waved good bye to everybody, grabbing with thankful hands the keys to their rooms.

- Get a good night's rest. Tomorrow we go visit the city a little then we are going to meet some interesting people, said Peter. We can meet for dinner at eight pm if you feel like eating.

Everybody shook heads as they felt fed up with so much meat and expected to have trouble resting. Liam, with his Texas meat eating habits, looked still fresh and said:

- I wonder if there is any remarkable difference between sheep and goat, in taste that is. I may try some goat this evening. Besides, it is almost evening, it is five pm. See you at eight for a fresh steak, he smiled while the others looked disgusted and tired.

The next morning, breakfast was light: everybody was mostly interested in juice and coffee, with the exception of Jean Yves who chose his favorite croissant and Peter and Liam, who chose boiled eggs and beans.

Upon leaving the hotel, another can with a beacon and the marks of the Somaliland Army was in the front parking. This time, a young lieutenant, armed as usual with a submachine gun, came to greet them:

- I am lieutenant Siyad – Major Bashir sent me to accompany you wherever you want to go. Please take your belongings and you are welcome in my car. Do not forget to take a cap or a hat; Sun can be very powerful at noon.
- Ok, thank you. I'll let the others know. Give us five minutes.

As soon as everybody was inside the car, the lieutenant drove outside and stopped at the first gas station to fill the tank of his car with diesel. He also bought 10 bottles of ice- cold water and placed them in a plastic bucket in the back of the car.

- Whenever you feel thirsty, please take water from here. No need to ask me.

As he was preparing to drive, he turned to them and said:

- I want to show you the central marketplace in Hargeisa. It is something you cannot see everywhere.

He drove towards downtown Hargeisa and by extensive use of his beacon and his horn, he succeeded to get to the market place in 20 minutes, apparently an outstanding time.

The market place was huge. On the left side were some shop buildings, a huge building on the right belonged to Dahabsheel Bank – a powerful local Somaliland bank. The rest of the territory was occupied by an extensive tent complex, with a maze of stalls and booths, all full of various and colorful merchandise. Clothing, toys, garments, shoes (some of which visibly worn out, but still valuable for bare foot clients), cheap car spares, bicycles, live animals, food.

Most particular were the street vendors having their whole business loaded on a bicycle or trike. They picked a spot on the side of the street, opened a few panels and a colored tent for shade, and visibly exposed their merchandise. In the evening they packed everything back and pedaled home, with a few dollars earned in the heat of the day. Cooked food – sort of fast food - sector was very impressive for the guests and one needed a less sensitive stomach to endure the smell and probably the taste of food. They actually saw an individual managing a charcoal grill. The grill was covered with smoking meat, some of its margins showing advanced signs of decay and smelling badly, but obviously greatly appreciated by those lining up to buy such "warm fresh treats".

- Mon Dieu, these people must have a strong stomach – Yves Durand made a face, while smelling the foul odor of rotting meat on the barbeque.
- Yap! Liam Johnson smiled in approval. Eat that shit and you be dead at home in a couple of hours.
- I am convinced I do not have to advise you to pass on this one – smiled Peter. Our hotel is one of the few safe places to eat. Ok guys, check what you are interested about. Here is an exchange booth. I am going to exchange one hundred bucks.

He went to the booth and came back with a large bag, carrying in excess of five kilograms of overused banknotes, some of which were torn.

- Big mistake! - he said. Keep your dollars, they work fine out here, I was told. Can you imagine I took millions of Somaliland shillings for my hundred bucks?

Jason Barr was laughing.

- It' good you did not exchange some bitcoin! We would have had to hire a truck.

- Ok guys. Meeting back in one hour and a half in front of the bank building!

Within the ninety minutes, all of them were gathered in front of Dahabsheel Bank. Liam Johnson and Yves Durand were enjoying some plain "Gitanes" cigarettes, from the personal reserve of Yves Durand, whose patriotic choice was also appreciated by Liam.

Joe Cooper and Jason Barr were chewing gum and threw disgusted looks to the couple of smoking colleagues:

- These things will kill you! Joe said to them, pulling back when a cloud of blueish smoke came his way.
- Yap, maybe, but I'll be in my bed. Listen brother, I am not afraid of getting old, I am afraid to die young! Better watch your own but!- Liam answered with a smile.
- Hey mister, I am not any brother to you! Besides, I was just trying to have a conversation, not to question your white supremacy! said Joe, still having the power to smile.
- Hey, no offence intended! I know it is a bad habit. I tried to quit, but you know how it goes – you can quit smoking every day!
- Come guys, drop it, Peter interfered! We don't have time for this bullshit! Tell me what you found? Did you buy anything?
- I got me a Somali suit – with the skirt and blouse and cap! Jason Barr smiled happy. I can barely wait to wear them.
- Try your lipstick with it – laughed Liam, while Jason threw a fierce look.

Lieutenant Siyad approached and greeted them, witnessing Jason's joy, mixed with confusion.

- Take care where you go dressed like that!- said Liam. You will look like a hot blonde chick in search for big size adventure. I do not think it is advisable to do it here, although I hear the criminality rate is very low and there are no gay people here.

Lieutenant Siyad smiled and said:

- That there is low criminality rate, I can promise you! Maybe police efficiency is not outstanding and we may lack modern tech, but if you will see the prison, you will understand no sane person wants to ever get there. As for the gay, I wouldn't know for sure. We met very few cases.
- I believe you for your word – Peter said. Come on guys, what else?
- I got some interesting embroider pictures and a pair of sleepers – Joe Cooper showed to his bag, where a pair of sleepers in the shape of camel head were smiling to their curious eyes. They are nice, aren't they?

Liam made a long face, then smiled, accompanied by Yves Durand.

- I got some powerful smelling incense and some toys for my little Marie – said Yves Durand, smiling while showing everybody the photo of his younger daughter, a little angel with blonde curled hair.
- What did you find interesting Liam? – asked Peter.

Liam smiled, took a glance around and got closer to the group and extracted from his pocket a pistol.

- Oh Mon Dieu! Yves Durand exclaimed with his eyes popping out. What are you going to do with that?
- Nothing! It is just for protection, The Lieutenant here or the Major will not always be with us to protect us with their guns. It is a Glock 17, 9 mm with 17 round - magazine. And in a pretty good shape, too.
- But you have no permit for it, exclaimed Yves again.
- So, who's gonna tell? You? The lieutenant here knows about it and if he decides, I will surrender it to him. I will do that anyway when we leave, although it would be a quite expensive souvenir. I paid 400 bucks for it and the bullets.

Lieutenant Siyad had a serious look on his face when he saw the gun, then spoke:

- It is all right! I trust your judgement and you can keep it while you are here – Siyad smiled. But you must abandon it when you leave, as you cannot board the plane with it.
- Agreed Sir! Liam placed the gun back to his pocket with satisfaction.
- I feel safer now, guys – he added, while the others smiled. A man gets more confident when carrying a gun.
- What are we going to do next, Lieutenant?
- Oh, I am going to take you to a visit to the environment Agency, the pharmacy depot, then we will visit the location where we have the water source for Hargeisa, and after we will go have lunch at a special place, called the Lion's Den.
- Ok. We are with you!

After visiting the objectives, they went close to the valley of the creek splitting the city to an open space restaurant called Lion's Den. The name was owed to the fact that the owner had a small zoo on the location, hosting lions, cheetah and small 4 fingered mongoose (Suricata).

The meal was highly appreciated and the Lion's Den was considered another safe place to eat. Liam Johnson has been impressed by the camel steak:

- It is not like our genuine beef, but it certainly kicks, with the herbs on it. It is good!

Jason Barr and Yves Durand looked at each other, their eyes expressing something close to disgust.

- Did you know that for camel steak they use only baby camel not the old ones? Jason asked.
- Whatever! As long as it doesn't crawl out of my plate or scream when I cut it, I like it! Liam smiled amid colleague's laughter.

Evening was rapidly casting its shadow on things, as they reached the hotel for a small break.

Lieutenant Siyad was again patiently waiting, discretely smoking a cigarette in the parking lot of the Continental.

– Where are we going now? Peter asked and the officer was swift in replying:

– I am going to show you how rich our country is in fact, in spite of seemingly being so poor. We will visit some friends in the outskirts then we go dine at Mansoor Hotel and Restaurant, where it is also safe to eat. Tomorrow arrangements have been done for us to visit the moors of what we call "Ground 0" and have some conclusions afterwards. I understand you will have to leave the day after tomorrow.

– That is true. We hope to have access to new findings tomorrow. We thank you very much for your guidance!

– Most welcome! Now we go to see some interesting things!

They left the Continental Hotel heading to the opposite side of the city. The trip was uneventful, except for sweating - not necessarily because of the evening heat, but because of the random traffic development they were witnessing. The driving side was apparently randomly chosen by drives, wherever it was room enough to go. Many cars were second hand imported from Japan and had the steering wheel on the right side, although officially normal driving was on the right lane. To the amusement of Lieutenant Siyad, Liam observed that almost nobody used left/right signaling, any intended move in the traffic being preceded only by obsessive horn blowing. The street was an almost deafening concerto of horn blows, on all tonalities and frequencies. A policeman here and there, in larger crossings, would try to organize traffic, still being hard to be noticed or respected, because of lacking a full uniform. Some of them had a shirt with flaps, or kaki trousers, some were even dressed civilian, while carrying a police cap on. Nevertheless, their presence there was picturesque, yet seemingly inefficient, as all drivers were choosing to ignore their signs. Like this, the traffic policemen were turned in weird characters performing a weird and hard to understand ballet.

They reached the outskirts of the city, into a rather poor neighborhood, where houses were made out of clay and covered with rusty tin or plastic bags. Few people were walking the narrow streets, and flocks of sheep and goat were roaming the area, to the irritation of the few drivers using the narrow streets.

Finally, they drove near one of the small houses with a large courtyard. One isolated bulb was lit and the dim light showed a welcome committee formed of two persons, one older with some grey hair and a much younger one, both dressed in traditional Somali, garments and holding cell phones in their hands.

Car stopped, and Lieutenant Siyad stepped down and spoke a few words. The men smiled and waited to be introduced to the group.

- This is Maxamed Omar and his son Yusuf! – said the lieutenant.
- Salam alekoum! - both men greeted.
- We came to see the results of their work. They are both some sort of free lance geologists. In other word, they go in the mountains and seek for valuable minerals. The minerals they collect are sold to local geology companies and some are being exported, But the price of rough, unpolished gems is rather small, compared to the final product. We would like to have industrial exploitation on these and sell them for the right price. He waived a sign to the waiting men and they rushed inside a small courtyard, chasing out a few goats. They took shovels and for a moment, Peter was afraid to think he would come alone, at night, in such neighborhood. The two men dug a hole in the ground and came back with a wax paper package. They placed it on a small stone fence and opened it. A bunch of row gems were glittering in the flash light beam. There were about two fistfuls of green emeralds, a few red rubies and many other gems like sapphire, opal chunks, and topaz. Everybody was stun.
- Are those things for real? -Liam asked.

– We think so – the lieutenant answered. Tested with this hand gadget – he pointed to a miniature hardness tester for minerals – they seem all right but a specialist opinion would be needed.

– If all these are genuine, we could buy with the money a small fleet of oil tankers – said Liam with a serious look on his face.

– Now you realize that we are not so poor as the word goes – the lieutenant said. He rapidly whispered a few words to the older man, and Mr. Omar disappeared for a couple of minutes, only to rejoin them holding a jar in his hands. He placed the apparently heavy recipient down with care.

– By God! This is raw mercury! – said Joe when he examined the jar. Look how heavy it is !

– Indeed, it is raw mercury! They collect it while dripping from rocks in mountain pits – said Lieutenant Siyad. But, as you know, it is difficult to export it and it requires special packing and monitoring conditions. This is next to impossible for us while being under embargo, as mercury is one basic ingredient for movement sensor detonators in artisanal bomb making. We are trying to prevent this stuff to get into the hands of Al Shabab or other terrorist groups. But we cannot seal borders and our infectious outbreak is proof to that.

– All right! This is awesome! Maybe sometime later we come take some samples and try to check their quality – Peter said.

– Sure thing. We could use some investors. We have to rely upon natural riches to begin with – said the lieutenant. Now we can go from this place. I will thank Mr. Omar for his kindness and invite you to have dinner with me at Hotel Mansoor, another safe place to eat for you.

– Okay Sir! Lead the way! – Peter smiled. We also thank Mr. Omar for sharing with us his work results.

Mr. Omar was smiling at them, next to his son. Obviously, he did not understand all the words in English and relied upon the brief and partial translation the lieutenant offered him. His satisfaction was betrayed by his large smile, exposing a few missing front teeth.

They went to Mansoor Hotel and dinner was full of culinary surprises, as they had the opportunity to taste more exotic plates.

- Too bad you cannot add a beer to all this! – Liam complained, to everybody's agreement, except for Lieutenant Siyad, who felt happy with his tea.
- Tomorrow you leave early in the morning! – he said. You need to reach the moors area and have time to assess the place and maybe go visit the surroundings.

They all agreed to go to bed early and get a good night's rest.

The next morning, Peter and Liam were the first to hit the lobby. Eventually, they moved on to the breakfast restaurant while waiting for the others to come. Joe Cooper showed up next, followed by Yves Durand and the last was Jason Barr, still yawning his mandible out and scratching his haystack hairdo.

After breakfast and coffee, they got in the car with Major Bashir and headed towards Berbera. Half way to the port, they turned right and drove east towards Maydh. The landscape was rough rocky mountain tops and deep shady valleys but the lack of green vegetation was desolating. The road had no asphalt, it was mostly reddish ground and pebbles, but satisfactory for the Isuzu Trooper they rode. The road was bordered with some bushes of an extremely aggressive plant, carrying 2 inches long thorns, large enough to perforate the tires, and this made Major Bashir drive very carefully to avoid going out of the lane, while trying to avoid road holes.

- Look close to that trees! -suddenly the Major stopped the car.

Everybody turned heads towards the mentioned direction.

- This is a blue antelope! – said Bashir. It is a rarity and it is protected by law.

The animal was rather small, smaller in size than a regular deer, but had the back covered with dark blueish hair and was shy, running for the bushes when the car got closer. Bashir eventually stopped the car next to some 3 m tall clay formation like a cone.

- This is a termite nest! – he said. There are millions of them inside. Never try to destroy the nest, as they will chase you and attack any intruder.
- Formidable! – exclaimed Yves Durand circling the termite nest. How long do they take to build this?
- A few weeks maybe! – answered Bashir.
- But tell me, Major, do you have poisonous snakes here? Liam asked.
- Not very common, but we have some in the bushes or close to water. There is a species of wasp and some pit vipers, and we are the Northern limit for the habitat of black mambas, but that one is scarce. Never saw one in the wild yet.
- That is something I wouldn't like to see, said Jason, looking worried on the ground around them, as if a snake presence was imminent.

They went on, encountering a dead hyena in the middle of the road and once stopped to allow a horde of baboons cross the road. Dozens of monkeys went by, some approaching the car and showing their canine teeth in defiance, but Major Bashir managed to scare them off by repeatedly blowing the horn and turning the lights on.

- Pretty aggressive when together – he made a comment – but shy when isolated. We had some attacks on farmers inland. These animals are not afraid of dogs and have very smart attack strategies. They are quite territorial and we cannot tame them.
- I see! Peter said. We will try to keep away from them.
- Well, we are getting close to ground 0. I'll take this side road to take us there. The moors are in the distance, where you can see the two small hills with some bushes around them.

The car took a bumpy ride towards the open field location and soon they were within 50 yards from the closest moor pond.

They got down and tried to do a few moves to warm up joints, Sky was blue, sun was shining, everything looked nice but the impression was different.

- Okay, said Peter. We should spread in order to cover most of the area. Each of us will take a 5 m wide strip, from here, parallel to the moor, towards those fallen trees.
- Ok Boss! Jason answered and they lined up, major Bashir joining them somewhere outside the inspected lane.

They slowly walked forward, stopping from time to time to inspect and sometimes collect tiny objects from the ground. When they reached to the trees, Peter inspected the results: a few metallic fragments, shiny but very small (millimeters across, impossible to figure out how they were assembled before.

As they were standing next to a fallen tree, Liam exclaimed:

- Holly shit! There's a bonanza here, guys! He turned to a spot on the ground which was apparently deranged and multiple metal fragments, some of which quite large, were stuck in the wet ground and the mud nearby.

He was ready to go collect some samples when Joe Cooper yelled:

- Sop Liam! Freeze! Don't make a move, or it will bite you! He pointed to a place in the high grass in front of Liam. Only a keen eye or a closer observer could see the coiled snake ready to attack.
- It looks like a pit viper – Major Bashir said. Dr. Johnson, please keep still. Now easily, without sudden moves, take a few steps back. Yes, do not rush. We don't want to disturb the local fauna, but we do not want to get bitten, either.

He took a side approach to the debris and collected some of the biggest, then returned to the group.

- I'll try to be more careful! Thanks Joe! I owe you one! - smiled Liam.
- It is all right! - answered Joe. I was lucky to see it first.
- We have to go back and we need to pass in between the two hills to get to the car – Major Bashir said.

Some howls and growls as well as high pitched screams interrupted him. They all looked as one of the hills came to life with dozens of baboons showing up across the crest.

- I don't like this – said Major Bashir. This horde must be local and resides here – in their eyes we are trespassing and we risk being attacked. Do not look towards them and we try to detour, to avoid coming close to them.

As he was speaking, another choir of screams and growls came from the other hill and another horde of baboons took position in front of them.

- I do not like this at all – we fell in the middle of a territorial dispute between these two hordes and they are very determined to sort out the problem. Unfortunately, we are in the way, so stick together and watch each-other's back. I will try to lure them farther away.

That was hard to accomplish as their position was at the moments on the battle ground between the two hordes of baboons. The animals were engaged in a prelude of screams and aggressive gestures in both hordes, menacing each other, as the tiny group of men was caught in between.

- I don't like this at all, Major Bashir exclaimed. I was inspired to take my gun with me – he added as he released the safety pin of his automatic pistol. He loaded it and set it from burst to individual fire. Dr. Johnson, I know about your Glock; if you carry it with you, it may be high time to get it ready for action.

– What do you suggest? – asked Peter. We do not stand a chance here in the middle, guns or no guns.

– Certainly doctor! That is why we will start moving easily towards the car. Do not run and stay inside the group back to back. Be as noisy as you can! Scream and shout but without too much gestures which might be interpreted as attack movements. Ready?.....Here goes! I will open the way, dr. Johnson you will be the rearguard. Shoot any aggressive male coming closer than 5 meters. Let's go!

They started slowly walking as a packed group, with Major Bashir leading the way and menacing the monkeys trying to outflank them from both hordes. Apparently, it was a new game; the monkeys seemed to have lost their appetite for war between clans over hunting ground and females, and focused their compensating attention on the alien group of humans, invading their territory. Soon, the men from the group observed this, as well as the tendency of both hordes to deploy aggressive males trying to cut their way to the vehicle. At a certain moment, Major Bashir started shooting in the air to scare them off. For a few seconds, attacking monkeys were stun and gave a swift retreat, but as soon as they realized nothing bad happened except for the noise, they charged again in a deafening choir of shrieks and barks. This was not going to be easy, and Major Bashir stood still and took aim for two of the most aggressive males: two rapid shots and the attackers instantly fell down, with head smashed by bullets.

– Come on, let us hurry – Bashir tried to get advantage of the monkey's amazement and the brief moments they shifted their attention to the dead horde members. They will attack again.

– I am also concerned about the hyena pack I see in the distance, close to the moors – said Peter, and everybody turned heads to see the few hyenas standing and waiting in the shade of the bushes.

– I guess they wait to see who wins and the looser is on the menu – Jason joked. I personally declare myself inedible, but I do not think those hyenas are choosy at this time.

–   They will adore your white skin and fine flesh, dude! Liam said. Besides this, they may try more exquisite "cuisine" with the Frenchie. Hey Yves, they'll have to chew more on us, 'cause we are both ripe!

–   Mon Dieu! You are right, cow boy! Only that I intend to provoke to them an indigestion! Me and hyenas will establish a rule – I do not eat them, they do not eat me!

Nobody laughed, but they started walking faster and this made the group spread a little. Spreading the group made Joe Cooper less careful. While looking back, he engaged on a divergent path leading to a pile of rocks, separating him from the group. More than that, while looking at the hoard and walking backwards, he stumbled against a rock and helplessly fell on his back. Once there, he would take a longer time to get back on his feet and reach the safety of the group. This disadvantage was promptly exploited by some large baboons, who outran him and reached first to the rocks, rendering Joe Cooper in the delicate position of being down and surrounded by enemies They were moving in for the attack. Realizing his unfavorable position, Joe raised to his feet and looked around for help. But the male baboons on top of the stone hill were in no mood for joking. They started both running downhill, obviously converging on him, while trying to separate him from the group. The closer one came within reach and tried to grab Joe by his leg. Joe was prepared for the attempt and gave it a powerful football kick which sent the monkey flying and falling to the ground some feet away, too dizzy to get up quickly. The other one became more cautious and delayed his attack, compensating with a solo of howling and barking, while restlessly jumping up and down and showing its teeth. The other one was coming around and the whole horde was approaching, when two loud shots thundered in the tiny valley, and the two larger baboons fell down. The others ran off, and the tall shadow of Liam Johnson, hat and boots on, and his smoking gun in hand, came out of the cloud of dust and smoke:

– Come on brother, why are you hanging on in these parts? I have a hunch those freakin' monkeys do not like you too much, in spite of your African ancestors – laughed Liam, pushing the corpse of the dead baboon with his boot.

– Thanks man! I never thought I may die being eaten by savage monkeys, and that before I grow old! – Besides, my origin is in Sene-Gambia, far from here! My blood is Mandinka! Joe tried to smile, while his gasping breath and grey face told a different story.

– Well, that would explain their grudge! You are from the West coast, they are from the East! You are not welcome as a male! But you know what terrifies me? This one- he said, showing the dead baboon – did not have any condoms with him. You were in danger to get some catchy disease! – he laughed and everybody smiled.

Joe was in no mood for jokes and preferred not to answer.

– It's ok, we are even now! – Liam continued. You saved me from being bitten by that viper! We'll have a "Jack" on that when we get home!

– You bet! Joe answered, shaking off the dust in his clothes. But we're not out of the woods yet.

They eventually got to the car and managed to lock doors before the vehicle was surrounded by howling monkeys, some of which jumped on the vehicle and were banging on the windows, without apparent success. But things started to change when some of them brought some wood pieces to slam them against the windows and Peter saw in horror as some baboons grabbed stones from the fields and were hopping on the car, trying to bang the windows with them. The rear shield suddenly got a crack and there was danger for it to give way, shattering in a thousand pieces. Peter yelled:

– Come on, step on it! Let's go!

The car swung to action, throwing sideways all the monkeys clinging to it. At a certain moment, they left behind the war zone and found the country road taking them back to the highway.

- Sacre Dieu! Please tell me somebody managed to grab the debris from the place! – Yves Durand said.
- I took some – Major Bashir answered.
- I got my pockets full of them! – Jason Barr informed them. We have plenty of the stuff, but I cannot figure out what the thing was, judging from the fragments only.
- Nobody could or did, yet! – said Major Bashir. We are still working on the debris we already have, right now.
- Let us hope the additional ones will help us. It would be worth the danger we went through – Peter concluded.
- Sorry for the monkeys we killed! – Liam said. But I saw no other way to solve the problem.
- Never mind! They are officially protected, except when they become aggressive or sometimes rabid. Do not worry, the local hyenas and the vultures must have consumed them by now. Monkeys are still afraid of hyenas and do not interfere. Maybe if it is about defending cubs, you may see a heroic baboon mother charging a hyena, but ultimately, they have to accept fate.

The car was going South, when Major Bashir took a rather unexpected left turn, on a side road.

- This is going to reach a crossing with Maydh – Burao road. I know the place. I want to show you something.
- Ok! Peter said. I didn't feel like going home, yet, anyway.

They traveled for almost one and a half hors until they reached a small village. On one side of the road was a barrier and a sign stating briefly – Laas Geel.

- Laas Geel is one ancient archaeological site in our country – perhaps the oldest and the most important. The site contains prehistoric cave wall paintings and they are remarkably well preserved, in spite of being at least 5000 years old. They hold some of the best images about animals of the savanna, especially the oxen.

They entered the barrier and went inland for about 2 miles, reaching a hill-side area. The side of the hill was made out of sand stone and there was a dent with a deep inside pit representing a natural shelter, probably much appreciated by primitives. There was good shelter from monsoon rain and room enough to make open fire. Some boulders might have had ritual roles, as they were painted in red and blue, but the best was an extraordinary fresca of hunted animals: antelopes, oxen, hyenas, birds, even lions. All members of the group were impressed by the paintings and the hand marks were tempting, having the similar size as modern men's hand.

The visit of Laas Geel was just the necessary ingredient to conveniently forget the morning adventures when they were chased by hordes of aggressive baboons. They went back to the hotel, where they observed a flat tire caused by giant thorns of the wild vegetation.

– It is good the car did not let us down in the field. You know – major Bashir smiled – sometimes hyenas await on the side of the roads for careless drivers and there were some attacks on those that stopped in the wrong place, regardless the reason.

The next day they took a warm good -bye from the Major and Lieutenant Siyad, Liam painfully giving up his Glock to Bashir, who promised to keep it safe for his next visit.

Dim light

Stephen Hicks was feeling so much pressure, he was unable to have breakfast. He difficultly swallowed his coffee, which seemed much bitter and hotter than usual, and then headed for his office. While driving towards GERMINA Inc., he took time to consider the possible questions his boss would ask, and kept wondering if and how much was Archie annoyed by his interest on GERMINA's exports.

He slowly parked next to the entrance, closest to the elevators and passed through all security tests (finger print, retinal scan), finally reaching the second underground level where his office was located.

No sign of Archie so far, and Stephen tried to recall if he saw Archie's car outside or not. However, atmosphere at work was cozy and welcoming, like in any other ordinary morning.

Hicks got in his office and threw himself on the rotating armchair, closing his eyes for a second. Why did it have to be so complicated? It was all fine one week before and now he was caught in something that could potentially endanger his career, to say the least!

He pushed the button of his intercom and shouted:

- Hi Audrey! Good morning!
- Good morning, Professor! – a crystal voice answered.
- Can you bring me the coffee, please!
- One moment Sir! – and she hung up.

Hicks tried to relax a little. He switched to Dave, the administration guru and the "know -it-all" person in the company:

- Hi Dave! Good morning!
- Good morning Sir!
- Can you send me the situation of this month's overall product – germs, garden soil, fertilizers, insecticides, whatever. And I will need the biological report on the lab tests on the bugs we have worked on – say - the last two weeks.
- Right away Sir! Give me ten minutes and you will see it on your mail.
- Thanks Dave!

Hicks was satisfied. The work routine made him feel good and helped him ignore his fears.

The door opened and Audrey, his secretary, came in with his favorite cup of coffee. Audrey was a well -made blonde woman, a bit plump, but it was easily forgivable considering her generous breast, thought Hicks. Even if her breast was inspiring and he sometimes had visions of him seeking refuge with his face deeply buried between her boobs, Stephen could not overlook the three kids that have suckled on them and the muscular auto-mechanic she had for a husband, strong enough to stop his exuberant imagination dead in its tracks. However, she was a nice and considerate person, always polite to him and quite efficient.

–   Thanks Audrey! You are sweet!

Stephen took a sip from the coffee which was sweet as he liked it.

–   Oh, Professor, before I forget! Mr. Donovan said he will be waiting for you in his office when you come!

Audrey smiled to Hicks, possible not noticing the acrid face he put on when hearing about the invitation. The new gulp from the coffee cup seemed bitter and tasteless, this time. So here it goes again! What the hell did Archie want from him? Probably Dave informed about his curiosity regarding the product stockpile. Well, he will find out anyway and will decide what to do according to Archie's position.

He took another 10 minutes to finish his coffee and then slowly made his way on the corridors towards Archie's office. He conveniently knocked twice and opened the door.

–   Good morning Stephen! Archie greeted him before he could say anything.
–   Hi Archie! – Stephen smiled like a professional clown. What's up?

Archie was looking into a file, and from time to time compared whatever he was reading, to some info on his computer. He pointed a short look to Stephen and half a smile, then carried on studying.

–   Have a seat! Do you want some coffee?

– Thanks, I just had one! That would be the second, if I count the one I had in the morning at home. I am getting too old for it – smiled Stephen, trying to bring a little laxitude in the atmosphere.

Archie took some time to answer, and then he continued:

– Not to old to score on ladies, Stephen!

Stephen froze – has Elizabeth been telling Archie facts about their meeting? But no, that was not possible, he realized. It would simply be against her better interest to go through such details.

– By the way – continued Archie. Thank you for accompanying Elizabeth during weekend. She said she had a good time and that you are a real gentleman. I may have misjudged you, all this time, Stephen!
– Oh, she is too kind. I just wanted to help and do what I promised to – Stephen managed to swallow his acrid saliva.
– However, you have something else to explain to me! Dave informed me you were preoccupied by the export proceedings and the stockpile of merchandise in the depot. For your information, such documents are not for the use of research personnel like you are, therefore access to such documents is restricted from now on, as previously decided for the contracts, for a fact.

Archie set back in his comfortable chair and removed his glasses, gently massaging his temples.

– Tell me Hicks! What are you curious about? What the hell is bugging you? – his tone ever increasing to shout level. Tell me what the fuck are you looking for? This has got to stop or I will be forced to consider you as untrustworthy person. Such thing may have other consequences, none of which to your liking, Stephen. Mind your own business and stop meddling into mine, I am telling you for the last time. Get of my back or I'll screw you! Do you understand this, Professor Hicks?

Stephen took some time to close his moth, opened as a surprise after this violent speech:

- Loud and clear, Director Donovan! – he answered in some defiance and rose to his feet, ready to leave the room.
- Stephen, we go back many years, good years, happy years. Do not ruin that over stupid reactions!.- Archie concluded in a friendlier manner, bringing his voice back down to conversation tone.
- Okay, Boss! Hope you do the same! - Stephen smiled, and left the office, with his heart pounding and the same acrid taste of fear in his mouth.

He went to his office, not before cheerfully waving to Audrey who was guarding the enclosure like a blonde Cerberus, her huge breast resting on the keyboard of the computer in front of her and a large lipstick- smile on her face.

Back in his office, he started checking on his papers and after one hour of boredom, raised to stretch a little.

- Dave, tell he guys in the lab I will come to see their progress. I'll be there in 5 minutes. Tell them I'll have brunch with them: a sandwich and a glass of milk.
- Yes Sir! Right away Sir!

Hicks went to the closet behind the door and extracted a white lab gown which he put on, in spite of not being very fresh and very white.

He went out on the corridor and got to the elevator which carried him to the fifth floor underground.

- Hi guys! Long- time- no -see!

The lab workers raised some bored eyes from their microscopes and machinery and some of them mumbled something close to good morning.

- How are things going, Matt? Stephen asked a man dressed in a complete protection overall, with a bio-hazard protection mask, operating a pair of mechanical arms inside an air-tight closed booth. The arms had operating counterparts inside an incubator like enclosure, mixing some fluids in various recipients.
- What are you "cooking" there, Matt?

The man took of his mask to show a smile and answered:

- Some cholera strain that can unexpectedly resist on dry stuff for 24 hours plus! Totally deprived of water!

Then he put his mask back on.

- Hm! Tough choice! The Vibrio Cholerae can survive only in water, but if you succeed to make it survive dry environment, for one hour, you are good. Make it two hours and you get the Christmas bonus!

Stephen moved to another booth and watched as a woman, also dressed in highly protective outfit was delivering injections to a bunch of mice in a small cage.

- Hi Sandra! How are your mice doing, dear?
- Good day Professor! They are fine for the moment, but not for long. I am trying to train them resist a powerful strain of meningitis. This becomes very destructive after first symptoms and induces potentially deadly meningeal hemorrhage within hours.
- Is it safe to make it that powerful? Stephen asked.
- Actually, Professor, I am trying to find a safe antibiotic that can offer solution to this problem, but I failed so far. I have tried almost all third generation cephalosporines.
- Hmm! ....Why don't you add aminoglycosides or Lyncosamide to your test board? Maybe those have better penetration through the meningeal barrier. Works for bones.

– Maybe it is a good idea! I will try them and even the cheaper Sulphametoxazole, see what happens.

– You do that, and let me know how it works! If somebody uses this out there, they are doomed without effective treatment. And we get no money – laughed Hicks.

Then Stephen went to another underground level where atmosphere was more relaxed. Some lab technicians were supervising a great reactor, like a giant pool, where a huge mixer was turning large chunks of something that appeared to be mud and was smelling as bad as it looked.

– Hi guys! How is your new fertilizer?

One older lab man, dressed in an orange overall, smiled to him and answered:

– Juicy and tasty! For the things we put in it, you could serve it as side dish for Kobe steak! And he laughed very pleased with his joke!

Stephen smiled politely and turned to the others:

– What can you tell me about sewage reactor flora?

One of them removed his gloves, and spoke coming towards Stephen, who could no longer avoid the hand-shake:

– It is good, Sir! We have managed to get good results! One hundred grams of reactor flora can decontaminate 5 ton of sewage water in 24 hours!

– Wow! That is good! Stephen was rubbing his hands. That will bring us great pay. But where is Greg?

Everybody indicated the next lab booth, which was closed and a man wearing the same orange protection outfit was working inside.

The entrance to the booth was card protected and Stephen used his to enter the enclosure.

- Hi Greg! How are you today?
- Fine Sir- the guy removed his mask and his gloves and shook hands with Hicks.
- Did you make any progress? You know we have three more months for this project, and the entity interested in it will not forward any more money unless we show some progress.
- Well Sir, I think we are about to succeed. The bacteria I am training becomes more and more effective by the day, but I have to select powerful and resistant colonies to generate a solid breed. So far, with 100 grams of bacterial suspension I can inactivate 1 ton of crude oil in 24 hours. We still have to work on the multiplication rate, which is rather slow, maybe more than 32 hours. We must drop it to 10-12 hours with logarithmic consequences.
- You can realize we are committed to helping all countries to be able to clean the accidental oil spills that pollute seaside areas and bring havoc to ecosystems. Besides, being the only ones having such tool, we can make a lot of money.
- Give me another 3 months and I will get an efficient product. Incidentally, suppose someone would inject 2 kilograms of this stuff in the core of a very productive oil field of an enemy country, say in Middle East, for instance. His oilfield will run dry in 2 months and he will start importing oil – and Greg started laughing, very pleased with his joke.

Of course, Stephen smiled like hearing a good joke and had no intention to confirm to Greg how close to the disturbing truth he went with his assumption about the less obvious advantage and possible use of these bacteria.

He went back up on the 5th level and joined the lab workers for a break and a sandwich. An uneventful afternoon passed and he was already yawning when he went back past Audrey's room. Audrey was seated in the exact position he saw her hours before, apparently doing the same thing, working on her computer. With her huge tits dangerously hanging over the keyboard, as usual.

Hicks smiled and entered his office, undressing the white gown, which he crumpled and threw in a basket for laundry service.

He sat down and resumed his search on the computer, opening his mailbox. Nothing unexpected though. Some courtesy invitations to local celebrations, a lot of promotion for various things, from detergent to salami – which made him regret he had not installed a more updated spam filter – and some communications from known subcontractors. But Stephen routine and curiosity worked without fail, so he mechanically opened the junk box. Among a pile of more annoying bullshit there was a message he opened immediately. With trembling hands, Hicks wiped his glasses and read:

"Dear Sir

I hope this message finds you well. I am writing to you out of professional interest. I remember that many years ago we discussed some potential characteristics of Lyme disease and the best approach to healing the disease, in terms of germ sensitivity to antibiotics. I also remember your lab was the leading facility in such research, until the unfortunate accident that convinced you to abandon the project. I have been contacted by some WHO public health officials regarding such research, with the occasion linked to a recent outbreak of a related disease in East Africa. I took the liberty of also directing them to you, as a better and more instructed specialist in this topic. I am opened for discussion and cooperation on this matter, as I also pointed out to the WHO representatives.

Please receive my best regards
Your sincerely
Professor Jan Schuster
Detroit"

Stephen mechanically pressed reply button and wrote:

"Dear Professor Schuster,

I remember about the time we were competing for researching the Borrelia strains and their pathological capacity and I certainly remember that your lab was the one in the lead, as mentioned by CDC. I hereby thank you for letting me know about this issue and I assure you I will have the same transparent attitude.

I look forward to cooperating with you and the WHO in the interest of public health and safety.

Kind regards
Professor Stephen Hicks
Milwaukee"

Hicks was devastated. Sweating abundantly, he checked for other messages but there were none of any importance.

He printed the message, and forgot to put his coat on while storming out the door, towards Archie's office, paper in hand. Sharing the news with Archie was the only thing he could think of right now and Archie will find a way out. After all, it was his ass at stake, thought Stephen, but Archie's "saving boat" was large enough for him, too.

He was almost running out of breath when he knocked at the door, hoping Archie had not left already. He knocked twice and without waiting, busted in. Archie was seated at his massive furniture office desk, busy to cut the tip of a fresh cigar and to his amazement, Elizabeth was provocatively half seated on the corner of the table, crossing her extralong legs in a cheeky, sexy attitude and offering a wide display of the panties and garters.

Archie raised his eyebrows and took a few long seconds to light his cigar, puffing two or three times before leaning back in his chair. Elizabeth did not react at all and was holding a lit cigarette in her left hand.

- So, you do like my birthday present, honey? Elizabeth asked.
- Sure! Archie answered throwing a passive look at the gift she brought, a small painting of herself – in the nude, and in a provocative position, placed in a complicatedly sculptured frame, full of embedded gems and semi-precious stones.

Kind of kitsch – thought Hicks, but managed to smile:

- Oh, sorry Archie, I completely forgot about your birthday and I think I can barely remember mine! Hello Miss Elizabeth! Glad to see you again and may I say what an exquisite gift you brought, although I fear it wouldn't be safe to have everybody see it. Stephen turned a meaningful smile to Archie, who continued looking at him expressionlessly, like the baked head of a mutton from the oven.
- I did not know you were busy, but there was an urgent matter to bring to your attention, that is why I took the liberty to disturb you! Here, this is a message I received today. See it and let me know what you make of it!

Donovan picked up the paper and looked through it, then let it drop on the table and hid his face between his palms, massaging his eyes. His face looked tired and eyes were red.

Elizabeth registered the awkward moment and jumped down from the office table, grabbed her shinny purse from a chair and went to the door, with a loud comment:

- I can see you boys are very busy, so I'll be on my way! I hope you enjoy my gift, darling! Elizabeth smiled viciously.

Archie stood motionless, and finally waived his hand good bye when she went out. He mechanically stumbled on his desk for the usual cigarette box, picked one and lit it, inhaling deeply the blueish smoke as if it were the purest oxygen. He started cleaning his glasses with a piece of cloth and spoke with his metallic voice:

- What the fuck is with this woman, it is the second time she comes here in one year. She could have waited till I got home! It was supposed to be all about sex and money, then why the fuck all of a sudden, she mentions love? …Darling? ……..Crazy bitch!

He puffed a little more from his cigarette, almost finishing half of it, and returned his sad look towards Hicks:

- Stephen, did anybody else contact you about this?
- Absolutely nobody, Archie! I swear it was a total surprise for me!
- Are you sure you did not stir them up with one of your stupid messages or something, having this come as an answer to your call?
- Come on Archie! You know me better than that! Would I be so stupid to stir things up when you know how much I wanted this issue to be buried and forgotten forever?
- It's just this thing that I know you and your blunder talent! It is not the first time you mess things up, giving me a hard time cleaning the shit you dumped!

Stephen was amazed. Of all the bad things he could hear, this was too much. He instantly understood Archie had something to do with the issue – who knows, maybe he was the one who sold the germs and the insects that were used in Africa – and now he was preparing to put the blame on him as a scape goat!

- Listen Archie! I had nothing to do with this shit, well nothing more than what happened twenty years ago, and you know it! I do research on germs, not sell them! Better think of our best strategy out of it, when the WHO will come to us!

With these final words spoken on a higher tone, Stephen sat up and went out of the office, banging the door a little bit, while Archie was biting his lips till they got white.

He stood motionless and when Stephen got out, he stuck his tongue out and cursed:

- Son of a bitch is mocking me! I know it better? Find a strategy? What the hell did he mean by that?

A second alarm bell started ringing in Archie's head: Stephen's words implied it was something Archie knew about or even did, and him, Stephen, somehow found out about it, but did not agree to take the blame or even worse, become a scapegoat. He knew Stephen to have from time to time such personality crisis.

He thought of the personal export of infected bugs he was doing in secrecy, but the people he sold the stuff to had nothing to do with Africa. Unless….maybe, …they sold the stuff to somebody else, or someone else was actually the true beneficiary. He will have to discretely dig in for some answers, and the best opportunity would be the tomorrow shipment, when he was supposed to deliver the package he had in the safe. But he needed to be delicate and avoid freaking them out of the deal. Oh, and he decided not to forget about the first alarm bell, triggered by the unusual behavior of Elizabeth. Her playing the role of a woman in love was simply grotesque, compared to what he knew about her. The crazy bitch had something in mind, and he had to find out what that was or better send her away before getting him into some mess. He decided to call it a day and took his coat and went to the parking lot, where he picked up his Mercedes and set off for the city.

In an obsolete building in the outskirts of Milwaukee, the tall man with grey hair stood in front of a computer with headphones on and said:

- Okay, I have a visual! Do we have audio?

Somebody answered in the headphones.

- I can hear loud and clear. Put everything on tape, guys! I want to hear a fly sneeze if it is inside his office.

He raised from his chair and went to the bathroom, leaving his coffee cup in front of the screen, where the image of Archie Donovan was frozen, as he was smoking, seated at his oak desk.

Back in business

Polivanov was early in returning to the ship. He was satisfied with his short vacation and now was contemplating the idea of setting everything back in motion. His reunion with Zarufin was sincere, even if less emotional, and was consumed using the common vodka ritualic sacrifice, which in this case meant two bottles of Moskovskaia.

Gradually, all crew members and mercenaries came back on board, except for one Albanian, who was involved in a bar brawl, booked by local police and further recognized by fingerprint as being the aggressor in a case of robbery complicated with manslaughter in Italy, wanted by the Interpol. He received a lawyer paid by Polivanov through a p.o. box company in Panama and also a large sum of retirement money, to keep his mouth shut. His contract anticipated such situation and also a gruesome death menace if he chose to become informer for the authorities. There was no mistake about this and two cases in the past stood proof to the matter; as manhunt was a pleasant hobby for GRU agents friendly to Polivanov. There was a team of two or three of them anywhere in the world, ready to help their comrades and get things done. The authorities who tried to use such informants lost them to odd accidents like falling from the fifteenth floor while smoking on the balcony, or drunk driving a car off a harbor key right into the deep sea water. This is how Luki's story remained a well- guarded secret so far.

They prepared the ship, and Polivanov checked fuel and supplies with Zarufin. When everything was in place, they set sail for Saudi Arabia, as ordered.

On the 19th of the month they anchored in Jeddah and after brief formalities (Luki declared sailing without cargo) Polivsnov and his officers could set foot on dry land. They went through customs and took a slow walk towards the city center.

There were a lot of small shops with souvenirs and a number of taller glass office buildings. In the back, older houses shadowed narrow shady streets and a glittering colorful mosque imposed itself amongst minor buildings, scratching the sky with its minaret tower.

On the other side of the market, there was some sort of food court, with three little restaurants serving coffee, tea and food. The one in the middle was "The Golden Camel", and Polivanov went towards it accompanied by Zarufin.

They chose a little table in the shade, under a huge umbrella, which was delicately sprayed with water mist from a ventilation and cooling unit. Since there was no alcohol there, they ordered tea and something to eat and started looking around. There were various people at the tables, some obviously working in the port area and out for a tea break, some having lunch on their way to who- knows where, but all of them seemed locals. Some had dark or even black skin, so Polivanov felt relief when he noticed a group of five white men, seated at a large table, drinking tea and smoking.

He made a sign with his head to Zarufin, who looked towards the men instantly and nodded. Polivanov got up and slowly walked towards the group at the table. He got there and he noticed that they were staring at him. He addressed to a solid blonde man with a rough face, dressed in a cotton suit, apparently the leader of the group:

- Gospodin Sokolov? Privet! (Mister Sokolov? Hello!)
- Dobre deny! Ia Sokolov (Good day! I am Sokolov)
- Dokumenty, pozhaluysta! (Papers please!)

Without a word, Sokolov put his hand in the chest pocket and came out with a passport showing it to Polivanov.

- Gospodin Sokolov, my ship is waiting for you and your men at pier 19. We leave tonight at 10 p.m. Please be embarked before 9,30 p.m. You have here travel permit cards for boarding our ship. Please fill in the names of your companions, for border control. Dosvidanie!
- Spasibo!(thank you!) We'll be there in time!

Polivanov extracted a small cigar from his pocket and asked:

- Gospodin Sokolov. Do you have a light?

Sokolov nodded, and raised his hand with a lighter. He lit Polivanov's cigar, the two men looking in each other's eyes, then Polivanov returned to his table, puffing vigorously on his cigar.

- It is ok! – he said to Viktor. They will come. Let us eat something. I am so hungry I could eat one of them camels on a shish-kebab.

They ate in silence and watched how Sokolov's group left the café, probably going to the hotel to pick up their luggage.

The two men finished their meal and served a coffee then slowly walked back to the harbor and to pier 19, where the Luki was waiting.

After the "Captain on board" signal was given, the ship seemed to come back to life, sailors and other crew members started going to and fro, preparing the ship to sail. By seven o'clock, the guest group boarded and they were invited in a secret cozy cabin under the main deck. That was one deck above the mercenaries' secret quarters, anyway.

Sokolov and his men were instructed to avoid going out on the deck, abstain from smoking in forbidden areas and be ready to receive meals at fixed hours, like the rest of the crew, at 8 am, 2 pm and 7 pm. Polivanov sent them a few bottles of fine vodka in the fridge in their room. There was no window there, but AC was creating a comfortable atmosphere. Finally, the pilot came and boarded the ship and Luki steered out of harbor, taking to the middle of the Red Sea at full speed. The sea was a bit rough, but pushed by its powerful engines, the Luki sailed on quite smoothly, as Zarufin managed to put some ballast before going away, rendering the ship a steadier buoyancy on the rough seas.

A quite thick cloud of blueish smoke lingered in Director Fujimori's Swiss office of the WHO. The new comers, Peter Bud and his companions, plus Henry Sutton entered and were frowning, with the exception of Yves Durand who enjoyed the atmosphere polluted by his favorite cigarettes.

Jason and Joe Cooper coughed politely, and Fujimori understood he must open the window wide. When everybody was comfortably seated, he spoke:

–   Good afternoon gentlemen! I am very pleased to see you again and happy you all came back in one piece. I have studied the material you have reported and it contains a lot of things I already expected. Our suppositions are confirmed but new details come to complicate this issue.

All the people in the room payed attention to him. Henry Sutton, a bit restless in his chair, raised his right hand and interfered:

–   Indeed, our assumptions were right! I have information on our channels and we share it with the American NSA. Looks like this germ is an "engineered" strain and the alteration was made somewhere in the US. This germ is older and some of its early versions accidentally reached Europe. We know about one specific case registered in Romania, confirmed by serious lab in Vienna, Austria. We tried to contact a hyperbaric oxygen therapy facility in Romania, and the doctor there confirmed the case. We also know of a lab in the US which allegedly worked on such germ in Detroit, and the former lab chief Dr, Schuster also confirmed their preoccupation.

Henry paused to take a sip from his coffee mug, and continued:

–   According to his allegations, there was another lab in Milwaukee called GERMINA Inc. with similar agenda, perhaps even more advanced in research concerning this bug. But apparently, their effort was abruptly cut off after an unfortunate accident, with two lab workers exposed to infected insects who unfortunately died. The story was deeply buried ever since, but I find it hard to believe the lab lost all interest in the research of this germ or failed to capitalize on the results. We thought of contacting a professor Hicks who still runs research there and was in his early days when the bad thing happened, but I think it would be more appropriate if information would be requested by WHO. Nobody can refuse that and get on with it!

- I totally agree with you, acknowledged Fujimori. We will send a mail with inquiry content tomorrow.

- I have a better idea to continue yours – said Sutton. Why don't we send a delegation there? I mean we have this team which knows all about the issue. They could leave tomorrow. We must not leave them time to imagine misleading stories.

- But Sir – Jason asked – are you sure these labs did alter the Borrelia strain and loaded it on to mosquitoes? We all know Lyme disease is not carried by mosquitoes.

- I am positive, Mr. Barr! I will share with you some intercepted messages within the last years! This Dr. Schuster seems a straight forward fellow and I trust him. I strongly believe the engineering was performed by GERMINA Inc. Additionally, they may have been able to develop able insect carriers in the mosquito family.

- Yes, maybe! Said Peter. But was this a licit contract or a black-market deal, because if so, we won't find any documents on this. And I feel we are in for the second option.

- Most likely, even exiting documents must have been arranged to look good! -said Fujimori. But this still does not explain how the disease made it to Somaliland and why there, particularly?

- There is more mystery in this – continued Sutton. What was the role of the Russian team coming there right after and harvesting fresh info on the cases? Are the Russian involved? My people at MI5 did not find any relevant info abut any Russian preoccupation in this matter, which I cannot say about the Chinese or the North Korean; still need some info on that, and waiting for details.

- This is indeed a problem that is worth further research – sentenced Fujimori, lighting a new cigarette, to the desperation of those around him.

- According to my sources in the NSA, they also set eyes on GERMINA and some of its prominent administrators for some time now. Something to do with poorly covered contracts with obscure beneficiaries, some of which incidentally … from Russia or Belarus, which is pretty much the same bloody thing.

- Cool ! Liam exclaimed. Now we are getting somewhere. But if Mother Russia is not directly interested, that means the Russians are just carriers or mules – intermediaries to be polite. Who is behind this operation? I mean the one interested to test this bio weapon-to - be in Africa?
- Hmm! That is a hard to answer question! Maybe we'll find out some more after you get to the US. I took the liberty to make travel reservations for all of you before asking, because I was sure Director Fujimori would not mind and you – with your young energy and determination, will not mind, either.
- Swell! Jason Barr exclaimed. Do we have time to take a shower?
- Monsieur Sutton, with all due respect! I did not have time to see my family and my little girl is waiting for me.
- And I have ignored my family lately as well! I need to go see them! – Jason smiled.

Sutton nervously puffed from his cigar and took a few steps in front of the group. Fujimori lit his new cigarette and was looking with interest, but managed to say to the audience:

- I completely understand and you are absolutely right. Normally you would be entitled to some free days after all the effort and all the adventures there. However, I am not the only one who sees the opportunity here; we can take some surprising steps ahead and get closer to the perpetrators in this biological event. Thus, time becomes a sensitive issue and we really need to send a team over there to investigate. We can already guess some political implications and we need to clarify the situation, so the interested parts – in this case states or governments like Somaliland – may take appropriate action. Of course, our main goal is to prevent disease spreading and eradicate cause. The economical and / or political implications are not in our courtyard. That explains the presence of Henry Sutton here and our cooperation with the MI5 and American NSA.

- Precisely! – added Sutton, this time seated in his armchair, in a posture resembling a bit with Churchill with the cigar in his mouth, thought Peter. The he added:
- I can understand your point of view, but delaying the mission is not an alternative. Who else is not willing to continue? – Sutton asked, looking at Liam Johnson and Joe Cooper.

They looked at each other than spoke together:

- We can go with Peter, Sir, no problem! It is
- Very well then! Tomorrow morning you have your flight to New York and there you will transfer for Milwaukee. We will have someone to wait for you there, and get you to the hotel. You will have a car and a driver assigned for the job. The person is instructed to take you wherever you go. Local expenses are covered by the NSA.
- Understood Sir, Peter answered. Perhaps you will tell us which are the main objectives.
- Certainly. But I cooked the plan together with Director Fujimori and upon leaving this office, you will receive an instruction guide. You will read the paper and safely discard it. From this moment on, you talk to no one about this mission, not even your family or friends. We do not know how wide is the coverage of this organization.
- Seems to be a reasonable approach, Liam answered. We'll be on to it, but what if someone kicks back. We may be needing to protect ourselves.
- You will be closely monitored by the FBI and NSA. There can be no better protection, if you ask me- answered Fujimori.
- One more thing – Sutton interfered – I must let you know that when you get to the US, a new member of the team will join you. I understand the person is a biologist working with the NSA. So, you will not be alone!

- Okay Sir! Let's go ! Peter said to Liam and Joe Cooper and waived good bye to Jason and Yves Durand. See you guys later!
- Sure- thing Peter! Jason said, as he turned to leave.
- One moment friends – Henry Sutton stood in front of Jason and Yves Durand. We must be very clear about the secrecy of this operation. Results depend very much in this case on our discretion. Most likely, this means you cannot openly discuss or debate on the topic for a week or so, but we'll keep in touch and you will be informed.
- Very well Sir – Jason replied. I think I speak for both of us in saying that we will not discuss the issue with anyone but you and Director Fujimori, and we are always open to cooperating when and if necessary. Do not hesitate to call us! Thank you!
- We thank you my dear friends! Henry shook their hands followed by Fujimori, and saw them to the door.

Henry Sutton took a seat in his armchair and lit a new cigar and Fujimori picked up the last cigarette from his second package that day.

- These things will kill us – said Sutton, looking at his gently burning cigar.
- Better these than a rogue bacterium! Or the wife! – said Fujimori.
- Do you have further feedback on the disease from Somaliland? – asked Sutton.
- Yes, as a matter of fact, I do. Looks like they have registered a total of 234 patients. Out of which 73 are already dead, so we are close to 30% mortality, even with enhanced treatment. We shipped to Hargeisa some antibiotics and other drugs and materials, but it seems that preventing the disease is better, and this includes having control on the vectors. Locals have tried to contain the alien mosquito species in the area and we observe a certain decline in the number of new cases. There is increasing hope the bug is not transmitted to indigenous mosquito species.
- You know, I heard rumors from the NSA that they have an already opened case on this issue – the company there – GERMINA Inc.

– being involved in illegal export of biological material. But all I know for now is this and I hope I can get further details.

- Well, keep me posted ! Such details might prove helpful for us in trying to prevent or limit outbreaks of this kind.

- You bet, my friend! Sutton extended his large and warm hand to Fujimori, who shook it and bent a little according to Japanese politeness code.

On the job

Travel to US was uneventful. All members of the team were pleased to get home, in a manner of speaking, Peter, Liam as well as Joe Cooper, being US citizens. La Guardia Airport was kind of crowded, but their Delta Airlines connection to Milwaukee was only three hours away.

They used the transfer routes inside the airport and safely boarded the plane in time. They landed in Milwaukee late in the evening and were a little tired when they finally recovered their luggage and set off for exit gates.

They went out in the arrival hall, blinded by powerful lighting and pushed around by the crowd. Peter was looking around the welcoming people, some holding banners in hand, for the biologist who was supposed to wait for them and further join the team.

He failed to see his name on any of the banners and turned on his phone, ready to call Sutton, when a nice- looking young lady came straight to him, smiled and asked:

- Dr. Peter Bud, I presume? Her smile unveiled a perfect set of pearl-white teeth. She had a little charm tan in spite of the season, dark hair with some fairly colored strands and her beautiful hazel-green eyes with rather oblique deployment betrayed half Asian ancestors.

- Yes, that's me! Peter answered. These are my colleagues, Dr, Liam Johnson and Dr. Joe Cooper.

- Delighted to meet you! I am Alma Matsumoto, biologist.

- Pleased to meet you – Liam answered, followed by Peter and Joe. All three sort of surrounded her.

She looked amazing in a light blue cotton costume, loose enough to let her breathe, but tight enough to expose her perfect athletic body, with a tiny waist and large sexy breast. Her neck seemed fragile and she was wearing only one jewel – a neckless with a golden pendant – in fact a Japanese word. She invited them to her car in the parking outside. The drive towards the hotel was rather dull. They were welcomed by a doorman in uniform at Cambria Milwaukee Downtown Hotel, and luggage was taken to the rooms.

- Look, I know it is late, but we invite you to joins us at the bar for a late coffee or something. We may get to discuss tomorrow's program – said Peter.
- Very well then! I guess tomorrow I can afford to be a little late at work. Alma smiled, displaying a pair of mesmerizing dimples in her cheeks. Her rather short haircut enabled full view on her charming profile and gracious tiny ears. She directed them towards the bar, and they took a free table in a discrete corner. They were already seated when a waitress came and took their order, tequila for Joe, bourbon for Liam, a glass of Connemara for Peter and a small gin & tonic for Alma. A plate of sandwiches completed the table setting.
- I presume you already know what we came here for – opened Peter. So, we can go to details already.
- First, excuse me for booking a three- star hotel, but I thought it is better to keep a low profile on our job. I came here for the same reason – said Alma. I actually live in LA., and I arrived yesterday, in time to rent a car, see around and prepare for your arrival.
- We are very thankful for your welcoming us! Said Joe, ordering another tequila.
- How can you drink that stuff? – asked Liam holding his Gentleman Jack glass. Smells like cough syrup! What do they make it out of - horse radish and cologne water?

- Actually, it is made from a species of cactus called Agave, also related to pineapple and lily. Fruit needs 10 years to get ripe and this Jose Cuervo is the first – and in my opinion the best – blend ever.
- So good that you need salt and lemon to avoid nausea -laughed Liam. Or maybe poisoning!
- Relax buster! You are not obliged to like it! It is only for people with exquisite taste, not for peasants able to drink the brake fluid of their car, when thirsty.
- Come on guys, we are not alone. Alma here will think we are a group of immature sissies or uncivilized rednecks. Let us know each other better, before we go on. Alma, tell us about you!

Alma smiled, showing again her charming cheek dimples:

- Well, I was born in Hawaii. My great grandparents came from Japan. My great grandfather was a merchant and had opened business at the beginning of the 20th Century, when Hawai'i was annexed territory to the US.
- Must have been before 1920 or '30 – observed Joe.
- Well, there were actually 42% Japanese people in 1923. During and after the war he suffered from persecution of post-war society simply because he was Japanese. Perhaps the post-war times were harder, according to his stories. He was a merchant but also an expert in martial arts and he developed the same passion in my grandfather, who was born before WWII. He, in turn, taught my father and me everything he knew and I inherited the family's passion for martial arts – I am very fond of jiu-jitsu and kendo.
- Wow – Liam interrupted her – one should be careful not to mess with you!
- I keep training even now – Alma said with a serious face. You cannot imagine how useful that proved to be for a young girl. Let's just say that I never fell victim to bullying, ever since high-school.
- So, what happened next? -asked Peter.
- My father was born right before Hawai'i joined the US community. His youth was still marked by random persecution because of

Japanese descendance. He thought to put an end to it by joining US Army and served in an anti-aircraft battalion defending the islands. Later on, he met the love of his life, my mother, who was a beautiful American girl from LA. She came for a post-graduate vacation to the paradise islands and she found her love here, so she decided to stay. This led to a 4- kid family in which I have 3 brothers and I am the youngest. Unfortunately, she died because of a terrible and swiftly progressing type C hepatitis; I understand she contracted it from her dentist. I was only 5 then. I can barely remember her, all I know she was very beautiful and she loved me very much. My father took over the family business and now he owns a few souvenir shops back home and runs them with the help of my brothers.

- And why did you decide to leave Hawai'i? -asked Peter.

- My grandparents from my mother's side helped me to settle in LA. I did not follow the commercial tradition of the family, because I liked biology and was good at it. So, I studied to become a biologist and I got so far as completing my PhD on bacterial metabolism and invasiveness at the University of California – Los Angeles. Further on, my competence was needed for some government agencies and I was thrilled to accept such cooperation, even if I cannot speak about it. I am very proud of what I do and the fact that I am at least half Japanese. Oh, and incidentally, I seldom get bored.

- And you should be proud! – rushed Peter politely. Now it is our turn.

- We were advised about your competences – all of them – said Joe. My name is Cooper, Joe for friends. I am a specialist in epidemiology and exotic diseases. Born in New Orleans, tried hard to get the ghetto mentality out of my mind and my behavior. I studied and completed my PhD in Florida. I live in Florida with my wife, Keyla and my two kids, Chet and Etta. I was hoping to get to see them upon our return, but it seems something hard to accomplish, at least for now

Joe smiled and he looked to Liam, inviting him to speak with a gesture of his hand.

- I am Liam Johnson, from Texas. Born in Austin, member of NRA, none other than National Rifle Association. I have competence in bacterial and molecular biology, so we can talk business. Got my PhD degree at Baylor, in Waco, Texas. I am not married and I equally like guns and Tennessee whiskey. Guns should kill only scumbags. Whiskey kills all germs. Liam smiled and raised his glass for cheers, accompanied by the others.
- Let me introduce myself now– I am Peter Bud, born in the US but half Romanian. Studied in DC but got my PhD in UK at Oxford on Public Health. I commonly live in the UK and, incidentally, I am not married, yet.
- My, my, I am blessed with such an elevated entourage today, right? Alma smiled and they were not sure if that was a honest allegation or just a bit of sarcasm. Her childish smile voted for the latter.
- Well, now we know who we are, and certainly why we are here, all of us. Let us meet again tomorrow at nine at breakfast and discuss our plan for the day - said Peter. Unless you have other details, some of which we had no time to find out about, we will start tomorrow by contacting our HQ and report our plans for the day. Then he turned towards Alma.
- I can give you a copy of our instructions – I may have saved one just in case.
- No need, I must have received it while you were flying. I know what we have to do. I got the car prepared for tomorrow.

Joe and Liam got up and asked to be excused, leaving Peter and Alma at the table, face to face.

- Alma, it is getting late! I really enjoy chatting with you, but you must be tired also and you need to get to bed as well.

Alma smiled and said:

– That is right, but it won't be a problem, because my room is one floor above yours! So, we've got time for another drink! That is if you are not too tired, too!

Peter smiled in turn and he made a sign to the bar tender for a refill.

– I want to ask you a personal question! How did your family get from Europe to US? – she asked.

Alma paused to take a sip from her new glass:

– If you think it's too personal to tell me, I'll understand.
– Oh no, it is no secret or anything embarrassing. My grandpa was a criminal investigation policeman and left the country in the aftermath of the revolution in '89. He went to the UK where he worked with the Yard as a counselor for Eastern Europe issues. His knowledge about the gang whereabouts and prominent or international perpetrators habits came in handy for the law. My father had the chance to complete his military studies and marry in the US, where I was born. He was a specialist in electronic warfare and we lost him in his first round in Afghanistan. His mobile radar and radio vehicle blew up because of an explosive device placed on the road by the Taliban. Mum was devastated, and her grief must have triggered the breast cancer that killed her shortly after. I remained close to my grandpa, and often stayed with him in the UK for months. He perfected my Romanian, because that was the language we used at home. There I met Henry Sutton, a good friend who works with the Yard, but also cooperates with SIS or MI6, as I hear you do with the NSA and FBI, if I am not wrong.

Alma put on half a smile and said:

– Those are collateral parts of our CV we do not need to talk about. The important thing is that I am here to help. There are indeed clues about one company producing what we call mirror bacteria, allegedly for ecological benefit, but there are suspicions about secret production of less common stuff. I am not implying it is totally unknown, some of it may even be of strategic interest for the US Army, but there's more to it and it appears there are some discrete beneficiaries of such merchandise from distant and even unfriendly countries.

- You mean they produce more than meets the eye and something else besides declared stuff ? -asked Peter.

- Exactly! It is important to know where does such products go. I have been informed that sensitive items have already been delivered to dubious entities and there are some "rumors" that the company exported more stuff than officially declared. Besides the biological interest in the matter, I think the IRS could be eager to know if export and the money coming from it was correctly and entirely declared, which I very much doubt.

- That's good – problem attacked from all angles! - said Peter. But I heard the company has successfully buried all its blunders in the past.

- You will be surprised to find out that all partners that GERMINA has come across with – legally that is, or in open competition – have lost the battle. Some "conveniently" perished even and I saw a list of unfortunate "events" ranging from deadly traffic accidents to explosions of ships at sea. Of course, such development was undoubtfully a "happy ending" for GERMINA every time. Nobody could ever prove anything, but I do not believe in coincidences and sheer bad-luck. The security director there, a man called Archie Donovan, seems to be the actual decision maker; the manager of the facility is nothing more than a puppet. But apparently, they make good money on fertilizers and similar stuff and company goes well. Pays nice wages in due time. Almost too good to be true – said Alma picking something from the tapas plate in front of them.

- Hey, I am still hungry! I'll tell them to bring something better! She waved to the waiter and ordered a plate of roast butter fish with guacamole salad and wasabi sauce.

- I think we can have a white wine with these – said Peter and called the waiter for a bottle of cold Sauvignon Blanc.

Both tired and hungry, they attacked the fish plate and devoured it in minutes. Half way through the bottle of wine, the dialogue continued:

- That is better! Alma said. You have another perspective on things. More optimistic, I'd say!
- Hmm, I was thinking about this Donovan guy. He could be a very dangerous man. I think we must be very cautious with him and his men. If we squeeze them too quick and too hard, they might respond violently. How about the Professor Hicks, who is the scientific Director?
- The professor was described as a touchy person. Very skilled in bacterial biology, I must admit. He is top. But I think he is becoming aware he sold himself cheap and I do not know how satisfied he is or how tolerant to compromise he must have become. I am sure that he must be acquainted with at least some of the fishy business there, if not all of it. He might prove to be the weak link in this build up. He might choose to wash his hands when the going gets tough. A fellow scientist from Detroit – a Professor Schuster – mentioned him concerning the Borrelia strain research in the past.
- We must assume they are still interested in it and possibly -as we can see – they might still be working on it. You may be right! I agree that we should contact him first. Besides, our WHO background entitles us to contact him and only after the administrator of the facility. There is something that bothers me though!
- What's that?
- We can ask for information about their research and production – and that within some limits – but we cannot actually search the place to check for evidence. We must be satisfied with whatever they choose to show us. An official search must be done by law enforcement and a warrant. Perhaps the IRS would find reason to

inspect first and then have an investigation that can be naturally and credibly amplified.

- That is a cunning plan, surprised to see it coming from someone who studied in a medical school only! Alma smiled. I am impressed. She finished her glass of wine and continued:
- That is exactly what we planned to do. We believe that all these things coming practically in the same time, I mean IRS investigation, WHO investigation, maybe even other type of investigation, would destabilize them psychologically and one of them might snap and do some mistake.
- I think the security director Donovan is an old fox. Maybe squeezing Hicks would work better, he is most likely less trained for stressful situations.
- Exactly! Alma smiled. I am glad we think the same way. I was afraid I would run into a bunch of stiff nerds, fond of taking selfies at museums and playing roles from Star Wars or Star Trek.

Peter smiled and answered:

- I am far from feeling like Captain Kirk. Joe is no Klingon and Liam is too violent to become a good Spock. But they are good guys, and they have come up with interesting information about the germ in the little time they had to study it.
- I am sure they are ok! Peter, can I ask you another personal question?
- Ok. Shoot!
- How come you are not married yet? I am not surprised about Liam, with his passion for guns and booze, but I do not seem to understand you!
- Perhaps this is the reason. Maybe I am wrong, but modern girls are generally either too afraid or too bored to dig deeper. I do not swim well in shallow waters. Let us say I did not meet the right person and besides, my activity, as you can see, is hardly appropriate for a cozy family program. They say marriage is the triumph of imagination over reality. Perhaps later... Now I would ask you the same question, in turn. How come you are still single?

– I kind of expected it, under the circumstances. Oh, with me it is simple. Part of my family wishes and expects me to marry a Japanese guy, others vote for a genuine American. I did not think about this, anyway not on these terms. I am not the shy "asking – for- protection" type of woman. I can protect myself and some uninspired men could testify for that, otherwise I feel free to live my life the way I please and that surely requires a little action spice. I mean I could always put on a cleavage dress and high heels with great impact, but I prefer my sportswear and the katana sword in my hand, whenever I do not handle my computer.

– There will be some time before you use your katana to chop veggies for a home- made Miso soup, if you go on like this – Peter smiled!

– Now that was mean, mister! I was being honest with you! Besides, I don't know why I am so curious about you. There is something intriguing about you. I'll figure out what it is in a couple of days, don't be afraid. I can usually read any person.

– I have nothing against it – I am an opened book for you! You can read me page by page! Hey, just to make up, I'll tell you a secret – I can cook all sort of things! Grandpa taught me! Perhaps this is another reason I did not really need the permanent presence of a woman in my life!

– Oh my God! This is gender discrimination, Dr. Bud. What do you need a woman for, then?

– Oh, I left myself cornered here! Women need men as well! Don't tell me you do not have a lover.

– This is something too personal to discuss. Nice try anyway! Men are infatuated. They claim to be modest, but they require to be the first in the love-life of a woman, to enjoy her while still untouched by another.

Peter smiled and poured the last drops of wine in their glasses.

– You know, Alma, I came up with a thought! I prefer to be the last man in a woman's life rather than the first!

Alma closed her eyes trying to comprehend the meaning then opened up and smiled:

- That is interesting, generous and very … demanding!
- Think so?
- Also, selfish and infatuated. Are you that good?
- Better than you might think!

Alma smiled and placed both hands on the table.

- It was nice talking with you Peter Bud! It is getting late and we have a long day tomorrow. Let's go to bed!

They went to the lobby and took the elevator. Being that late, the lobby was quieter and elevators were free.

Inside the cabin, Alma pushed button number three, but Peter was hesitating.

- You? Alma smiled.
- You said let's go to bed!
- Your personal bed, mister! Why are men so boringly predictable? Your room is one floor lower, which means here! – she said, pushing the number two - button.
- And a Very Good Night to you, miss! – smiled Peter, getting out on the second floor. Doors of the elevator closed while Alma was looking him in the eyes. He then turned around and walked the hallway to 221, his room.
- What an exotic creature! I wonder if the likes me! -he mumbled opening his card lock. He turned on the shower and finished it with cold water. Shivering a little he turned in and fell asleep immediately, leaving the TV displaying a boring snooker game.

The next morning, Peter was the first in the breakfast room. He chose some salmon, avocado, cheese and a hard- boiled egg, a strong black tea and some lemonade. Joe and Liam came next, with plates filled with omelet and sausages. Large cups filled with coffee completed the menu. Alma joined them, with a modest tray on which she carried yoghurt, cheese and a fruit salad. The appetizing aroma of a cappuccino came from her cup.

- Good morning boys! I hope you had a good night's rest!
- Slept like a baby! – answered Liam, struggling to swallow his omelet. I feel good and ready!
- I had a good rest! – said Joe. But I woke up in the middle of the night twice because I overheard through the walls someone snoring so loud, I could not believe my ears. Was it by chance you, my dear colleague? Your room was next to mine, and mine is at the end of the corridor.

Liam pretended to be attentive to the food in his plate. Seeing everybody smile, he kicked back:

- Yeah, so what! I snore when I am tired, but it is not my fault; it is the dry climate! "Snow-White" here is very sensitive!
- Dry climate in Milwaukee? Joe was rolling his eyes like snooker balls waiting for a reaction from audience. What the hell did you smoke?

Alma opened her eyes large, expecting things to blow up, only to see Joe smile at the racist remark.

- Even ogres can get sleep apnea – he concluded.
- At least I don't smoke – Liam defended himself.
- Come on guys, break it up! We got work to do. Last night I talked with Alma about our plan. We will go visit GERMINA Inc., most likely just to see how they react. We do not expect them to show us anything interesting, nevertheless this visit will put some pressure on them.
- This is just for starters. I already called my friends and hopefully tomorrow or the day after they will get a surprise visit from the IRS. We will discuss the matter and decide further action after they give us additional clues.

- Looks like a good plan, if you ask me! – said Joe.
- It is a good plan! – emphasized Peter. We are going to visit first a Professor Hicks, who is the Scientific Director of their research facility. We will see if we can get to talk to the almighty Security Director – a Mr. Archie Donovan, a bad ass, if you ask me.
- Then it is settled! – said Liam finishing his coffee. I'll go dress for the occasion. Give me fifteen minutes and I'll meet you in the lobby.
- Me too! – said Joe, raising from the table.

Once again Peter and Alma remained alone at the table.

- Do you always eat so little for breakfast? – asked Peter.
- Nope! But I ate much last night and it was late. I hate to put on fat. You know, I was a bit chubby as a child. Sports and martial arts saved me, I guess. How was your night?
- I think it was restful! Mattress a little soft and fluffy; I am used to sleep on a harder one.
- All right, Peter Bud! I'll go get my things. Meet you in the lobby in ten minutes.

Fifteen minutes later the group was ready to go. Alma was dressed in a corporate business outfit, a light blue deux pieces. The rather short skirt allowed the view of a pair of perfect legs and she wore a pair of elegant but discrete shoes.

Joe had his usual brown jacket with some grey trousers and a dark tie to match the light green of his shirt.

Liam wore a pair of fresh jeans and a leather jacket over his checkered shirt. Both were freshly shaved. Peter wore his grey jacket over light green shirt and black trousers. The green shade of his tie matched the color of his eyes and somehow made them express better. Seeing the boys in the lobby, Alma smiled and asked:

- Going to a wedding or something?

Confused smiles from everybody was the only answer she got. She led the way to the parking lot and she said:

- I will drive because I was here before you and I know my way around. I programmed my GPS for GERMINA Inc. address. Our visit was announced yesterday by our Public Health Authority. Please remember I officially work for that entity.
- Okay sister! Liam answered.

They got into the car and set of for the outskirts of Milwaukee.

- Let me introduce myself first on arrival, and I will present you after! -said Alma. Later on, we can ask questions, but none of those implying any of our suspicions. We don't want to spook them.
- Right! We will ask to visit the research lab and the biological products factory, see how much are they going to show us!

Minutes later, Alma took a right turn on a wide alley, leading to a huge parking lot, situated between three windowless hangar type buildings. No smoke chimneys, only a few ventilation exhaust pipes perforated the walls and there were chiller units on the roof tops.

They parked close to the middle building, which seemed to be the main one.

They approached the entrance and an armed security greeted them. They had to pass through and airport like scanner and show ID cards to the other man, seated in front of a table full of video monitors showing images from the outside cameras. Other monitors displayed images of the interior hallways.

- Please leave your mobile phones on this desk! – he asked, with a voice that did not stand any denial. When all the phones were lined up in front of him, the man picked up his own and called someone:
- Hi! They are here! – that was all he said and then hung up, staring at the visitors, like looking to a poster hanging on the wall.

The embarrassing moment was interrupted by the arrival of Dave, the administrator, who greeted them and successfully composed a smile, which was generally a difficult task for him.

- If you will be so kind as to follow me, we must provide you with protection equipment.

The whole team followed Dave who led them to some sort of locker room, where he opened a cabinet and took from there 5 protection kits, the kind visitors receive in a hospital, blue cap, gown, surgical masks and slippers included. Each of them also received a yellow visitor badge, which they had to wear attached to their chest. The team being prepared, Dave took over and led their way to the main hallway. They were at the ground floor of the middle building, which seemed to be a huge deposit, full of grates and packages. Some workers, wearing fully protected suits, were busy arranging and superposing the crates in piles, awaiting loading to transport vehicles. Two large trucks were parked for uploading, and some workers, helped by an electric forklift, were busy loading the semi-trailers.

- As you can see, we have quite many contracts, our best products are top quality bio fertilizers and reactive mud for septic tanks and sewage systems sells like hot cake.

Peter and his colleagues walked past the loading dock and Peter asked:

- The other two buildings are also depositing facilities, like this one?
- Most of their surface is used for depositing, but there are also some packaging units, and the southern building has inside a plant for processing garden soil and natural fertilizers. We also have there some quality testing labs.
- According to our information, which is backed by your own site, you also have a well -equipped biology lab and some of your

products are within the range of mirror bacteria. Can we see the lab? – asked Alma, looking into Dave's eyes.

Dave's face seemed clouded for a moment, Peter observed, then he almost smiled and said:

- Of course, we have a lab, not so large, but quite effective. I understand you also want to meet Professor Hicks and I will leave him the pleasure to show you to the lab!
- We'll be delighted to do so ! – Liam interfered.
- Follow me please – said Dave and went towards the end of the corridor where the main elevators were.

They called one and stepped in, only to silently go to the second floor under.

They took the main hallway and arrived at Stephen Hicks' office. Door was opened and Professor Hicks was apparently busy with his computer, while repeatedly sipping from his coffee mug on the table. He was dressed in white shirt and dark green trousers and his face was enlightened by a generous smile.

- Hello and welcome dear guests! He raised from his office table, while taking a few steps toward them.
- Greetings Professor! I hereby transmit to you best wishes from Director Fujimori of the WHO, who also told us he regrets being in the position of disturbing you, if it weren't for this Lyme like disease outbreak in Africa, -Peter said.
- Let me introduce you to my team: This is Alma Matsumoto, biologist, Liam Johnson – bacteriologist, Joe Cooper – Epidemiologist and I am Peter Bud – Public Health specialist. Guys, this is Professor Hicks, Research Director of GERMINA Inc., and for a long time now, if I may say so!
- Glad to meet you! I understand there is some debate over the etiology of the African outbreak. It seems that the responsible germ is a Borrelia strain. Having that in view, I wonder what

the purpose of your visit could be? – and Stephen gave his best innocent smile ever.

- Professor, we have been advised by one of your colleagues from Detroit, Professor Schuster, that some years ago you were studying Lyme disease and Borrelia bacterium. – spoke Alma, smiling in turn. We have monitored that activity, and it appears that you have lost interest in - so to speak – this disease, following an unfortunate accident that killed two of your lab employees.
- You know, you are right on this one! We were running some tests to assess the germ's survival on insects and its resilience to various antibiotic, when the misfortune happened. After this incident, the company considered the topic as plagued by bad omen and no further funding in such projects was approved.
- So, let me understand! - said Liam with a rather nervous voice. You stopped any type of research on Borrelia strains ever since and you left all previous experience and results go to waste?
- Oh, no Sir! We have tried to be eclectic in our approach to such bacteria. We even communicated our results to CDC and also the set of partial conclusions we could formulate, based on our expertise. But given the unfortunate accident we have experienced; no further funding of the project was available by our company. Maybe others took over, I wouldn't know. However, our lab workers did not die due to the infection with the mentioned bacteria; they were actually killed by the direct exposure to automatic poisonous gas release, meant to control loose insects within the enclosure. Unfortunately, they were careless and operated without protective gear, as it is specified in investigation official documents. We have increased our protection and awareness level ever since.
- Could we take a look at your lab, Sir ? - asked Peter putting on an equally generous smile.
- But of course! I will show it to you – said Stephen, while grabbing his protective white gown from the hanger behind the door. Please follow me! An unctuous smile was painted all over his face – too greasy to be true, thought Alma.

He went outside and took the main hallway to the large elevators, where they called one. They went to a lower level, and Professor Stephen Hicks led the way on the hallway and started opening the automated doors on both sides with his card, allowing the guests to peek inside:

– Well, this is the bacteriology lab, all renewed!

He went on opening another door:

– This is a workshop where we produce culture media for bacteria! – most of them based on gelatin – agar, but we also do special ones if need be. Let us go to the next one! – and he led the way to the next door:
– This is the lab where we are selecting the best recycling bacteria for sewage water treatment. We have come to great results on these, the water coming out of our reactors is so clean – well, better than drinking water in some African countries, anyway!- and he laughed like sharing a good joke. Then he continued:
– We are testing biological material filters that can render this water the actual drinkable quality, with very promising results – said Hicks, showing them a glass of water from a nearby table. He took it and swallowed a few gulps.
– The next one is very interesting:

He went across the hallway and entered a wide lab with numerous booths.

– This is a lab where we design eco-friendly biological material. Our preoccupation for environmental safety is very steady and profound!
– In other words, what is happening here? – asked Joe Cooper with a genuinely curious face.
– Well, this is one money maker for us – here is the place where we design bacteria that can clean oil spill in the sea. We obtain considerable quantities of this biological material, starting from

ordinary Escherichia Coli, and we further mix it with peat dust, all softened with a moist nutrient solution until it looks like mud. The substance is held in barrels and it is deployed by shovel or mechanically into contaminated waters.

- How effective is your substance, because I heard of similar products back home in Texas – asked Liam.

- Oh, our substance is most effective! We can use one barrel for a square mile of polluted water. There will be no trace of oil within 24 hours, and the process is not harmful for local fauna or sea weed.

- I see! Most impressive! - said Liam and gave Peter a discrete wink. Hicks went on with his presentation.

- We have exceeding export orders for this, we can barely cope up with the demand, more than two thousand barrels per month all over the world. The variants of this product are effective also for detergent spills or other substances, and I can show you something quite secret, -said Hicks, pointing to the next door.

- This is a lab where we are selecting and brewing bacteria that can eat plastic – and that is a wonderful solution for the millions of tons of plastic debris. Returning plastic to organic substances to enrich the soil is a dream come true, and we are very close to fulfilling it! And very proud of it, but we still need to perfect the product and the procedure, so that makes it sort of a secret, yet! – smiled Hicks.

- Professor, please excuse me for interrupting your very elevated and interesting presentation, but I want to ask you to help me with a quite trivial problem – I need to go to the bathroom, please! – and Alma put up an embarrassed smile.

- Sure, Miss! Let me show you!- Hicks went outside the lab door and pointed towards the end of the corridor they came from – Take this corridor to the elevator area and there is an entrance on the left!

- Thank you and please excuse me! I'll be back in no time!

Peter gave Alma an interrogating look; he grabbed her arm and pulled her to one side, further away from the others:

– Do you want me to accompany you? – he asked.
– Nonsense! I will be ok! Be back in a minute! Did you see the elevator panel? There are six underground floors, and we saw just two! – said Alma departing on the corridor.
– Alma, don't do anything stupid! – he said, with the distinctive impression that she either didn't hear or did not care.

She looked back to see if anyone came to follow her, then she looked to the ceiling corners, checking for live cameras and there were some, including one facing the elevators lobby. In front of the elevators she wondered around a little, pretending she cannot find the way and then pushed the button for the closest elevator. It came presently, announced by a pleasant bell ring. She got inside and pushed the lowest floor button. The elevator gently descended and stopped at the lowest level. Alma got out on the corridor, pretending to hesitate like a lost person, but keenly registering everything she saw. There was a line of doors, apparently labs, like the ones they have just visited, only there were no inscriptions on the doors. All doors were card protected and all she could do was peek through the tiny secured windows. Doors seemed to be air tight with gaskets and there was no chance to open one without a valid card, While Alma was trying to see what was happening in the third room, some heavy steps sounded behind her and a man's voice called her:

– Hey Miss! Please come back, visitors are not allowed in this area! Please follow me!... Miss!.... I am talking to you!
– Excuse me Sir! – she smiled nicely to the security guard, a six-feet tall uniformed African American, with the constitution of a professional military or a football player – she thought. I was searching for the rest-room and I must have taken a wrong way!
– You took a very wrong way, and at the wrong floor, Miss! – the security guard answered without smiling. I will escort you back! Please follow me! – he finished, calling the nearest elevator.

They went up 4 levels, then got out and he accompanied her to the entrance to the rest room. He invited her in with a sign and spoke:

- Here it is Miss! I will be waiting here to accompany you back to the group!
- Oh, thank you very much, Sir! You are very kind! – and Alma smiled again, although she knew that will trigger no reaction. She pretended to get busy inside for a couple of minutes, then got out still smiling:
- Here I am, and relieved of my problems! – she declared, and she was dissatisfied to see again the lack of any empathic reaction of the security guard, who led the way towards the visiting group.

The group was stationed in front of another door, and Professor Hicks was explaining something, when Alma returned being escorted by the tall and bulky security guard. Peter saw the situation in a glance and took two steps forward ready to react, but Alma smiled and loudly spoke:

- Hi everybody, I got lost on these corridors and I would be wandering in this labyrinth even now, if it weren't for this good man who was so kind to bring me back. Thank you once again for helping me! – she smiled again towards the guard, apparently without any effect.
- You are welcome Miss!- and turning to Professor Hicks the guard continued: Sir, I found this visitor down on the 6th level in the lab area, which is restricted for unauthorized personnel.

Hicks made a serious face while hearing the report, then recomposed himself and smiled to Alma, answering:

- It is okay! It was near the elevator, you were not in need to use the elevator! My fault! I failed to explain it properly, or maybe I was even better accompanying you! – he turned to the security guard – Thank you! You may go now!

– Sir! – the man turned around in soldier manner and walked away towards the elevator area.

– That is interesting! Peter observed, without giving Hicks enough time to react. So, that means you do have other labs apart from these! Can we visit those, too?

Hicks conveniently coughed to cover how displeased he was with the question, but he had to answer somehow. He did it eventually, but in a softer voice:

– Yes, we have some extensions of the labs that you visited, but they are actually the same as procedures and activities. Part of the activity was reassigned there, because there was not room enough for the full deployment of our programs. However, I must inform you that access in those labs is restricted for unauthorized personnel. Security regulations! There are aspects of the company's production proceedings which are subject to intellectual property protection, We are particularly careful with Korean, Chinese and Japanese visitors. I am sure you will understand that we can make no exceptions!

– Sure, Professor! Never mind! – said Peter, smiling. Joe was having, by contrast, a very serious look and Liam was pretending to speak to Alma, who was also caught in the dialogue and did not react.

– Okay, then I hope the visit was helpful for you! Once again, I am sorry that we cannot help you more with the bacterial problem you are trying to solve, but any resemblance to that strain is long forgotten to our labs. We are trying to keep away from dangerous items, even if we have been entrusted with some government contracts, or maybe especially because of that – said Hicks and continued. I would like to invite you in my office for a cup of coffee if you have the time, now!

– Thank you very much, Professor, for your tour and all explanations. I am afraid we are on a tight schedule so excuse us for skipping the coffee break! However, we were hoping to meet Director Donovan, for a few minutes. I understand he was fresh in security management when you had the Borrelia strain accident, and I would expect him to remember some details about the incident.

The red spots on Stephen's face vanished and his appearance turned pale; eventually he spoke:

- Director Donovan would have liked to greet you, but unfortunately, he had some scheduled meetings at his office downtown! I am sure he will be happy to receive you there. I will contact him and arrange a meeting for tomorrow. I will call you tonight to give you further details! – he continued in a more considerate way, showing a smile, while holding their business cards in his hand.
- Very well Professor! Allow me to thank you on behalf of our team!
- Please let me know if you find something interesting! And of course, if you think I can further assist, do not hesitate to call me! – he continued, handing them his card.
- Rest assured we will share with you the conclusions of our investigation – Peter smiled. They are bound to be interesting,- Peter added, and he was pleased to see Hicks startle. Come along, team! Let's go!

They took the elevator to the ground floor, accompanied by Dave, who escorted them to the locker room where they dumped the protective outfit in a yellow box, then went to the main entrance counter, where they recovered their phones.

Two minutes later they were getting out of GERMINA's parking lot and took the highway towards the city.

- What do you think? – asked Peter,
- He lied his ass out – said Liam fixing the road in front of them.
- I went on the bottom level which was packed with secret labs. We have seen 20% of the real thing, I guess, said Alma. For sure they still work on mirror bacteria.

– You bet they do ! – said Liam. Remember about the ecological cleansing mud for oil spills? Imagine I inject 10 pounds of that bacterial shit in an oilfield in Iran, which is the eighth crude oil producer in the world. Next year they will be importing oil!

– That is indeed sensitive stuff! Joe Cooper said. That is why he mentioned about government contracts, maybe they have contracts with the military and they hope we will stay away from those.

– I can tell you for sure they have – interfered Alma, but none on such crazy thing. However, we must have a delicate approach, we must avoid throwing the shit upwards to the fan! The last contract I know of, was before the war in Afghanistan, when they helped the Army develop the so called "life straw". You dip the red end in the water puddle you found – otherwise looking as bad as it can, and drink from the green end with no fear. It all started with the implication of Carter Center in the eradication of Guinea worm in Africa, but Army was interested to place it in the survival kit of special forces.

– Well said, sister! – smiled Liam. Now I have a question – did their involvement in the Lyme disease issue start from some Government contracts and is it still running, or they went rogue and thought of selling stuff to make a buck?

– Hard to say! Peter exclaimed. Maybe we can have a more adequate conclusion after we talk to Mr. Donovan.

– When we get back, I have to do my reports: I guess you have to do it as well! We meet downstairs at 5 p.m. I am going to take you to a special place for dinner – said Alma.

– Okay, sister! – exclaimed Liam, smiling. While looking at her elegant profile, he gave Joe, who was seated next to him, a nudge, and continued:

– I like her! Trust me, I rarely say that about a woman! It gets to their head!

Everybody laughed, including Alma. She parked the car and they all went to their rooms.

- I may be down at the bar half an hour earlier, to get a drink! Anyone interested? – said Peter.
- We'll see – answered Joe, calling the elevator.

Once inside the room, Peter threw his coat to one chair and grabbed the phone. He chose Fujimori's number and switched to WhatsApp messages:

"Hello Director! We have visited GERMINA. Theatrical display – everything is perfect! Many secret labs with no access. They appear to be dirty. We need further inquiry. Keep you posted!"

Then he closed the phone and undressed, entering with pleasure under the hot shower coils of water. He finished his shower with ice cold water, as usual and felt refreshed. And hungry. He got dressed in a more comfortable outfit and went on the hallway to the elevator. He did not have time to recover about the surprise of immediate opening of the lift doors, as he was in for a bigger surprise seeing Alma smiling at him, all dressed in a jeans costume, fitting her perfectly. A hint of light makeup emphasized her good taste and modesty, which he considered to be consistent with her Japanese heritage. Her beautiful teenage face was radiant, with a large smile, showing pearly teeth and rosy lips. A hint of exotic perfume lingered around her and Peter found himself desiring to get closer to feel the luxurious but quite discrete scent.

- Hi, going down?- was all he could utter, struggling not to stare at her like paralyzed.
- Yap! Thought you need someone to join you for drinking. She smiled
- We'll get a cab, I don't drink and drive!
- That's ok, no problem!

They entered the bar, where Joe was already enjoying his preferate tequila and Liam held a large Gentleman Jack in his greedy hand.

- I'd like Santori whiskey! – Alma said smiling. It is Japanese, but very well crafted!

- I trust you! Peter smiled and turned to the bartender – I want the same but make it double! Some ice for me, please!

They chatted a while and then Alma called a cab. Upon having everyone seated, Liam asked:

- May we know where we are going; I am so hungry I could eat a horse with its halter and saddle on!
- Be patient! I know a good place- answered Alma and she turned to the driver: Take us to "Five o'clock" steak house.

Then she turned to the boys and said:

- I heard only good things about it, and they have homemade bread of their own!
- Yippee! – exclaimed Liam with a serious face. I just hope it is as good as you say.
- Come on guys! What can be bad in a steak? – asked Peter. Company pays, so relax.

They went in through the wide door, admiring the raw brick exterior, which gave the place a vintage look.

They were ordering food, when Peter' s phone rang discretely. Peter took some steps away from the table and spoke for one minute. He came back to the table and said:

- Well guys, we're in business! That was Professor Hicks! He arranged for us a meeting with Director Donovan. We are to meet him in his downtown office, tomorrow at 11 a.m.
- Cool, man! – said Joe! We are going to see what the guy is made of!
- Yeah! And see what lies he can come up with! – completed Liam.
- I guess it will be very important to look neutral to him – said Alma. I have a bad feeling about this person, we must be careful with him. If we become offensive, he will cover in impenetrable "armor".

- So, we'll be careful then! – answered Peter. We shouldn't worry right now. Let us enjoy our steak first – we have time for philosophy later!

They all laughed and the rest of their meeting was uneventful. Peter found himself surprised by his tendency to stare at Alma. He realized he had this urge to look at her all the time, because her presence made him feel good. His persistent eye contact was perceived by Alma, who pretended to ignore it, but it was so obvious that Liam gave Joe a nudge and pointed to Peter.

- I think he's been hit by Cupid's arrow! Only the arrow is as big as an RPG and sent shrapnel! Whispered Liam in Joe's ear and Joe laughed and acknowledged.
- What secrets are you talking about, guys? – asked Alma, while Peter, a bit embarrassed, pretended to do some glasses refill.
- Nothing important sister! – said Liam. Here is to you and friendship!- he continued rising his glass.
- Here is to love and friendship! – raised Joe, smiling.
- To love and friendship! – everybody repeated.

The rest of the evening was uneventful. They took a cab back to the hotel. Peter invited Alma to remain outside for a walk around the block and she accepted. Liam and Joe smiled like Cheshire cats and went up, saying "good night" and "sleep tight" and laughing like young boys.

- What do you think will happen tomorrow?- asked Alma, while stepping next to Peter on the deserted side-walk.
- Oh, nothing much! – answered Peter. I expect this guy to be reserved and suspicious. After all, it looks like they are hiding something and with his position, he would be more acquainted with the facts than Hicks, However, he will be very careful not to betray anything and he will consider very carefully everything we say. I bet he will avoid any technical or medical dialogue, pretending it exceeds his competence.

- I think we'll have to speak less, maybe ask some questions and let him speak! - said Alma.
- True! But I doubt he will chirp like a happy sparrow! Besides, we must be very careful about what we ask! We are not law investigators and there is a limited entrance gate for our questions, so to speak. By the way, how is it going with the IRS investigation?
- Oh, that is on its way! Both the Feds and the NSA have been trying to build a case on this company. I understand they have some inside info and some recordings. I did not get all details, although I have some clue about who their source is. When I'll know more, I will share info with you.
- Sure!....answered Peter. Tell me Alma, is it not stressful for you to be mingled in such sordid cases? After all, you are actually a scientist, and a very good looking one, if you ask me. I can better picture you happily enjoying life, rather than chasing perpetrators and exposing yourself to danger!
- That's the "what's a nice kid like you, doin' in a place like this" kind of question, right?
- Sort off!- smiled Peter. Can you answer it?
- Well, first let me thank you for complimenting me on my looks! And you've seen only the public part of it! Secondly, I find my life fully rewarding – I make enough money and I get plenty of challenges and action.

Alma looked around, and, a bit shivering from the chill of the night, took him by the arm and moved closer to him.

- I am not the armchair knitting type of woman. My best cooking talents range from boiling milk to spaghetti, and I know how to mix veggies in a Japanese style salad. The rest is training. I seldom get involved in relationships – hard to find a man to worth it! At least, until now! I am not fond of socializing, but I have no stress doing it. I am trying to be practical and to live my life the way I like.
- Which brings us to the problem – looks like you have little room for a man in your life!

- Oh no, don't push it that way! I am straight, if that is what you mean. What I am trying to say is that I do not exactly fit in the preference pattern of today's men; they dream about a helpless fine young lady, asking for their help when she has to cross the street or walk barefoot on the grass! Not my cup of tea! World is full of lazy damsels and sissy males, all shaved, artificially tanned and with blonde hairdo! I am sick of such cliché!
- Can't blame you! I do not really appreciate that style, myself! But the protective urge is embedded in males, regardless the species.
- That is an unnecessary feature – if you ask me! Some thirty thousand years ago, women were in charge! And there were not so many wars, apparently!
- Arguable point of view! Men are creatures of multiple talents – they are best chefs, hairdressers, gynecologists, psychologists, etc. Otherwise, why does a woman have to struggle for recognition? I agree there is a lack of respect and sometimes terrible manners addressed to women in societies governed by traditional old mentalities, like in remote underdeveloped countries and some Muslim areas – like Afghanistan or Iran, but according to my knowledge, the number of female orthopedists is insignificant, compared to men.

Alma smiled:

- That is true! We appreciate and sometimes even enjoy men muscle domination – makes some moments of life spicier! But men shouldn't always count on it as their prime quality!
- Men are always counting on that!- said Peter. It is impossible to ignore that!
- Well then, I must confess I do appreciate that man type; furthermore, I do not place you in that category!
- How come? Do you find me special? – smiled Peter.
- I don't know! You seem different, I have a good feeling about you! I kind of trust you before you even flex your muscles! You have something peculiar about your personality, which does not

require lousy reassuring gestures. And that is a good thing, in my opinion, because it is a rare thing!

- I am glad I meet your best standards!
- Hey, don't get carried away! Wait a little! I have many standards, and you haven't been checked for all, yet!
- I am looking forward to it !
- You know, I haven't decided yet on you! Your personality goes deeper than meets the eye! I will need more time for adequate assessment!
- How can you tell? When will you decide?
- I don't know! – Are you in a hurry? - said Alma, stopping her walk and looking at him in the eyes. It may be something about your eyes. They seem to be the gateway to much deeper thoughts and a totally different world, one that you keep to yourself for now!
- I wouldn't mind sharing this world with you! – said Peter, without thinking twice. He gradually came closer to her face and ended his phrase with a passionate kiss, to which she willingly responded. He was amazed by the sweet taste of her lips and mesmerized by her scent – a discrete exotic perfume that he could not describe in words. He realized he did no longer care where he was and why he was there, a sensation he had never experienced before.

After a certain moment of abandonment, she suddenly pushed him back and smiled:

- Hold it stranger! I said I did not get to know you well yet and this will not help, you know!
- Looks like I did not need that much time! I like the world beyond your eyes and I want to further explore it!
- Presumptuous and macho! I think we shouldn't rush to conclusions! Let us sleep on it!

Alma took him by the hand and they returned towards the hotel:

- Let' go! It's getting late and we must think about our strategy with Donovan.
- Okay, Alma! But remember, I am not sorry for getting carried away!
- Who is ? – smiled Alma, as she was entering the hotel door.

The next morning, they all found Peter already at the breakfast table, dealing with his second coffee cup.

- Come on lazy ladies! You are still asleep and it is nine in the morning. Open your eyes to see the coffee machine!
- Did you wake up earlier, or you haven't slept at all? – asked Liam smiling at Peter and Alma.
- I had a good rest, thank you!- said Alma trying to warm up her cold grapefruit juice between her hands.
- But you Peter, look like you forgot to remove your yesterday make up! – Joe was laughing.
- Come on, guys, drop it! I just took time to think about the mission! I find some things very intriguing!
- So intriguing that you didn't sleep a wink! – Liam said. Good for you Alma! But do not destroy our leader to soon! Let us finish the job first! Then you can finish him!

Alma smiled from her grapefruit juice glass and decided not to answer.

- All right, guys! I want to ask you to let me do the talking with Donovan! Alma, do you have any idea when will the IRS move in on GERMINA?
- I don't know! I will call today for details. Today is Wednesday. Maybe tomorrow or on Friday! Better tomorrow, so the impact of cross checking will be greater! I will tell them!
- I agree! – said Peter. Ok! Meet you in the lobby in twenty minutes!
- Sure – said Alma. We take the car and I drive. I got the share location you forwarded me on WhatsApp, I know where it is!

It was five minutes after they left the hotel, when Liam, who was seated in the back seat, said:

- Guys, I have news for you! Bad news is we have a tail! The black SUV – the Lincoln, has been following us since we left. Good news is they seem to just observe us, and made no move to attack us! Anyway, I got my piece with me! – and he waived his gun under her noses!
- What the hell is that? – asked Joe with a perplexed look on his face.
- A fully licensed Sig-Sauer P226-MK25 – Navy Seal gun. Loved it when I was in the army. Fifteen rounds in a clip. Powerful deterrent!
- You were in the army?
- Used to be a Navy Seal! I was not a rich boy! The Army paid for my medical school. I did quit when I finished my second contract. I wanted to deal with something less brutal. But I can see life keeps putting me in situations where I can use my training and skills.
- Sure- thing buddy! – Joe exclaimed. But keep the freakin' gun out of sight, otherwise some cop will come chase us!

They pulled over in front of the office building where they were supposed to meet Donovan and went to the front door. A bizarre deja-vu sentiment occurred when a security guard welcomed them and registered them at the desk. This time they were not obliged to leave mobile phones, but Liam congratulated himself for leaving the gun inside their car. They waited in the lobby until a pretty young lady, wearing an exquisite green deux pieces with a very short skirt barely covering her beautiful long legs provided them with yellow visitor badges, like the ones they had at GERMINA factory. They were invited to the elevator and went up to the third floor, where a large lobby accommodated two secretary booths. One secretary was the one accompanying them; the other one, older by age and with a more austere appearance and no smile on her face only looked at them and nodded for good morning.

- This way please! – the younger secretary showed them in, shaking her blonde locks and spreading an interesting wave of spring floral scent perfume. This is my colleague Wilma and I am Sheila.
- Thank you, Sheila! -answered Peter, as they were approaching a sumptuous mahogany carved door which opened in front of them. Silenced and possibly armor-plated, by its thickness – thought Peter.

At the other end of the wide room, air perfumed with cherry blossom mixed with cigar smoke, there was an equally sumptuous office desk with a throne like chair behind. On the chair, Arche Donovan himself, reading on some papers in front of him and absently puffing from a Cuban cigar, thought Peter, judging by the smell. "Cheap staging" thought Peter and looked at Alma, who answered with an amused look and winked.

- Oh, here you are! – Archie Donovan raised from his desk. Allow me to introduce myself – I am Archie Donovan, Security Director of GERMINA Inc. Welcome to our office in Milwaukee!
- Thank you, Sir! We are a group of medical specialists representing the WHO. My name is Peter Bud, this is Alma Matsumoto, biologist, Dr. Joe Cooper and Dr. Liam Johnson, bacterial biology specialists.
- Glad to meet all of you – answered Donovan, shaking hands with everybody. He then turned to a meeting desk occupying the other half of his office and made a wide gesture around him, at the comfortable chairs around the table. Please be seated!

He grabbed his cigar and a giant metal ashtray, occupying the seat at the head of the table. "Transmitting the message, he is the boss" thought Peter, but managed to smile while Donovan produced a box with cigars and invited them to pick one, but all guests refused.

- Do you mind my smoking? Donovan asked.

– Not at all! – answered Peter. Please excuse us for disturbing you! I was wondering if you can clear for us some aspects able to help us in an epidemiological investigation.

– No problem at all! I only hope I can help you with something! I understand you have already visited our factory and probably that gave you the answer to some of your questions.

– Yes Sir! You see, this infectious disease outbreak we are investigating in Northern Somalia – Somaliland, to be more precise - seems to have been caused by some odd Borrelia strain, using a particular type of mosquito as transmitting vector.

– Northern Somalia? Never had business over there, as far as I remember. Or Africa, for a fact!

– I believe you, but according to our information, GERMINA was dealing, at a certain moment, with similar bacterial material and also studied insect vectoring of some infectious diseases.

– That might be! Please understand that I am dealing only with security problems. Many of the projects GERMINA is working upon are politically and economically sensitive and therefore subject to intellectual property regulations. There is a wide world out there, full of competitors and they are not always loyal. Getting back to our subject, I think you should have this scientific talk, if you didn't do it already, with Professor Hicks. He is our Scientific Director – I can imagine he can better answer all these questions.

– Yes, we talked with him, but we were interested about the incident twenty-five years ago or so, when two of your lab workers died being exposed to such bacteria.

– Oh, so that is the problem! Well, I was a junior security specialist then and frankly to say I do not remember too much.- said Donovan trying to put on a smile, denied by the cold look of his eyes. He rubbed his chin, puffed a little from his cigar, pretending to concentrate and trying to remember:

– At least something is clear, for me! – The two workers did not die because of the bacteria, they actually died from shock induced by multiple insect stings and because of inhaling heavy insecticide mist set off by the security system. There was a crate full of insects that accidentally broke and they were caught without the full equipment which included protective suit and gas masks. The investigation ruled it as accidental death and they bear full responsibility for going inside the depot enclosure unequipped – Donovan said.

"How easy it is to wash your hands, with convenient circumstances explaining the incident" Peter thought. Without betraying his disappointment, he insisted:

- Professor Hicks was kind enough to explain that! But my question for you, as you must be acquainted with and protect all activities of the company, is the following: do you remember of any bacterial products with a more sensitive character having been recently shipped to external beneficiaries, with or without insect vectors?

Donovan listened carefully the question, then puffed again from his cigar and raised eyebrows:

- None that I know of! All our products, types and quantities are mentioned in the books for accountant operation and double-checking. All of them meet the regulated standards and have the approval of interested state agencies.

Peter was taken by surprise when Alma interfered:

- Obviously, Mr. Donovan, we are sure that every product you showed us is fully approved. How about the products you and your Scientific Director, Professor Hicks did not mention?
- What projects do you mean Miss….
- Matsumoto is the name! -spoke Alma with an energetic look on her face and grasping the handles of her chair in a visible effort to contain her anger.
- Yes, Miss Matsumoto, you were asking about other projects. Which projects are you referring to ?

– The ones you are dealing with in the lower level labs – that would be level 5 and 6, I guess.

Donovan was pale in the face, but he tried to control himself, puffing vigorously from his cigar and finally crushing the stump inside the plate size ashtray, next to another one smoked earlier.

– I do not know what you are implying. Perhaps it is better to talk to Professor Hicks once again. I do not think I can further be of help for your visit here! Now if you will excuse me, I have a scheduled meeting to attend to at the County Council! Thank you for coming by! We will be glad to forward all required documents, in proving WHO that we have nothing to do with the unfortunate epidemiological event in Africa. – Donovan pressed an intercom button and spoke: Sheila, our guests are leaving! – and rose behind his desk.
– Thank you, Sir!- answered Peter and they all rose, being escorted by the young blonde secretary out of his office and the building.

Inside the car, Peter asked:

– What was that all about? I thought I asked you to let me do the talking – said Peter with a discontent look on his face.
– Well, I was sick and tired of his bullshit! He was taking us for fools, that's why I got angry!
– You got visibly angry, and now he correctly suspects that we actually know a lot more than we claim. You spooked him and tomorrow's IRS visit is not going to help.
– I think the guy will try to take revenge. I fear some sort of preemptive strike – spoke Liam. It will not be direct! I wonder what he will come up with or he will simply deny everything and let us go emptyhanded.

During this time, Donovan gritted his teeth, biting the tip of a new cigar, which he forgot to light, He suddenly grabbed the phone and dialed a name in the agenda:

–   Hallo Stephen! Glad to hear you! I wanted to tell you something! You are the most stupid moron on the face of the Earth! If your stupidity were painful, morphine would be powerless in your case! You despicable jack-ass, shut the fuck up when I talk to you! What did you tell these tourists?

A short answer came out of the phone and Donovan continued:

–   Nothing my ass! And how the hell did they know we have active labs on the lower floors?

Again, there was answering in the mobile speaker.

–   Fuck! And you fell for the toilet trick! You are indeed stupid! Trust me, this Japanese bitch is poison. She wanted to eat me alive. They will not stop here. I have to think of something to keep them closer in view. What?..... Ok, I have the mobile phone number from the business card. Where do they stay?... Aha, Cambria Hotel. I know I can, I had their telephones tagged. I'll keep an eye on them. You keep your filthy mouth shut, understand? Otherwise you will regret it.

Donovan hung up and he dialed another number, this time on WhatsApp, to avoid some of the detection:

–   Hi, it is me! I know we are going to meet on Sunday! Listen, what the fuck did you do with the cargo in Africa?

A man's voice answered, and Donovan continued:

–   What? If it wasn't you, who the fuck it was?... Who was your beneficiary? ....Ok Ok, don't get hectic, we are not going to go through it over the phone, but I have some problem because of this shit. Some representatives of the WHO are here asking about the bacterial source of an outbreak in Northern Somalia. .... Ok, talk to you on Sunday. If you have something I should know of, keep me posted. For the moment, my official position is "I know nothing about it". No more loose ends, please! – and Donovan hung up again.

Sheila, the blonde young secretary came in and opened her mouth to ask something. Like getting up from a dream, Donovan looked at her with fierce eyes and shouted:

- Get the fuck out of my face! Who told you to come in? Let me think and close the door behind you.

The poor girl choked on her words and turned left-around, running out of the room.

Donovan lit his cigar and he felt he was on to something. He looked at the picture of Elizabeth, scantily clad, almost naked silhouette, placed in the same kitsch frame full of gemstones like the one he had at his GERMINA office. She might finally come to earn the money he spent on her ass. He grabbed the phone and dialed her number:

- Hello darling! – he unwillingly put on an unctuous smile. How are you? ….. Listen, are you busy this afternoon? I want you to come with me to visit some guests at Cambria Hotel around 5. I am taking them out to dine and I feel the need for your company…….What? No - no, they are civilized people, all of the doctors from the WHO, … Then it's all set! I'll meet you outside Cambria at five minutes to five. You know, it's on West Clybourn Avenue crossing N. Plankington. Ok, thanks!

Donovan called in his favored restaurant to make a reservation for six persons and the put on a coat and got out of his office:

- Sheila darling! – he started, reading the surprise in her eyes. I am going out on some business. I want you to do me a favor. Call me up on my mobile at eight p.m. and remind me to come to the office. Now don't worry, I am not going to call you at the office, I just need to pretend I am busy to get out of a boring meeting.

- Sure thing, Mr. Donovan! – was all Sheila could answer, her heart pounding fast.
- Ok, then it's settled! Bye girls! – said Donovan and left the hallway. He needed some fresh air and to relax his nerves. Once in the car, he took out his phone and called the escort company Hicks was using, upon his advice.
- Hi ladies! … Yeah, it's me! I need some relaxation massage. I feel tense!... Ok! I'm on my way to you!

He drove to the known address in the outskirts. He stopped in front of a classic looking villa, parked to the side of the lane and stepped in. A young lady in a spa white gown greeted him and accompanied him to a room on the first floor, where he entered silently. He first picked up the phone and dialed a number:

- Hi Dr. Bud! This is Archie Donovan speaking! You visited me today! I live somehow with the impression that you are dissatisfied with your visit and I felt guilty for not being able to help you more! And for this I take the liberty to invite you and your colleagues to dinner at five pm. I'll have a car waiting for you, so you won't bother about the transportation…..Yes, that's right!... see you at five then at your hotel. Yes, I know, it is Cambria hotel. He closed the phone and looked around.

He saw the massage bench to one side and a jacuzzi tub on the other. He got undressed and when naked, he tied a fresh towel around his waist and laid down on the massage bench.

A gentle oriental music – possibly Indian mantras – was playing in the background and air was saturated with mixed incense and exotic perfume aromas, some of which very penetrant. It took two minutes for him to control himself and switch to relaxation mode.

A female silhouette came from behind a white colored curtain. She was wearing only a towel around her waist, like him, but her visible breast was consistent, elastic and upwards tilted, in a perfect match with her intense tan- possibly natural. Maybe she is Latino -thought Donovan, as he reached with his hand, grabbed one of her nipples and squeezed it until she cried and backed up!

- Sorry – just checking if they are for real – he smiled, but his cold eyes told the different story of his finding pleasure in cruelty. Lots of women use silicon these days!

The girl pretended to ignore the moment and took a special massaging oil that she spread on her hands. She started massaging his feet, slowly going upwards.

Again, he interrupted her by leaning forward. He took her hands and moved them directly to his semi-erected penis. The girl understood his request and started performing a very exquisite hand job on it, with positive response. Donovan enjoyed it for a couple of minutes, then he grabbed her by the hair – she had a pony tail that came in handy – and pushed her face towards his genitals. The girl understood the gesture and slowly started to perform a comprehensive blowjob, while Donovan was getting excited and his erection became complete. At this point, Donovan tore at her towel and plucked it away, leaving her superb body all naked, with a shadow of pubic hair which made her appearance even sexier. She must have been eighteen or even less, with a very fragile appearance, with delicate but superb proportions of her body.

He got up and grabbed her by her loins and pushed her towards a coach to one side of the room. He threw the screaming girl on the coach and rushed between her thighs, penetrating her furiously without any foreplay, while she was still screaming. This bothered him, so he silenced her with a powerful slap in the face, so all she could do was cry her eyes out, unable to make a sound, still noisily gasping for air. The brutal assault on her vagina seemed to last forever – although it took only several minutes – and then Donovan decided he needed more fun. He turned her with the back towards him and stuck his thumb in her asshole, which made her scream with surprise. Once the path was free, he penetrated her anally, with the brutal force of a buffalo, as the girl was screaming again and he had to punch her in the head and pull her by the hair to make her shut up.

After a few minutes of frantic movement to and fro, Donovan felt like needing to cum and after the climax he rested in for a few seconds more, shaking in pleasant agony. Upon withdrawing his penis, he observed some blood drops around the anal orifice of the girl, who fell on one side like a broken toy, sobbing.

He went to the jacuzzi bath tub and stepped in, cleansing his body with fresh soap and water. Without a word, he got dressed and left the room, while the girl was still on the coach, crying.

- Finished Mr Donovan? I hope you feel better now! – the girl at the reception desk smiled.
- Yeah! That was good! Put everything on my bill! – he answered, winking to the receptionist, and stepped out towards his car.

At the Cambria Hotel, the atmosphere was rather tense. The whole team was at a table at the bar discussing the day's outcome.

- Rather odd this Donovan with his invitation! – said Peter. I left the office with the distinctive sensation that he would never wish to see us again.
- That is true! – answered Liam. Actually, he hates our guts. I wonder what made him change his mind about us?
- It's very simple. Guys! – said Alma. He hates us all right, for mingling in his business, but he is probably unsure of what we already know and what we are actually after! So, he wants to keep us close until he finds it out!
- That's correct, sister!- said Joe, holding his cup of steaming black tea.

Liam poured himself another whiskey from the bottle next to him and added, with an amused smile on his face:

- Well, we're just about to find out! Here he comes and he's got company!

All eyes turned to the lobby where Donovan entered accompanied by Elizabeth. He was wearing a cozy brown woolen jacket over comfortable black shirt and black trousers. Elizabeth was stunning in her glittering black dress, with a deep side cleavage and a small fur cloak on her shoulders. She was wearing "simple" pearl jewelry, hanging heavy on her generous breast, which instantly became the target of Joe's and Liam's starring mode. When they reached at the group's table, they smiled – a technical grin from Donovan, displaying his almost too perfect set of teeth, possibly peroxide whitened.

- Good afternoon or is it evening already! – Donovan said. Allow me to introduce to you Elizabeth Walker, and these are our guests from the WHO!
- Hi, I am Dr. Peter Bud, this is Alma Matsumoto, Dr. Joe Cooper and Dr. Liam Johnson.
- Pleased to meet all of you!

Elizabeth smiled to every one and made a longer eye contact with Peter, who felt a bit embarrassed, probably caused by Alma's presence, but most of all, because of Elizabeth's breath - taking appearance and her mind-blowing perfume scent.

- Well, now that we are introduced, how about dinner? The black Mercedes in front is waiting for you. See you when we get there, fox!

Donovan took Elizabeth to his Mercedes Coupe and left with tire screeching acceleration. The rest of the group embarked the 500SEL luxury Mercedes and soon were on their way.

- Where are we going? – asked Peter who was seated in front with the driver.
- Lake park Bistro on Newbury Boulevard! – answered the man with the cap, presently. No more than twenty minutes away from here, considering traffic.
- Okay, thanks! -Peter answered.

- I smell danger! – whispered Alma. Although I was warned! Joe and Liam were the only ones to hear her and smiled.
- One steak cannot do any harm; can't be considered bribe! – said Liam. For other kind of danger I am prepared- he smiled petting his pocket where he kept his Sig-Sauer gun.

Joe made a funny grimace:

- Not that danger, fool! The lady seems dangerous! We'd better tell Peter to be careful. I live with the impression she set eyes on him. Who the hell is she, his wife?
- Nope! No wife acts like that. And he wouldn't expose family, if he had one! Some sort of mistress maybe! One he pays very well and probably a woman of many talents! – observed Alma, biting her lips with worry. There is little we can do about this – she murmured.

They arrived at the restaurant. Donovan's order was absolutely exuberant, thought Peter. They started with Beluga and Champagne, followed by lobster and duck, only to finish with an exquisite steak and divine deserts. Expensive wine started pouring in the glasses, replacing single malt whiskeys – with the exception of Liam Johnson, faithful to his Gentleman Jack.

They were about two hours in the dinning process when Arche Donovan's mobile started ringing, and he answered presently.

- Yeah, that's me!....What the fuck? …..I see! Okay! I'll be there in half an hour!

He turned to the guests:

- My dear guests, fate is unfair! The pleasure of having you around has to be interrupted. I am called with urgent business at the office. Do not worry, nothing wrong happened. Just need to sign some things for tomorrow morning and it cannot wait.
- So sorry to hear this! -Peter said. We are ready to go as well!

Liam and Joe were already rising to stand up.

- Nonsense, my friend. Please do stay and enjoy! Elizabeth, darling, order the best and tell them to put all on my account. Do not forget what I asked you! … And something else, I leave you my car so you can get safely home! I'll take a cab to the office. Besides, I had some drinks, so I would be risking my license.
- Okay! – Elizabeth said and kissed him good-bye as she received keys of the car; he formally pretended not to observe her kiss.

Donovan waived good-by to the group and stepped outside the restaurant towards a yellow cab.

- Now that we are on our own, let us celebrate this meeting! – Elizabeth turned to the waiter and ordered two more bottles of Champagne.
- We are going to regret this! – Alma smiled. It is too much for the evening.
- Nonsense, that will only happen if you go to bed. Hope you are not thinking about sleeping right now, smiled Elizabeth and threw herself on her comfortable chair with a kinky move that made her side cleavage open wide and exposing her perfect pair of legs up to the garters.
- Like I am surrounded by drooling wolves! – mumbled Alma and took an irritated side position to the scene. Eventually, the three men finished staring at Elizabeth's legs and continued the conversation, Alma keeping quiet.

Meanwhile, Elizabeth was pouring Champagne glass after glass, and by desert she was visibly affected, finding it troublesome to spell complicated words and avoiding to stand up, even if that meant giving up on her regular visits to the smoking booth. Liam and Joe seemed pleased to conversate with her, enjoying her direct addressing style and uncensored language, which seemed to conveniently dodge political correctness. Peter was quitter and looked a bit worried, barely touching wine, and Alma was also quiet, looking at him from time to time, and watching Elizabeth's glittering performance in general.

- Have you been working with this team for a long time? - Elizabeth asked Alma, directly.
- Not so long! We have been recently cooperating on various projects! – answered Alma cautiously.
- So, you have not decided on any of the boys! – concluded Elizabeth, with a cheeky attitude and a somewhat glued tongue.

Alma smiled. Joe, who was witnessing the dialogue with the others, interfered:

- I am married, so you can rule me out! – he laughed loud, betraying a dangerous level of Champagne uptake.
- Why, married men are the safest kind! – answered Elizabeth and she gently caressed Joe's cheek, giving him shivers up his spine. All he could do to respond was a silly smile all over his face.

The situation was rather sensitive – thought Alma. Elizabeth was getting wasted visibly, but she was acting as host and still ruled. It was hard to confront her on anything. They finally finished dinner deserts and Peter agreed with his colleagues it was time to go. The exuberant Elizabeth managed to sort out the payment formalities and then she took an evasive path towards the restaurant entrance. At the door, they were pleased to find out that the Mercedes car was parked upfront. Elizabeth took a few wobbling steps towards Peter, grabbed his lapels and spoke to him facing him at 10 inches distance, forcing him to inhale her alcohol breath, in a kinky mix up with her perfume and her body sweet odor:

- Peter darling, I am embarrassed to admit I over did it with Champagne tonight. Must be your enchanting charisma and your lovely colleagues' entourage! But I do not feel able to drive my car properly, and I would not like to leave it here, 'cause Archie would get very upset. Maybe not about the car, as much as about my over-drinking. I noticed you drank very little wine, if any. Can you do me the favor to drive me home,and our company car will come for you, after the driver takes you colleagues to the hotel. I am sure your colleagues won't mind a half hour delay!

Peter was surprised but managed to smile politely and, after looking to the others (Liam and Joe wearing some greasy smiles on their faces, while Alma displayed a worried one), nodded and said:

–   Of course, Miss Elizabeth! Allow me to thank you for the wonderful dinner, in my name and for my colleagues as well!
–   Nonsense! – a small hick-up shook Elizabeth's shoulders. So, you will return presently. Meanwhile, our car will take you to the hotel. She spoke to the driver: Take them to the Cambria Downtown where you picked them up, then come to my place and wait. Let me know when you get there.

As they boarded the Mercedes, Alma said loud enough for Liam and Joe to hear:

–   I must confess I didn't see that coming! – as she was starring at the empty boulevard ahead.
–   That's all right, sister! – Liam answered, careful to spell word correctly. Peter is a grown - up boy, he can take care of himself!

Meanwhile, the Mercedes Coupe was slowly making its way to the streets, Elizabeth directing the way towards her home, as Peter was trying to drive as cautiously as possible, to avoid being stopped by local Police. His moderate attitude paid off as a police car was parked on the side, beacons glowing, but nobody stopped them. Probably they were waiting for someone else – thought Peter, slowly passing past the standing by police crew.

–   What's the matter? Scared? – Elizabeth asked. Don't worry, you are with me! Nobody is going to harm you!

Was it just an impression? -, or Elizabeth was already sobering up, because Peter observed she was no longer hesitating in her speech. He ignored the thought, but soon he had to admit that something must have happened – Elizabeth took out a cigarette case and a lighter from her purse, and her precise movements were no anymore the ones of a hesitating drunk person, but those of a sober and a bit nervous person.

–   Stop here! Park the car in that area, next to the fence! -Elizabeth said, with a firm voice and unrecognizable sobriety.
–   Okay! – and Peter parked the car where instructed. He then turned to her and said:
–   Okay! Thanks again for the invitation! I'll be on my way now!
–   Nonsense! Besides, the company car did not arrive yet! I guess you have enough time to join me for a cup of late coffee?
–   I don't know, I do not want to be late. My colleagues are waiting for me and besides, what will Mr. Donovan say if I join you in this late coffee meeting?
–   Mr. Donovan can go fuck himself – observed Elizabeth without batting an eyelid. He is not my husband or my boss. I am a free woman and I am used to do whatever I please!
–   That sounds familiar ! – smiled Peter. However,…
–   What's the matter, are you afraid of me ? or you are afraid of your Japanese girlfriend?

Peter closed his eyes and reassessed the situation, which was getting very complicated at the moment. He decided to play things cool.

–   No! – he answered. I am not afraid of anyone, and she is not my girlfriend, but, on the other side, I do not know you any better!
–   And wouldn't you like to know me better, my dear? she whispered, grabbing his hand and pulling him towards the entrance to her building. They took a short walk to the apartment door, she opened it and then invited him in. She turned the light on, then set on a musical tool providing a soft blues program, to upgrade

the ambient. She then took his hand and placed it on her breast at heart level.

- See, Peter, that is an honest beating heart, and you will probably understand that only later, if you cannot realize it now. I do not blame you, and you shouldn't blame me! I just felt attracted to you in a way I have never been before. I feel I can trust you with my life, and that is not something I commonly share with the dozens of men I've been with!- she admitted with a smile.
- Should I feel privileged to be an exception, then? – smiled Peter, who finally decided to join the game and see where it was leading to.
- My dear Peter, in spite of your impression, I can judge men better than most women, because I always felt free to test them, all dozens of them, as I said.
- So, you decided now you need my name on the list? – Peter was a little upset with her presumptuous allegation.
- I decided your name on the list could be a precious rarity, and I can't place it there unless you accept it! I still have some pride left, you see!

She grabbed him by the backbone and forced her way up in kissing him possessively, but with the elegance demanded by her physical appearance. The kiss was as divine as it could be – thought Peter, still being unable to compare it to Alma's. It was a totally different sensation, and her perfume was so mesmerizing and bringing him to another unexplored universe.

- You will not be sorry for trusting me! - she said, starting to unbutton his jacket, then turned to one side and went to a little bar-table in the room.
- This meeting calls for a celebration! I want you to join me! – she said extracting a bottle of first- class Hennessy Cognac that she poured in two fat glasses.
- Here's to happiness! May it happen, if it exists! – she cheered and stroke his glass, gulping half of the content of hers, then touching his lips with a phantom kiss.

- What will Mr. Donovan say about this? – asked Peter, a little embarrassed by this direct attack.

Elizabeth sat down on the armchair with a tired smile:

- Mr. Donovan doesn't know or care about my life. He doesn't own me and I hereby confess I do not love him. I am conveniently using his money to have the good life I am used to, as he conveniently uses me and my body, but only as much as I allow him to. I don't know how long this will last, but for now, because of reasons I might tell you later, I am stuck with him. It was his idea of having you lured into this approach, but I am glad to do it once I know you. I mean he doesn't have to ask me, and consequently cannot stop me either.

Elizabeth smiled sweetly this time and turned to him with a fresher, radiantly vivid and sober look in her eyes.

- Otherwise, I would like to take you on a deserted island, and stare every day into your deep green eyes. Did I mention I would fuck you every day and night, exactly the way I am going to do it now?

Peter barely wet his lips in the booze and nervously waited for the follow up. He did manage though, to put on a smile. What if all this was just a hoax? Ok, but why would she unveil the corruptive plan, then? She started unbuttoning his shirt and released her fur cloak. Then she made a wide move which removed her black dress entirely, leaving her bra barely harnessing her generous breast and her black panties, stockings and garters being left in place, for the moment, but so inviting for a total tear- off.

She grabbed him by the neck and gently, but hungrily started to kiss him, until Peter started to gradually and visibly melt. When he became more obedient, she pushed him towards the sofa nearby and threw herself there on top of him, still suffocating him with a complicated kiss.

- You are so sweet and I like being with you!
- Maybe you can find for me that special place in your agenda! – whispered Peter, smiling.
- You are already on the cover, silly! – Elizabeth answered, pushing her way down his waist and undoing his belt.

Peter took over and removed with an expert move the back locker of her bra, rendering her breast free, allowing it to burst out of its "cage" into a consistent and charming cheeky shape, which definitely made her look divinely sexy. She smiled when freed from the bra and took advantage of the moment, burying his face between her tits, digging it out only to cover his mouth with wet kisses, to which Peter, to his amazement, responded happily.

The rest of the clothes went down, as well as her panties, showing her pubic hair as a discrete triangle of love and working her way down to his genitals. She grabbed his penis and started working it with an expert handling, and after a few seconds she started using her mouth in a way that tormented Peter. He was solid up when she made a break, then she sneaked under him and opened legs wide apart, her inviting split pink being an image hard to resist. He reached for it and felt it silky and wet. He went down and grabbed it gently with his teeth, kissing his way up and down until she started moaning louder. Peter let go and complied with the call of nature – he followed her lead and penetrated her vigorously, still trying not to hurt her, but she seemed to enjoy a bit of a rough play. After some time, not accounted for, both being covered in sweat, she grabbed him by the waist and turned him over, facing up. She climbed on top of him, riding him and impaling herself with his penis as deep as she could, moaning with satisfaction:

- Oh, baby! That's the way I like it! Push it hard and deep! Yeah! and she kept on moaning. You silly, I feel it up to my throat! Come on, I just want to see how it feels to be impaled by Dracula! She said, while shaking wildly on top of him, like he was a rodeo bull.

Peter was totally mesmerized by her riding talent, as she would lean all over him from time to time, to kiss him and rub her consistent breast with stingy nipples against his chest, in a recurring movement that drove him crazy and left him speechless.

Then she suddenly unmounted, turned with the back towards him and waited until he penetrated her again, this time from behind. Elizabeth seemed to enjoy the ride, as her moaning was getting louder, and for Peter was just another amazing experience, having her perfectly round but, banging gently and repeatedly against his belly, while he was working on her. Things were getting hotter when she suddenly stopped, and without changing her position, she grabbed his erect penis with a soft hand and brought it just outside her ass hole. She spit her right palm and wet her perineal area around it evenly.

- Are you sure? – asked Peter.
- Don't stop now, please!- was all she could say, as Peter gently pushed his way in. He didn't expect to get this intimate with Elizabeth, but she was really divine and it would have taken an army to stop him now.

The initial sphincter resistance dissipated and, as he went deeper inside her, he reached to a wider and softer space, where his penis seemed to grow larger and roamed freely or that was his impression. This was the ultimate union between him and this unknown woman. who was surrendering to him entirely, for reasons unknown, with surprising passion and honesty. He was unable to detect any fake gesture so far. He postponed his analytic thoughts for the end of action, as he was getting carried away. Their effort increased, until close to the end. When Elizabeth felt he was almost ready to cum, she moved from under him, came forward and grabbed his penis with her hands and mouth, sucking it loudly and powerfully until he released his cum with a moan. She then completely collected it in her mouth, opened it to show him the white creamy result and swallowed the whole lot, with a satisfied smile on her face.

Peter crushed on the sofa, all beat with effort and sweat. Elizabeth was gasping next to him and still moaning gently.

- I feel I'd like to have a baby with you! – she suddenly said…. Hey, don't get scared! It's not really going to happen, it's just that when a woman trusts a man so much as to wish having a baby with him - well, that is something! – she continued sipping on her cognac and lighting a cigarette.
- I'm glad you think it this way! You are a wonderful woman, but I didn't have the time to think of you as most likely to become a mother, much less the mother of my kids. ….Maybe I sound superficial or misogynistic! …..It's not that you could not become a mother, I'm sure that you could! …..What I'm trying to say is that I haven't seriously considered it – I mean having a baby in general - and I am definitely not prepared for that, yet! – said Peter, catching his breath. And he continued:
- Well, anyway, I wouldn't know you as a mother, but as a lover, you are absolutely divine! I think this was the best love making I got in years, if ever! When you get some experience, you can tell a heartfelt fuck from cheap sex! – said Peter, smiling.
- That's why you must appreciate the exception! When I say I feel like I would like having a baby with you – which is most likely never going to happen – that fucking means I feel like I can trust you with my life.
- You can trust me, Elizabeth! Peter rose his head and stared at her blue–grey eyes You can be sure now you can trust me! I will not let you down, although we will be just acquainted, I guess.
- Let karma decide on it!- smiled Elizabeth. And, for the record, I did not fake my orgasm with you this time! I really enjoyed fucking you! I feel you as being my soul mate, or better said my kindred spirit!
- And I did, too! ….. Maybe it is better to leave it at the level of soul crossing! …I think it is time for me to go! – he said, trying to raise from the bed. Elizabeth pushed him back dominantly.
- Yeah, sure! But not before I'm done with you!... No, silly!- she said smiling, I don't want to fuck you again, although I feel very

much tempted to. I don't know when I will get another honest fuck like yours, anytime soon! Even if I repeat myself and excuse the tautology, it was fucking good, but now we need to talk, and trust me, you won't be sorry about that, either!

- I am here for you, said Peter, placing his arms in a large embrace, which she enjoyed childishly.
- Well, let me go to the bathroom first and you get dressed! Pour us another cognac and I'll make coffee too! I'll tell you the story of my life. It starts dull, but this last chapter is most interesting.

The next morning, Peter was the last for breakfast, to his regret. Joe and Liam had a wide smile all painted on their face, Alma was having a sour attitude, although polite.

- Hi guys!
- Good day,boss! – observed Liam. Morning is already gone.
- So, what's new?
- Oh, nothing much! – answered Alma. The IRS went this morning to investigate GERMINA; they are checking them as we speak. I sure hope Mr. Donovan is not so cheerful now.
- Mr. Donovan! – exclaimed Peter. He is got a lot to worry about, trust me!- he said enigmatically. Do you have info on the other investigation from your people?
- I think they're on to it, but they will wait for some preliminary results from the IRS to have a reason to barge in. How was your evening, did you manage to get your princess to her castle in one piece? I hope you were not attacked on the way!
- Unless the princess herself attacked him – observed Joe sipping on his coffee. "It's good to be the dragon" – said he, mocking the "It's good to be the king!" expression of Mel Brooks in 'History of the world".
- Hey, cut that out! Yes, she got home all right and I found out interesting things from her, some of which I need to check if they are true. Trust me, I am on it!
- Yeah, I bet you were on her, too! If it wasn't the other way around! – charged Liam, smiling! And everybody laughed.

They all relaxed, and Liam added:

- I don't blame you! I was poisoned too! You could have sent me! I would have gladly sacrificed.myself to protect you! – charged Liam. It would have been a pleasant death for a hero!
- Cool! Now let us get serious! I spoke home and we are supposed to go back to Africa, in light of new evidence.
- What new evidence? – asked Liam, serious all of a sudden.
- Something about the disease! They successfully lab-tested the germ and there is scientific proof it was "engineered" to become more invasive and more toxic.
- So what Donovan told us about the death of his lab workers was a lie, wasn't it" – asked Alma.
- You bet, sister! – answered Joe. The man is a professional liar.
- I wouldn't' take that for grunted, but it very much looks like it or maybe it was a mix-up. Remember, we have no solid evidence yet – answered Peter. Let us see the result of the other investigations. By the way, preliminary tests on the metallic moor debris show they were stained with a powerful anesthetic. Maybe they were insect boxes where they kept sleeping mosquitoes.
- You have no idea how close to the truth you could be! Dormant insects wake up and start biting in new location. Scary! I think we should keep a low profile now – said Liam
- Indeed, we do not want to push them into connecting us with the other investigations they pass through! – completed Alma. At least, not immediately!
- That is a wise thing to do! So, we are leaving tonight! I found a connection via Dubai, but I have to call them up and confirm the three passengers!
- You mean the four passengers! – Alma said with a dry voice.
- Oops! – Joe smiled. Check mate! Atta girl, Alma!.... Sure, you come with us! – and he started laughing like a child.
- That was not in our plan! – said Peter. We are going to encounter adverse circumstances, potential danger and harmful situations. Even if Yves and Jason will join us there, we cannot afford to

babysit anybody! – Peter burst in a rough response, without thinking twice.

- Dr. Bud! If you imply someone has to babysit me, you are dead wrong! – Alma was dead serious and not smiling. I can assure you that I am fit for the occasion and all I have to do is make a phone call and they will inform about my departure. Alternatively, I can make one to ask them to provide you with my assignment paper as special envoy to Africa and there's nothing you can do about it. Your call, mister! – smiled Alma.
- Uppercut and knock-out in the first round! – interfered Liam. I vote for Alma to be on our team! I already have a feeling we won't regret it! Alma, you are welcome to join us!
- Then it is settled!- Joe smiled like a carved Halloween pumpkin lantern. All right Alma, go pack your bags.

Peter smiled.

- All right! I enjoy the idea of your coming with us too, but I am just worried that something might happen to you, that's all!
- I am a big girl now! I can take care of myself, trust me! – smiled Alma. ...Ok. I return the rental car and we meet in two hours in the lobby.
- You heard the lady! Let's go! -said Liam.

They grabbed a taxi for the airport. Peter used his time to make phone calls, including one to Major Bashir, asking for visas. To his surprise, Major Bashir confirmed Somaliland visas were grunted all right, even for Miss Matsumoto. Henry Sutton – thought Peter and smiled. He always knew what would happen ahead of others. He called Sutton as well, but the answering machine came back. Instead, he got a message on WhatsApp.

- Guys, things are warming up! I was informed that my friend Henry Sutton is coming here! It sure looks like this business is just the tip of a much greater iceberg and our inquiry opened a

Pandora's box. They will pick up the investigation from where we left - he said, turning to Alma.
- Yes, I was informed as well! Let us hope they will break the iceberg!

In the same time, Archie Donovan was steaming like a tea kettle forgotten on the stove. He took all necessary measures to soften the impact of the WHO visit, and surely Elizabeth did have a massive influence on the team leader, as far as he understood. Besides, they were leaving, but the freakin coincidence was that the IRS decided – out of the blue – to inspect them, and they were on to their most sensitive part, the exports. Upon being informed about the inspection, he used the early morning to take care with Dave of all sensitive files, making exported quantities match money and paid taxes and all sort of accessory accountant cover up. Of course, it was not his job, but the CEO was not aware of all his maneuvers and might have reacted inappropriately if there were problems.

Suddenly, he had a thought! What if this check up from the WHO, followed by the IRS are not really random, but somehow related! Nah, he thought! Maybe he was getting paranoid! Still, he was not the man to trust coincidence, and he promised himself to stay aware, no matter what.

Later that day he got the unpleasant news that IRS inspector have found some "inaccuracies" in their financial declaration of exports and they are still registered with some missing export merchandise for which GERMINA never got the money in its bank account. The best excuse would have been material error -highly unlikely, with computer cross-checking - or the alternative idea that those sensitive materials were stolen, which was even worse, likely to open a cascade of investigation missions from police, FBI and various agencies, all on their ass. He asked for a 24- hours- time to verify the issues, and he ordered Dave to work overtime and try to "debunk" the errors. Dave was supposed to get a lot of money if he pulled things out credibly, and he sparred no sweat and put all his talent to it.

The next day, when Donovan was hoping to solve the problem, he learned it had only gotten worse. The General Manager called him personally and said:

- Hi Archie! I heard you had some shit happening in your sector! First the WHO delegation, then the IRS. I've got more bad news, even! The FBI and NSA called me and asked me to see you about suspicion of illegal exports! What the fuck, Archie? Are we doing such things behind my back? Trying to put me in jail or what?
- Nonsense, boss! Some mismatching between exported and invoice declared quantities! Dave is working to clarify things as we speak. I'm on it! Don't worry! I'll keep you informed!
- Well if you say so, I feel much better! I am not in a mood for such adventures, Archie! Besides, they are not welcome to stain my image before retirement! Better make things right so we can go on with our lives, like usual! Otherwise, we may need some drastic measures, and someone will have to take responsibility and we'll have his head chopped off and fry for it! Bye for now! – and he hung up.
- Good bye, mother fucker! …. You stupid good-for-nothing bald moron! Adventures? You constipated jackass! Even shedding a solid poop is an adventure for you, filthy ox! – Archie was having a burst of loud monologue. This bastard is going to ruin all my plans! He picked up one of his favorite cigars and cut its end. He lit the cigar and tried to calm down, but he was still too nervous to react properly. He started puffing from his cigar, and this sort of calmed him down a bit. Intercom beeped.
- Yes Sheila! What is it!
- Sorry to bother you Sir. There is a request of an appointment that I registered for Monday. A Mr. Davies from the FBI, Mr. Hughes from the NSA and a Mr. Sutton from the UK Scotland Yard, would like you to receive them on important business.
- Shit! Fuck! … Okay Sheila! When exactly?
- They said they can be here on Monday at noon.
- Okay, set the meeting for Monday, twelve o'clock. And Sheila, did you talk to the CEO?

– No, Sir. The request came to his e-mail address and he forwarded
  it to me without any comment. Anything else, Sir?
– No, Sheila, Thanks!
– Very good Sir! Thank you! – and the intercom muted.

Now that was too much, thought Archie. First WHO, then IRS
and story goes on with the FBI, NSA and God only knows what
fucking international agency. Something was going terribly wrong
and someone was on to them, that was clear. But who? And why?
That looked very much like an inside triggered job. Hey – he thought
– wait a minute! The first to be interested in the missing merchandise
was Steven, when he poked his long nose in the depot archives and
export situations. He remembered Elizabeth saying something about
Stephen being interested in export quantities. Yes! Which means
Hicks was singing like a bird! However, he thought, giving this to
authorities was a suicidal gesture for Hicks, as he was the scientific
author of all the bad stuff! But what if the yellow rat had already
negotiated his way out? Meaning the "give us Donovan's head on
a silver plate, and you can go free!" kind of deal. After all, he knew
only too well how hysterical Hicks was becoming whenever and if
his career was at stake! He should have replaced the old vulture years
ago – he thought.

In a gesture of nervous defiance, Archie swept all things on his
table, coffee mug included, as well as Elizabeth's framed portrait. It
fell down with its back upwards, and the coffee mug spilled all the
remaining coffee on it.

Archie was stun, holding his head with his hands and observing
how his lifetime effort was about to be ruined in a couple of hours by
a bunch of morons.

He tried to calm down and started to pick up the things he threw
on the floor. When he got to Elizabeth's picture, he observed that the
back - cardboard cover of the frame became unstuck and was coming
off, displaying a short hair size metal wire. He took the frame closer
and pulled by the wire, which went deeper under the cardboard.
With a black premonition in his heart, he tore the whole cardboard
cover and a small electronic device appeared at the end of the wire.

He checked the circuit and, with his expertise, he realized it must have been some type of radio transmitter. He then turned the frame and depicted two odd looking gems, one of which was actually a microphone and in the middle of the second one - a blue Lapis Lazuli bigger stone - there was the millimetric objective of a miniature camera. He immediately remembered he had a similar one at the factory. With great difficulty, he resisted the immediate temptation to destroy the surveillance equipment. He tried to mount back the cardboard and put the frame on the desk, as if nothing has happened, hoping the guys at the other end will not realize his discovery.

He leaned back in his armchair, combing his hair with both hands. So, Hicks was a traitor, and Elizabeth, too. But why would Elizabeth blame Hicks in front of him, or even incriminate him? Clearly, they were not working for the same entity. So, there was more than one agency on his ass. And he still had to do a delivery the next day, or he would lose half a million, which was inconceivable. He grabbed his phone and dialed for Elizabeth, but the answering machine confirmed she wasn't close to the telephone. He left a message "Hi darling, I wanted to take you for lunch at two pm. We meet at the Bistro, as usual". Then, there was the problem with Hicks. He could not believe a nerd like Hicks could betray him. After all, in his case there was no direct evidence as he unfortunately had about Elisabeth. He decided to check how deep was Hicks involved in this.

But the next annoying question was, what will he do about Elizabeth? The most elegant way was to ditch her. Full stop. The "thrill is gone" as the song says. But doing it all of a sudden, under the circumstances, will show he is scared and will give his followers the information he became aware of being under surveillance. He must play on the role for some time, but that was depending on what the tomorrow's delegation wanted from him. It would be so stupid of him to blow his last shipment and loose the cash. He could quit anyway after. He decided that all he needed was the next day in office, because the day after he would be in Mexico, spending money on tequila and Latino mamacitas with hard tits and tight pussies.

He tried to relax a little, but he was overwhelmed by novelty and felt the need to clear his mind. He went to the giant globe in the corner, which was in fact a hidden bar, opened it, and extracted a bottle of Beluga Vodka, from which he poured generously in a water glass. He took a few gulps without thinking and then sat down, trying to act normally – after all, he was on line full time, he thought, main actor in the movie. He could not resist and even smiled "accidentally" towards the miniature camera in the picture frame.

In the same time, somewhere in the outskirts of Milwaukee, the elder grey- haired man watched the monitors - with a nervous Archie Donovan in full act – and called loudly:

– Billy, come over here! …

The person called Billy rushed to the room, just in time to see some disturbance followed by a distinct image of Archie Donovan exposing his grin to the camera,

– I think our cover has been blown! The moron somehow figured out he is tapped! Better inform our agent about this and tell her to bale out! We can send a recovery team there in thirty minutes.
– Yes Sir! Right away Sir, said the one named Billy, already dialing a number.

Beyond waterfall

Elizabeth was starring at the phone, experiencing a temporary paralysis. She learned about the message Billy posted and also the one received from Archie. Too close to lead to misinterpretation. The next few minutes she had to make a life saving decision. And she did! She phoned to the airport:

– Hi! I want to reserve a flight to Canada! First plane available! …. Aham!…. Okay! Register for Elizabeth Walker. Yes, I can be there in one hour!

The doorbell rang and Elizabeth froze. She did not expect anybody under the circumstances and she feared for the worst. Her car was in the parking lot, so she could not pretend she was away. She answered the intercom:

- Yes!
- Hi Honey! Did you get my message? I reserved lunch! Coming? I'll wait for you downstairs! – the voice of Archie Donovan was hard to mistake.
- PS – he added. Every time I look at your picture makes me missing you more!

Upon listening to the message, Elizabeth was frozen with despair! She called Billy's number, with no immediate response! When the robot beeped, she said: "Hi Billy! I am being abducted! I can't make it to the airport! I will try to improvise! If something bad happens, avenge me! Trace my phone!" and then she took her purse and went downstairs, where Donovan was waiting for her smiling.

Meanwhile Peter was in his plane to Dubai. His thoughts were split between Sutton, who was supposed to take over the investigation on GERMINA, with his American colleagues, of course, and Elizabeth. A woman of voracious sexual conduct, but with an incredibly gentle and pure soul. And incredibly sexy, as he felt a thrill in his lower abdomen while remembering his experience with her. He was worried about her, as he had reasons to believe she was not mixed in Donovan's businesses, but expected him to react violently, if offended or exposed. He decided to contact her on arrival in Dubai. Nothing could be read on his face, as he was leaning back in his chair, next to Alma, pretending to be asleep. Sutton had been informed about each of their steps and Peter was convinced about one thing: if anyone strong enough could ever hope to nail a big player like Donovan, that would be Henry Sutton. He was a little concerned about the beneficiaries Donovan worked for, and from whom he has probably got large amounts of money, help and influence. Those were bound to react somehow if Donovan was nailed, but he hopped Sutton had the proper approach for that.

- What are you thinking about? – said Alma, also pretending to be asleep, but far from being good at it.
- Oh, nothing! Just trying to get some rest! – lied Peter.
- Was she that good? – asked Alma, opening her light green-hazel eyes on him with interest, and a large smile.
- Good? Who? Oh, come on! Are you still obsessed with that lady? – answered Peter, pretending to be upset. What is it? Jealous already?
- Oh, nonsense! You've got to prove worthy of that, first! If I were really jealous, I would kill for you! Or you! Right now, I am preoccupied of your wellbeing, as my business associate.
- Let me tell you something Alma! The woman is not mingled in Donovan's business. On the contrary, I might say! She is no danger to us!
- I knew this! I guess I knew it before you did! I was informed she was no danger to us before we even met her, but I feared she might become a liability for you. Danger is not only about explosives and weapons; there are softer and more deceptive ways of setting events in a desired direction – and that may not always be the good direction! – she smiled. I guess I was afraid she might try this game with you, even if meant only using you to cover herself up!

Peter smiled – "You have no idea, sister!" he thought. Instead, he reached out for her hand and he held it dearly to his chest. Alma pretended to ignore the gesture, but complied and kept on "sleeping".

In the cloudy Friday afternoon, Henry Sutton was in a meeting with FBI and NSA partners. They were discussing all sorts of legal administrative measures on GERMINA, short of a direct, decisive confrontation. They already had received the IRS report on alleged differences between production of sensitive material (like mirror bacteria concentrate, carrier insect colonies, etc.) and deposit registers.

Part of this sensitive material was obviously missing and it was not registered as exported, and no money cashed for any national sale.

- I am afraid that they will try to dodge, and at least try to stall any official paper request and answer. But if we go there, we put pressure on them, and that might make them snap.
- Yes, maybe! But if we are wrong, and it is proven a simple case of material error, we get to the newspapers as oppressors of the private economical sector! Someone will demand our asses and they will get them and we'll be screwed! And what's worse, they win big time and can carry on their fishy business.
- Come on, lads!- Sutton insisted. We know there's no bloody material error! Think of what you can achieve with 1 kilogram of bacteria concentrated sludge. If it is poisonous and you place it in a water source, you can poison an entire city! So, you see, a few kilograms can be very significant, when we talk sensitive stuff!
- What do you suggest, Mr. Sutton? – a bold serious character from NSA asked.
- I say we bloody go over them, asking unpleasant questions, and see what we can harvest! It is like drilling a volcano caldera instead of waiting for it to erupt. In such cases, we can even divert the lava path where we want and minimize destruction!
- It is important we keep track of all factors – continued the NSA man.
- I totally agree with that! We kept a close connection with our partners in Somaliland, and as far as I know, they also sent an independent investigation team here, in the US, and we've been sharing with them all relevant information.
- Yes, we have monitored their coming here! Are you aware of any action from their part that we don't know about?
- None so far, according to our information, and I think you can agree on that. We'll try to contact them to see what they are up to.

Donovan was hyperactive. He had taken Elizabeth from home and took her to a remote restaurant in the outskirts. Wednesday was a regular day for having lunch together, so there would not be any suspicion.

Following lunch, they stopped in a parking, him pretending he had an urgent need for a leak.

Elizabeth saw her chance to smoke a cigarette, seated on a bench nearby, and was texting on her phone, totally unaware of Donovan's coming from behind. He got out his silencer pistol and executed her brutally with a bullet in the back of the head, like Nazis used to do on Russian prisoners. The entrance hole was decent, but the exiting bullet took off half of her forehead and a consistent lump of her brain. He dragged her corpse in the bushes behind the parking lot, smashed her phone, then cleaned himself and then drove back. He hoped to get a few hours before the owners of the microphone and camera would come in searching for Elizabeth. Meanwhile, he had to complete his deal in the parking of the Bistro restaurant and then go to Mexico with the first available flight. He had just about enough time to pass by the office and take the metal recipients with the bacterial spores he wanted to smuggle.

There was one last thing he needed to do - he was already sure of Hicks' treason and his only thought was how to nail the bastard.

He grabbed the phone and called Stephen.

- Hi Stephen! ... How are you?.. Fine, fine, thanks! Listen, Halloween is coming! I thought about you being alone at home in this chilly weather. I took the liberty of inviting a very talented young lady to your place in about one hour. Hey, trust me, I tested her! She's dynamite!... What? You already have a guest? Doesn't matter, another one will keep you young. Come on, Stephen, this is not a gift to refuse! Besides, I will pay the bill for both of them! – added Donovan the overwhelming argument. Ok, she will come at around five pm.

He knew Stephen would agree, especially if such treat came for free, and hung up. He revised his route and headed for the western exit, to get just in time to Stephen's villa. Meanwhile, he made a lot of calls, some of which international. He got there when almost dark, putting car lights out on the last hundred yards. He saw with satisfaction that lights were on everywhere, including the greenhouse area, where Stephen had his jacuzzi tub and there was a back entrance which Hicks would always leave open, just in case. Donovan stepped out from the car, went to the front door and rang the bell.

The next morning, Sutton went to the breakfast hall of his American hotel and was enjoying his boiled egg with a piece of ham and guacamole, when Frank Davies of the FBI and Edmond Hughes of the NSA came to his table with troubled faces. As Sutton insisted, they mechanically grabbed a cup of coffee and sat next to him.

- Hi lads! Where's the fire? – asked Sutton smiling.
- Oh, it's a total mess over there! Sutton, finish your coffee, and you'll come with us. The pile of crap just got bigger!

Henry took one last gulp from his mug, grabbed his coat and said:

- Ok guys! Let's go! Hope it is something that is worth rushing my digestion like this!
- Oh, you bet! You'll get constipated when you see all of it! Let's go! Car is waiting outside.

They went west until they reached a quite compact neighborhood of villas and small farm -like buildings, car parking outside Stephen Hicks's house.

- Excuse me Sir! – one FBI agent came rushing to their car. He came near his boss and gave him a piece of paper, that the man presently read, the he got his face between his palms.
- What? – the NSA man asked.
- Our agent "Angel" has been compromised three days ago. She was supposed to pull off and relocate to Canada immediately. Our shadowing agent lost her and she missed the booked flight. We couldn't contact her for the last two days and now she was

found dead. She was shot in the back of the head, in a parking lot outside the city, about three days ago. According to witnesses, the likely suspect is Director Donovan of GERMINA Inc., her so-called fiancée and I'll bet this wasn't a case of blind jealousy.

– Oh my God! – Sutton borrowed his face in his hands. I told you these guys are evil! One more reason to squeeze them hard like with dry lemons!

– I think I can consider this a proof for our now justified suspicions. Let's get on with it! – suggested the FBI representative. No need to wait till Monday, we go in now!

Everybody agreed. Sutton was aware about Peter meeting Elizabeth, however, short of the profound degree of their personal involvement. He was thinking it would be useful to inform Peter of this game changing move, so he texted him a message. Peter was supposed to receive the message while already in Somaliland. The strange thing was he saw no reception confirmation for his WhatsApp message – maybe he was flying or the bad connection in Somaliland could be the reason, so he didn't think too much about it.

They finally arrived at the entrance of Hicks' house, where a yellow belt labeled "Police line; do not cross" was placed and circled the whole building and courtyard. They went to the door and they saw that someone has taken a shot through the door visor. Inside, a very dead Stephen Hicks laid on one side, half naked with a nasty shot entrance wound in his right rye, the bullet probably still resting in his brain.

– Must have been someone who knew he is going to check the incoming guest through the visor! The device slowed down the bullet, and there is no exit wound, that is why I think it is still in his head! – said Sutton, and everybody agreed.

Stephen's body was already starting to decompose, and the eroded margins of his uncovered left ear proved that his hungry tomcat, Bruce, left for three days without food, tried to get a taste of his owner, literally.

\- That is not the only surprise! – said Davies. Follow me!

He made his way through the living room, where some rotten food leftovers smelled bad in a bowl -possibly some salad – thought Sutton, or else the cat would have eaten it. They went pass a small lobby area towards the greenhouse, where the jacuzzi bath still worked, in a terrible display of bodily fluid foam. In the water, half afloat was the body of a young lady, later identified as Stacey, the niece of the local escort company managing madame. Stacey's body was decomposing even faster, the action of warm water and bubbles literally shading the skin off her body until she looked like a hideous human écorché, with wide open, but opacified eyes, and lipless opened mouth, tongue sticking out because of hyperhydration. Verdict – one shot in the base of the skull, part of her brain contributing to the warm soup the jacuzzi bath was cooking, feces and urine from spontaneous release included. The whole body had the appearance of boiled ham and was not a pretty image to see. Later on, her colleagues remembered how Stacy volunteered to replace Lila on the fatal call. When the story was out the next day and after having the usual police statement, Lila signed off, went home, took her daughter and left for a long drive to California, never to be seen again there.

Davies called the center and said:

\- I want backup at the following address. I am going to operate arrest at the downtown office of GERMINA Inc. at the following address – and he sent them location. He continued: Okay guys! Let's go nail him! I'll bet it is Donovan's hand here too! He must have felt betrayed! I told you that cornering them with investigations will make them do mistakes, but I didn't think of anything like this! This is carnage, as if he wants to take revenge on the entire world. I wonder if we will find him!

They got back to the car and left for the downtown office. When they got there everything was quiet. Nobody in view, as it was Saturday morning. Davies was forced to call on Sheila – whose number was available – to ask her to come over and open up the facility, as he hated to destroy doors, even if he had a warrant.

Sheila came within fifteen minutes and opened up. They went upstairs, Davies examining Donovan's door, but nothing proved any trespassing. Donovan's office was not locked, and they opened the mahogany door and entered, only to find Donovan in his chair breathless and cyanotic, starting to decay, with a Cuban cigar box opened in front of him. His right hand tightly held a gift card. Sutton unclenched his tight cyanotic fingers and took the card which was saying: "Compliments from the citizens of Somaliland. We sent over our co-national Black Mamba to convey our best wishes!" and it wasn't signed. Sutton looked briefly at the corpse than shouted:

- Everybody freezes! Nobody moves! There is a venomous snake in the room and it's deadly! The critter killed Donovan and whoever moves near it comes next. We have to find it and get rid of it. Davies, call someone trained to contain a venomous snake.'

Davies shouted some orders in his telephone and within minutes, a specialist came over with a protection suit and adequate gear and started looking around. He found the snake coiled behind the bar-globe and he collected it with a hook quite easily, before it could harm anyone else. Once the snake was safely locked in its plastic container, they started investigating the body.

- Apparently, the snake was hidden in the cigar box – it is not very large, more like a young snake. It is like 2 feet long now, supposedly reaching up to five meters at adulthood, but Black Mamba is deadly since hatching – said Henry Sutton. He must have opened the box and got bitten by the neck – he said, indicating a double sting mark on the right side of Donovan's neck and right cheek. The victim obviously did not expect this, and the bite was so close to his brain and vital organs and no tourniquet possibility. He must have started to agonize within 30 seconds and died in 5 minutes, very likely, unable to move, do anything or even breathe.

– Do you think he got to understand the message? – said Hughes of the NSA.

– We can only assume that! We do not know if he was aware of how the materials he provided were used and where! It is possible that he didn.t know and didn't care about it! If you ask me, I would put my money on this version! But he must have ultimately realized it! - said Sutton. Then he continued:

– Someone from our friends in Somaliland understood that he is responsible for the shipment of deadly infected mosquitoes and took a stand in the name of the citizens to punish him. I think this is a classic case of heart attack at the office, caused by burn out. Otherwise, accidental access of loose exotic pets in transport crates is not something new !

– Yap! I reckon its hard to pull a homicide case on this – answered Davies. Whoever did this was more efficient than we were prepared to. I only regret we did not have the occasion to talk to him!

– I disagree with you, my friend! – Sutton answered. According to his profile – the one I worked on so far – he was a very clever and shrewd character and a very stubborn man. You would have gotten nothing from him!

– Heart attack would be a convenient death reason for his age and his exposure to stress! – said Hughes, in his turn.

– We'll go on that one! - answered Davies, and he welcomed the coroner who was just making entrance. … How are you Charlie? We got here a case of heart attack and it is a misfortune it happened on Thursday afternoon and we were notified just today.

– Huh! I can see that! – said Charlie, the coroner, looking at the snakebite on Donovan's neck. Hey, you contained that source of the "heart attack" so I won't get bitten, as well, didn't you?

– It is all taken care of, Charlie! Do your thing! The true file will stay in our drawer, the heart attack is for the press. We do not know who else has got eyes on him. We'll draw the line at the end.

Davies turned to the group and showed to the safe box in the wall, half way uncovered by a monumental painting. He dialed a number and called a specialist who arrived in 5 minutes. He attached to the handle and cypher indicator of the safe box some electric wires, then started scrolling until he found a relevant number, dialed it and opened the safe-box.

They could recuperate the two half kilo containers with deadly bacterial spores, vast amounts of money and a few foreign passports, all to Donovan's name. One of the passports was prepared on top and was meant for a Mexican citizen born in the US, Arcadio Guttierrez, next to a plane ticket to Mexico City. Donovan's mobile phone had 2 registered unanswered calls, both the day before what appeared to be his death date.

- These must be the Russians he was selling the stuff to – said Davies. We saw them waiting for him at the Bistro parking, but we didn't know at the time why he didn't show up to complete the deal.
- Evidence points out to a Russian connection. They seem to have been involved in the distribution of vector – we still do not know how – and in trying to collect data from the test field. – said Sutton.
- However, we do not know if they are directly involved or working for someone! I have my theories about that, said Davies, and Hughes made a sign he had, too.
- Let's see what we can find from the evidence! – said Davies. I want all computers from this building and from GERMINA dismantled and all information available, as well as the one from Hick's house. Only then we will know how large the conspiracy was! Come on guy, I want them opened yesterday!
- Excuse me Sir! An operative came in with a yellow envelope in hand. He continued:
- This is an envelope with documents signed by the late Professor Hicks! A lawyer just brought it over from the bank following our asking information about his bank accounts. He said Hicks ordered this to be handed to authorities in case of his untimely death. I think this was the opportunity he had in mind.
- That should be very interesting reading – smiled Sutton.

Life on the brink

WHO team's flight to Dubai was uneventful, according to standards, However, thinking about their job, Peter was afraid about the magnitude of the connections Donovan appeared to have. He was so nervous about the issue, that when somebody would speak Russian next to him, he would shiver and instantly depart. He noticed they arrived at the old airport in Deira, which meant that Al Maktoum airport was not ready yet.

They took the large transfer bus to Terminal three for Africa and got there in 15 minutes or so. The expected crowd was welcoming them, picturing monumental piles of luggage built by Pakistani nationals, all dressed in their long shirts and fabric vests, their colorful presence being spiced by persistent aromas coming from chicken Marsala and Tandoori food Indian restaurants scattered around. Qawwali music from their mobile phones featured Nusrat Fateh Ali Khan, their great singer and active groups alternated with resting ones, displaying ten to fifteen individuals sleeping on improvised blankets on the floor.

The WHO group found a few free chairs to "set up camp", waiting for their 5 hour connection to Somaliland. Alma caught Peter by the elbow and said:

- I want to go to the toilet! Maybe we go together!

Peter agreed, and told the others they were going to the rest rooms. They crossed the crowded hall towards the closest rest room available. Peter saw Alma get in safely and then he entered the man's facility.

As soon as he got in, he saw a bunch of solid built, colored characters washing hands in front of the mirrors. Seeing they wear airport staff uniforms, he ignored them and went to a more remote booth at the distant end of the room, expecting better privacy. The odd thing, he thought, was that in such great airport facilities, personnel has specially destined restrooms, thus avoiding annoying meeting with passengers. But who knows, oriental world was not exactly based on precision and obeying rules, and besides that, the wheelchair brought in by them perhaps belonged to an accompanied disabled person, so he dismissed the thought. As soon as he got in, someone came to that area, knocked at the door and tried to open the door. He shouted "Busy", to no result. The person forced his way in and Peter suddenly found himself embraced by a solid guy and another one rolled up his left sleeve and injected some drug in his forearm. He thought he could try to overpower them, but soon became unable to move or react and blacked out. The solid man took him over and placed him on the previously prepared wheelchair, getting him out of the group's sight and towards a distant gate.

A similar procedure was inflicted upon Alma and another wheelchair took the same direction, towards a private embarkation gate. The "care-takers" walked quickly, but not running, avoiding unnecessary attention. Both "patients" were covered with thin blankets and towels, having their faces practically hidden from exposure to the ubiquitous surveillance cameras.

When the two wheelchairs got to the destination gate, they were admitted in without any delay, and they rolled the "patients" on to a private jet parked outside.

The personnel received them, strapping them to their seats. The little staircase was lifted, door sealed and the private jet started engines and requested taxi permit for take- off.

As permit was swiftly acknowledged, the Pilatus PC24 jet taxied to the end of runway and shortly took off, quickly disappearing into the night.

Meanwhile, joe and Liam were still waiting for their comrades to come from the restrooms. The wait was not very long, after some fifteen minutes Liam complaining to Joe:

- I hope they did not forget about us. I hear they have an airport hotel here. Hope they didn't go that far!
- Hmm! Peter would have told us something! I am going to search a little for them. Maybe they went for a cup of coffee or something.

Minutes passed, with Liam looking hard in the crowd from time to time, to no result. After twenty minutes or so, Joe was back and with a worried face he said:

- I checked all male rest rooms available in the area. No sign of Peter. Same with Alma, although I couldn't go inside the female restrooms. I looked at the bar and the smoker's booth – nothing. It's like they disappeared.
- Shut the fuck up, Snow White! You have a foul mouth, you know! – answered Liam! You bring bad vibes!

He then took a deep breath and sighed:

- I told them that car following us was no good! Remember when we left our phones at the entrance desk of GERMINA?
- Yeah, what about it?
- Well, out of curious boredom, I opened the back of my phone to check the battery. Look what I found – and he showed to Joe a small chip device the size of an M&M candy.
- Good heavens! You think mine was tapped as well?
- There's only one way to find out! Give me your phone!

Liam took Joe's phone and with an expert move, he took out the back cover of the phone. He removed the battery, only to find beneath it a similar device, which he grabbed and placed it in front of Joe's eyes.

- We must assume Peter and Alma have the same problem. Those guys knew all the time where we are and what we're up to, including where we are going. Give me that – he said and grabbed both chips. He went inside the nearest toilet and threw them in a garbage bin. He went out and said:
- They will keep on emitting from here, even after we leave – he smiled and winked to Joe, who agreed. Next they took turns in trying to call Peter and Alma, but phones were unresponsive, like being switched off.

- Let me call base! – said Liam and he dialed Fujimori.
- Hello!.. Oh, Hello Dr. Johnson! What's the matter calling me at this time of night?
- Well it is almost morning here in Dubai, Sir! I think we have a problem. We have been stalked during our visit in the US, and things got even worse. We are now inside Terminal 3 of Dubai airport, awaiting our connection for Somaliland and we lost contact with Dr. Bud and envoy Alma Matsumoto. I think they may have been abducted by someone. Can't find them anywhere! What should we do ?

Fujimori first hesitated, like thinking for a second, then answered:

- Well, first declare them missing to the airport authorities and the police. Meanwhile I will try to call them myself and I will also inform Henry Sutton. The WHO supports you. Talk back to you in one hour, ok?
- Very well Sir! Over and out!

Liam turned to Joe and said:

- Come on brother! We've got business to do!

Within five minutes, the airport audio system was calling for Dr. Peter Bud and Miss Alma Matsumoto to report to the nearest information booth, to no result after a quarter of an hour.

Liam and Joe did not waste anymore time and spoke to the airport security officers. There was a brief moment of frantic communication in Arab and then, one official in a white long Arab costume called them:

- Please follow me!

They went towards a lateral corridor and entered a room with desks full of IT equipment and monitors.

- I have been instructed by our superiors to assist you in finding your colleagues! We have here images from all our surveillance cameras! Where do you think they went?
- They said they are going to the restrooms! – answered Liam. My guess is they chose the ones closer to the place where we were stationed ….which would be around here, I guess – Liam answered, pointing to a line of seats visible on one of the screens.
- Aha! That would be sector 5B! – said the clerk.

He then turned to a technician and quickly gave some orders. The image shifted to another monitor.

- This is the entrance to the rest-room area closest to your location, Sir. Let us watch what happened in the past two hours!

The rapid scan of images was eye disturbing, but eventually, everybody saw Peter and Alma entering the rest-room door.

- There they are, Sir! – Joe exclaimed.

They waited for about three minutes, and soon everybody saw the two wheelchairs carrying covered allegedly sick people getting out and being pushed by assisting personnel, wearing common airport uniforms.

The Arab official demanded something and images were brought back like fifteen minutes or so, and they saw assistant pairs, men and women, pushing wheel chairs inside the restrooms seconds before Peter and Alma went there.

- It looks like they were stalked and everything was prepared, said Liam, watching the two wheel-chairs coming inside full of towels and hygiene stuff.

The official demanded something in Arab, and the faces of the assistants were brought in a screen close up frozen image.

Another technician opened a personnel info folder on his computer and started cross checking the images with the photos from the data base. There was no positive identification.

- I am sorry! It appears your colleagues might have been abducted. They were most likely drugged and put to sleep. The people that took them over are not hired by us; they are not part of our airport personnel. We should forward their photo to the police. We will commence an internal investigation as to find out how they got the uniforms.
- I see! – said Liam. Maybe we should inform the police about all this asap!
- It is being done as we speak! Meanwhile, we can speed up the process by following the wheelchairs.

They switched to various cameras until they saw the wheelchairs driven through a private VIP gate and outside to a private small plane. An outside camera showed the "patients" in the wheelchairs being embarked into the Pilatus. Soon after, the plane taxied for take-off. At this moment, the official paused the registration and called the tower. He spoke to them for a couple of minutes. Then he turned to Joe and Liam.

- The airplane belongs to a private company in the Philippines and they have declared their destination as Mocha International airport in Yemen.
- But that is almost Houthi occupied territory – observed Joe, looking at the map. And Houthis are not very friendly with the Americans, to say the least.
- Not quite; I mean Mocha is officially still in government backing forces, but that doesn't mean they are not infiltrated by Houthis! And you are right by saying we have to actually assume that! I will inform my superiors about this development! I am sure there will be a coordinated international effort to set them free! We must be coherent and optimistic! – he tried to cheer up the two men.

- Thank you very much Sir! We are indeed preoccupied by this situation and I only hope it can be solved as efficiently as you dealt with problems here!
- Inshallah! And please be attentive if someone might contact you for ransom or something, in which case you should notify the authorities. … Speaking of which, may I present you captain Mohammad Al Qasimi, Chief Investigator of airport police.
- Salaam alekoum everybody! Pleased to meet you! – opened up the Captain in an impeccable English, apparently with British accent.
- How do you do, Sir! Pleased to meet you under the circumstances! – Liam found the power to smile a little.
- First, I want to clarify some facts that would explain the situation! Do you have any idea about the reason for which your colleagues were abducted?
- Beats me! – answered Joe with a surprised mimic. For all we know, it could have been us going to the toilette.
- I think I have some idea! – said Liam. We come from the US, where we were part of a very important WHO investigation on a powerful chemical and biological company. Our visit was – in a manner of speech – not expected, and also proved very uncomfortable for the company. I think we may have triggered some big problems for them and I suspect they have international connections and may try to retaliate. However, I would have never imagined they are so powerful or will go so far. One more aspect – following our visit there, our phones were bugged and someone tracked us, probably even here – continued Liam, - and he explained how they found the electronic chips and tossed them in the garbage bin.
- We need you to come with us to the office to give a full statement and maybe you can give us some recent photos of your colleagues.
- Sure thing, Captain! Lead the way! We lost our connection to Somaliland anyway and our motivation, as well; our program has changed already.

Liam went out dialing Fujimori's number.

Meanwhile, inside the Pilatus there was a paradoxically joyful atmosphere, owed to the fresh morning sunlight pouring through the side windows, all blinds being raised. Peter was seated in a comfortable chair, but coughed and with the seatbelt strapped on. The seat beside him was occupied by Alma. Both were apparently sleeping but the powerful sunlight started to wake them up. Peter slowly opened his eyelids a little, to take a look around. He guessed he had been drugged and taken away and found some comfort seeing Alma in front of him, most likely in the same situation.

There was a person next to them, on the other side of the cabin, seated on a couch and watching them, with a gun in hand. The man was solid, even obese, dark in color, with a moustache and beard according to typical Muslim tradition and was wearing a curious overall outfit, with straight neck collar and no lapel, like a Chinese or Vietnamese uniform. There was no one else in view. A bell tinged and a woman appeared from behind a curtain. She observed Peter as he opened his eyes and also shook Alma, who was trying to focus on things, in her turn.

–   We are going to land in ten minutes! Please remain seated and use the safety seatbelt! – she said with a gentle but firm voice!

The smile was meant for them, as they had their hands cuffed and tightly strapped in their seats, anyway.

–   That goes for you, too, she said without the professional smile, towards the armed guardian.
–   Yeah, whatever! He mumbled – struggling to buckle up, as he needed adjusting his seat-belt according to the considerable dimension of his belly. He was doing it without letting the gun go from his hand.

The plane started descending and followed a rapid approach corridor to the smaller strip of Mocha airport. The landing was impeccable and the plane taxied towards a distant hangar, stopping in front of it.

The guardian unstrapped himself and the prisoners and pushed them to the door without any grace:

- Come on! Get out! Get out! – and he rushed down the small stair behind them.

A black SUV – a Toyota Landcruiser, observed Peter – was parked next to the plane. The man invited them with the gun to go to the car and get in, occupying the back seats. He mounted in front and told the driver:

- Salaam alekoum Yousef! All good?
- Alekoum salaam Tariq! All good and ready. We leave for Dhubab and will be there in a couple of hours or so.
- Okay! Hey you, Americans, sit still and do not make noise, or I shoot you!

Alma looked at him for a few seconds, then spoke:

- Can I have some water? I am thirsty and I understand we go a long way.

Tariq looked at her with cold eyes, but then he reacted and opened an icebox at his feet, grabbed two small bottles of fresh water and handed them one by one to the prisoners. The cold water cooled them and cleared the fog on their mind. With refreshed attitude, they started assessing the situation, looking at each other from time to time. Being hand-cuffed, closely guarded and on unknown terrain, it was not a good idea to try any desperate escape move.

- Where the hell are we? - asked Peter, not really convinced they would answer.

Youssef, the driver, took the liberty to answer:

- You are in the part of Yemen being freed as we speak by our glorious leader Abdul-Malik Al-Houthi. We go to the city of Dhubab, where you will be taken to another place to meet some of our friends.
- Why did you kidnap us? – asked Alma.

Tariq smiled, allowing them to see his set of strong yellow colored teeth, stained by cigarettes smoke.

- Because you are a pain in the ass for our friends. That is why you were "invited". Someone wants to meet you and convince you and your group to stop meddling in other people's businesses. Or else you can be fed to the sharks – plenty of them in the Red Sea – and he started laughing loudly while Youssef barely smiled.
- I like sharks! And I like to feed them, if you know what I mean! – finished Tariq, with a glorious smile on his face.

They were almost one hour later on the road. Highway was deserted – if one disregarded the numerous military armored cars being parked here and there, or organizing check-points that they passed without even stopping. The car seemed to somehow have a priority pass.

- I need to go to the bathroom! - said Alma at a certain moment.

Tariq wasn't smiling this time and chose not to answer. But Alma insisted:

- I really need to go to the bathroom! It will only take a couple of minutes! Come on! What's wrong with you people? Is this the way you treat guests?

The two abductors exchanged some words in Arabic and the car slowed down, conveniently stopping at a parking lot where a low building hosted a small shop and a toilet. Tariq got down and he opened the door on Alma's side, waiting for her to get down. Peter pretended to be in a state of slumber, but opened one eye and whispered to Alma:

- Hey, take care!

She said nothing, pretending she did not hear anything and followed Tariq towards the toilet. She entered the wooden door in a very dirty room, with a fowl smell coming from the wet floor and the filthy toilet consisting of two holders for your feet and an ugly looking hole. A small tap with a tiny hose would provide the water for rinsing, according to the Muslim tradition. But more importantly, Alma saw she could lock the door and on the opposite wall there was an open window. She solved the biological problem she needed, then pulled a hair clip holding her hair laterally, and she bent it open and making a small hook at the end. She then inserted the tiny hook in the handcuff's locker hole and had her hands free in two seconds. Going out the window would serve for nothing; there was no place to hide in the middle of the desert and no one would be able to survive to the next day. Tariq was geting anxious and started banging on the door:

- Come on out, woman! Come out or I break the door!
- Just a moment – answered Alma, fitting the handcuffs to her wrists as if they were locked. The she got out smiling:
- See? It was not so painful! We can go now!

Tariq was satisfied to see her and escorted her to her rear seat, closing the door and securing it.

- Daena nadhhab! (let's go!) he said to Yousef, who took to the highway immediately.

Alma was leaning back with a satisfied posture. Seeing Peter who had opened eyes and looked at her, she chose a dead angle for the front passengers and showed Peter she was free from the cuffs, but kept them until a good moment for action came. Peter opened eyes wider a little, then smiled at her and signaled her to keep calm and wait.

The rest of the trip was uneventful, in the same desert like landscape, Alma taking care to conceal the fact her cuffs were actually opened.

As they arrived in Dhubab, they took a ring road circling the city and got to a wider uninhabited place, hosting an improvised football stadium at one end. On the distant end, placed on a wider patch of concrete, there was an Airbus H 145 helicopter adapted to hot climate, similar to the ones ordered by Bahrain. This one had no badge, but the letters USO and a serial indicative number. The SUV parked near the helicopter and the hostages were silently transferred into the large cabin of the helicopter, fitted with 10 seats for person transport. There was only one pilot, whose face full of speckles and blonde hair betrayed a Russian origin, confirmed by the language he spoke on the phone. He hung up when the passengers entered and smiled to them like setting up a prank:

- Welcome aboard our helicopter! Our company invites you to a private ride to the Mayyun or Perim Island. We go pass Masjid Al Rahma on to a beach location, just good for vacation- and the young pilot laughed amused by his joke.
- What company did you say invited us? – asked Peter, a little nervous about the joyful attitude of the young pilot.
- The company is called Neptune Investments! The USO letters come from "Unum Super Omnia". This is the motto! Maybe you did not hear about it!
- No, we did not! – answered Peter thinking he knew nothing about this entity. "Unum super omnia" – "The one above everything" – just another egomaniac exhibiting his powers.
- Well, hold on! We're dustin' up!

The helicopter was brought to life and soon took off and was directed towards the sea. It took like forty-five minutes to reach to the small island, where everything was seemingly waiting for them to arrive. They passed over the small city of Masjid Al Rahma, and continued their low flight to the South-Western seashore of the island, where a well- known beach pavilion with great local food was located. The helicopter landed on a green little field outside a small farm like enclosure nearby; a little golf with some scattered fishing boats was in view and the location did not miss charm, with all the palm trees shadowing the narrow habitation quarters. The air ship was immediately welcomed by two armed guards who directed them to the middle path in the center of the lawn. They took that way, led by Tariq, who exchanged friendly signs with the surrounding warriors. They seemed to relax when they entered the nearest building and cruised the crowded hallway to a separate office room that was heavily guarded.

They entered the room and started waiting, while Tariq was nervously plugging hairs from his nostrils and checking messages on his phone. The wait was not very long, enough to measure the crowded enemy presence, and think over any escape attempt, if any, regardless the fact that Alma was virtually free. They decided to wait for a better chance.

After having animated dialogues with some of the occupants of the building, Tariq was allowed to take his prisoners to the leader of the facility. They crossed some heavily guarded space and reached for a distant main office, where they were invited in. The lobby was literally cold because of the excessive use of AC, but that did not seem to bother anyone.

They entered the office and saw a small man seated in front of a huge wooden desk, with a powerful lamp lighting on each side. The man had an apparently paradoxical in-between positioning, so that his face was difficult to see. But from the appearance, he was Asian, yet Peter had no clue about his nationality, so he took a glance at Alma, hoping her Asian ascendance would help her identify this person's nationality. At a closer look, the skinny face, with prominent yellowish front teeth and vivid black eyes would match the portrait of the elusive Mr. Lu. This time his grin had the significance of a convenient smile and he waved off Tariq.

–   Welcome to our summer retreat! – I am Mr. Lu and you are my guests! - he said with a high pitched voice, resembling the one of a teen boy undergoing puberty changes, still being dissatisfied by it.

His courtesy, however, did not go as far as to remove the handcuffs.

Peter did not fall for the temptation to underestimate him; he knew Asiatic cruelty can be ferocious and this man obviously had other reasons to be physically frustrated and tempted to play with them a "cat and mouse" game.

–   What did we do to deserve the honor? – Alma entered his game.

Mr. Lu pretended to read something from an opened file in front of him. Then he bothered to answer:

–   When you were invited – so to speak – in Dubai airport – we were in the situation of having you and your team going too deep into our business with an American contractor, who is very important to us. The idea was to make sure that your investigation gets to a dead end – as usual, I might say - and he squealed a short burst of laughter at his joke – or else we would hold you until this happens. I heard that meanwhile, by a decision independent from you, who were in our custody at the time, this investigation is about to extend and this has made our American partners very nervous. We are currently holding you as a precaution to make sure they do not have problems.

At this moment, the obsolete telephone on his desk rang and he jumped up when he answered:

–   Yes Sir! They are here with me Sir! Everything is under control!... What? How did that happen?.. No I am not asking you Sir, I was just surprised!... I am sure! Yes Sir! Understood Sir! No loose ends! Thank you, Sir! We serve Unum! – the unmistakable sound of the other person hanging up was perceptible.

Mr. Lu sighed, took his seat and leaned backwards in his chair. He absently picked one plain "Ligeros" Cuban cigarette from the pack on his desk. He puffed a choking blue smoke out of it and extracted from under his right drawer his preferred bottle of Son Tinh. He heisted to bring it up and decided he would not share it with anyone, so he continued smoking.

- Well, my dear guests, the situation just got more complicated! What I was afraid of just happened and I just hope your organization will comply with our demands, otherwise we will have to dispose of your presence, so to speak.

Peter froze. He was wondering what may have happened as to radicalize these people. By now he expected Joe and Liam have triggered the alarm and a full search was on the way. Only he didn't know the evolution of events and anything about the steps taken for their rescue, and Mr. Lu was not in the exact mood to inform them. The alternative of "disposing of their presence" reminded him of the shark menace of Tariq, and it wasn't very comforting. Alma looked worried herself, but kept a brave posture, still posing as being handcuffed. All they had to do for now was wait to see what happens.

Mr. Lu picked his phone and dialed a long number:

- Hallo! This is Lu speaking! Give me Richard!.....Yes! Hallo Richard! I have a message from the "Unum"! You are to contact our informant at GERMINA Inc. The secretary named Wilma will provide you with a list of some investigation delegates. What?.... No, the usual. FBI, NSA and some old "turkey" from UK, who is especially dangerous. You have to make them understand this investigation is not welcome and we are decided to protect our operations. For this we must eliminate all loose ends and you know what that means! I know you are resourceful

and you are not scared! Activate our cells in America and UK!…
Yes! Furthermore, if you are still in Dubai, contact the rest of the
delegation. I will send you some telephone numbers immediately.
The deal is this: they drop the investigation or better bring it to
dead end or they never see their colleagues again. That is all! We
serve "Unum"! – and hung up.

– Now – he turned towards Peter and Alma! Where were we? …
Ah Yes! We were at the point where we were ready to feed you to
the sharks! Ha, ha, ha! He laughed in the Asian theatrical style!
Please give me the telephone numbers of your colleagues – we
may need to communicate with them for your better interest!

He pushed a button on the intercom and a heavily armed guard
entered the office.

– Take them to the "guest" quarters! Give them water and food for
now! Keep an eye on them at all times. We will see what happens
tomorrow

Then he hung up and dialed a longer and more complicated
number:

– Hallo captain Polivanov! I am glad to hear you! The situation
requires your presence in the strait of Bab-El-Mandab starting
tomorrow. "Unum"'s orders! Recovery of your team in Somaliland
is secondary! Please acknowledge message receival. Over and out!

Without any other word, Mr. Lu left the room and soon the
hostages did the same, politely "invited" by a heavily armed guard.

Meanwhile in Dubai, there was a bit of rushing activity at
Za'abeel Palace, the Sheikh's home. Peacocks in the green garden
were launching loud calls for mating, also showing their wonder fully
colored feather display.

A sweaty officer dressed in a police uniform was almost running
towards the main office, where he got almost out of breath. Controlling

himself and his rapid breath, he froze in a standing position in the presence of the Sheikh. The leader took a seat at his desk and invited the officer to sit on a chair in front of him, which the officer denied politely. The Sheikh expected this, nevertheless, said:

- I was informed that two American citizens, also delegates of the WHO, were abducted in our Airport, Terminal 3. How was that possible?

The man gasped for fresh air, made some breathing space by dragging his rigid collar and answered.

- It was a very professional action! Somehow, their people got airport personnel uniforms – something we are already investigating. Furthermore, it is related to retaliation in a file of bio-warfare investigation in the US, your Excellency! We have information the hostages were likely taken to Houthi territory in Yemen !
- Listen to me, officer! I want this problem solved asap! You are allowed to swiftly proceed with the investigation, Use anything and even special forces to recuperate hostages, if necessary. We are in contact with the Yemenite Government and have their approval for discrete intervention, if needed, in Houthi occupied territory! But we have no guarantee for the Houthi! I would prefer to be very cautious about the safety in those parts!
- We will proceed as instructed, your Highness!
- I want a feed back on this business! It is very important that the Emirates proves to be a safe country for everybody and we have no such events in our area. Especially if it means American citizens! Am I understood?
- Perfectly Your Highness! We will do anything possible to solve the problem!
- No, no! You did not understand me correctly! I expect you to do the impossible! This is a very sensitive issue for our Emirate! - said the Sheikh, and dismissed the officer. He then checked the emergency call list he decided and grabbed the phone. The list had a few emergency calls to deal with: the Yemenite Presidential

Leadership Council Chair, Ismail Omar Guelle – president of Djibouti, Muse Bihi Abdi – president of Somaliland, Prime Minister of UK, Vice-president of USA, and Vice President of Russian Federation.

In the same time, Henry Sutton had been informed about the bold move their bio-warfare enemy was trying to inflict.

He discussed a work strategy with Davies and Hughes. The idea was to go deeper, to the mastermind of this whole operation, but the deeper they went, new and fresh ends were uncovered, like the hydra regenerates fallen heads.

One thing was becoming clear – the Russian connection was involved all right, but mostly in terrain work and brokerage, probably all for vast amounts of money. The decision maker was somewhere in the far East, possibly an Asian organization, and the first that came to mind were Chinese and North Korean. But they would need serious investigation in order to prove anything and then the time, the way and the resources to react. After all, it was a problem of international interest, but so sensitive that they could not react publicly on it, at least not immediately and in a detailed manner. Besides panic or political interpretation, there would be voluntary obstacles from confirmed enemies and the danger of information leak. Sutton expressed his concern over this to both FBI and NSA, but also in his dialogues with Fujimori, asking him to be very discrete about the mission led by Peter.

The fact that Peter was gone missing, along with the NSA girl, proved he was right, and perpetrators were on to them, aggressively defending their operations. This was becoming far more important and more involving than the epidemiological investigation of the WHO itself.

It was rather cold morning at Arlington Military Memorial Cemetery and a small crowd was gathered, half of the group wearing military uniforms and there was an armed guard platoon.

Sutton was accompanied by Davies and Hughes on some chairs to one side. The burial ceremony for Elizabeth Walker was completed, and a uniformed guard brought the wrapped American flag to Elizabeth's mother and handed it to her. Both mother and father burst into tears. The serjeant gave the order and firearms shot three salvoes, while the pipers were singing Amazing Grace.

Sutton, followed by Hughes and Davies, went to the parents and presented their sympathy:

- We are very sorry it happened like this! Your daughter was a hero and she helped us uncover a powerful terrorist organization, dangerous not only for the US, but for the entire world – said Sutton, taking the hand of both elderly.

Still shedding tears, Elizabeth's mother was sobbing:

- My God, this crushed us like lightning! We never knew that she was dealing with such dangerous activities! I was so blind!
- Yes, we were! – continued the father! We always picked on her for not marrying, having a family, kids, and the common way of life she was raised with. And now….she's gone, and she was our only child! My princess!
- But that doesn't mean we are not proud of her – mother raised her still trembling voice! I can only hope her sacrifice is worth and something good will be accomplished!

Sutton answered for the whole group:

- I can speak for all present here that she hasn't sacrificed in vain; we are on to those who created this whole situation. Her murderer is already dead, as he turned the evil he did, against himself, but others who are involved with him, will also surely pay! We will never be able to thank you enough for your daughter's sacrifice!

The three men left to the car waiting on the side alley.

- She was a good and talented agent! – said Hughes. It is hard to find a replacement for such operative.

– And she was a beauty as a woman!- said Davies. It is a miracle she decided to work for the government, after all! She could have lived the way she liked anyway!

Sutton smiled and answered:

– I guess she had a conscience drive for this! After all, her parents are common sense people and probably she had her own balance, but was good at exploring the limits and decided to be useful while doing so! It is kind of returning something or giving something as your contribution to the others. She ultimately gave her life to it.

Sutton sighed as he climbed in their SUV and said:

– Yes, friends! Let us make her death count!

Meanwhile, in the city of Burao, Major Bashir drove along the main street. He was accompanied by a couple of armed militaries, with very serious appearance. He was investigating a tip about a crime organization in the city, linked to the disappearance of two locals.

Being dated approximately in the time or slightly before the epidemic incident, suspicions about the two men actually being some kind of couriers grew. Major Bashir concluded that the two men coming from Maydh area could have been the carriers of the insect boxes, and that wouldn't be such a wild guess. Why they disappeared was a mystery, but simple judgement pointed to the theory of silencing witnesses. However, there were only two people that saw them, one being the truck driver who brought them to Burao. He also said he had time to speak to them and heard one was called Youssef and the other Maxamed. He also said they were pleased with results of a good business and wanted to get to Hargeisa, but he was not going that way. The other witness was an old lady who said she directed them to an auto mechanic, where there was a chance to find transportation. She indicated Tahoot's shop, which consequently became a legitimate target for inspection.

The military police SUV of Major Bashir stopped at a certain distance from the entrance in Tahoot's yard. The three men, weapons in hand, got down and stepped towards the house, where they knocked at the door. There was no answer, as Tahoot was hidden in the dark shed, door closed, watching through the dirty little windows the three policemen in front of his house.

He stood there for about ten minutes, waiting for them to get bored and leave, which they eventually did.

He then relaxed, his mind nursing one powerful thought – Sadhanny betrayed him! It was impossible for the police to get to him without Sadhanny's betrayal! Sadhanny will have to pay for this immediately!

Tahoot was a quiet man, but with strong convictions and resolute in action. His mind was already nursing the clear plan of retribution for Sadhanny. It simply had to be done immediately, decisively and if possible, discretely.

He waited until the police car left, then mounted in his old truck and headed for the marketplace. He had his machete on the seat next to him.

He got to the marketplace and drove on purpose straight to the tent that hosted the little ka'at shop of Sadhanny. He got down, machete in hand and entered the tent, where Sadhanny was enjoying his afternoon slumber!

When Sadhanny saw him, his eyes opened wide and he tried to say something. Tahoot was swifter and placed his shovel wide hand over Sadhanny's mouth, dragging him to one side:

–   Waxaan ku idhi ha igu khaldin! (I told you not to mess with me!)
    – he said coldly, and with an expert move he slashed the victim's throat, starting a geyser of blood inside of the tent.

Tahoot was unable to control his compulsive need to completely behead Sadhanny; then threw to body to the ground. Now justice has been served and his killing routine accomplished, but Tahoot did not have too much time to savor his victory.

That very moment, a woman tried to enter the tent and saw the scary scene in front of her, Sadhanny's beheaded body on the ground and Tahoot standing tall and holding the man's head in his hand by the hair.

The woman opened eyes wide and before Tahoot was able to move, she started screaming as loud as the siren of a coming train, until the whole market place was alarmed.

Tahoot took advantage of the surprise moment, threw down both head and machete and ran outside to his car. He turned the engine on and took off leaving behind a nasty cloud of smoke and dust. Meanwhile, the woman kept on screaming, until two policemen arrived at the scene. They entered the tent and went out horrified by the image inside, both with grey faces, and one of them threw up. The other managed to make a mobile phone call, and Major Bashir's car came within minutes, as he was in the area. Major Bashir took a glance into the tent and the horror inside, and said:

- It was him all right! We spooked him! Hey woman – stop crying please! Did you see the man who did this?

The woman, still trembling with fear and shedding tears, spoke:

- Haa (yes), I saw him! Tall and strong! Had a red car, a truck. I think! He ran away 2 minutes ago.
- Which direction? – asked Major Bashir.
- That way! – said the woman, pointing with her finger the direction where Tahoot's car disappeared.

Major Bashir spoke to his men:

- He is going out of the city! Let's follow him! We need to catch him and find out his story!

They rushed to their vehicle and left almost as quickly as Tahoot's car.

Tahoot had no idea where to go. At first, he simply thought to get out of the market exposure, where he was sitting duck. He then started wondering if his swift reaction to kill Sadhanny was appropriate, as this was able to trigger even more misfortune. He did not question, even for a moment, Sadhanny's guilt of betraying him; he was a man of simple and direct versions of the truth. Consequently, he honestly believed his action had been justified, and if he were to get in trouble, that would have made him hate Sadhanny even more, even if already dead.

A fresh idea came to him – he would go and hide in the valley of the hyenas; no one would even dare look for him over there. He drove on to the outskirts of the city, heading on the country road towards the savage landscape of the hyena populated hills.

But before the dust raised by his truck could settle, a dark SUV hurried along, following him. Major Bashir and his men tried to temper their hurry, allowing him a reasonable advance, to see what his target was.

A bit surprised by his apparent random driving towards wilderness, they slowed down and waited for his truck to reveal direction. When getting over the top of the hills, the red truck stopped. They approached cautiously.

Meanwhile, Tahoot reached behind his chair and got out of a hidden place a fully loaded 7,62 mm Kalashnikov machine gun. He grabbed the gun and went towards the edge of the cliff, jumping on the other side, yet careful not to slip downhill towards the bushes and the hyena's den. He could already hear some barks and growls in the darkness of the bushes down below. He took the gun and took position towards the direction he came from, using the margin of the cliff as battlement. He could see Major Bashir's car approaching, until it was parked behind a small rock pile some two hundred feet from his truck. So, they were already hunting him down. Tahoot was not afraid; it was not the first time he was cornered and forced to fight for his life. Giving up and going to prison was not an option. He would have to kill these military police agents. If they sent military police, things were serious – he thought. The three men got down, sneaking behind the rocks. After they took cover, Major Bashir spoke:

– Mudane Tahoot! (Mr. Tahoot!) This is Major Bashir of the military police! Put down your weapon and surrender to us! You are under arrest for the killing of a citizen in the market place half an hour ago. You are also a suspect in other cases of murder. You will be place under arrest and accompany us to the police headquarters for statement and inquiry. We are authorized to use force, if necessary!

– Jid la'aan! (No way!) I had nothing to do with it. If you harass me, I will shoot!

– Mudane Tahoot! Be reasonable! We are armed and we will shoot if you do not obey orders or resist arrest!

– Cadaabta gal! (Go to hell!) If you want me, come take me! – and Tahoot defiantly opened fire with a short burst towards the rock pile.

The policemen did not respond. After a brief indication given by Major Bashir, the other two policemen split and each of them started crawling sideways, trying to outflank Tahoot. He fired two more short bursts from his machinegun, then took time to replace his magazine. The policemen took advantage of this break to go even further around him, around the narrow entrance to the valley. Tahoot felt trapped, but he still was not afraid, He rolled a few meters to his right, changing firing position, hoping to get a better shot towards Bashir, but the Major was well hidden behind the rocks.

Suddnely, Bashir whistled, and the policemen placed on the lateral sides of the valley opened fire with their machine guns, pinning Tahhot down in a quite uncovered position.

Apparently one bullet hit him in the shoulder, but without a sound, Tahoot rolled back to a more covered position and started firing on the policeman on his left. The other policeman saw his opportunity and fired a long burst towards Tahoot, putting a bullet in his thigh.

Tahoot was in pain and bleeding, but he kept silent. This was his battle and he had seen worse during the war in the army of General Aidid.

He thought he saw Major Bashir moving and rose to his knees to get a more precise burst at him, but instead got a bullet in his chest.

The bullet yanked him backwards and out of balance, and before he could control himself, Tahoot slid down the slope towards the bushes and the hyena's den. He eventually stopped within a few feet from the bushes, grasping with his bleeding fingers the red ground, and watching with horror the scattered bones in the dust, many of which human. His gun was lost during the fall and was yards away from him and he felt it was beyond his power to try and reach for it. The hyena family was gathering around him, while Major Bashir and his men approached and were watching the scene from the cliff.

Tahoot saw with the corner of his eye his hyena friend, Shakka, coming in front of the pack. For a brief moment he hoped Shakka will recognize him and spare him, but that was wishful thinking.

- Shakka, Shakka! – he called gently, with his bleeding mouth. I love you Shakka and I fed you all the time. Help me Shakka!

Apparently, the large hyena did not understand him, although it stopped to listen to his words. However, the smell of his blood was getting hyenas crazy, as they started barking and growling, still holding their attack until approval from the leader of the pack came.

With the red eyes piercing through him, Shakka gave a short bark, which was an open invitation to the feast. Tahoot felt in horror as one of the other hyenas grabbed his right forehand and started ripping it furiously, eventually severing it from the arm, which remained a hideous stump with some bleeding rags at its end. He was so terrified he couldn't feel any pain. The next thing he saw was Shakka opening her mouth large and grabbing his face. The last thing he felt was the fowl smell of her breath and then a bone cracking sound ended his life, while Shakka was enjoying licking his crushed skull.

- I do not think we are going to find any more information from him! – said Bashir to his men. We cannot retrieve the body from there, it is too dangerous. I will mention in my report this was the marketplace killer and most likely, the one who killed the two Hargeisa curriers. I think I know now what happened to them. Let's get out of here!

Things happen

Polivanov went on the bridge, where he lit his favorite pipe, filled with Capstan tobacco, and, looking over the dark night sea, let himself fell prey to thoughts.

Quite disturbing, this radio-call from Mr. Lu – "Be in Bab Al Mandab straights", priority mission, etc. Bullshit! He would have gladly disregarded the message, if it weren't for the confirmation, he got from GRU unit 29155, within less than one hour from Mr. Lu's radio-phone call. The cyphered radiogram stated: "Sledovat' prikazam Bambuk! Dyadya Piotr!" (Follow orders from Bamboo! Uncle Peter). Bamboo – was the code name of Mr. Lu and uncle Peter was his GRU commander. That meant he was in the situation to put Sokolov and his group on hold – hopefully not for long – until he solved this new problem occurring in Bab El Mandeb straights. Polivanov waited for Mr. Lu to explain the nature of the action, unable to guess why Mr. Lu actually required his presence there. Besides, Sokolov was silent for now and a message from him was expected three days in advance of recovery. This was convenient, as being in the straights area made it possible to reach the recovery point comfortably within 48 hours, with one day to spare. Polivanov only hoped the two missions will not overlap. In this case Sokolov would have to wait, hopefully not for long.

Meanwhile, Henry Sutton was arriving in London for a rapid debriefing.

He was invited in an older building in the City, not far from Downing Street, which was a meeting place for officials and operatives, practically unknown to the public and the press. He left his car in a public parking, at the margin of the neighborhood and walked a few hundred yards to the meeting place. High SIS or MI

6 officials, Scotland Yard, military intelligence specialists and even a state secretary sent by the Prime Minister were invited to attend the meeting. A heavy dark wood table was placed in the middle of the room. The wood paneling of the walls going up to the ceiling, had the same color with the table and provided the room with a warm atmosphere, enhanced by the joyful glow of the fire burning in a black granite fire-place. Two great metal ashtrays were placed in the middle, hosting some expensive cigar stumps; in between the ashtrays, there was a bottle of Macallan 12 years old, a bottle of soda and a bucket of ice for those too scared to try plain.

All men gathered around the table, cigars lit and glasses filled. One of them, a director in SIS, opened discussion:

- Gentlemen, we are confronted with a new and complex challenge. It is not directly involving us now, but it soon could, if we choose not to react now. Incidentally, our American colleagues are also on it and they had the time to dig deeper into it, but agreed not only to share with us all information, but also to fully cooperate, in the meaning that we need to guard each other's back. In order to have a pertinent view over things, our outstanding colleague and cooperator - Mr. Henry Sutton here - is ready to share with us fresh information from the field.

- Good day, everybody! I believe we have been introduced, so we go straight to the subject! I just came from the US where, accompanied by FBI and NSA representatives, we have investigated the collateral extension of an African case.

Everybody in the room focused attention to Sutton and the monitor on the wall presenting a quick salvo of slides, correlated with the information of the storyteller.

- A couple of months back the authorities in Somaliland (The independent Northern province of Somalia, formerly British protectorate) started investigating an epidemic outburst of a previously unknown disease. This has caught the attention of the WHO, which sent there a team of medical investigators, led by our representative – Dr. Peter Bud. The first information was far from being comfortable, as it resulted the disease was induced by highly modified Borrelia germs, carried by an alien species of mosquito, which does not exist in Africa, but in North and Central America.

There was a small rumor in the room, as Henry went on with his story, displaying images of the patients and the incriminated bacterium and mosquito species. He continued:

- We have reasons to believe the biological material – bacteria and insects – were illegally provided by a bio-chemical plant in the US – Milwaukee, to be more precise. Some of the leaders of this company, called GERMINA Inc. – were already undergoing FBI and NSA surveillance when we got there.
- How come you got there to investigate them? – someone in the room asked.
- We didn't, at first, but the WHO did. There is public information they dealt with some similar strain of mirror bacteria – Borrelia, to be more specific – some decades before and they were stopped by a horrific lab accident. The WHO decided to ask them for details, without incriminating anybody, although we got reasons to believe they still have the capacity to produce the bug and use different vectors than common ticks. It seems that the investigation led by their team there (us having representatives in the group who previously inspected African site) - was able to generate discomfort. Apparently, some of them freaked out – I am talking about their Security Director, and he got paranoid enough to believe he was betrayed by his fiancée and his Scientific Director, killing them both in cold blood.
- And you have got him, right? – said another person.
- No need to! The bloody bastard conveniently succumbed to a heart attack in his office – at least officially, for the media, until the investigation concludes. Unofficially, he was bitten by a Black Mamba snake sent as "gift" in a cigar box by anonymous citizens

from Somaliland. But we do not risk to disclose that information yet and for sure, the origin of the reptile must be verified.

–   Oh my God! – someone exclaimed.

–   What is more interesting is the fact that Mr. Donovan – that was his name – probably never knew what happened to the materials he had secretly sold. I assume also that he was ignorant about the fact that someone used Somaliland as testing ground for this new bio-weapon, maybe until recently. Furthermore, it appears that these materials were smuggled out by a powerful Russian connection, but we have no indication that Moscow is the mastermind behind all this. It is a possibility they are just intermediaries and the moral author still remains bloody unknown.

Sutton interrupted his speech, took a gulp of Scotch and interrupted the whispers and low voice conversation by continuing his presentation:

–   How powerful are they? Well, they are bloody powerful, if we consider that yesterday they kidnapped two members of our joint team – Dr. Bud and biologist Matsumoto (American citizen and NSA operative) and they expect us to drop our investigation, or the hostages will be executed. They have somehow been moved on the west coast of Yemen, practically in Houthi covered territory. Now with your permission, I would call that a crisis situation and I feel that we are free to use all our means in order to assist. This is no longer an African problem or a WHO problem, but international terrorism. I do not know who is behind it and what the real target is – as I strongly believe Somaliland was only a testing ground, and the real target or targets come next. Imagine London receives a few crates of bacteria infested mosquitoes; they will bite tens of thousands until we figure out the right way to get rid of the insects. However, I do not see this happening in winter, if you ask me, so we have time to move. But other populated areas with tropical climate might be targeted.

– Do we have any information about the kidnappers? – said a representative of SIS. My opinion is that we can guess the mastermind behind this if we identify the kidnapper.

– All we have for now is the registered telephone dialogues with our team members prior to the abduction, and there is nothing significant in there. Maybe it is worth mentioning that apparently, their mobile phones were rigged while they were visiting the incriminated facility, and they were constantly followed during their stay in the states. We took that as a gesture of intimidation, but apparently it was not a bluff.

– I see – another official said. On the other hand, I am sure you are on line with the Emirates and cooperating with them already!

– More than that! – answered Sutton. I have also contacted authorities in Djibouti and the American base there. They are assigning one of their patrol ships for covering the straight of Bab El Mandeb in search & rescue operation. I spoke to officials in Somaliland and South Sudan. Unfortunately, we cannot rule out Iranian helping the perpetrators but we have no dialogue with Tehran. That goes for the Russian too! As you know, our relationship with Russia got very cold since they decided to invade Ukraine, starting with Crimea; for some reason, they are particularly upset with the British. I think it would be better if I went there myself. Until then, I informed our Prime Minister and the Foreign Affairs Secretary and we have the liberty to proceed as the situation requires. I have the approval of the Director of Special Forces for one ship of our Navy to cover the area. It has two helicopters on board and a team of highly trained special operations SBS (Special Boat Service) men.

– Do you have other information on the abduction, surveillance cameras, satellite photos, etc.?

– Certainly! We know already they were likely both drugged by injecting anesthetic while visiting airport restrooms. They were disguised as sick people and carried with wheelchairs to a private jet, a Pilatus, which took off immediately and landed at Mocha, according to our information. We believe they were taken by car deeper South, probably to Dhubab. – said Sutton, projecting a local map. Our local stations depicted a low flying ship- probably a helicopter – from Dhubab to the Perim Island, and we are currently investigating the possibility of our hostages to have been taken there. The odd thing was the airship had its transponder off throughout the flight.

- Mr. Sutton, I think the situation is quite well covered, if I may say so! We have received the file with all sensitive information and I want you to rest assured that we will do our best to react promptly and decisively on this.
- That is something that I very much appreciate; the same goes for me!- for tips and details you can call me at any time, day or night!
- I will then close this meeting, hoping we will get good news shortly.

Everybody in the room raised and one by one they stepped out in various directions. One last official shook Henry Sutton's hand and asked:

- We are with you Henry! By the way, can I give you a lift?
- Oh no, thank you very much, indeed! I have my car in a parking nearby!- he said showing his car keys, with the bulky remote connected to it.

Still smiling but with his head swarming with thoughts, Henry Sutton walked towards his car, a bit deranged by the chilly breeze which contrasted with the warm atmosphere of the meeting room. Besides, he even regretted now he took his car, as the meeting house was well within walking distance and he had to give up having a decent glass of that excellent Scotch that he could only taste a bit.

Getting closer to the car, Sutton thought of having a compensatory treat from his Balvenie bottle at home and take a hot bath to remove the autumn chill. Two minutes later, a giant explosion rocked the neighborhood, and police cars rushed to the parking lot.

Meanwhile, the speaker of their meeting received a call from another attender and answered him:

– Yes John!... Aha! …. What?.. You got to be kidding me! Good Heavens! – and he closed the telephone slowly, with very delicate moves.

Then, as if woken up from his sleep, he grabbed the phone and called a number:

– Hello, Michael!... Yes I know! …No Sir!... I just called to tell you that two minutes ago Henry Sutton's car blew up in the parking, as he was leaving from our meeting. His body is probably minced meat, according to John, who was there and called me! … Yes, I know! … Blow your horn! We are under attack! I guess Sutton was right all along!

Clearing path

The man who Mr. Lu talked to was called Richard; he stood at his desk and contemplated the beautiful sunshine in Dubai streets from the height of his office window. He was thinking how to solve his problems. That poisonous Lu character, he was fast in throwing the hot potato to him. He had already given the necessary orders to the cells in UK and US and they were being carried out already. At least that uncomfortable SIS investigator Sutton was blown to pieces in the sky, with confirmation from the local police. He was waiting for the reaction of the other two "messages" he transmitted.

Little time before that, a white Ford van stopped beyond the group of photographers keeping an eye on the NSA building in Fort Meade, Maryland. The van was parked in an oblique position, near the bridge of Savage Road, leading to the detour motorway, the rear of the car facing the building assembly. The driver opened one of the doors in the back, left it like that and then ran away and jumped in a car stopped next to the van. The car disappeared in traffic. After a few seconds, an explosion followed by a "swish" sound accompanied the remotely controlled launch of a Javelin RPG. To the amazement of the present photographers, the trail of the rocket drew a straight line towards the dark new glass building in the back, where the impact of the explosion performed a hole with a visible diameter of about 30 feet. As if this was not all, the van suddenly blew up and started burning furiously. It was almost completely incinerated before any firemen got there. The dazzled photographers, some in a state of panic, were already being identified by some police agents, others being preoccupied to establish a security perimeter around the burning vehicle.

In the very same time, another white van with a lateral door left open slowed down in front of the sign which was bearing the inscription "26 Federal Plaza" in New York, in front of the FBI building. The van was actually between two police cars waiting in front and the perimetral security fences and the metal poles preventing it from riding the sidewalk. The moment it stopped, an explosion and a "swish" sound accompanied the launch of yet another Javelin towards the entrance of the building at the ground floor, destroying it completely by shattering all the windows and glass structures there. By chance, there was no person entering or leaving the building at that moment. Like in the previous case, the van blew up and caught fire immediately, catching the agents in the police cars unprepared and ducking for cover. The investigation started right away, by establishing a security perimeter.

Hughes and Davies met in an office in DC and after receiving a cup of fresh coffee, started examining the situation.

- First, Sutton's car blows up in London; we still do not know anything about what, and especially how it happened – said Davies. Then some lunatic fires a Javelin towards our HQ in Fort Meade, Maryland. I got 6 wounded persons there, three of them severely. Nobody saw anything. Car was abandoned and destroyed immediately after and the Javelin seems to have been fired remotely. Not a shred of evidence there. We thought maybe it was the work of an ISIS self -radicalized terrorist, but then we got an anonymous message claiming that was punishment for mingling in African business.

- We got our Javelin in the front door at the FBI HQ in 26 Federal Plaza New York; same system with a van, but that was remotely driven and the rocket was also fired remotely. We currently search the local cameras, maybe we find another suspect support vehicle nearby. We got the same message all right! Lucky for us we got no victims, only two residents with panic attack.
- Poor Sutton was right! This is no longer a WHO business, this is a National Security problem. Or should I say international.
- Can you imagine the nerve of these guys to attack our HQ-s in a demonstration of force? It's like saying: "We know who you are and we don't give a fuck! Next time we can even kill". Pretty scary! We don't even know who they are and they demonstrated they have organized groups here on American land. And those groups are operational already and efficient! Only God knows when they started putting this circus together! How come we knew nothing about this?
- Yeah! -replied Davies. And with access to sophisticated weapons like Javelins. Where the fuck did they get them from? Those are not freakin' fireworks on sale at the Walmart.
- We must think of a security breach and probable accomplices. Maybe even some people in the army! We must verify our personnel who had access to this file. I am on to it and you call your Internal Division. They may find some dirty cops covering issues. I'll keep you posted! – completed Hughes.
- Understood! Will do so! – said Davies and each of them went to his team.

Richard was thrilled to see that his messages have been received. He was watching the CNN breaking news report about two allegedly terrorist attacks on American soil, one in New York where the headquarters of FBI was attacked with military weapon and the other report was about a similar explosion inflicted upon the head office building of the NSA in Fort Meade, Maryland.

Richard started laughing, displaying his small and rotten mouse like teeth. The NSA, the most powerful agency, supposedly defending the nation, being unable to protect its own building! That was a laugh! Americans! Stupid truckdrivers and rednecks! Their intelligence would be surprised to know how many subterraneous organizations the American state nurses.

He took the phone and dialed Liam Johnson's number.

At the other end, Liam picked up the phone and hesitated a little, seeing an unknown local number with 971 code.

- Hallo, hallo! – a quite thin, still coarse voice spoke in the phone.
- Hello! – answered Liam, waiving a sign to the police officer seated next to them and was satisfied to see the guy turning on the recording device.
- Mr. Liam Johnson, can you hear me?
- Yes, I can hear you! Whom am I speaking to?
- I am a friend willing to help you and your colleagues!
- Help me about what? What are you talking about?
- Come on Mr. Johnson – or should I say Dr. Johnson. I have an information that you are missing two of your colleagues, that is Dr. Peter Bud and a female biologist called Alma Matsumoto. I might be in the position to help you find them or even set them free, as I have the capacity to negotiate such thing!
- Negotiate with whom? Who abducted them? – asked Liam, looking at the policeman who wrote on a paper "here in Dubai, but rerouted; keep him talking!"
- Wouldn't you like to know immediately, my dear? – sounded the unctuous response of the thin voice. Someone very powerful, someone who was able to take all of you, but chose to keep things at reasonable proportions. I can give you details if you agree to meet me. I am an intermediary, but I must also protect myself and if you chose to call the police – which I imagine you did – you will lose the chance of seeing your friends again and alive, that is what I was instructed to tell you.
- Okay! Tell me where do you want to meet me?

– I prefer a public place, still discrete enough to be protected against any disturbance. If authorities choose to retain me, I will forget completely about your friends and you will never find them. Let us meet tonight at 7 pm at the bar at the third floor at Towers Rotana hotel, here in Dubai. You can take your colleague Dr. Joe Cooper with you as witness and of course, you will be able to record our discussion. Once again, consider my position as intermediary! Good bye Dr. Johnson! And one more thing! Watch the news on CNN!

– Ok! See you at seven! – closed Liam.

He turned to the police. The man said:

– Difficult to locate. Apparently somewhere here in Dubai, maybe Sharjah, but call was rerouted three times so it is difficult to find out the real number of the caller.

– Doesn't matter! – answered Liam. We are going to meet him anyway. I wonder what did he mean with the CNN news? Turn the TV on, Joe!

– Maybe going to meet that man is not entirely wise – tried the policeman to talk him out of it. I am sure he will call again.

– Nonsense! – Liam was confident. We'd be wasting even more time. Besides, I am not buying the bullshit with the intermediary; he is one of them all right! And only by meeting him we can find out more about their organization and about our friends.

Meanwhile Joe had turned on the TV and once he selected the CNN channel, the breaking news about the terrorist attacks in the US and London came as a total surprise.

– Do you think he would be boasting about this if they weren't involved? – asked Joe?

– I don't think so! This was the message meant to scare us! – said Liam. If they are not afraid to attack NSA and FBI, then small flees like us stand no chance – to translate it in English.

- I think you are correct! – said the policeman. My boss called me because of this. I am going for a debriefing and I will leave my colleague with you.
- One more thing, officer! – said Liam. First, thank you for your help and secondly, I think we can afford to play it their way, for now. They will not harm us during negotiation time. But if we freak them out with police presence, or even arrest the intermediary, he might choose to enter the mute mode and we consequently loose any connection to our friends.
- I think you are right, but, you know, we can be very convincing when we have to make someone talk. We have high orders to do everything possible to solve this problem, and everything means a lot of things, trust me! – smiled the officer. I'll be back soon to organize your meeting.

Polivanov reduced speed and was more or less idle towards the eastern part of the Bab El Mandeb straight. He instructed Chief Engineer Didenko to smoke the exhaust pipes from time to time, mimicking some main engine trouble, that would explain his idle position within the waters of the straights.

He was wondering about of the nature of his assignment when he received a scrambled call from Mr. Lu :

- Hello Captain! Can you hear me?
- Yes of course!
- It is possible that tomorrow you will receive two important guests coming from Perim island by helicopter. I remember your ship can offer landing to a small helicopter!
- Yes, we can receive small helicopters! Call me half an hour in advance!
- I will do so! And I will tell you how to dispose of the guests, according to our needs. We serve UNUM! Over and out Captain!
- Yeah! We serve….Whatever! - mumbled Polivanov after Mr. Lu closed the radio-telephone.

He turned around and told the young sailor staying on the wing:

- Go fetch Captain Zarufin! Bistro! (Quick!) On the double!
- Tak iesti! (yes Sir) – answered the young sailor and ran down, coming back in 3 minutes, accompanied by Viktor Zarufin.

Polivanov was thinking while inspecting the map and the radar screen. He then turned to Zarufin:

- Viktor, we must linger on this side of the straights. I want you to be prepared for short notice helicopter landing sometime tomorrow. Check the machinery and tell me how it works.
- Very good, Commander! – answered Zarufin, then turned around and left.

Few minutes later, testing of the ship's handling gear was on the way. The bow derrick was turned aft and the cover of the bow hold remained clear on a surface of 20/20 meters, enough for a skilled helicopter pilot to put the bird down. Once the test was completed, operation lasting about 3 minutes, Zarufin reported to Polivanov. Their wait was going to be longer and the "Luki" was still pretending to have mechanical failure, communicated to authorities in Aden and dropped anchor right where it was, a bit out of passing cargo vessel route.

There was a discrete presence in the third-floor bar and restaurant at Towers -Rotana hotel. The evening lights were dazzling outside and Burj Calipha was glittering less than one kilometer away. The sixteen - lane Sheik Zayed Boulevard in front of the hotel created a continuous humming sound, while inside it was cool and perfect silence, broken from time to time by the elevator bells. Inside the restaurant there was a discrete café-concert music sound.

Liam and Joe got down from the taxi and declared their visit to the restaurant at the reception desk. They took the elevator to the third floor, observing the hotel had 30 floors available.

They descended directly inside the bar enclosure, where hundreds of fine drink bottles awaited western tourists, all arranged in view on superposed bar shelves. They looked around and, on the left, in a quite shady extension of the bar, a man seated at a table raised his hand. They followed his invitation. They took a better look at Richard. He was a short chubby person, with a haystack of white hair combed "Einstein" style, but with a pair of extremely imposing side burns, possibly mingled with his ear hairs – thought Liam.

- Good evening gentlemen! Allow me to introduce myself! My name is Richard Apollo Yerihoff! I am – like I said – merely an intermediary in solving your problem! And you must be….
- Liam Johnson! And this is my colleague Joe Cooper!

Liam placed his telephone set for recording on the table in front of him, quite defiantly – thought Joe.

- Shall we drink something? – said Liam, calling the waiter and asking for a double Gentleman Jack. And for you? – he continued.
- One ginger- lime tea for me – said Joe.
- Absinth for me! – called Richard Yerihoff.
- So, Mr. Jerrycove, what is your message? – asked Liam smiling.
- Yerihoff, the name is Yerihoff! – said Richard with a crooked smile, blinking nervously.
- Okay! Sorry for misspelling! What is it they want?
- My message is the following: dumping your investigation on the epidemic in Somaliland may raise an eyebrow or two. It is better if the investigation stalls, unable to find relevant facts and the whole thing is gradually forgotten. Your colleagues go free the day the WHO presents the boring results of a common epidemic outburst. Any intrusion and further investigation will determine an unhappy fate for your colleagues. In this case, you may consider you saw the last of them.

Liam and Joe did not even blink. It was basically the scenario they expected and have already discussed with the Emirati authorities. Liam asked:

- Where are they now?
- Unable to tell you precisely – smiled Yerihoff. All I can say is that, according to my knowledge, upon a positive result, they will be returned to Dubai.
- I don't think I have the power to negotiate such thing directly. I will have to consult my boss and the other authorities; people have died on this, I understand there have been also some terrorist attacks linked to this event.
- How unfortune, isn't it? Yes,- said Yerihoff, but I understood it was not ISIS. But then, ISIS was just a subsidiary of our powerful contractor. And he smiled, displaying his mouse -like small teeth.

He wiped his glasses and put them on, and his eyes seemed in the distance ridiculously large on his tiny wrinkled face, doubled by an enormous goiter. His laughter sounded like an unpleasant screech, something like chalk on a dry blackboard.

- What exactly are we supposed to do and how exactly do we get our friends back? – asked Joe.

Liam took a deep breath and answered:

- What Mr. Jerkoff here wants is that we play stupid and try to close the investigation. Our leaders are not morons. More likely, they will send others to finish the job.
- Yerihoff! The name is Yerihoff! Richard Apollo Yerihoff! – and the little man was hissing like a tea kettle forgotten on the stove.
- Oh, excuse me! Can I call you Dick Jerkoff, then? – smiled Liam.
- You are not in the position to offend me personally! This will cost you and your friends a lot!

- But you were saying you are just an intermediary! – Joe interfered, still smiling but trying to calm down the spirits. Why are you so touchy?

- Yes, I am an intermediary! But make no mistake! I am doing this because I volunteered to, and I still have the possibility to do it. I can also mind my own business starting tomorrow morning and you would be clueless. Oh yes, and your friends will probably be dead!

- Listen to me! – continued Liam. It is like I said. I need time to discuss this with our authorities. I cannot guarantee they will not send other investigators to replace us and try to search for you and your contractor. Even if we promise we don't, I think you are mature enough to see I am right and what I promise wouldn't matter.

- I am sorry you want to play it this official way. It was supposed to be a mutual understanding situation. Your leaders would not necessarily have had to know it all. Think of it! Your friends would be free by the time you release the new update of your investigation. This could be done tomorrow, if you want!

- Okay Dick! We have plenty of food for thinking! How can we get in touch with you?

- The name is Richard! -puffed the little man. Never mind! You have 24 hours to send a rectifying report on your investigation. I want a print-screen of the sent report on this e-mail address. – and handed a small card to Liam. And a copy of their answer.

Liam took a glance at the card, then finished his whisky and rose to his feet, shadowed by Joe. They went to the elevator, pass the bar tender:

- The little man pays for all – Liam smiled, and they disappeared in the elevator. They got to the street and took the first free cab.

Yerihoff remained at the table. He pulled out a mobile phone, dialed and with a bitter voice he said:

- Hello! It's me!.... Yes, I talked to them! I chose to meet them as intermediary! No, no I didn't disclose anything! …. Calm down, nothing like that! I am an outside person who does the service of facilitating a deal, that's all!.... Yes!... No! They said it is not up to them and if they ditch the investigation, others will come to finish it. They are reluctant to work discretely, as requested. They want it all in the open. I think this story with the abduction was a bad idea and has gone too far!- Yerihoff scored in turn.....No, it is ok! The rest is done, as you can see! … Yes! I will be around! Yeah, we serve…...!

Yerihoff put his phone inside his pocket and said with low voice:

- You serve who you want, yellow moron! I feel the climate is too hot for me here! Think I will change some things in my life, starting now!

He ordered another absinth and enjoyed it, trying to forget the meeting. He made a funny grimace when going to the bar and seeing the check, but paid everything without any comment and took the first elevator down.

He went to the boulevard and concentrated in locating a free taxi, when luck smiled on him; a taxi came out of nowhere and stopped in front of him.

- Get me to Deira! – he told the driver, a solid guy with a light brown Pakistani clothing.

The man nodded and went into the traffic, while Yerihoff fell to his thoughts. He was still contemplating what to do next when he had the odd impression that the car was not going the right way. He looked at the panels and saw they were on route to the harbor, to Jebel Ali. He could already see the lights of the villas on the palm island beyond the port facilities.

He spoke to the driver:

– Hey, where are you going? I said I want to get to Deira, and you are going in the opposite direction!

The driver turned a little, smiled foolishly and said something in Urdu, which obviously Yerihoff did not understand. Meanwhile the car arrived at some distant berths at the end of the inner water body.

– Stop the car! – said Yerihoff, which the driver did presently.

To his surprise, the driver got down first and came to open his door. At this moment, Yerihoff's surprise turned to horror. In the split of a second, he understood what Mr. Lu meant by "no loose ends" and that he exceedingly exposed himself, thus becoming a liability for the company. So, the company was not wasting any more time and decided to dispose of him. This simple thought had the power to paralyze him, like being hit by a stun gun and rendered unable to react. The solid driver, still silent, bent and cuffed his right ankle, then rose to his level and hit him by surprise with his left fist. Yerihoff was knocked out instantly, and dropped on the rear bench of the taxi. The driver took him out of the car on the concrete of the pier, searched his pockets and transferred the content – wallet, papers and other smaller stuff – into his pockets. He removed from his own pocket a large photo of Yerihoff – used for identification – and placed it into the unconscious man's coat. He went to the back of the car and took from the trunk some barbell weights, five of them equal to five kilogram each, and attached them with a bicycle locking cable to the ankle cuff of Mr. Yerihoff, who was still asleep after the left hook blow to his chin. The driver took Yerihoff, together with his weights, and threw him into the dark water without any ceremony. The body, plus the weight, splashed quite high. The driver looked around, but there was nobody in the area and no camera because it was a no interest area. He remembered he needed much time to find such good place for delicate businesses like the one tonight. In that moment he saw water swirling a little and some air bubbles coming up and tried to imagine the surprise of Mr. Yerihoff when waking up submerged and feeling unable to swim to the surface. Ugly death, but technically, the person did not die by his hand. The man simply drowned. Satisfied with his interpretation, the driver extended his hand to the right pocket to feel the advance money he received for tonight's service and from the left pocket he grabbed his mobile phone, dialed a number and said:

– Hallo! It's me! The problem is solved! I will be at your place in half an hour for the conclusions. – he smiled with satisfaction that he was going to cash the other half of the pay.

There was also a generous bonus from Yerihoff's wallet money, so that was a good day's work.

Rush-hour

It was the third morning of their captivity, when Alma and Peter were brought in the office room of Mr. Lu without receiving food or water for breakfast. The massive Tariq entered the room with his inexpressive poker-face and waited near the desk.

– An egg white omelet for me, with baked tomatoes and cheese. And an orange juice! – Alma tried to defy him, but surprisingly, Tariq did not overreact as usual.

For Peter, that was a bad sign. Something more important was on the guard's mind. So far, Alma kept her hands freedom secret, but to no immediate use. They waited for a few minutes, then the yellow phantom of Mr. Lu appeared from a lateral door. He sat at the desk, looking at them through the small slits of his eyes, like a cobra snake before striking prey. He tried to smile, exposing his yellow rotten teeth in a toxic grin, then spoke:

– Good morning, if I may say so! You will finally decide if it is good or not! I am afraid I have bad news for you.

Peter observed that their phones were still on his desk, probably Mr. Lu had not reached to a decision about them.

He made a pause for suspense increase, lighting up a "LIGEROS" Cuban cigarette and puffing from it. Alma coughed politely, to no consequence, as Mr. Lu kept on smoking until the cigarette was halved.

- Your investigation already made victims – some of our cooperators in the States died. It seems your people do not want to negotiate or cannot do it at their level and the problem went out of hand now. We tried to send messages about our serious commitment: the car of your boss Henry Sutton blew up in London, there were explosive attacks on NSA and FBI headquarters in the US – you will see them on the news, if you survive. But they do not seem to care!
- You killed Henry Sutton? You, miserable scum! – Peter jumped from his seat, but Mr. Lu promptly directed to his chest a Glock with a silencer mounted at the barrel, and smiled again, like an absurdly oversized tickled gecko lizard :
- Temper, temper, Dr. Bud. Save your energy for when you will really need it and be sure that time will soon come! For us you are no longer useful and we should dispose of you, preventing any disclosure of identity – like mine - or other sensitive information. Same with your girlfriend here! However, I have to take into consideration that you were just doing your job and many things happened while you were in our custody, so you were not directly responsible for them. I still have consideration for the people who doing their job no matter what. Therefore, I am reluctant to the idea of killing you directly, without giving you a fair chance. My men will take you by helicopter to a ship at sea and you will be disembarked close to the shores of Somaliland. I hope you know how to swim. If you manage to swim to shore before sharks get you and survive further on, good for you, but I do not see city kids like you resisting such challenge. You will take minimal clothing with you but no supplies. Think of it as a "Survivor"

contest – Hi, Hi, Hi, Hi! His laughter seemed like a rat's squeak – thought Peter.

The situation was bad, but being executed immediately was even worse, by all means.

- Now you will eat your last meal and prepare to go in 1 hour! Do not try anything stupid, or you will be shot on sight! Understood?

There was a moment of silence, then Peter answered:

- Yes! – and Alma nodded, trying to cover her wrists with the sleeves of her blouse.
- Okay! – said Mr. Lu. One last check for your safety! Show me your cuffs!

Peter and Alma were paralyzed. Peter stepped forward first, hoping to give Alma time to conceal her opened cuffs. Mr. Lu checked his, and turned towards Alma. She extended her wrist with the back side up, trying to conceal the opened cuff, but Mr. Lu had keen eyes and grabbed her by the loose cuff. While blocking her hands with the cuffs, he slapped her face with all his might, rendering Alma almost unconscious and splitting her arcade above the right eye. Some blood drops found their way on her cheek, but she still smiled defiantly.

- Tariq? – yelled Mr. Lu. To no result, as Tariq was already viewing the scene with wide open eyes and mouth.
- How did she get free? And when?
- I don't know, Sir! – Tariq let it go without thinking twice, and that was not in his favor, to say the least.

Mr. Lu was boiling and he was moving his gun like directing an orchestra:

- So, you want to tell me that you were assigned with the security of two prisoners – only two! - of which one is a woman!

At this point Mr. Lu was rolling eyes in his head and puffing like a boiling kettle:

- She manages to break free from handcuffs, and you don't even know when that happened, much less understanding how it happened! You must be the champion of morons! Gold medalist! ....Give me another handcuff set!

Tariq handed him another pair of cuffs, which Mr. Lu mounted on the equimotic wrists of Alma, removing the old ones. Then he turned towards Tariq:

- I demand total obedience and professional attitude. Such indolence cannot and will not be tolerated. Tariq, you are relieved of your duties regarding the prisoners. Call Youseff here immediately!

With trembling hands and furious looks towards the prisoners, Tariq made a 5- second mobile call and in 30 seconds Youssef was in the doorframe.

- Mr. Youssef, as off today, you are assigned as guardian of the prisoners, replacing Mr. Tariq, who was unable to fulfill his duty properly. You will accompany them by chopper to the motor vessel "LUKI" at sea and will stay with them until they are disembarked close to the shores of Somaliland but not closer than half a mile. Their performance in swimming is not our concern; and no water and no supplies. Understood? I won't accept any alteration of the plan.
- Yes Sir!
- Oh yes, and Mr. Tariq, you know we do not encourage failure and we do not leave loose ends!

To everybody's surprise – maybe less Peter – Mr. Lu grabbed his Glock and shot Tariq in the chest. Two shots – "Plop1 Plop!" – and the big guy was down, and all the people in the room turned yellow, with the exception of Mr. Lu, who was smiling defiantly – thought Peter.

–   Mr. Youssef, one extra job for you! Take our late Mr. Tariq out of my office and clean this shit – he said showing the large puddle of blood created under Tariq's dead body.
–   Yes, Sir! Right away, Sir!

Mr. Lu turned towards the prisoners and, like trying to somehow excuse his reaction, said:

–   I said I like people doing their job in spite of adversities! So unprofessional!

Then he turned to Youssef who looked like shot with Amazonian poison darts or in a vigil coma:

–   Well, why are you standing like a stuffed monkey there? Do not waste my time! ….And when you finish, feed the prisoners!

Prisoners looked at Youssef and shook their head:

–   Thanks, but I lost my appetite! – said Alma.
–   You, young lady, you will not try any more of your tricks with me! – interfered Mr. Lu. I am not stupid like Tariq! Beware not to follow him soon! You are worthless now, do not forget that! – emphasized Mr. Lu.

Alma bit her lips until they turned white, trying to keep quiet, as "instructed" by Peter's intense look. Mr. Lu took his heavy phone and dialed a long number.

–   Hallo Captain! Be ready to receive guests tonight at 7 pm. The rest of the instructions remain valid. You are supposed to be waiting not more than 10 miles out west of Perim Island. We serve UNUM! Over and out!

Finally, Mr. Lu decided to exit the room. Youssef dragged Tariq's corpse outside and placed it on a cart, covering it with a canvas. In the evening it will be easier to carry the body to the nearby shore wharf and get rid of it into the sea. Sharks will do the rest.

He returned and used a mop to clean the floor of the room, finishing with some perfumed detergent. Nothing showed the drama that happened there.

Peter and Alma were removed and sent to their quarters, without having the chance to discuss a plan for their escape. As Youssef has become very motivated to be an example of good guardian, there was little chance, if any, for them in diverting his attention.

Meanwhile Liam and Joe were trying to keep up with the news. They had been unable to find out details about the terrorist attacks in London, Fort Meade and New York, for the time being.

- However – said Joe, I heard the American Navy will send help and I think the British will do the same.
- Not to mention our Emirati friends! – completed Liam, greeting Captain Al Qasimi.

The Captain was dressed in uniform, but wearing the traditional Arab kafya headscarf with Aqel rope.

- Greetings everybody! I come with good news! According to our intelligence, your friends were indeed taken to Mocha, then carried by car to Dhubab. From Dhubab they were flown by helicopter to Perim island here – he said pointing to a map. And we think they are held as hostages there.
- What about local authorities in Yemen! – asked Liam. Will they help?
- I very much doubt! – answered the Captain. You see, that region is indeed officially held by pro-government forces, but we are informed they are massively infiltrated by Houthis and a takeover of this area by the Houthis is imminent, I presume.
- That is bad! – said Joe.

- Yes! – completed Liam. Let us hope the Houthis do not become interested in the prisoners for getting ransom! If they take them inland, we're going to search for the needle in a haystack!
- Hmm! I do not think so! I think the abductors, whoever they are, went on discretely about this. I are say they are accepted by local authorities, and presumably also by the Houthis. Corruption there is as dramatic as their poverty! – completed Al Qasimi.
- But now they are upset about our non-complying position! -observed Joe. Think they might retaliate on prisoners?
- That I cannot say!- the Captain followed. However, things have got beyond control and I think they will soon regard the prisoners as an unnecessary burden, eager to dispose of. I am afraid of what they will decide then. But I have other good news, in exchange!
- Let's hear it! – smiled Liam, rubbing his tired eyes.
- Well, we have been informed that the British have prepared a war ship, a destroyer or something, anchored in Aseb area, behind the island of Fatma in Djibouti territory, hidden below radar from the view of Houthi observers in the West channel. We don't want to stir them up and create a conflict situation able to paralyze the passage through the Bab Al Mandab straights. Secondly, an American frigate, often patrolling the Gulf of Aden, will be waiting in the straights. The US Navy "Astrid" is known and still tolerated by the Houthis, as it has never shown offensive intentions while roaming the area in search of pirates. However, it will be prepared, with a team of Seals and two helicopters on standby.
- Swell!- said Joe.
- And more than that! By direct orders of our Sheik, two Emirati war ships – a frigate and a fast torpedo-boat – together with two helicopters and a team of special marines, are already in standby a few miles across Al Bahyah, which is government Yemen territory. We do not want to stir up the Houthis either.

Liam shook hands with the Captain:

- The Sheik of Dubai is my favorite country leader! Give me a President like him and I will happily reorganize the entire world!

The Captain laughed with satisfaction and he thanked for the appreciation:

- We are indeed a happy community! We have a good cooperation with both America and Europe. We believe in mutual understanding and creating a safe balance between western and Muslim values. Ultimately, everybody has the right to live a good life, Inshallah!
- I like your thinking Captain! – smiled Joe with enthusiasm. Let us discuss our next step.

Meanwhile, Captain Polivanov still held his phone in his hand. Zarufin stood in the captain chair on the bridge, close to the gyro-compass repeater and the radar screen. Navigating the waters of the Bab-Al-Mandab straights was no easy task; after all that was the reason for its name – "The Gate of Lament/ Tears". Treacherous shallow waters, rocks and random currents could drag the less skilled sailors to their doom, but the "LUKI" was a large ship and Zarufin a competent navigator. He was observing Polivanov and he sensed that the commander was in the process of making an important decision. He slowly got up, and extracted from a small fridge a bottle of vodka and two glasses. Further on, he got from the shelf next to his chair the Commander's pipe and tobacco box. He placed everything on a small table in front of Polivanov, who sort of woke up from his thoughts and smiled to Zarufin.

- Viktor! A man to my soul! You are like my son or my little brother! Pour some vodka! I need to talk business with you!
- I am here for you Commander! I am whatever you want me to be, because I have a new life due to you. But you are aware that all I know is navigation and I have poor skills for business, so do not take my advice on anything. I might be wrong!
- Never mind, my dear boy! I have quite taken the decision but I need someone important on the ship to understand what I want to do and help me. The only one I trust is you!

- That is okay Commander! Nu davay zhe! Govorit so mnoy! (well come on! Speak to me!)
- You know Mr. Lu! The Vietnamese guy we both disliked, not long ago, with the mission to Somaliland, when we lost Kruger and Kraichuk?
- I remember him! – said Viktor. And I remember I was glad when he left. Dangerous man, but he comes highly recommended, I understand.
- That is true, this is why I cannot ignore him. This time he wants to get rid of two hostages that will come on board tonight at seven by helicopter!
- Tonight? – asked Viktor. But we never tried helicopter landing on that small space during night time.
- Oh nonsense! I am sure you will succeed! I am sure they have a skilled pilot. But here is the deal. We have to conceal prisoners and carry them to the same waters where we have to pick up Sokolov and his team. By the way, any message from Sokolov?
- No message Sir! Total silence! Hm! I have a bad feeling about this pick -up job. Maybe they got caught or are already dead, who knows.
- You are right Viktor, but our orders are to be there for them. I will report them being late with message, to the best. After the job tonight, we can get there in 24 hours at most and we have a three- day margin. I say we are in time for everything, plenty of time to think. Now here is the deal.
- I am listening!
- I don't know why they want to erase any track of these prisoners or what are they involved in. The devil Mr. Lu told us to throw the prisoners to the sharks, at least half a mile from shore. They have no chance of getting there alive and even if somehow they manage to swim ashore, they have to walk one hundred kilometers in the desert in any direction, without clothes, water or food, to find a decent human settlement to help them. So, for Mr. Lu they are as good as dead. But what if we keep them and use our friends in Puntlands as intermediaries to get some ransom for them. We can ask for at least 4 million dollars and can easily afford 10%

for our intermediaries. For them it is a walk in the park; they will be happy to oblige. The important thing is "LUKI" stays out of trouble and so are we. Prisoners will be blindfolded till Puntlands outpost. Money will go to one overseas account I have, and you will have your share. I may even think of a bonus for all our team members, even if they do not – and should not - know what is all about.

- What if they make their official appearance somewhere after and Mr. Lu will understand they are alive because we did not obey orders.

- Hm! I thought about this, too! Suppose they were so good as to escape swimming to shore without a shark bite and lucky enough to encounter some isolated fishermen camp to help them! Or they were "saved" by Puntland pirates roaming the area. To me, this is a credible enough story! Who can prove otherwise? The hostages will be happy to get out alive.

- I think you are right! As usual! Four million is good money! A piece of that pie will enhance my pension! – smiled Zarufin.

During this time, Peter and Alma were ignorant of the multiple plans regarding their future, as they wondered what the next few hours would bring. While staying in their rooms, a thousand thoughts came to their mind, but they kept a silent and dignified posture. Around six in the evening, while still having enough light and with a beautiful sunset on the sea, they were escorted outside and left with a guard next to the helicopter, where the pilot was busy checking his systems.

Youssef took the wheeled cart carrying Tariq's corpse from the little barn in the back of the farm and pushed it calmly to the wharf nearby. There, he unveiled the victim by dragging the stained canvas placed on top of it and rolled the corpse directly into the water, without any ceremony. He stood there for a few minutes, like expecting something to happen, but then he turned around, grabbed the canvas and stuffed it into a metal barrel, setting it ablaze. A column of black smoke from the lubricant used as fire accelerator rose straight up – there was no wind.

He than hurried to the helicopter, checked on the prisoners' cuffs and then pushed them inside. Peter and Alma were in the back seats, looking towards the front of the helicopter, and Youssef sat down on a chair looking towards them, that is with the back to the pilot. He gave the Russian pilot the ok to go. The engines were turned on and the huge rotor started slashing the air with ever increasing rotational speed. Eventually, the machine took off and slowly moved towards the sea, hanging below radar, not more than 200 feet above the water. The pilot set course directly to the West, expecting to find "LUKI" somewhere towards the middle of the straights. Upon leaving the area, Youssef observed with satisfaction some shark fins coming close to the wharf. The "cleaning agents" were coming, most likely attracted by Tariq's blood from miles around. Youssef smiled, unaware that behind him Alma moved like scratching her hair and produced a hair pin that she used to open the cuffs. She had just the time to wink to Peter, who was surprised, but tried to stay very solemn and used his most boring attitude to repel Youssef's attention.

Minutes passed and they felt the helicopter raising higher and heard the pilot communicating:

- This is USO J 44 – motor/vessel LUKI, please respond!

There was silence. The pilot changed frequency and tried again:

- This is USO J 44 – motor vessel LUKI, please respond! I repeat, LUKI, please respond!

This time the message was heard by the operator on Luki. For a better understanding of events, it must be specified that the message was also picked by US Navy frigate "ASTRID", who instantly set an intercepting route. Details were communicated to the British destroyer and the Emirati vessels, all set in motion instantly and converging on Perim Island area.

- This is motor vessel LUKI, I hear you loud and clear USO J 44! Now I have you on my radar!

There was a pause then:

- USO J 44, we have light for you on helipad! Are you able to put it down?
- Ciort! Am I able to walk?
- Wait USO J 44! Are you Russian?
- Da! Ya uveren chto ya russkiy! (Yes! Sure I am Russian!)
- Then you will manage! Over and out!

The dialogue was closely monitored by all approaching ships, and all shared the radar signal of the coming helicopter, trying to meet the motor vessel LUKI and land upon it.

Aboard the American frigate, the navigation officer reported:

- Commander, this ship is known to us! We even came to check it once for suspicious behavior, but with no material finding. According to our statistics, it has been around in 75% of the investigated piracy events in the last 3 years, but never in the exact location of the attack. It sails very often in these seas and oddly enough, it never reported a piracy attempt even, in years.
- That's bizarre! Who owns it? – answered the commander.
- A Russian commercial company in Malaysia; declared crew is international, mostly Russian. One Igor Polivanov is in command, older and experienced seaman. Not on any wanted person list. The ship is in view, Sir! – said the officer, handing over the binoculars.
- We will see! Looks like he stayed undercover for a long time. I have the feeling this ship will show us interesting things. Prepare to board it and we'll search it to the keel. Keep an eye on the chopper! Observer on the bridge, now!
- Sir, the helicopter is approaching the target ship! – the observer reported.

Aboard the helicopter things started to happen. As they were approaching the cargo ship, they observed the wider space created on the cover of the foremost hold, with white light all around and the loading derrick turned aft to make room for the improvised helipad.

Being so close inspired Alma who got up. Still pretending to be cuffed, she turned to Peter and slapped him in his face, a movement that took him by surprise:

- That was for you, because you are an idiot. I got here thanks to you and I am going to be eaten alive by sharks! – and she started hitting him again and again.

Peter was genuinely surprised, but realized Alma was trying to create a diversion, so he stood up and pretended to defend against her blows, shouting loud:

- How was I supposed to know what will happen, woman? This is because they sent a woman to do a man's job and that ruined everything! – and Peter almost tried to hit her in turn.

Although a promising show in the beginning, things were coming out of hand now, just before the delicate operation of landing on the ship, so that Youssef decided to interfere and calm them down. He got up and said:

- Now calm down woman! And you too, or I throw you directly into the sea! – and he opened the door, chopper almost hoovering about one hundred feet above the ship.

Next, he made a mistake, as he tried to get in between Alma and Peter, to separate them. As he did so, Alma freed her hands and grabbed him by the neck with a skilled grappling martial arts technique. While Youssef was fighting for his breath, Peter found the cuff keys at Youssef's belt and freed himself. The chopper was still hoovering but the pilot was unsure of what was happening behind him. The moment Alma turned her attention to Peter, Youssef jerked out of her grip and jumped to block Peter, only Peter moved to one side and gently pushed him to pursue his trajectory, leading out the opened door of the chopper. Youssef cried helplessly as he fell and shortly landed on the ship's hold cover, cracking open his skull and exposing the jelly consistency of his brain. That was a view which paralyzed for the moment all witnesses, with the exception of Peter, who grabbed Youssef's gun from the floor and placed the cold muzzle of the gun into the pilot's backbone:

- Abort landing! I may survive if I kill you, but you will surely be dead!
- No problem my friend! - smiled the pilot, apparently used to confront such crisis situations. He stalled the helicopter: Now what?
- Give me the radio!- said Peter, and the pilot handed him the headphones.
- This is USO J44 – Doctor Bud speaking! I am in control of the helicopter! Anybody hear me?
- This is the US Frigate ASTRID at 2 miles west of you. We have helipad and we wait for you!
- Thank you, ASTRID! Glad to hear from you! We can see you all right! Be there in five! – and Peter showed the pilot the American frigate with all lights on not far away.
- You can choose to be dead, a convict in Gitmo or a protected witness in America! Which one shall it be? – he asked the pilot.
- I am a very honest witness and I can barely wait to tell my story in America – said the pilot, looking ahead of him, ascending the helicopter and abandoning hovering position, to the amazement of the people on the ship, already waiving to him.

The chopper slowly departed LUKI, leaving those on deck baffled and staring at the dead body of Youssef on the deck. After a few minutes, the derrick came back to its original position, some hands on deck took the body and threw it into the sea, and all ship's lights were turned off. A cloud of blue smoke rushed from the exhausts and the ship's aft got splashed with sea water foam. The "LUKI" was pushing hard to get out of the frigate's vicinity, while the military ship was busy recovering the chopper.

Indeed, the ASTRID slowed down to minor drift while enabling the chopper to land safely on the aft helipad. Peter and Alma got down and the pilot was taken in custody by two armed sailors. As soon as they were down, Peter hugged Alma, who nestled in his arms and kissed him dearly. Then suddenly she grabbed him by the lepel of his coat and shook him, asking with a cold voice:

- And what did you mean by "never have a woman do a man's job!"? Better think of a rational explanation...
- I was trying to blend in the role – you know – pretending we have a fight – came the unconvincing answer from Peter.
- So this is it, right? - said Alma pretending to be upset. You mindlessly spoke your truth, that's it! That is the way you think! I mean that's your philosophy about women, right? – this time she sounded more serious.
- Come on, I am a bad actor! You know I was not talking my mind! – smiled Peter and prevented her from answering by kissing her again, which she consented undecidedly. All those on deck smiled discretely.

At this moment, a sailor came and handed Peter a radio-telephone:

- It is a call for you Sir!
- For me? Thanks!... Who the hell knows I am here! I myself didn't know I will be here twenty minutes ago, for Christ's sake!

Peter grabbed the phone, nevertheless and answered:

- Yes Hello! Who is it?

A man's voice was speaking through the phone.

- Henry? Henry Sutton? .... Is that really you, old man?
- You bet, Buddy Boy! I believe you Romanians have a proverb: "Horses don't die when the dogs want them to"
- How come? They told me they blew up your car!

– That part is correct, only I was not in the car when it happened. Remember the smart remote gadget I bought for my car? It can open the trunk or start the engine remotely so you warm up your car before entering it. That's what I did – better said, what I tried to do, because when starting the engine, the whole bloody car went up.

– I am so glad you are good! Where are you? I would be very glad to see you!

– Well, I am not so far away! I am on a British destroyer you can see, a few miles North from you. We will meet soon. Tell me, can you give me some details about the person who abducted you on Perim island?

– Yes, it is a Mr. Lu! But he is not the brain of this. He works for somebody calling himself "Unum Super Omni" – whoever he might be. But Henry, I have a better idea. Mr. Lu will try to run after realizing his plan failed. I don't want to miss him. I'll tell you what is my idea – and Peter continued to speak for the next 5 minutes, turning his back on the audience.

– Thanks for the phone, but I will need it again soon! – he smiled to the sailor, who remained close to him.

– What are you up to? – asked Alma.

– I want to settle my accounts with Mr. Lu! Let me quote – "we must not leave loose ends"!

– Come on, we got out all right! What else do you want?

Peter smiled and embraced her:

– I want him to pay for hitting you!

While they were talking, phone rang again and the sailor passed it to Peter:

– Yes Henry!

– Peter, we are within 2 miles across from Perim island! We launch now and you do your thing in exactly 4 minutes! The ASTRID captain has been informed about our move! The Emirati ships will cut any retreat South.

- Understood! In four minutes, I have a go!

Peter was impatiently waiting for the chronometer to reach the 4 minutes figure. When it did, he dialed his own phone number, and to his satisfaction, it was ringing which means battery was still holding. A hesitating Mr. Lu answered the phone ringing on his desk:

- Hello!
- Oh, Mr. Lu! Long time no see! I wanted to speak to you before I leave the area! By the way, Henry Sutton says hello! He is not dead as you thought!
- You, stupid city boy! Wait till I get my hands on you again! You and your woman will feed the sharks!
- That is not going to happen, my dear Mr. Lu! Now please get to the window! I suggest you take a look outside! It is not dark yet! What do you see?

Mr. LU took two steps towards the window and looked outside, just in time to see some black flying objects rushing directly towards him. He instantly understood that by talking to Peter's phone, he became a sitting duck for the kamikaze drones they sent for him, guided by the phone in his hand. It was already too late, and the vision of a great ball of fire terminated his last thought.

Actually, the observers on the two war ships registered 3 explosions in rapid sequence. Sutton's ship sent one observation drone – which registered the whole thing – and not one, but three kamikaze drones, every one packed with a six kilogram highly explosive bomb. They hit the target one by one less than one second apart.

- That was brilliant idea, Sir! The frigate Commander spoke to Peter!. How did you manage to target them so accurately?
- Oh, it was simple! I knew he holds our telephones on his desk. Tracing the active phone was easy business for the drones and the outcome is visible! Mr. Lu was in for a surprise!

- Well the history is not over! Looks like the cargo vessel LUKI is trying to flee.
- For all I know, they could be doing dirty the business for Mr. Lu! – answered Peter. Maybe they are the ones that brought the illegal contaminated insect shipment.

Peter never knew how close he was from the truth then, but for now he congratulated Henry for the well synchronized attack on Lu's headquarters.

The British destroyer was coming to assist, cutting any escape possibility to the North, while the Emirati vessels went out and were blocking LUKI's access towards South. Zarufin was throttling his engines this time to the limit, and the two oversized Diesels pushed the ship with a staggering 25 knots trying to outflank the Emirati ships Southward.

The ASTRID was on her tail. The frigate's Commander invited them on the bridge in a side corner, where they could not be in anybody's way.

- Can you look at this guy run? It is the first time I see a normal cargo vessel this size doing 25 knots. Almost faster than us. It is probably customized for smuggling or piracy, I guess! And it is a twin screw, highly maneuverable! – said the Commander.

He made a pause in comments, then he spoke to radio-communications officer:

- Hail the ship! Tell them to stop engines and prepare to be boarded. If they do not comply, we are authorized to shoot!
- It takes just one missile to blow them out of the water! – observed Peter.
- Sure, but I do not want to kill them all! Besides, I am very interested about their life story on this ship and their activity in the past – say three to five years! And I confess I would like to see that ship on the inside! Must be well made! Actually, I think they took a regular cargo vessel and secretly tuned it in some lousy repair shipyard.

The com officer was doing his job:

- This is US Navy ship ASTRID; We are authorized to check up vessels in this area. Stop your engines immediately and prepare to be boarded; You are to obey order immediately!

The cargo ship LUKI was not responding, but managed to somehow increase speed, almost finding a free path South of the Emirati group of warships.

The Commander was responding to a call from them:

- No, please do not fire yet! We are on to them! Just a few minutes and we will discuss further attack, if necessary! Thank you, Sir! – and to the others on deck – The Emiratis were ready to open fire if needed!

The Com Officer spoke again in his mike:

- This is US Navy ship ASTRID, authorized to check maritime passage! Stop your engines completely and prepare to be boarded. This is a warning! If you do not comply, we are authorized to open fire.

He waited for a few minutes and spoke again:

- Cargo ship LUKI! Stop your engines immediately and prepare to be boarded! This is US Navy ship ASTRID and we will shoot if you do not comply! This was our last warning!

Apparently, Polivanov had no intention to surrender.

- ASTRID crew! Action stations! – spoke the Commander on the intercom. A siren honked twice with an ugly sound.

The frigate Coomander took the mike and spoke:

- Commander Polivanov, we know you are on the ship! Stop engines and allow inspection! Otherwise we will consider you are hiding something and have hostile intentions; that is reason enough to shoot! Do not endanger the life of your men!

Polivanov chose to keep quiet and the LUKI was speeding faster South, despite the continuous menace coming from the Emirati ships. It was getting darker and soon visibility was going to become scarce.

The Commander switched observation tools to infrared, displaying a colorful and vivid aspect of the cargo ship.

- Wizzo! – called the Commander.
- Yes Sir! – an officer took position in front of him.
- You are authorized to shoot the 30 mm all-rounder; short bursts, 300 feet in front of the ship. Shoot three warning bursts; let's see what happens.

He then grabbed the mike and said:

- Cargo ship LUKI! Stop your engines and allow inspection. This was your last warning and we will start shooting.

After a few seconds, a short burst of 30 mm shells exploded one hundred yards ahead of LUKI's bow, followed by other two short bursts, aimed at the same distance. But the cargo did not alter speed or course and pretended to ignore the fire upon it. Or so they thought! Oddly enough, they saw the middle derricks turning in the direction of ASTRID and two small explosions were depicted at the tip of the derricks.

- Incoming- shouted the Commander, and everybody ducked for cover.

Two shells zoomed by a few feet over the bridge.

- The villain has 75 mm guns concealed inside the derrick arms! – said the Commander. I never saw anything like this before! Wizzo, use the 30 mm all-rounder to pierce through the hull of the vessel, one foot above water level. I do not want to sink them yet.

The automatic gun erupted in a few bursts, digging large holes in the hull of the cargo at midship level.
The SCO communications officer shouted:

- Commander, it is the Sonar! I put him on the speaker:
- Commander, this is Sonar! I heard two noises like the opening of torpedo tube hatches!
- Observer! Shouted the Commander!- then he completed: Torpedoes! That would be hilarious!
- Nothing Sir! If they have torpedo tubes - they must be opening underwater level somewhere aft....What the ...! Torpedoes coming from port-bow - bearing 300 - distance five thousand yards - he shouted still holding his binoculars.
- Commander, this is Sonar – two torpedo launch confirmed; confirm bearing 300, distance 4700 yards, estimated speed within 50 knots.
- Ok! Hard starboard, full ahead port engine; full astern starboard engine. – and he continued: Smaller, slow torpedoes, possibly custom made!

The ship started to pivot to the right and after a few seconds, Commander ordered:

- Hard port now! Full ahead both! Launch counter-measures!

Meanwhile, the ship increased speed so abruptly, that everyone on the bridge had to hold on to something, while the hull was vibrating with engine power and a giant wave of "boiling" sea water formed at the aft, marking the curved and almost interrupted wake of the ship.

The torpedoes near missed the frigate and exploded on the decoys, raising geysers of sea water at the impact.

- Wizzo!
- Yes Sir! – the Weapon Systems Officer responded instantly.
- Let us launch a helicopter! Approach the ship from the aft, with caution! Fire missile in their aft. We need to stop them! Destroy their rudder and the props! This villain is a twin screw, like a warship!
- Understood Sir! The men gave some orders through his walkie-talkie and within a few seconds, an AH 1 Z Viper helicopter was out of the bow hangar and started engine. Within seconds it took off and started circling the cargo ship.

There was a frantic report from the helicopter pilot:

- Base – this is Viper 1! The cargo ship opened small caliber fire! I am taking evasive action! RPG on deck!

The chopper came on a long arch trajectory, avoiding exposure to the sides of the target ship and flew farther North until it was far enough from the ship – about one thousand feet according to the spectators on the ASTRID.

Peter was as amazed as everyone else on board. The Commander had denied military help from the British or the Emirati Navy vessels, but asked them to close the map North and South for the targeted ship.

Meanwhile, the chopper arranged its position and accurately fired two missiles that produced havoc at LUKI's stern. The ship started steering uncontrollably to starboard, like trying to cross ASTRID's path and the bow foam wave decreased, while the ship was losing speed. In spite of all this, the LUKI opened fire again with its guns. This time one of the shells hit ASTRID"s deck, close to the anchor winch at bow. There was no one on deck there, but it looked like ASTRID will not be able to lower its port anchor without repairs.

– The villain still shooting gun towards us! Viper one, shoot under water line. One missile, so we have time to divert it away from the passage area before it sinks. We cannot endanger other ship's path later.

The Viper came towards the ship, aiming its starboard side and launched another missile. The explosion created a water geyser and the whole ship shuddered and slowed down even more. The ship had now a visible starboard heel and had almost stopped. Defiantly, she fired one last salvo with its guns. Accuracy was poor this time, shells flying some feet over the ASTRID, with a sinister whistling, only to blow up almost a mile away at sea.

– That behavior is suicidal! – said the Commander. Then he ordered:
– Open fire at will with the 30 mm gun! Short bursts! Aim for the hull!

New bursts from the 30 mm gun holed the hull of LUKI, as smoke was coming out of them and sea water started pouring in. Shortly after, the heel of the ship seemed to rebalance because of incoming water on the opposite side, but it was visibly sinking, as the water level increased at least two feet over the red line and the stern was almost submerged.

There was a bit of movement on the deck of the sinking ship. Both lifeboats were being lowered down.

– Cease fire! – ordered the Commander of the frigate.
– Aye Sir!- and the 30 mm all-rounder stopped firing.

The cargo ship was now well beyond passage path of the Western channel of the straights and it was motionless. A white flag was raised on the mast. She was finally surrendering.

– Cease fire, but remain on stand - by! Launch rescue team!

A rubber speedboat was lowered instantly and a team of 5 marines jumped into it, weapons in hand! The boat was quickly pushed by its Mercury engines and was trying to approach the vessel from the stern, avoiding exposure to potential enemy fire. They were supposed to make contact with the lifeboats as soon as these were seaborne.

The two boats were almost in water when a series of internal explosions shook LUKI's hull, which broke somewhere at the middle although the two pieces of the hull did not come apart. A cloud of black smoke erupted from the aft habitation structures and some people were shouting. The hands of some blocked sailors came out through the opened round windows, almost at water level and their movement stopped after the sea water started pouring in through the windows. The scene was dramatic but it was impossible to save them at that moment.

The two lifeboats were at large now and both had white flags raised on improvised masts. The attack speed boat circled them shouting orders and directing the lifeboats towards the ASTRID.

- Prepare the quarantine rooms for the newcomers – ordered the Commander. Large crew – he mumbled – I see around forty or more likely they have mercenaries on board, too.

At this moment, a life raft was lowered from the bow and two men started rowing towards the ASTRID. They were soon observed by the military speedboat, which shouted some orders to it. However, it was clear that the raft would be slower than the lifeboats.

Meanwhile, the LUKI continued to sink, water reaching beyond main deck level. At this moment, the ASTRID came across to its starboard side, three hundred feet away. The silhouette of an apparently older man, with grey hair and thick moustache, came on that side of the bridge, wearing a white shirt and a commander cap.

The frigate Commander saw him and used his megaphone:

- Commander Polivanov, save yourself! Take a life vest and swim toward us! You will be treated as a prisoner of war!

At first, Polivanov did not seem to have heard the message, then he turned towards the ASTRID and made a goodbye sign.

He defiantly poured some vodka from a bottle in a glass in front of him, then raised the glass as to cheer the frigate commander, then drank the glass as water was reaching his feet. Then he turned towards the ASTRID and gave a military salute, as waves engulfed the last parts of the bridge together with him and a bubble storm erupted in the place where the ship sunk.

– It is a pity such man chose the wrong side! A fighter, nevertheless! – said the Commander, impressed by Polivanov's show.

The first of the rescued men arrived on the ship. Some had papers, some did not. They were identified provisionally, disarmed, given fresh clothes and blankets and sent under the main deck to quarantine rooms.

The two men in the raft were eventually rescued and presented themselves:

– Viktor Zarufin- second officer.
– Andrei Didenko – Chief engineer!

They were enlisted and followed the others below.

– The investigation will not stop here. The scuba diver team will check the ship now. There may be survivors in air pockets. The water is not deep here – about 230 feet. I have the hunch we will find very interesting things from the wreck.

Everybody agreed on that.

– Okay! Battle stations at ease! Wizzo, secure weapons! Viper, this is Base! Final check for survivors and come back home! Over and out!
– Viper one, Roger and out!
– Com?

- Yes Sir!
- Alert port authorities in Djibouti. There will be an oil spill from the wreck and a special processing ship is needed. We will assist in every way possible, but specialized ship is mandatory asap.
- Understood Sir!
- Captain on deck! Mr. Smith – the bridge is yours. As soon as we recover our investigation team, you are authorized to set sail for Dubai; let me know when we are within 50 miles from the port. Yes, and have the com officer come to my cabin to edit telegrams and reports. Make sure our guests have everything they need.
- Aye Sir!

Is it over?

Peter and Alma enjoyed the warm hospitality of the crew members of the ASTRID and used the time to rest and recover after the adventures they endured within the last several days.

In Dubai, there was a meeting set up by Liam Johnson and Joe Cooper at the third-floor restaurant of the Towers -Rotana Hotel. A large table was all set with tea, food and beverages. Among other guests, Peter noticed Henry Sutton, Major Bashir from Somaliland, their colleagues Yves Durand and Jason Barr. An Arabic officer, later proved to be Captain Al Qasimi – the Emirati Airport police officer entrusted with their investigation and some other people. Peter thanked all those present in his name and for Alma, who was a little emotional, especially when seeing Liam's grin and Joe's motherly attitude.

- I don't know which one will kill you first – alcohol or caffeine? -said Joe, looking at Liam, who placed in front of him a huge steaming coffee mug and a generous dose of Gentlemen Jack.
- You are dead wrong, brother! They both keep me alive! – answered Liam, cheered by everybody at the table.
- I take this opportunity – said Henry Sutton raising with a glass of Champagne in hand – to thank his Excellency, the Sheik of Dubai,

for the determining help he offered us in finding our colleagues and for assisting in an investigation of major importance for local and global safety. I want to also mention the Emirati Navy represented by a frigate and the patrol boat that cornered the enemy from the South. The same thanks I extend to my friends in the NSA and FBI, who were unable to join us now, always proved reliable companions. I also thank American Navy and especially frigate ASTRID and the destroyer type 44 – Daring class, CLYDE, of the Royal Navy, for their support and their successful military actions. Many thanks and our friendship to the authorities of Somaliland, represented here by Major Bashir. Peter and Alma, we hereby declare this party as an opportunity to tell you how important you are to us! Dear Alma, you may not know me, but I became aware of your skills and value, and this is why I volunteered to take part in the quest for your freedom. Peter is like a grand-son to me, and I couldn't stand knowing he is in danger. Luckily for both of us, he was with you! – and everybody laughed.

- Hey, I was going to ask you! – Peter turned to Alma. How did you free yourself from the handcuffs again, in the chopper?
- Oh, it was very simple! I carry more then one hairclip in my hair, and they didn't check for it! – smiled Alma. Another woman's job we can't count on for being done by men, isn't it?

Peter received the hit with a smile.

- Touché! But how can you keep it there all the time? Doesn't it bother you when you sleep?
- No! I wonder if it won't bother you! – Alma smiled defiantly.

Everybody laughed and Joe started whistling; the situation was funny enough, as Peter remained speechless.

Just to make up to him, Alma came to him in front of everybody and kissed him on the lips, while their colleagues cheered or whistled, creating a joyful moment in the restaurant.

An Arab gentleman, with a white traditional costume, rose and spoke up:

- I am entitled to transmit my best wishes of behalf of our excellence the Sheikh! We were happy to assist in your mission and we hope you will share with us the results of your investigation. We equally hope you will share with us the knowledge about the healing of such infectious disease, as we are preoccupied particularly about the well-being of the people of the Emirates and preventing such epidemics. Our laboratories and medical research facilities are opened for you and willing to help day and night.

Henry Sutton was warming up on the Scotch in his hand:

- We are most indebted to the Emirates for assistance. I can assure you on behalf of my friend, Director Fujimori, of full attention and cooperation from the WHO! And since we are in Dubai, let me suggest a western traditional cheer for his Excellency the Sheik! Here is to His Excellency, the Sheik of Dubai and to all the Emirates. – and Sutton raised his glass full of single malt Scotch!

Everybody cheered and shouted, glasses in hand, with the exception of the Arab guests, who were holding their cup of tea. They most likely found alcohol cheering at least controversial, but respecting guest welcoming tradition and good intentions made it easier to accept the compromise, so they thanked and smiled politely, but keeping a safe distance from the bottles on the table. Sutton continued:

- You must know your visit in the US induced havoc. The Scientific Director Hicks, as well as our agent Elizabeth Walker, were killed by Security Director Donovan. Donovan himself was killed by a black mamba snake sent as a gift by his "fans" in Somaliland.
- Elizabeth Walker was killed? – Peter asked in total surprise, falling back on his chair, while Alma made a grimace. She told me she is in danger but I didn't understand well why, at the time.

- Yes! She had a military funeral as any fallen agent and was buried like a hero! – answered Sutton, and then continued:
- I think you need some answers about the ship you were bound for, in the straights. According to the report of the scuba divers and the other things we managed to put together, the LUKI was a customized cargo ship – actually a phantom ship, specialized in piracy and smuggling sensitive cargo. It held within its hull 4 speed boats; it would launch them from a safe distance against ship targets. The speed boats would perform the piracy act, coming apparently from nowhere and below radar, and when the attack was completed, they would return to the ship. This ship was in the area when most of the piracy attacks took place, but it was able to stay at a safe distance by sending the speed boats. The ASTRID succeeded in destroying two of them some time ago, but they couldn't find out then the origin of the boats.
- Who owned this ship? – asked Peter?
- According to our information, it belonged to a Russian company called Nymrod, in the Philippines, directed by someone named Nemirov. The commander named Polivanov and most of his crew were Russian, but also carried international mercenaries. Among the dead ones, we found people declared dead decades ago and others with fake IDs. Most likely Commander Polivanov was also working with the Russian secret service of GRU. But they were only subcontractors and were doing well paid jobs for a foreign entity, someone who calls himself "Unum super omni" ("The One above everything"). The pilot you brought to us proved to be very cooperant. We believe this "supreme leader" is North Korean, and we are currently trying to find his whereabouts. And you were right, Peter!
- What about? – asked Peter with curiosity.
- We had a moll in the system! Director Fujimori had a helper – Ben Johnson, whom he sent to China to investigate the debut of some coronavirus epidemic. He knew some details about our operations and he delivered it to a well-paying beneficiary there. Many things went bad because of him.
- What happened to the chopper? – asked Liam

- Ah, chopper was confiscated and added to WHO air-fleet. I can't see a better use for it!
- Whatever happened to that guy we talked to…Mr. Jerkoff? – asked Joe?
- I think I can answer that question, said Captain Al-Qasimi. The police are about to conclude the investigation. The person you ask about was found drowned in the port of Jebel Ali. By the time he was discovered by a fisherman, he must have been dead for three-four days, possibly in the very evening he met you. The man saw him floating midwater.
- Strange time to take a bath in the sea!
- Even stranger if you think he had twenty-five kilos of iron tied to his feet. He seems to have been unable to climb up to surface to breathe. According to investigators he was thrown into the water alive and drowned there. He had been picked up by a taxi when leaving this restaurant, which makes you the last people that saw him alive- he continued, looking at Liam and Joe.

The two men looked at each other then tried to speak.

- It is clear that you had nothing to do with it! We have you on tape! Besides, we have as witness the taxi driver who was assigned on that car, but who borrowed the car to a fellow Pakistani countryman – it is a matter of time before we find this person, probably the killer.

Major Bashir stood up and spoke:

- We were also successful in capturing a group of Russian spies or agents, probably Spetsnaz, led by a man called Sokolov. They have entered the country illegally, possibly brought by sea by that ship. We hope to get some information from them before they are convicted. Charged with espionage, they are facing at least 15 years in jail and in a Somaliland prison, but they may not last that long.

- If they are Spetsnaz, you will never get any information from them -said Peter. These guys are tough and will resist even torture.
- You will be surprised! It may take us a longer time or special treatment, but finally they all talk – smiled Bashir.
- Like having them bitten by a poisonous snake, right? – smiled Sutton and winked to Bashir.

Major Bashir looked him in the eyes for a moment, then his face was enlightened by a smile:

- Maybe Sir! You have no idea how talkative they become after they get bitten and they see the antidote in your hand! Of course, most people have poor knowledge about snakes, and do not realize they have actually been bitten by a non- venomous species! Consequently, they are actually safe and need no venom antidote! But we only tell them the truth after!
- Well, you should be more careful. Some of them are really venomous!

Everybody laughed and Sutton asked:

- Now that you finished your mission, Peter, where will you go next?
- Actually Sir, I thought I'd hang around here for a few days, to get some rest and recover!
- Aha! So, I get back with Liam, Joe, Jim and Yves! Alma darling, will you join us on your return to US?
- I will …. Sure, I'll go! But I thought I should stay and recover for a few days, too!
- Well then, may I suggest you join Peter; he was quite recently in Dubai and he knows all the good stuff. And make sure you visit the Burj Calipha – it's a bloody high tower. I'll bet you can see the white cliffs of Dover from up- there! – joked Sutton, finishing his glass.

Two days later, Peter was taking a walk with Alma in the singing fountain area, close to the Calipha tower. They were strolling slowly, hand in hand, barely talking, but looking at each other from time to time.

- I think I finally started to understand you – said Alma. Now I feel I can relax with you, because I came to trust you.
- Yes, like all women feel the urge to tell me that! – smiled Peter, having a brief vision of Elizabeth talking to him. Alma's look made him immediately regret his words!
- What women? – or that's what I was supposed to ask -right? – said Alma, smiling sweetly. But surprisingly, I can tell you I don't really care. For now, I enjoy your presence here, with me! Tomorrow, I don't know! We can wait and see what tomorrow will bring us!
- I don't care what will happen tomorrow, as long as I am here with you today. Let's go eat something and then we go to the hotel. You make simple things sound very complicated! And I love it when you do that!
- Totally agreed! But tomorrow I want to dine on a boat in the Dubai Marina. And before that, we go to desert safari!
- Good idea! – smiled Peter, and in that moment telephone rang. The screen showed it was Henry Sutton.

Alma grabbed the phone from Peter's hand and answered, saying with a metallic, robot-like, voice:

- You have reached Dr. Peter Bud's phone. Peter is not available right now, because he has been abducted and carried away to an unknown destination. Wait for my instructions about the ransom! - and she hung up.

A message from Sutton followed shortly and it said: "Need invoice! Company pays!"

Peter was smiling! Henry was acting as his Grandpa. At the other end of the connection, Henry Sutton was laughing. He poured another glass of good Scotch and lit a Churchill cigar and mumbled:

– I love that girl! Peter should think about it!

Meanwhile, in the western Sea of Japan, at the same level with Munchon – North Korea, at exactly 38° 36' 10" N and 125° 4' 12" E, there is a tiny island belonging to North Korea, called Ung-Do. It raises 78 m above the sea. Nobody lives on it, but the military North Korean regime placed there a small four men guard outpost on the Eastern shore, mostly to take care of the remote radar facility placed in the highest place of the island.

Unknown to the North Korean public, much less by others, in a small valley in the Southern part of the island, there was a fortified small castle, built low and covered with indigenous materials and so perfectly camouflaged that from the sky, a satellite or even a drone camera would have taken it for a pile of rocks. A larger flat terrain next to it – lighted at night time when needed – turned itself into a very comfortable helipad which at the moment hosted a black small size helicopter for persons transport. It had the USO badge on it and the J 33 indicative.

The little castle had its own power and water source, both hidden in caves nearby. In the front window with bulletproof glass of his office, the grey - haired man calling himself "UNUM SUPER OMNI" stood and looked at the cloudy sky outside. It was a cold and dark day, both outside and in his soul. One of his best businesses collapsed. The pirate ship financed by him with the help of Nemirov was sunk during a fight with American Navy; he lost his best operative Mr. Lu and some other men in the process, the germ weapon testing, although promising, was blown up also by Americans and those restless investigators from the WHO. The abduction of the two delegates and the terrorist explosions at the FBI and NSA headquarters were satisfactory: at least they became alert and afraid they can find no safe place to be protected against him. Not to mention he lost a chopper and a pilot who probably spoke a lot, but fortunately knew little, and never flew a chopper around his base on Ung-Do.

He needed to boost his morale. He extended his hand, mechanically took the tea cup and a red telephone. He dialed a short number and spoke:

–   Hallo! How are you?.... Things did not go very smoothly lately. What are you doing?

The man he was talking to was in a hurry to speak and say a lot of things, but the UNUM cut it short:

–   Spare me the bullshit! Your Grandpa and especially your Father were very efficient! You grew fat and lazy! Too much foie gras and French wine! You will lose grip on the party and they will not spare you. My impression is that your sister is barely waiting for you to have a stroke – and UNUM smiled, considering he had his interlocutor scared enough. He continued:
–   Ok! Now it is time to show something, flex a muscle or two! Do you have any results with the ICBM project?.... What? …..Almost ready! Well, fire one across Japan skies, for testing! You let them know in advance! Even better! …. What? No payload? Send it without payload or put some buckets of shit inside so they can study it! - he laughed alone at his joke.
–   And one more thing! I spoke to the Russians! We'll keep connected with the Spetsnaz. I promised I will convince you to send some more troops for training in Russia – like 10-20 thousand soldiers. They might prove helpful when they will have the full-scale attack on Ukraine in spring... Oh, you didn't know? Well, I know for sure and I'm telling you!

The other man spoke something in his phone, and UNUM answered:

–   Geuleohge haela! (Yes, you do that!- in Korean) I will monitor the international impact! Geogjeonghaji maseyo! (Do not worry!-

in Korean) They will end up by taking you seriously! Naega malhaneun daelo hae! (Just do as I say! -in Korean) – and he hung up.

He picked up a paper from his desk, which looked like a grocery list, but it held much more interesting content. The list was written with a pen and contained a few lines, where he started noting down:

1. Increase migrant exodus to destabilize European countries – empower ISIS and proxies (weaponry and money)- targeted: France, UK, Germany; – accomplished; bonus -UK brexit
2. Help North Korea complete its nuclear weapon program – in progress
3. Bio- Weapon triggering engineered bacterial epidemics – Africa test – failed!
4. Spreading of SARS type virus; vaccine business investment – China interested – Big pharma notified! – work in progress.
5. Acclimatization of deadly Irukandji jelly-fish in the Gulf of Mexico to undermine American tourism – project undergoing documentation
6. Hunting down Starlink satellites – China and Russia interested!- project undergoing technical detail design; note – psychological approach on Space X decision makers;
7. Initiating the yearly "arson season" – targets: California in America, Greece in Europe, Australia, Turkey – in progress
8. Attack on Israel by Iran and its proxies; more modern weapons to Hamas and Hezbollah – in progress
9. Helping Iran with its nuclear program – in progress
10. Control of Red Sea passage by helping Houthi in Yemen – in progress

Unum put down his pencil and paper and sat down to drink his tea. There was a lot of work to do.

ABOUT THE AUTHOR

Marius Dumitru Enescu is a Romanian author whose novels explore the intersections of history, science, and human nature. He is the author of *Clisma cu săpun de rufe (Laundry Soap Enema)*, the allegorical satire *Me and My Tapeworm Isobel*, the geopolitical thriller *Lime Squeeze*, and the historical epic *The Impaler*. A physician and researcher by training, Enescu brings the precision of science and the depth of lived experience into storytelling that is both compelling and cinematic.